THE WATER MEADOW MAN

Nöel Murphy

To Sabine

There is no way on any earth that I would have even started this let alone finished it without you.

To Zuzu

Thank you love, you're always an inspiration.

Huge thanks to Marcus for fact checks and proofreading.

Tel: +44 (0) 7983 428 704

21 Third Avenue, YO31 0TX, UK

noel@crosschester.co.uk

Copyright © 2021 Nöel Frances Murphy

Table of Contents

PROLOGUE

WELCOME TO CROSSCHESTER

The ancient city of Crosschester used its history like Cleopatra used asses' milk. It luxuriated in it. Misty memory and selective history were its lifeblood. It fed off the faithless payments of tourists who had superseded but not entirely replaced the subscriptions of pilgrims from a thousand years before.

Like Cleopatra's baths, however, the longer it lay there, the more the milk softened its body, the more time it took to shower and scrub away the sourness, and the feeling that everything was forever held under a thin layer of white scum. Modernity would occasionally mount an assault on Crosschester but it would inevitably be forced back out to the big cities, or to 'Abroad' where it had come from, leaving only shallow scratches behind.

The local newspaper reported cattle auctions, garden parties, cricket scores and jumble sales. Crime and dread happened somewhere else.

Mr and Mrs Craven's Little Sweet Shoppe in Jewry Passage had
recently been sold to Mr and Mrs Aditya Kharbanda from Southall.
The Kharbanda family had been keen to buy, they wanted to relocate
as soon as possible. They wanted to experience the country they'd been
born in.

Mr and Mrs Craven wanted to do the opposite. They liked where
they were. They knew where they were. They knew their customers
and suppliers, their bowling green, their places on the pew, their seats
in The City Tavern, their allotment and their plots in the graveyard in
Commiton where they'd been born.

Their son Darren wanted more, and he'd been the king of the
family since his sister died of the measles when they were both eight.
What Darren wanted from his parents, Darren received, with thanks.

What he really wanted was anything at all that would get him
away from the stifling, ball-aching tedium of the "ancient and historic
cathedral town of Crosschester". He would move to London. He'd
work in a bank, any bank or he'd take a sales job, any sales job. As he
said of himself, he could sell sand to Arabs; snow to the Eskimos;
scotch to the Scottish.

Darren had shown the Kharbandas around the shop and the nice
parts of the city, highlighting the loyal customer base, making sure
they were aware of just how peaceful and friendly Crosschester was.
He guided them around the cathedral and its grounds, enthusing about
the stability and history of the place. He avoided taking them anywhere
near The Sleepers Hill or Stangate.

The money was almost his, he could feel it like the first cigarette of the day. The first thing he was going to do was to buy a Ford Capri in Maize Yellow with a black vinyl roof. A mate of his had done one up and was offering it at a knock-down price because he was leaving the country to go and live in Australia. Darren had considered Australia or maybe Canada or South Africa but not until he'd got rich quick.

What he hadn't mentioned to the Kharbandas was the flak head chopped in The Green Man about the sale. Some of his pals had cut him out of their lives completely when he'd explained the deal.

"Fuck them anyway, small townies going nowhere", he thought as he looked his old mate Kev up and down. He'd leave them to deal with the fall-out.

"You know what you've done don't you, Daz?", said Kev over a pint. "You've only gone and opened the floodgates to Paki cunts. Man, we've known each since school, I'm fucking staggered you let this happen and just for the fucking money. I thought you were a decent bloke. You're more like a fucking Jew, mate, all about the money and no loyalty, no honour in sight. You really are, you really, really are.

"See, one of them Asians moves in and they all do. They start charging all sorts of prices to us but then their family moves in - and I mean extended to all fuck – and it's different prices for us isn't it? Higher prices? And you can't even fucking understand them jabbering at each other, they could be talking about any fucking thing.

No booze or fucking pork out of them shops either", said Kev over the last pint in the last pair of pints they'd ever share.

"It's a fucking sweetshop, Kev, they never sold pork or beer. Jesus mate, move on. Get with it, pal or get left behind".

"I'd rather be left behind than have to put up with that lot and their stink and their jibber-jabber. Crosschester is a white town, always has been, always would've been if it wasn't for you Darren. If I have my way, me and some other like-minded blokes, it will be again. We fought wars for it", said Kev, born ten years after the war. He drained his glass, got up and left with the nobility and courage of St George after defeating the dragon coursing through him.

None of this was a problem any more for Darren. As soon as the Paki money was in his pocket, and his folks were moved, he was gone. Out of Crosschester for good.

CHAPTER 1

DARREN IS A SKILFUL DRIVER

1977

A month after the sale, Darren was driving down The Old London Road into Crosschester at a speed that was okay for him but not so for a less skilful driver. It was November, the mist coming off the River Icene was freezing in the air. Darren was in control. Darren had demob fever after a long day at work, a double shift of chickenshit and dust collection. He didn't know it, but black ice was forming. He knew the road and he knew his car.

He was a little late as he approached the roundabout in the middle of town, but he was nearly home. Saturday tomorrow, a morning to spend under the car, then to the footy to watch Rovers lose for the last time, and then his last ever night in this shitty little city. Patricia was going to buy an LP from Starkey's in town, ABBA or something poofy. He'd pretend to like it, and eventually they'd both be singing along. It kept her happy and that was important right now.

Tonight was cod and chips with thickly margarine bread from The Dolphin chippy near the barracks. Then a snuggle, maybe a blow job at last?

The Capri was going too fast for someone else to handle, he was sure of it. He was certain he could tame the car and the landscape so that tomorrow he would be saying goodbye Crosschester, escaping the ancient, dusty old dump for good. For very good.

The brakes seemed only to work when they felt like it.

The steering wheel was impossibly easy to turn but had little effect.

The Maize Yellow Capri slid disgustingly.

Darren would make it all ok in the end. Darren was in charge. Darren was free and clear.

It was all going too fast.

He had the money at last.

He could go to London. He was going to London. Tomorrow.

He pressed the brake pedal, and he felt his foot hit the floor. He had no control. No control at all. He was going to die alone in a cheap, second hand Ford. He had all the money, and he was going to London. Crosschester would not let him go. The engine roared. He pulled at the wheel. He'd work on the car tomorrow. He would.

The Capri skidded around King Egbert roundabout onto Kings Gate Row and the Guildhall. Darren was proud that he'd managed to stop the car from smashing into the plinth of the bronze statue of the city's Saxon queen Eadburh that stood in the centre of the roundabout.

Darren was elated. Darren was under control.

He meant "in control". In control of the babyshit coloured, secondhand Ford Capri that his mate had not fixed at all. Darren would fix it. Good as new. Then sell it for a profit. Good as new.

He tried to close his eyes but they forced themselves open again.

"Fuck you Crosschester", he thought.

Curse your bones and your foundations.

The Capri slewed. He felt tears on his cheeks as the walls of the city closed in on him.

He stamped on the brake pedal; the Capri slid. There was only ice, slush and snow for the tread of the tyres to bite into. There was no hope.

Everything was shrouded in fog but everything that was about to happen was finally and entirely visible. No lying to himself now.

He tasted egg and chips and salt and vinegar, his favourite plate of food. He thought about a prayer he'd not thought of for many years. One his parents had taught him.

He screamed. He stamped on all the pedals. He sobbed. He was angry and affronted. The car was not sane, it was working against him. It was enjoying playing in the snow.

If only this prayer would come back in full, he might make this life work. He could be back in control with God and his Guardian Angel back by his right and lefthand sides.

He could still see an old man in front of the Guildhall, and another trying to walk across the road from the bus station to the first one. The second old man was waving his arms and shouting something. The first one had his head down lighting a fag. He was wrapped up tight against the cold, he wore a hat. It was warm looking, one of those Russian jobs, it had flaps, they covered his ears.

Darren felt he knew the old man that this car was about to hit. They'd met before, at the football or in a pub or somewhere like that. They'd exchanged pleasantries. Darren knew him, maybe just the smell of him. He knew his name, it was Mick or Mike or something like that. He had always seemed polite.

The car was going to kill him. Darren took his hands off the wheel and his feet away from the pedals.

The prayer returned as he saw the old man's face in full. Mick looked surprised but not scared, this was a comfort to Darren. He finally managed to close his eyes.

> Guardian Angel, bold and bright
> Help to guide my way tonight
> Help me follow our Lord on High
> And if Guardian Angel I might die
> God bless Mummy
> God bless Daddy
> God bless Patty
> God bless All the men at sea
> And Guardian Angel, God bless me
> God, help me

Darren was such a young man. From the upstairs bar of The Crown and Anchor came a song.

> Guardian Angel, bold and bright

Help guide to my way tonight
Help me, help our Lord on High
Don't know what I want
And if Guardian Angel I might die
But I know how to get it
God bless Daddy Mummy
I want to destroy passerby
God bless Mums and Dads

There was someone's blood on the windscreen.

God bless Aunty Pat
It's coming sometime and maybe
God bless all the men at sea
I give a wrong time stop a traffic line
And Guardian Angel, God bless me.
Your future dream is a shopping scheme.
God bless Mick
Cause I, I wanna be, Anarchy.
In the city.
God bless Mike or Michael

Darren tugged on the handbrake and pulled the ignition key from its slot. He finally closed his eyes and he screamed.

CHAPTER 2

LAST ORDERS

1977

The night Mick Downes died, the weekend was only a quiet whisper away. Mick and Lunsford had put their coats on in preparation for leaving the Civil Service Social Club and going home. Lunsford had asked Mick if he had the negative of the photos of them and their wives, Chloé and Jeanne at the beach in Porthampton that summer. He said he'd like to get a copy developed.

Pictures of his past with his wife were his present now. He didn't have many photographs of his Chloé. Like everybody else, for sanity's sake, he had assumed he had all the time in the world to spend with her. Now he had so much time to spend without her, so much time left to go. Now is more than a single moment. It reaches forward, it doesn't want to disappear.

Mick and Lunsford were draughtsmen with the county council, they had been leaving school with a brief stint in the navy fighting U-boats, sleeping with women in New York City, and facing down the Kamikazes. Both men enjoyed their jobs with the City Council. The Council Officer grades meant that they could gradually climb the salary ladder all the way to healthy pensions and quiet retirements with no fuss or bother.

Like almost everybody else in The Social, neither man talked about their war experiences. They didn't want to, and people there knew not to ask.

One or two blowhards became loud about their exploits when they were pissed. Nobody judged them out loud. Everybody dealt with their own experiences of those excitements and horrors and boredoms, sadnesses and terrors in their own ways. For many they those things weren't memories, they were firmly in the Now. They lived in those experiences each day. So, why give them more light, more air and sound? So, for the most part conversations were kept very much to the pleasantly mundane and everyday.

It had been a fair old Friday night, with a few pints downed, some fat chewed; darts thrown and dominoes pushed; a bit of chat about the horses and the usual mediocre state of Crosschester Rovers FC. They'd also talked about their boss, Mr Donald 'Call Me Don' Jarvis.

Don, as usual, had spent the week at work wandering out of his office giving unwanted advice that he'd been ordered to give by someone higher up. Both Mick and Lunsford had been at their jobs for a decade before Jarvis had arrived, what he said was rarely more than chatter.

Lunsford was a short, thin man, quiet man who loved his wife. He had no great ambitions to be anything other than contented at home, at work, at the football, in the pub and at The Social. The lines on his forehead had been driven in deep by worries, memories and concentrating on his work. When he thought about himself, which he did rarely, he liked to think he was a nice man. Chloé had said that. Chloé was gone now so nobody said that. It was a simple thing to say. Not hearing him made him feel lonely, so he got on with things. Other people thought highly of him as a colleague and as a friend. His wife, Chloé, had loved him.

Mick once had ambitions to have kids with his wife Jeanne. This never happened. Some people mention it, Mick and Jeanne just get on with things. He concentrated on work, wife, fishing, football and never looking back unless he absolutely had to. She worked hard at the hospital, quietly going about her business. He was a tall man, taller than Lunsford anyway, and never less than dapper in a suit, with waistcoat, razor creased trousers, shined shoes. She was short put powerfully built, she was elegant and she inspired confidence in her staff. They were still in love on the night Mick died, still in love after many years.

Lunsford's wife, Chloé had died of cancer a few years before. They'd buried her up at St Eade's Church in Shalford. Quite a crowd had come to see her off: friends from school, friends from university, friends from the war, friends from the Shalford and Crosschester, friends from bowls and bridge and the WI, from painting and cooking and the theatre, colleagues who didn't like her but respected her greatly, and family from all over the world who she had made sure to keep in touch with despite all the usual familial ups and downs. The reception in The Bugle pub was a good one, it didn't go on for too long and no one misbehaved.

Mick had been guiding him back into the world, pint by pint, game by game. Pint by pint, game by game, day by day. Lunsford would never be totally whole again, not without Chloé but at least with Mick and Jeanne at his back, he could start to pick up some of the pieces.

As Mick and Lunsford stepped out of the warmth and conviviality of The Social and into the cold of Water Lane. It was 11:30pm. The snow blown hard by the wind from the coast was gently smothering everything in deathly quiet. The streetlights that were still working flickered and fizzed putting up a poor fight against the night.

As the chatting pair reached Kings Gate Row they saw some drunk lads scrawling chalk marks on the Guildhall before running off, laughing.

"Wogs Out!" one scrawl.

"Pakis Go Home!" another.

"Down with the Unions! Up with the Workers" and one more.

"Fuck Foreigners!"

"Britain for the British!"

The boys had been busy.

Lunsford tutted at the vandalism. Mick was furious. Seething. He stopped for a cigarette.

"See you tomorrow, mate. I'll bring the negatives. Sunday lunch in The Bugle with the girls?"

Lunsford nodded and put one thumb up.

Mick's house was a 20-minute walk up past the train station, up and up the hill where the prison officers and their families lived, and across The Green, a small grassy island hemmed in by roads.

Lunsford started to cross the road to the bus station, he looked back and saw his mate leaning down to shield his match from the wind. He continued to make his way out onto the road and slipped on his front foot, sliding a little way before righting himself. He wanted to get over the road quickly to the last bus to Shalford. Otherwise, it was an eight mile walk home to his empty cottage.

Darren's wild, baby shit yellow, broken, insane Ford Capri sped and skidded across the road, clipping Lunsford and smashing into Mick who didn't see it coming.

Mick's body was wrecked. Simple as that. Destroyed. The car rammed the man into the Royal Mail pillbox that stood next to the Guildhall. Darren came through the windscreen, headfirst into Mick, off the red post box, into the wall. Their blood and flesh and bones mixed and flew at The Guildhall wall spattering the fresh graffiti.

In the moment of Mick's death he felt no pain but so much grief.

In the moment of Darren's death he felt rage and outrage.

Jeanne was at home. Mick was dead. He had not seen the car sledding toward him before chopping into his legs, dragging his body into the red post box. Mick was dead, there was no question of it.

Lunsford was injured, badly so. The Capri has clipped him, breaking his legs and ribs as it made its way to Mick. Lunsford had been conscious when Mick died. He saw Mick's death. Ugly and mundane, warm blood creating disgusting slush on the pavement. Then he passed out.

Jeanne Downes was reading a book on the sofa under the light from a tall, slender lamp at the moment before Mick's death. She was sipping a dark rum at the moment of Mick's death. She was relaxing, not thinking about much else other than the book and her first long weekend in months. Three whole days. Mick and she were going to try once again to get Martin Lunsford to come out of himself. Maybe a trip down to Porthampton for the sea air. They'd try to get him to talk about Chloé again. Her name had been reduced to her gravestone, it had slipped from their conversations. They were all so close before. There'd been a few difficulties over the decades, of course there had, but they were close, that couldn't be denied. Jeanne turned the page of her novel and took another sip of her drink.

Mick had just died. Right that second. Gone. She felt a sharp sting in the air and wrapped her cardigan closer around her.

CHAPTER 3

IF ONLY THERE WERE WORDS

1977

If Jeanne was honest with herself, which she invariably was, Chloé was the only real friend she'd made after she'd moved down south, to this small, fat town so bloated with history. Jeanne's family were, for the most part, in Birmingham where she had been brought up in a lovingly strict, church-going household.

She was working there in Accident and Emergency when she first met Mick. He'd travelled up from Crosschester to attend a course on a new design technique or brickwork or window structure and had ended up in A&E with a sprained ankle. While she was treating him, they started to chat. He was shy but asked her about her work and about life in Birmingham, which was as alien to him as Mars. She was at the end of her shift and sick of the abuse or groping or combinations of the two that she'd endured, so one man's being less like a pig than the other drunks was very appealing. In point of fact, and pigs aside, they liked each other immediately. She was professional and lovely. He was shy and kind. They agreed to meet again a month later when he'd travelled up to see a football match. He, Lunsford and Jeanne had gone to the game, her first ever. Mick had stayed in the city in a cheap hotel so he could go dancing with her all night.

For the next few months he would visit her whenever he could (he'd feel emptier and emptier on each return trip) and write letters to each other. Finally, he proposed to her with wide eyes and the expectation of kind rejection. She'd accepted with relief and love. Then decisions, decisions. The wedding, with Lunsford as his Best Man of course, was in Birmingham with much outrageous joyfulness, music, dancing, hugs, handshakes and love. Then a honeymoon in Scotland because neither of them had ever been. Up and down Ben Nevis, a visit to Loch Ness, and three nights in Edinburgh, and then she agreed to move to Crosschester.

Now Mick was dead, and Jeanne was in their house, reading and oblivious. Midnight came and went. She was cross and concerned because it was so unlike him. She hoped he was in the kitchen of Lunsford's Oak Cottage home, tipsy and playing dominoes, talking about work and football. She couldn't call Lunsford at that time of night to test that theory though, that would be rude. At twelve thirty she went to bed with plans for wrath and forgiveness in the morning.

The telephone rang just a few seconds after she fell into shallow sleep. She knew exactly what it meant before she went downstairs in her dressing gown to pick up the receiver.

She knew the bloody junior doctor on the other end of the bloody line, so she asked for the exact details. She breathed deeply and calmly.

She hung up. Her professional responses slipped off her like dead skin. She fell to her knees in an agony of sobbing. Unable to breathe or see, she felt her tears impossibly cascading from her eyes, stinging like acid. She allowed this chaos and loss of control for some minutes, then gathered herself, was gentle with herself, held herself, and raised herself up.

She stood and went into the cupboard under the stairs where she found her sewing box. Slowly and deliberately she chose a length of red ribbon which she tied around her wrist.

She left their home, closing the door and laying the flat of her hand on it for a moment, then she rode her bicycle up to the hospital. She thought about going straight to the morgue but decided on seeing the living first. She went to see Lunsford. He lay in a side room unconscious, bruised, hatefully, precariously alive. She examined his notes, kissed his forehead and left.

Only then did she go to the hospital's small morgue. There, in the low light and cool air, lay her beautiful man's hideous body. Some residual heat was left calling to her as it dissipated out into the night to join Crosschester's thousands and thousands of dead down the centuries. She had no tears, they were all gone. There were now nine days of mourning on her own to occupy herself with. Nine days, and after that she had a plan for the future. She left the room and the lights shut off with the closing of the door.

"Don't worry. He won't be left alone in the dark, we'll make sure of that, we'll look after him for you", one of the people in the room told her. Someone with a familiar voice and a family and a home to go to. Someone she knew had cups of tea to share and bills to complain about and beds to make at home. Someone who didn't have to say anything at all to her but, "Time to leave now, love", but instead had taken the time to care for her. She would always remember that.

There was nothing more to be done that night for Mick. The future like a bareknuckle fighter wouldn't back away for anyone. Jeanne headed to the staff bicycle rack. She tried to get there without meeting anybody along the way but the further she went, the slower she went as more people approached her with condolences so formal and mannered that they could have been the serving of legal writs.

"Sister Downes, I just heard I don't know what to say", she nodded and walked on, not knowing why anybody needed to say anything.

"If there's anything you can think of anything we can do, Sister Downes..." on she walked unable to think about anything except why she was expected to reach such conclusions. She was only vaguely aware of what she could do, let alone what anybody else could.

"Jeanne, if only there were words..." she walked on.

"We've never really talked but I want you to know how terribly shocked and sad I am for you" she walked on and on and on, never fast enough.

"Jeanne! Jeanne! Hold on, wait! Was it your husband? I heard the name from Sam Kenyon, and I couldn't believe it... Jeanne! Wait!" on and on and on and on, she began to run, she fled. Finally, she reached her bike and rode home in the darkness and freezing cold of her new life.

CHAPTER 4

THE BIRTH OF THE WULFRIC HALL

1976

A year before the fatal crash that killed one and nearly killed the other, Mick and Lunsford were called into a meeting with Donald - 'Call me Don' - Jarvis, the deputy department head at the City Council. It was a Top Secret, Need to Know, Eyes Only meeting to discuss an exciting new project. Mick and Lunsford were always wary of Jarvis. He was a bureaucrat not a technician. He had no skills, none at all, and he didn't realise this.

The bigger problem with Don, however, was that his mediocrity came with a huge dose of subservience to any higher authority. He thought of this as loyalty or even clever networking. His colleagues saw it for what it was, obsequiousness and lack of imagination. Any idea that came from Don was inevitably someone else's. His recent passion was for anything that resembled the work of Owen Luder, although he'd been told that his new hero should be Luigi Piccinato.

Lunsford hoped to heaven they weren't going to be asked to do something challenging again. Challenging? Who wanted to be challenged by a building? Certainly no one who had to use one. He didn't see the point.

Take for example the recent carparks project, completed six months before. On their exteriors both the North Gate and East Gate municipal carparks were unremittingly bleak with straight lines where curves would have been in keeping with the surrounding landscape, and so much grey against the green of Mizmazz Hill and her sisters.

On their insides where being able to park a car and then find it again was the entire point, there were curves where straight lines would have helped confused car parkers orientate themselves. All of these misplaced lines and curves also allowed for small, dark, foetid places where pissing boys and the city's pitiable addicts could carry on with their lives in peace. Four concrete and wire mesh sculptures of leaping female figures (all elbows, chins and sharp breasts) had been hauled and nailed up; one sculpture on each face. There was no beauty. There was only dominance and threat. The gargoyles and grotesques on the great Cathedral, the corbels on the inside, those ugly, thousand-year-old things, cruel sometimes, had more style and humour, more humanity than the sculptures that crept along those carpark walls and threatened the citizens of Crosschester every day.

Lunsford wasn't one for theories. If the explanation behind a plan for a building took longer to read than the building itself took to erect it probably wasn't worth the bother. Elongated, gassy theories also inevitably made for ugly buildings. It irked him to see the buildings going up and then standing in the town like self-regarding bores ruining a friendly local pub.

So, it was with mounting trepidation that Mick and Lunsford watched Don's take out a large, black leatherbound book and lay it on the desk in his cramped, little office. It turned out that the meeting was to discuss a brand new building called The Wulfric Hall. The plans for the hall had been handed to Don by Robert Harding, the 82-year-old former mayor of Crosschester a month before he had passed away quietly in his swimming pool.

It was a phoenix of a plan born from another failed project that Harding has been involved with in Belfast in the early 1930s. The old man had asked Don Jarvis to his home for a pint and to explain his vision for the new building. Don was both amazed and honoured because Harding was still important in a few local circles. Harding was a jagged man, Crosschestrian born and bred, even his grey hair was sharp. His eyes were grey, his lips were thin, his body was always encased in tweed, and he wore half-moon spectacles for an effect. He and Don were sitting in the withdrawing room of Harding's mock Tudor home when he took the younger man into his confidence and presented him with a gift.

"Don, I'm not a well man", he grabbed Don's hand and held it for a long moment.

"I've had a full life but it's caught up with me. So, I need to pass my great project on, and Don I've chosen you. Yes, I want you to take charge of this plan, which is precious to me".

Don sipped his beer.

"We've got lots of beautiful old and ancient buildings here in Crosschester, but so have London, Exonbury, Porthampton and

Saintsbridge. We need something more, something bigger, something rejuvenating, or life is going to pass us by. British life, Don. Of course, we need to preserve and conserve our past, we fought wars to do that, some might say we shouldn't have, but I strongly disagree".

"As do I Mr Harding, as do I".

Harding sat up a little straighter and grabbed Don's hand.

"Good Don. Good. Good man. Because we, the good men and true of British stock, we are builders, Don. Not of consensus. Of powerful direction, Don. We need to build, we must build, building is in our Anglo Saxon blood. We must build solid foundations for the future, Don, we must but we are not!". Harding always spoke as if he was orating to thousands. Jarvis was hanging off his every word.

Harding continued, "Crosschester was once a place of significance and pilgrimage. It was at the heart for a healthy body of national feeling. But Don, we've become an historic sideshow or worse, a nowhere, a memory, a lost dreamland like Camelot or the new Jerusalem".

He paused, squeezed Don's hand and sat up a little straighter still.

"The crying shame is that the same can be said of the country at large. Where we once saw greatness, resilience, tradition and invention, we now see stagnation, laziness, unionisation, torpidity, people Jewing their own people, and the coloureds we civilised coming to turn us savage, Don. And we are not the savages, Don. We are the civilisers.

But our national imagination is being replaced by the ideas and dreams of others. Other races and cultures, all of which have their places in the world do not misunderstand me, are replacing us in our own lands. Where we once had a vision for the rest of the world, a good, honest, healthy vision to raise up the others to be like us. We need that vision again. Don, we are going to make a building of honour, legacy and the future right here in Crosschester, and you're going to lead the project.

Another pause. Another drink. A squeeze of the paternal hand. A sharp intake of breath from the acolyte. Harding continued.

"We desperately need a way of declaiming our blood truth proudly and with strength from the rooftops. And if that means making our own rooftops then so be it Don, so be it. We need our message to resonate with our British people, sleeping as they are like the Round Table Knights, like The Warrior Monks of our long destroyed Crosschester Abbey. What better way than a meeting hall as of Anglo Saxon days for the people to gather and make their will, their hearts and souls apparent? The Wulfric Hall, Don! Named after a legendary English chieftain. Constructed from the mud and memory of our city, county and country made real in stone, Don. Imagine it!"

Harding took a long drink, and with a conspiratorial tone he told Jarvis, "We need to build alliances too, Don, alliances of the like-minded. The Wulfric Hall will be a place to focus those alliances. There is already a group on the council keen to push this through. We've got the media on our side. We've got the money. Most importantly we've got the will, and now we have you, Don, the expert, the Master Builder. Soon we will have the People too".

He poured himself a drink and sipped it.

"It's all in here, Don", he placed a large, black, leatherbound book and something small and metallic into Jarvis's hand.

"I want you to have this ring, Don. I had it specially designed. It's a limited edition. Only given to the right sorts. Treasure it, Don".

It was a signet ring, and it carried a lion rampant in gold on a union jack. The lion was standing on three letters: B.D.F.P.

"It stands for The British Democratic Freedom Party. This will open a few doors for you lad, wear it with pride but not in public quite yet, and be a good, loyal soldier".

After Harding finally died, he was given a two column obituary in the Crosschester Chronicle written by its editor Bill Symonds who also gave the eulogy over the graveyard hole into which Harding's body was placed to the sound of a six shotgun salute. It was a well attended affair with people travelling from all over the country, and from Europe to pay their respects with breast hammering salutes and drinking contests in the city afterwards. Along with the boisterousness, however, smaller groups came together in upstairs bars in down-at-heel pubs outside the city centre.

Jarvis was wearing the B.D.F.P. signet ring, and Harding was in his soul as he began speaking at Lunsford and Mick.

"Gentlemen, I want you to look at this book and then think for a minute, and then we'll get into the detail". He sat back, put his hands behind his head and closed his eyes.

On the front cover in a Germanic, Fraktur typeface were the words: The Wulfric Hall. The contents of the book were a mess. It was filled with handwritten notes, photographs, sketches and photocopies of other people's work. These fragments were connected by slices of typed text which were pasted in and then linked back to each other with red or blue or yellow tags. It all looked as if it must be highly significant. Harding's notes mixed with his drawings, which mixed with his Polaroid photographs of cement and steel buildings, mountaintop schlosses and grandiose places. Don let them soak it all up before opening his eyes and standing up very straight indeed.

"The Wulfric Hall is a distillation of all you can see here, all this knowledge and learning and insight, chaps. It is a hope made solid. It is a building for the people by the people, and it must focus the power of the people on the will of the people. It will glorify not just Crosschester but also the county and finally the entire country", it was as if the late and lamented Robert Harding was speaking, or rather orating.

Lunsford was gazing out of the window at an aeroplane that was on its way to somewhere much more interesting. The office was warm and the day was nearly done, pints and wives were waiting. There might even be time to take in the last few overs of the Test Match on the telly. Mick looked over to Lunsford and coughed. They both looked back at Don and nodded.

"May I ask a question Mr Jarvis, sir?", Mick was bored with being bored.

"As I keep saying chap, call me Don. Ask away?"

"What's it actually for?"

Lunsford perked up.

Jarvis went into full flow, he wanted these good, salt-of-the-earth lads with him. He wasn't surprised that they might need several runs at the intellectual, cultural and ideological underpinnings of the mighty project. The Wulfric Hall was to be the venue that would host his other great passion: the first meeting and then, until the Albert Hall, subsequent meetings of The British Democratic Freedom Party.

"Well, it's great that you ask that, Mike, it will be used for the good of wider society and…"

"Thanks Don, got it. When do we start?" Lunsford cut him off.

"Immediately, my lads. Right now".

There had been no problem getting The Wulfric Hall through the planning committee because most of the members were tractable or lazy enough not to want to go into too much detail if the contracts went to all the right people.

"There will be nowhere else like The Wulfric Hall anywhere in the county. Nowhere outside London for that matter", he declaimed.

Unfortunately for Mick and Lunsford this didn't mean the end of the meeting.

"Before we go, let us take a few minutes to explore and appreciate these ideas. Soak them up. Then I want to hear from you. This is an important project for us all. An historic opportunity. So, please chaps, please give your first encounter with The Wulfric Hall your full attention".

They looked through the notebook again. Neither of them had ever encountered anything like the proposed design before. The final sketch in the book covered two pages of A3 paper that had been folded in. It depicted a building that managed to be both stark and sickly, and sentimental and overbearing. There was nothing warm, nothing human. Everything was huge, too big for any space available in Crosschester.

Even in the sketches it seemed to bully the tiny people who were pictured adoring it at the same time as it dominated the roughly drawn landscape it was squatting in. The Wulfric Hall was long and oblong with over-ornamented Doric columns seemingly everywhere they could be crammed. The windows had red, white and blue leaded thirds so that the people gathered within the chamber would be suffused in a light that never illuminated.

Mick and Lunsford re-read some of the texts. One piece kept recurring, sometimes as a single quotation like this:

"Building on Our Past, Creating a Stronger Future"

At other times in blocks like this:

"Building on Our Past, Creating a Stronger Future"

"Building on Our Past, Creating a Stronger Future"

"Building on Our Past, Creating a Stronger Future"

This quote appeared repeatedly:

"The purpose, the site, the material determines the shape. Nothing can be reasonable or beautiful unless it's made by one central idea, and the idea sets every detail".

They raised eyebrows at each other. Surely Jarvis couldn't be serious about this?

In the middle of the book, in slanted handwriting was the following paragraph:

"Our new building, like our new movement, must be daring and must endure. Our new building must worship and be worshipped by the land and the People that give it life. The Wulfric Hall must dominate the people like a father does his children. It must predict the era to come but it must not forget our sacred history. It must act as a prism, a lens to focus the attention and the natural motivations of the People".

Jarvis explained that both the land and the budget had all but been allocated, The Wulfric Hall was on the starting blocks waiting for the starter's pistol, he said. He was the coach, they were the athletes and the building was the race that they were going to win the gold medal for Great Britain. He then asked for observations and contributions.

Mick had piped up with an observation, "This is that piece of land by The Chronicle's offices next to D-Day Green isn't it?"

"Yes, spot on, nicely-dicely that man, well observed", replied Jarvis, his skinny frame vibrating with excitement.

"Are you sure about this?" Mick asked. "That's not a lot of land".

Jarvis was getting used to this sort of small thinking. He understood that the two working men in front of him did not have his vision yet. Workers, like Mr Lunsford and Mr Downes could be nurtured so that they would grow to embrace the vision and the future. They were, after all, ex-servicemen.

He did a breathing exercise and replied, "Martin, chap, it's enough space for the people to come and enjoy the society of other likeminded folk", he was pleased with that. "And it goes back a long way", he added for good measure.

Mick and Lunsford looked at each other and blinked because they knew each other so well that a blink of a certain length and force was as understandable as a sentence.

"Hold on a minute, Don", Lunsford had flipped to the end of the notebook and had seen the deadline date for their final drawings. "It's a project from scratch and this deadline looks tight. We've got the carpark on Roman Road to complete. The swimming baths for Beauworth School aren't even started".

"Thank you Martin, I appreciate that matey. You are to drop all your other work, hand it off to your juniors. Wulfric Hall is to take priority. You'll find that you've got plenty of support where it matters. Now, let's crack on and make this a better place to live for all the good folk".

With that he stood, picked up the notebook and left the room. In front of both Mick and Lunsford were two files filled with photocopies taken from that notebook, and schedules including the reporting dates and that hard deadline.

Mick looked at Lunsford.

"Madness" said Mick.

"Corbels!" Lunsford replied.

Within the month the drawings were signed off by a willing committee. A year later the Wulfric Hall was up and ready for its grand opening. A ceremony that Mick would never see, and that Lunsford wouldn't want to see but would be drawn into.

CHAPTER 5

THE BIRTH OF THE PARTY

1977

Crosschester had a theatre, two cinemas and a football team, although not one of them was worth more than local attention. There were no places for bands who didn't want to play covers or be pastiches. It had pubs though. Hundreds of pubs, inns, coaching houses and hotels. Every street and alley had a place to get drunk traditionally.

Take for example the St Mary Godwin Tavern. Built in or around 1380 and added to ever since by breweries who knew the value of nostalgic novelty. The ancient pub was two storeys tall but still managed to seem squat. The height of its front door meant that anybody over five feet eight had to crouch slightly to get in. The width of its stairs was so narrow that patrons were forced to turn on an angle and carry trays over their heads or out in front with outstretched arms to navigate its dark, fantastic twists and turns.

It was generally so quiet that you could hear the scratch of a pen on a crossword or on a postcard home. The City Tavern was "The Oldest Pub in Christendom", a Grande Dame, a pillar of the community, it was at the epicentre of all things Crosschestrian.

However, elsewhere deep inside Crosschester's guts, in a mean spirited pub called The Green Man, a new political party of old rages, griefs and nostalgias was gestating. The British Democratic and Freedom Party and its proposed new HQ, The Wulfric Hall, would build on memories of indistinct occasions, triumphs in brief, asymmetric wars. They would build on the current, dreary, dreadful state of the country. The BDFP would build what its members felt but never saw as grief for all those things they never had but felt that they deserved.

Two men walked into the small upstairs bar where William 'Bill never Billy' Symonds the editor of The Chronicle was speaking at Don Jarvis. Also at the table was Stephen Hedges, the general practitioner, a man so grey you would miss him in the smoke of a small campfire was keeping his counsel as usual.

"Alfred, Reg, good of you to come", Jarvis welcomed the older men. Both he and Symonds stood up and held out their hands for the formal round of over-firm grips and staccato shaking. All four men then sat at a Formica-topped table in hard-backed chairs. Jarvis poured each one a measure of Bell's Whisky.

The tallest and oldest of the four, Mr A.K. Jordan, was leader of The National Party of St George and a man whose right fist, like his teeth and soul, was painfully white and permanently clenched. The initials in his name stood for 'Alfred, Ketilbert' but he preferred to be called plain, old 'A.K.'. He was a self-described intellectual heavyweight with a Double Starred First in Latin and Greek from Cambridge. But, like the man himself, the party he led was not living up to its early promise.

According to A.K., "The National Party of St George's Christian, British, white policies and philosophical position had been driven out of public favour because of the Permissive Society". This in turn was a construction of the Jewish news and entertainment media.

According to A.K., the British People had been, were being, terrifically misled by the Hebrew machine. Indeed, it was that machine that had embroiled The Party in a cheap financial scandal that had lost it much of the good will it had fought so hard to garner. The so-called scandal had seen its treasurer, who was also A.K. 's granddaughter, abscond to Spain with all its members' monetary contributions. She had also leaked the list of party donors to the liberal New Reformer magazine, "because those bastards deserve it".

That list was a cross-section of society that included a rock star, a jockey, a Cabinet member, a Shadow Cabinet member and a senior member of the Royal Household. So, with his reputation as a masterful leader and organiser destroyed by his own daughter's daughter, A.K. was now looking for a new party to lead.

As was his former close ally, and now arch-critic, ex-Special Forces officer and leader of The Britannia Party, Major Reginald "Reg" Fountaine CBE. The BP had come under harsh censure from all political positions when eight party activists had been implicated in the death of a Dr Dean Mahomed and his young family in a house fire.

There were many acts that the British public would overlook for fear of making too much of a fuss but leaning two stolen motorcycles against the front and back doors of a small suburban house in Leicester, and then dropping lit rags into their petrol tanks was going a bit far.

Dr Mahomed who was a popular GP, and his two children Shuhul, aged 11, and Zoya who was four, had all died in the fire. It meant that Major Fountaine, who eschewed all responsibility for the "unfortunately tragic occurrence", was looking to lend his formidable abilities to another outfit while the court case played out.

Reg was the first to speak, "Cards on tables gentlemen, we're all of a mind here. I know where we should be, and I know how to get there, I should be the leader and here's why", he placed a black attaché case on the table, opened it, took out four slim, beige folders, and handed them around.

"Reginald, Reg, as Virgil would have it, sunt hic etiam sua praemia laudi, sunt lacrimae rerum et mentem mortalia tangunt", said A.K. not looking at the document but looking directly at Major Fountaine.

"Speak English please, Alfie", Reg Fountaine was not having any truck with dead Romans or Greeks or Thunderbirds, "ensuring we all do that is, after all, one of the main reasons we're all here", he downed his scotch with a grimace.

Alfred looked about him, and said, "Ὡς χαρίεν εστ' ἄνθρωπος αν ἄνθρωπος ἤ" before putting his hand out and onto Reg's. "You make a fair point, Major. An undeniable point. There are so many things we agree upon", he smiled as genuinely as possible.

Bill Symonds took the floor by the clever tactic of standing up and pouring everybody but himself another slug of whisky. His usual cigarette was necrotising the far left of his thin lips, which opened slightly as he spoke in a papery voice, "Reg, Alfred, you're both respected men. Staunch men. Strong men. You've both fought hard in your own ways for the cause of British freedom and democracy. The time has now come to pool your resources, our resources. Britain needs a new party of the true Right. Here in one of Britain's most ancient cities we hold the promise of such a new party, such a Grand New Party. But we need to stop bickering, we must put aside pettiness and fringe concerns. Right is Right! That must be our headline".

He sat down, pushed his full glass away and lit another cigarette. In his mind he had set the tone for the evening's business.

Don Jarvis took a turn, "I am here because I believe in our cause. I believe in our children's future".

He paused and took a breath, "I believe that some races are better than others. I believe that, while other races have their places, their places are not on our shores", he waited for applause, he got nodding.

"I believe that queers should have no part in our culture", he said for good measure. He sat down and looked for support.

Each man looked to the other to proceed and as Reg and Alfred prepared to rise, the door to the private room swung open and a fifth man, with a woman, walked in. All eyes turned to them.

"Kamarades!" boomed the fat, short, but imposing man. "Gentlemen! What a sight! What a sight to revive the hearts of good folk. Reg! Major Fountaine! Colleagues! What a night! What a famous, historic night. Let's get down to the business of forging The British Freedom and Democratic Party", Mr Eric Benson beamed and turned to the equally wide woman, his wife, Edith.

"Get your camera ready, my love, it's time to document this tectonic moment. The moment that Britain was reborn! Stand up gentlemen, gather around". They aligned, faced the camera and performed their smiles. The camera flashed, and the door, pushed over the sticky carpet, closed slowly with a creak.

CHAPTER 6

THE HOSPITAL

1977

Since arriving at The Royal County Hospital Lunsford had started hearing voices. At first, he heard Chloé telling him he was going to be fine. Soon after that a darker voice made itself heard, that of Frank Lunsford, his long dead and unmourned father. Lunsford didn't mind, it was company without the inconvenience of actually being company, and after all it was only him talking after all.

The Royal County was a Victorian shell that had been gutted and refitted in 1948 and then left to get on with it. Despite its grandiose moniker The Royal had no claim, aside from its enormity, to be further up the pecking order than Porthampton or Stouton's general hospitals; no obvious claims to fame other than a very brief, ribbon cutting visit from Edward Prince of Wales en route to a horse race or brothel. There had been no Royal births, no rock star drug car tragedies, no famous sporting heroes in for knee rebuilding, just run of the mill birthing, fixing and dying.

The Royal boomed and echoed and confused with its size and a layout that years of panicked running or sad trudging to navigate still didn't quite clarify or make comfortable. Despite this monumental scale it could in places also produce a submarine claustrophobia. Even if you had worked at the Royal for years, it still felt as if you were passing through it. Its size wasn't what grabbed most people's attention though, the feature that grabbed the attention of passers-by was its towering chimney stack. Anybody who saw it only thought one thing, "That's People coming out that tower, that is. I must look away, that could be grandad".

So many people had thought this was a fact that the hospital had been forced to issue a bulletin to The Chronicle:

"It has been stated that the black smoke being emitted occasionally from the hospital's main chimney indicates that the old incinerator is burning cadavers.

"This is not and has never been the case.

"The truth is that when boilers in the building were switched over from one to another this resulted in a brief expulsion of said smoke.

"As a result of switching over usage, oil will accumulate and be burnt off all at once, causing the black smoke. This will stop once the flame within the boiler has stabilised".

People reading The Chronicle who had never even considered that their local hospital was incinerating the results of failed operations, the cold contents of evacuated beds or the bodies of those who had simply fallen foul of the Accident and Emergency waiting times, were now wary. The other readers, those people who had seen the smoke, were unconvinced. Whatever the opinion, the smokestack remained occasionally ejaculating the contents of The Royal's guts.

The poor old, unloved Royal, all the art by all the local children in every country in the world couldn't make the hospital feel anything other than a place that people needed to escape from more than any other prison.

Somewhere deep inside it Lunsford sat up in bed and asked a passing nurse if he could have a glass of water. This was on that first day, a Wednesday, that he was able to sit up. This was after the opiates had worn off, the tubes had been pulled from his arm and throat, his voice unsealed. This was after several months of dreaming unconsciousness.

"Certainly, love. Anything else?"

He wanted to say something like, "No thank you", but nothing so well formed came to him. He couldn't think of anything else to say. He couldn't think of anything else he wanted. He felt hungry but he didn't want food. He realised that he just wanted to be left alone forever. His mind went into a slow spasm and he closed his eyes again. There was a spotty darkness, every so often a vein of pink light would wriggle across his vision, sometimes a green speck.

After sitting up in bed and asking for water he was simply compliant and polite, which he knew was the best way to remain alone. When time came to bathe, he was bathed and dried and taken back to bed. When time came to have his bed linens changed he went to the end of the ward to the balcony to look over into the gardens with their islands of trees and patients being cheered up by their visitors. He wished he smoked. He returned to bed. He ate his food without a word or any enjoyment. If the visitor to another patient asked to borrow a chair or a beaker, Lunsford nodded and smiled. He responded to the medical staff truthfully and with the minimum of time-consuming chatter and never with a question. He was the perfect patient if a little quiet, a little reserved, a little pale.

During the previous six months he had slipped in and out of morphine caves exploring as he went, getting better and then slipping away again. His broken bones had healed. His workmates had visited and left. Swings, roundabouts but no fun. The drugs and trauma to his brain following its bounces and play down the road under and over the car, under and over his friend meant that he had no memory of visitors during that period. When he had first regained consciousness all he could recall was snow, mist, ice, him screaming, a song, skidding, breaking, braking and Mick.

Every so often he thought he could see Mick on the ward, near the nurses' station, standing with scornful looks and jerking, broken movements, facing into the grey corners, standing over the bed, floating over the bed, everywhere in that half-light that was as dark as the hospital ever got. Mick was insistent that Lunsford should visit The Wulfric Hall, the building that they had both worked on and had left mementos in the form of small, grotesque sculptures of themselves hidden in the rafters by their joiner pal.

"Have you seen the building yet? Get out of bed, mate. Get up", Mick was there but only just.

I can't. I can't move.

"He's lazy. Always has been lazy. He was bone idle when he was a boy and he hasn't changed yet and he won't", his father, Frank was there and full-blooded, loud, vicious.

That's not fair, dad. I wasn't.

"That's not right, Frank. Not right at all", whispered Mick.

"Then why's he just lying there like a lump? Moping, like a teenage girl?"

Leave me alone.

"You know I won't leave you alone, how are you ever going to learn?"

Obviously, this was the drugs thought Lunsford, but still. During his wife Chloé's descent into cancer someone had told him that if your deceased (she had said, "Passed") loved one visited you in dreams, then they were giving you their blessings. It certainly didn't feel that way. If anything, he felt he just wanted to join Chloé. He didn't even know if he loved Mick, that wasn't a word he'd use about another man, especially not his best friend since school. He'd known Mick for most of his life, they'd holidayed together, been Best Men, fallen out and fallen in with each other but did this add up to love? He was absolutely certain that he didn't love his father, Frank. And where was his mother? What did the rules of postmortem dream visitations have to say about people you liked a very great deal? Why was his dad bothering?

Live people did visit him: friends from work and the pub, but all the visits dried up once everybody was certain that he wasn't going to die. People were busy. Life went on. He didn't mind. Most likely he'd just been there for too long, and only ghouls enjoyed hospitals.

"They blame you for what had happened to Mick, and you deserve it, you've always been useless. Look what happened to me. To your family", his dad just kept going. Just stuck to this one job, as he hadn't in life.

For Lunsford, memory was no more solid than a piece of caul hung over the present. Feelings had taken over from memory. He felt guilty about Mick and so he was guilty. He felt lost and he was lost. His feelings were curious cats in the presence of hard facts. He didn't want to ask anybody anything, he had no room for anything new. His feelings smothered and kept him snug in the face of the icy blasts from the nights that his life descended into untethered, unrelated, tangled darknesses of his loss. Chloé, his dad, Mick weren't actually talking to him, he knew that.

He was talking to himself in a circular race to a final, devastating crash. He'd never been taught about how, in their profusion and noise, feelings can distress and ruin everyday life. He wanted reality back but was so terrified of the emptiness of Oak Cottage, his and Chloé's home, that he wanted nothing, nothingness, no touch, especially not that. No sound, no sight, no prickling nerve endings assuring him of his life. He wanted this but his body and his loves and upbringing by a single mother who wouldn't let him stop, they mediated against the death of his deepest self. Somewhere in there was life. That's why the voices of Mick and Chloé seemed to come to him.

"Oh, my feelings hurt. Oh, I can't take any more. No son of mine".

Lunsford shrugged and put his magazine to one side and lay back on his pillows. He drifted into an unsteady sleep. His bed was one of seven along one side of the long, overheated ward. The side with a nurse's station at its head took five beds. The paint on the walls was a pale green. The paint on the floor was red. Neither colour had seemed to Lunsford to be encouraging of healthy improvements.

It was a male surgical ward that seemed to be named after someone called Beacham. The Randolph Beacham Ward. Attempting to construct some sort of reasonable world Lunsford decided that Mr Beacham must have been some philanthropic Victorian gentleman, maybe he owned flour mills or had shares in the railways. Possibly he had led an early life of licentiousness, lust and greed out in the Empire. Ravaging people as well as lands and landscapes in industrial violence as he brought Christianity and syphilis to grateful natives.

Lunsford pictured Mr Randolph Beacham, bearded and dressed in his black suit and gloves, tall and haggard by his travels and his diseases. He was returning to his home in the county's lush green winter countryside to attend to the funeral of his father. His mother saw into him and judged him.

"Randolph", she said, "you are now in control of the estates, of your family's legacy, of its traditions and of its future. Your time as a young man has ended as it should with the natural death of your father from old age and hard work".

She brooked no response other than a nod of this head. She expected his eulogy to his father to be biblical in content and extent. She knew that she only had another two or three years and in this time her role was to support her son and put this stamp on the estate. He needed a knighthood of some kind, something her disgusting husband had failed to achieve despite the opportunities presented by war and commerce.

Lunsford imagined the damp Wednesday afternoon on which the paterfamilias had been dropped into the ground. He saw the church, St Eade's of course. He also saw himself listening to the interminable and shallow eulogy falling from the weirdly formed lips of Randolph Beacham.

Following the funeral and in the sanctity of money and security, Randolph Beacham wholeheartedly embraced the church. He had been cured of the clap by regular ministrations of mercury and prayer, and he had taken to philanthropy with immense brio. Lunsford, with a sadness that reflected his own situation, intuited that Randolph's children would inevitably end up insane, or dead in the trenches, or both. Randolph's wife Cecile would flee inwards to despair and mourning, leaving him with plenty of time to atone for both his guilt and sin.

Lunsford wasn't at all sure if he felt much sympathy for Randolph Beacham, or whether a hospital ward should have taken this name. But there it was.

The reality was that there was no Randolph Beacham. The plaque had been nailed on to commemorate Mr Derek Beacham who had died on the ward in 1965. His pals at the golf club out in Bursley village had clubbed together literally in a charity round to raise funds for the plaque. This had then been hung up by the door outside the ward leading people to call it The Beacham Ward. Its official names were Ward 12 or The Bursley Ward, as all the wards were named after local villages and hamlets.

Elsewhere in the Royal in Shalford Ward (Ward 9), Darren Craven had died some months previously. The steering column of his slipping, sliding Maize Yellow Ford Capri had entered his brain through his mouth putting all the billions of his lights very much on for a microsecond before extinguishing the overwhelming majority of them in dribs and drabs.

To all intents and purposes, he was dead on the spot but where there's breath there's hope according to his mother, so he was put on life support on the Shalford Ward. This is where his parents left him because they'd booked a round-the-world cruise and had to be in Porthampton docks early the next day.

As his brain died, it filled with wonderful sounds and sights. He was as content as he'd ever been. This was strange because he'd never thought much of contentment other than as a soft thing that would kill you with comfort. As he died there was no pain, no regrets, no desires. His mind produced angels carrying baby angels, it produced a child, and he felt proud of it.

His girlfriend Patricia visited him. She brought his son inside her. She brought her love and her tears and her regrets, and she left them there. She cried in private. He was dead, she didn't need people to see her, no one but him and the new boy, their boy.

She had a new future to consider. She never reckoned he was going to marry her. He wasn't even taking her to London with him. So, his early death presented a tragic bump along the way rather than a major disaster. She was certainly upset, but as the weeks went on she realised that she didn't love him. He was great fun and everything, but she didn't love him. She knew where some of the cash was, so she moved to London and without the problem of continuing to argue with him about it. She disappeared and brought up the little one on her own.

Darren had a beautiful funeral in town at the Roman Catholic Church with a priest wrapped in a black cape and an Irish accent, all paid up front by his folks. Incense swirled everywhere stinking up the mostly sober crowd of mourners: footy friends and former choirboys, girls from work (he was a very handsome man) and relatives from all over but not far or wide. He was buried at eleven o'clock in the morning. In the pub after, everybody agreed that he'd be at the Pearly Gates and smiling down on them all despite the rain and the inflation and all.

Lunsford didn't know this of course. As far as he was concerned both car and driver had continued to spin off into the night, into a universe of sparks and stars that had taken over from Crosschester. He drifted back into his search for Mick and Chloé. His wife Chloé had passed life like an exam, she was clever, always had been. She was an industrial chemist in Crosschester, mostly researching new ways to make herbicides more herbicidal. Her death was no surprise but it was such a shame, she was so much of a good thing. Chloé was grand in a way that made everybody around her elevated. She was grand in size and in the breadth of her everyday humanity. She had a temper that was legendary because it was so rarely experienced. Chloé liked to expand her horizons, from the library to the theatre to the ballet up in London, to singing loudly as she worked in their garden, her body moving heavily and gorgeously from bed to bed to bed to lawn and then to bed again.

She had cancer of her whole body. Lunsford had stopped listening to the details after they'd been told, "less than two months". Of course, she lasted longer but when the end came it came as fast as the first thousand hummingbird pecks. He didn't care where her cancer was because try as they might to hide it, it was everywhere: in the house, in the fields, in his heart, in hers, in their futures, in their cups of tea, and in their kisses; in the walks they took along the River Icene and in the Water Meadows to the fringes of The Hunters Wood. He knew he could never clean her of it or be washed of it himself no matter how he tried.

Her friends, other researchers or ladies from the bowls club came in, day after day and week after week with jokes and tears. They held her hand like he couldn't, and they fiddled with her hair putting bows in as it disappeared and then they came in with smart bonnets and caps. They held her and read to her, talked about life. Mostly their lives but they never held back. Not like him, only able to look at her and squeeze her hands and talk about getting a dog when she came home, or how they would go on holiday when she got better. Nonsense. Both of them knew it too. She let him waffle on, and then her friends came in with crosswords and word searches, a novel to read to her from. She lay back on the bed, closed her eyes and wished hard for death to catch up quickly.

The night-day she died, she screamed but not in song so loud and long that even in her demented state she prayed for him to hear her and come. She left the world as high as Icarus and alone except for two nurses that night at three in the morning when the stars nibbled in through the curtains.

"She can die at home. Let her die at home", he'd said to someone in white every day after she'd been swallowed up by the Royal County Hospital. "Let her come home, there's nothing else you can do here, he pleaded.

He'd been told, "We can ease her pain, Mr Lunsford. You can't do that", the man in white had let that sentence go out because it was true and he was busy with families.

> You can't ease her pain like we can
> You can't ease her pain
> There's nothing you can do here. Go home

She died in The Royal County, he wasn't there. He couldn't be there all the time, he had other responsibilities. He couldn't be there all the time, the vicar told him this. So did her friends. Mick said the same thing. He wished he could have died with her or instead of her.

He remembered so many things. She used to ride her bike until it was beaten and it had to lie down on the grass. The cancer had come quickly for all they knew. Someone said it could have been in her for years, since before they were married. Someone said that lots of people are born with cancer in them and it just took time to manifest itself. One person from St Eade's Church hinted that it would only manifest itself as a test to be passed or failed.

Gone. Painful. In the Royal County. A surprise announcement. Her legs were short and strong. Her warmth was all over and perfect. Her cancer murdered her voice after a while so she couldn't sing. She weighed nothing at the end but they both kept smiling for as long as they could.

Now he lay in bed imagining or dreaming about what had become of Chloé and Mick. How could he have helped? Why was everything good so far away now?

He searched for those kisses on the picnic blanket in the summer after he'd put the camera away in its leather box and lay down with her as the Dotterel flew over, and the sky set orange and warm over the Water Meadows, reflecting off the pools and streams like forever.

He searched for the first kiss, the second kiss, the third and fourth and fifth kiss. He searched his dreams but only found himself watching Mick in spastic pieces near a red Edwardian postbox.

He wasn't gentle with himself down there in his dreams. He was hard. No sunset and daiquiris down there, just facts and not being there.

There's no way you can ease her pain Mr Lunsford.

No way you can ease her pain.

We can do it here.

Go home Mr Lunsford.

You can do nothing here.

You can't ease her pain.

There is nothing you can do.

Go home".

Doctors came and went over him as he mended. Nurses, including Mick's wife Jeanne visited him.

"I know you probably can't hear me, love, but I thought you might like to know that Mick's funeral was a lovely affair".

"Such a shame you couldn't be there, Martin. Peter spoke for you. He did a reading. I know you can't hear me, maybe you can, but I've brought it to read you. We all missed you. Mick went quickly. We buried him at St Eade's overlooking the river, facing the sunrise. Mr Holland the vicar was wonderful. Such a dignified young man. Everybody from your work was there, even Mr Jarvis turned up. He was in bits at the end, sobbing his heart out, more than me. Very sentimental. I didn't even know he knew Mick that well. Anyway, I must get back to my ward now Martin. Here's what Peter read, he said he was doing it on your behalf, I hope you don't mind, of course you don't. Get better soon love". And she read to him from Corinthians 15:50-57:

"Listen, I tell you a mystery: We will not all sleep, but we will all be changed in a flash, in the twinkling of an eye, at the last trumpet…"

Lunsford was so deep down by this time, lost to everything and everybody except the painkillers and his own body, which was doing its damnedest to save itself for a reason it was unable to fathom, that nothing came in. Only old, ancient relics.

Go home Mr Lunsford.
We don't need you here.
You can't ease the pain.

The next time Jeanne visited him she had news.
"Martin, I hope you can hear me. I've left my forwarding address in your jacket. I have to go home now. Back to Birmingham. Now Mick's dead there's nothing for me in this city", she paused and sighed.
"At least back in Birmingham I can feel a little more wanted. Aside from you and lovely Chloé, if I'm honest, I've never really made

a lot of friends down here. Twenty-five years, Martin. A quarter of a century and only two real friends to speak of. That's not a life. I know I have good, decent colleagues but it's not the same thing. My nephews and nieces are in Handsworth, my sisters too.

"I know the names that people have been shouting at me in the streets recently. Or whispering about me behind their hands. Crosschester, it's a small town no matter what it thinks of itself, Lunsford my lovely man. A very small town, with some very small minds and even smaller hearts lately. I will miss you. Do write, please take care of yourself".

She kissed him on the forehead and left the ward for the last time dressed in her smart, going out clothes, her blue suitcase in her right hand. She headed to the railway station and didn't give Crosschester a second glance when her train left.

Later or earlier in time, he was sure he had looked up to see a face and a neck and a stethoscope and a white coat and some long hair and red lipstick floating over him. A doctor maybe? A dream doctor, a pain specialist, a saviour machine, some kind of help. Or an avenging angel.

There was mumbling. There were more faces. The red lipstick and stethoscope remained in focus. Now the eyes, blue, shadowed, and friendly. Now the voice, which he had no way of characterising; it frightened him but only a little. It was both male and female, at once as loud and commanding as the voice of God to Abraham and as silent as the sound that comes after the final reading at the funeral of a child.

"Mr Lunsford, can you hear me? Your friends from work are…"

"Doctor Lees, can you spare a moment to look at charts?"

"Doctor Lees, are you available to talk to Mr Hodges' family?"

"Mr Lunsford", continued the voice. She was in control of him, of everything really. He'd never known anything like her voice and it almost picked him out of his tarpit.

"Mr Lunsford, you're doing well. We'll see you again soon. You should be proud of your progress. Your friends from work tell me that your or you're or your or…"

"Dr Lees, it's very urgent that you…"

"Mr Lunsford, if you can hear me, you're doing very well, very well indeed. I will come back to see you next week. We will come back. Your friends from work…" What if he couldn't hear her? Where was Mick?

Go home Mr Lunsford.

We don't need you here.

We can't ease the pain.

CHAPTER 7

GOING HOME

1978

Time to go. All his bone and muscle healing were done. The breaks
had knitted as well as they were ever going to do. Everybody from
Cleaner to Consultant was convinced that Lunsford would be happy to
go back to his house, not that any of them had any idea what this house
was like, or whether he even lived in a house, nor if it was a home. But
consensus is consensus.

"Get out of bed, mate. Get home. No more lying about", Mick
urged him.

"Lazy. Just a lazy, lazy little tart", Frank, his father was on his
case.

I'm going mental now. I'm going to be all alone in that house.
Alone and crazy. What do I do in it? What's left to do?

"Wait for somebody else to tell you as usual", said Frank.

"Frank, leave him just for a while".

"Fuck off pal".

Lunsford did not want to go home. He couldn't imagine it. He could imagine it; each effort resulted in loneliness and loss. He genuinely feared going home. Oak Cottage, the beautiful little house that Chloé and he had cherished was just bricks now. Its view over the Water Meadows, its wonky stairs and wooden floors. Its kitchen that only ever welcomed people was empty now. It was never untidy, never unclean, in fact Jeanne had written to him to explain that she'd cleaned it thoroughly for him before she left town.

He had become less and less forthcoming in the months approaching his release. As his bones healed, his mind and his emotions – things he'd rarely had many dealings with outside of birthdays, Christmases and funerals – began to bend and break. As the drugs were withdrawn, he withdrew with them.

"Self, self, self. As usual", said Frank.

He slept or looked as if he was sleeping for most of the day. He was lost in his mind most of the time, with no desire to unfold his thoughts to anybody else. People were worried, no one in particular, but people generally around the place, fleetingly.

"I hope he's not forgotten how to talk to people", said a nurse, "that happens, I've seen it".

"I hope he's got someone at home", said one of the visitors across the ward.

"Never gets visitors though, wonder what he's done?" said another.

"He's so slight and he looks so alone", said a patient.

Lunsford's thoughts focused on what had happened to get him into this ward in the first place. Jeanne Downes had done her best to get it through to him that he had been involved in a hit and run but what hadn't yet quite stuck all the way inside was that Mick was dead. Mick was nowhere to be ever seen again: not later not in the pub, not in the street nor by the Market Cross nor at the football. Mick wasn't coming over to play dominoes and drink blended whisky while Chloé was out at the cinema in the city with her friends, with Jeanne. Mick was obliterated from the future and fading from the past already. Lunsford struggled to remember his friend's voice which evaporated and condensed and evaporated and condensed and dripped away.

Mick's death was surely not allowable.

Chloé had taken some time to die, and her illness was such that the end was a dreadful, atomising misery but he'd seen her buried, watched her descend and let her go.

Mick's death was purely a fiction.

"It isn't mate. It's real. Get up. Let's see what we did, let's see what they did with that daft Wulfric Hall. We can go together. It'll be a laugh"

But why would anybody lie about something like that, let alone Jeanne? She wouldn't. She mustn't have.

The more Lunsford tried to relive the moments of that night, the more he found himself removed from it. Further and further away he went from place, time, events, smells, lights and sounds. All the memories revoked themselves, redacted themselves from the record of his life. Lunsford had no control over this part of himself, nor did he want to have. The sooner everything left him alone, the better.

Memory relies on outside influence, it needs to touch and be touched by outside realities to come into being, and then it needs reasons to remain. There's no hope in remembering a feared one or a loved time if there is no sense to realise it: no smell or taste or sound or sight. Without at least one of these, there are just fleeting feelings. Feelings can reorientate and reinterpret past realities. Feelings can create myths and legends when no supporting realities ever existed. In fact, feelings will form a simulacrum memory with nothing more solid to cling onto than the desire for it to be.

Lunsford's memory from Kings Gate Row that night was mediated and narrated by the sight of falling snow, the feeling of cold, the sound of a brakes screaming and a car skidding on the black ice, the feeling in his head and stomach of a pint too many, maybe even a hint of boredom with Mick.

When it was time to leave, he picked up the holdall he'd been supplied with, patted down his pillow and started walking to the exit. He stopped. He was staggered by the weight on his heart of the idea of going back into life, into the world. He turned back and sat on his bed, he took the plastic water jug and began pouring water into his beaker. He sipped it and shook, he started to feel an intense pressure all around his head. The moment this began he knew absolutely that it would never stop. His hands were icy stiff, fragile and breakable. The longer he sat, the more danger he felt. From his bones to his organs every part of him was liable to tear and fracture at any moment. At the same time, he felt indescribably leaden. He began to cry, quietly at first.

"Mr Lunsford! Haven't you gone yet? You're as fit as a fiddle, now go home", laughed the nurse who began to guide him to the door. She could see his distress and she deeply, deeply wanted to help him emerge from this pain. She knew, however, that this sort of thing happened to a few long-stay patients, especially the older ones. But what could she do? He was physically as fit as they could make him, and it was time to go. She didn't want to humiliate him, so she closed the curtains around the bed, wiped his face, brushed him down, and helped him on with his thick winter coat.

"Stand up now, Mr Lunsford, British fighting spirit and all that. You'll be amazed how much you'll enjoy your own home and your own schedule", she stood in front of him, at arm's length placing her hands on his shoulders and straightening his coat lapels.

She smiled, "So much life ahead of you. So much. You've been a wonderful patient, one of the best, all the staff say so. We'll miss you that's for sure but you can't stay. So, up straighten up", she dropped her hands to her sides and looked him in the eye. "Remember your comrades, they wouldn't have given up the ghost, would they? And here we are, lucky to be alive. Let's honour their sacrifice, let's remember what you all did", she created an exit slit in the folds of the curtain.

He said nothing. He had no language to use, all outward communication was devastated and useless. He hated her for saying what she'd said. He mustered a shrug. Then he shuffled a little on the spot as if preparing to move.

"Come along Mr Lunsford, it's time now, there's nothing more we can do for you here. It's time to go home", the nurse was alternating between extreme frustration and mild panic. She didn't want this to escalate. Her working life was hard enough, her shift had just begun, and this bed was absolutely needed.

Lunsford started to move forward out through the curtain, holdall in hand again, a shuffle into a step. A delicate step as if he was walking on ice and could slip and smash into smithereens at any moment.

The young nurse helped him along, locking his arm through hers. No one said, "Goodbye", only one person looked up from his newspaper briefly and then went back to stories of vandalism, immigrant floods, inflation and Punk Rockers spitting at Chelsea Pensioners.

Lunsford moved slowly, the further from his bed he got the more he wanted to return to it, to curl up and drowse in it like he had on so many Wednesday afternoons. No one asked any questions, he didn't have to talk or make any sense. He was happy to end his days there.

"Lazy. Lazy little bastard".

"Leave him alone, Frank".

"Leave me alone".

"Lazy, cowardly little bastard. I'll do what I want with you. You're mine. My flesh and blood you little prick".

"Go out, get better, see our building, mate".

"Lazy, self-pitying little fucker. Nosey bastard".

Suddenly, with a final goodbye from the young nurse, he found himself out in the corridor. He was looking back, frail, stumbling, half on earth and half suspended above it looking down on the hospital's shining, ageing floor. There was a radio blaring something awful from the cleaner's cupboard.

He was on his own. Standing in the corridor, just looking at a locked door. He turned and looked for the sign that said, "Exit".

"Let's go mate", Mick tried to sound jolly.

"Make a fucking choice you little bastard", Frank remained on duty.

CHAPTER 8

THE PARTY IN THE GREEN MAN PUB

1978

The Green Man pub on The Sleepers Hill just out of the city centre was a grim place. Squat, beige, flat roofed and mean spirited with more bars than drinkers most of the week. Outside, the carpark was pockmarked with a few cars but it was mostly a venue for fights and the Friday night chip van.

At the private upstairs bar, sitting on high-stools, facing each other and drinking cheap fizzy white wine from abroad; deep in conversation were the landlady Mrs Meredith Brewer and her best friend, Mrs Edith Benson: Sub and Dom, opinion taker and opinion maker. Behind the bar stood Assistant Landlord, Harry Mottram. H' was waiting for a fight, eager for a brawl. He was waiting for orders, hoping no one thought he was too stupid to carry them out, not caring if they did because there was nothing worse than a clever-dick. Tense, always tense, everything tense even his veins, even his blood. Ready to go.

Always ready.

On a midweek evening in October, The British Democratic Freedom Party was finally close to revealing itself to the world and this revelation was being brought to fruition in the private room over the public bar. Downstairs the regular drinkers swayed and discussed the acceptable sports. A jukebox oozed rock'n'roll songs into the fug of fag smoke and aftershave.

The locals down there were mostly prison officers, a few ex-cons, pensioners and a group of Teddy Boys in their thirties. They all loved The Green Man because tourists, of which there were always thousands in the ancient city, never ventured in. There were rarely any women in the place, there were no fancy drinks or crisp flavours, there were no fancy ideas, no fancy conversations. There was a sticky, faded red carpet. There was a stag's head with a single remaining antler that jutted out of a wall over the electric fireplace in the lounge bar. At least once a night somebody said that it must have been going at a hell of a clip when it hit that wall, and everybody else laughed because the joke was so familiar.

Every wall in every bar was lined with pictures of fox hunts, fields with hayricks, ships firing cannons, Spitfires, Winston Churchill, horses, pigs and sportsmen. In between these were crossed cricket bats and oars, football boots and a single, tarnished horse brass nailed into the flock-covered plaster. Cigarette smoke pervaded and obscured everything.

The Green Man had been hastily thrown up by the brewery in the 1950s to take money from the newly developed Stanhope housing estate. No one ever looked at The Green Man and thought, "We could do a lot with that place, make it really cosy and welcoming" or "let's pop in there for a pint", because The Green Man whispered, "Fuck off" to anybody who passed by. This was another reason the pub was beloved of the local drinkers. "A man's boozer", "A professional drinker's pub", were some of the names given to it by those who appreciated its claustrophobically dark interiors, its lack of choice and its testy service.

Harry walked back into the upstairs bar from the Gents and made his way over to the dartboard to watch the game. Two men were playing a game of Killer darts, badly. Two other men were sitting at a table nearby, Thomas Vyvian Sarson-Taylor was trying to avoid the stare of Stephen Hedges, the thin, grey, terrifying man. Sarson-Taylor nodded a hello to Mottram, then looked at his empty whisky glass and raised one eyebrow. Vyvian might have seemed out of place to the uninitiated because he reeked of solid wealth. Not of money but instead of never having to worry about money, not in this life or in the lives of several preceding generations. He was in his thirties and dressed in the kind of hardwearing, shabby countryman's cloths of tweeds and leather that would last forever and soak up a great deal of gore. Vyvian fitted right in, he was one of those professional drinkers who the pub's darkened spirit welcomed.

And his family owned the pub.

The game of Killer ended with a lucky dart. One of the players, Mr Eric Benson joined Sarson-Taylor at the table while Don Jarvis went to the bar and brought back three pints of dark beer: one for him, one for Mr Eric Benson the portly shop owner and nominal Party Leader, and one for Vyvian who looked at it and grimaced.

"So, Don, how go the preparations for the grand opening of The Wulfric Hall and the launch of our great new Party, Donald?", asked Benson who thought he already knew.

"Nicely, nicely-dicely, Eric. All ahead full. Mr A.K. Jordan has confirmed that he will be coming down from London to speak", he paused, "if we will provide transport. He'll be speaking about Communism and immigration", replied Jarvis, moving away from Benson's vile smelling cigar.

"The tight bastard. Too bloody self-important. Sooner he's off the steering committee the better. Still, he's a good speaker, there's no arguing with that. What about Reg Fountaine? He's coming?"

"I've had trouble reaching him. He keeps changing telephone numbers and moving from house to house since the unpleasantness in Leicester with those coloured boys".

"Fucking Paki nonces", muttered Mottram from the bar where he was polishing glasses.

"Harry, it's talk like that in public that's led to the Front being boxed in by the media. We're a respectable organisation of forward-thinking ideas that any Briton can readily support. Remember that".

"Well, they were Pakis weren't they? Spade a spade and all that. Honest English language, nothing wrong with it", he thought for a moment. "There are Pakis taking over Mrs and Mrs Craven's sweetie shop in Jewry Passage. Better watch out Eric, it'll be your place next. Think of it, Nignogs in Shalford". Harry returned to the bar and continued to wipe pint pots and whisky tumblers with a greasy, old cloth.

Benson turned back to Jarvis. "Don, make sure that Mr Fountaine is still available and confirm ASAP".

He turned to Thomas Vyvian Sarson-Taylor, "Vyvian".

"Please call me Thomas or Tom, Mr Benson. I would appreciate that. The name Vyvian is, well, I'm sure you realise, is a little" he paused, "a little fey. It's an old family name and every generation someone is made to bear it. As you can see, I am not a little fey", he flexed his muscles but no one could see them.

"Certainly, I won't forget. So, Tom, how are you getting along with your task?"

Sarson-Taylor sighed, "You've yet to give me anything to do, Mr Benson".

"Righty ho, we'll remedy that. For now, pop over to the bar and ask Harry to invite Mrs Benson to the table as soon as it's convenient for her".

Sarson-Taylor stood up and went to the bar where Mrs Benson was chatting with the landlady, he was immediately replaced in his seat by the gaunt figure of Bill Symonds, the editor of The Crosschester and District Chronicle.

"Good of you to join us Bill. How goes the war on lies?", said Don.

Symonds shook hands, took a sheet of cheap paper from this suitcase and handed it to Mr Benson without a word.

Whenever he did speak, each word Bill Symonds exhaled had maximum stage time given to each syllable. He was particular in everything he said and did from keeping his exotic fish to his quiet, committed and mostly private drinking. He was also particular in his view of humanity. For the most part, when taken individually, it was poor, very poor in fact. Most people never achieved anything because of who they were. If someone had the ability to do something, then they would do that thing. This was a failsafe proof. People were born not made. The making of them merely brought out what was already there. The making of someone didn't just mean that a person came into their own in the finest aspects, it would also show them for cowards, mountebanks, dullards and fools. He'd seen this during the war. Heroes were few and far between. Cowards were two a penny. For the most part everybody sat in the middle just about living. As for the self-made man, that went both ways as well.

He looked at Eric Benson who was a fine man, self-made, not old money – which he despised, "I want to run this as a reader's letter in tomorrow's second edition, Eric. Tell me what you think?". What Benson read was typewritten and not entirely to his taste.

AN ASSAULT ON EDUCATION

The Messiah of excellence has been persecuted by the scribes and pharisees of envy and mediocrity and condemned to death. Moreover, anything that has as much as touched the hem of the robe of excellence has also been condemned and sacrificed to the false god of equality.

Envy is the driving force of this new religion of equality, envy that knows but never will admit that people are not equal in their abilities; envy that relentlessly and malignantly prosecutes its unholy cause through politics, through education, through the arts and in many areas elsewhere.

Envy in its many forms, it could be argued, makes an effective recruiting sergeant for most political systems. For instance, the communist covets his neighbour's ox; the socialist has no ox but hates anyone who has one; the capitalist covets all the oxen; the liberal treats the ox as his equal. On the other hand, the nationalist will endeavour to see to it that everyone deserving of an ox shall have an ox.

The equalisers have infiltrated the field of education to hunt down excellence on a mission of search-and-destroy. Teachers who had swallowed whole the pernicious nonsense of Das Kapital but had no more than nibbled at Real English literature, began to 'harmonise' ability by teaching children that spelling, punctuation and grammar were 'elitist' stuff that only the bourgeoisie bothered about. The miasma of envy lay so dense in the dank educational hollows that some so-called teachers went as far as to reprimand parents for teaching their children to read, protesting that this gave the children an 'unfair advantage' over others.

Those children lucky enough to circumvent the comprehensive slough and stay on the straight and narrow of grammar and assisted-places schools found further perils waiting for them at the colleges and universities. These also had been infected by the bug of equality and began to 'harmonise' exam marks by robbing bright Peter to pay dim Paul.

Sincerely, T Burgess,

14, The Verges

Commiton

Benson nodded, "It's quite wordy don't you think Bill? It's a bit theoretical. I mean, Oxen? Let's have another go, eh? Let's attack the enemy more directly. Let's try and appeal to the parents and the children, the pupils, the students. We need young blood infusing the Party".

Symonds took the paper and replaced it in his suitcase. He nodded almost imperceptibly. He had nothing to say. He preferred the sound of a rapidly hammered typewriter to a yaddering tongue. He did have one thing to say before he returned to work.

"Eric, Don, this Sarson-Taylor chap, is he solid?"

Mr Eric Benson looked to Don Jarvis, a solid bureaucrat.

"Don?"

"As we know, he comes from an old County family with good, deep roots".

Bill leant in, "Where did you meet this particular Sarson-Taylor?"

Jarvis thought, "In The St Mary Godwin, drinking a pint".

"When?"

Again, Jarvis had to stop and think. Mr Eric Benson meanwhile was scribbling in a small, black notebook. He looked up, "Well, Don?"

"I'm not certain", naturally a follower, Jarvis began to doubt his own memory, and started to feel guilty about something or all his old guilts clamoured for more attention.

He laughed nervously, "Shall we let him know he's not wanted?" He laughed again and then his eyes widened as a horrible thought dawned on him, "My god, he could be undercover police!"

In a rare outburst of emotion aside from icy anger or mild despair at some else's stupidity, Bill laughed fit to suck the joy from a four year old's birthday surprise. His entire laugh was the sound of the final second, the whispery tail in anybody else's. It was almost there, almost not there at all. It moved the air in front of him causing it to chill slightly, and it sent ripples of chaos to flatten Barbadian flies.

"Calm down Don. There's not a copper in the county I don't know or who wouldn't have given me the tip".

"What if he's out of the country though Bill? What if he's the Met or Special Branch? Jesus Christ, Bill".

Mr Eric Benson put a hand on Jarvis' arm, "Look around yourself, fella. We're not even noticeable to the people in this pub let alone to the Special Branch. Calm down Don for goodness sake.

"As you've already pointed out, the Sarson-Taylors are a highly respected family in the county. Sir Philip is well thought of in the right circles further up the chain".

Bill looked up, "Sir Philip is also senile and believes he's head boy at the college".

Eric continued, "We need to keep young Vyvian close, that's for certain. Give him some attention. Make him feel wanted. His family have money and connections. It's all well and good being a party of The People, that's where the muscle is".

"And the heart and soul, let's not forget those", said Don.

Eric went on, "Yes, those. The People will be the beneficiaries but we must be the vanguard, and a vanguard that's well supplied is more likely to pull the main force along. We'll make Vyvian Sarson-Taylor a valued member. I'll give him something to do, keep him occupied".

"The more the merrier", chirped Don.

Bill was vexed by this nonsense. He stood up, bowed slightly to Jarvis and then more deeply to Mr Eric Benson. He ghosted his way out of the pub to his desk at The Chronicle where he proceeded to red pencil the latest feature story from a senior journalist for no good reason other than authority.

"Right, Don, now that minor panic is out of the way, let's get down to brass tacks. How's recruiting? Who have you got in the schools and at the football?" Jarvis' reply was lost in the general hubbub.

Mrs Eric Benson was at the bar end sitting on her stool, drinking a glass of port and lemon and chatting with the landlady, Meredith Brewer, who was ignoring a tourist who had wandered in having become lost on his way to the bus station.

Vyvian has passed on his message and was hunched over sucking down scotch. Harry Mottram coughed at Mrs Benson, and waited.

Mrs Benson noted him out of the corner of her eye but continued her conversation, "…you will never believe how much it cost just to get some banners made up. Absolutely shocking unless you want to have it done by some of the sort of people who will work for peanuts. But you can never tell what you'll get back from those sort of monkeys do you? Also, it's taking the wages from decent tax-paying folk, even though the tax we're all being asked to pay is extortionate, daylight robbery by this spineless government".

Miss Brewster, a stocky woman with her black hair pulled back into a painful bun, her eyes smaller than seemed feasible for seeing, and her mouth that made everything she said sound like hissing, refilled Mrs Eric Benson's glass. Harry coughed again.

"What is it H'?!", she snapped and avoided looking at him. She despised her second-in-command but he was necessary, he worked for booze and he cooked food in a way her patrons appreciated, although she had to correct nearly everything he ever made. In fact, her habit was to correct everything he did. He knew she hated him. He understood why: he was an angry man with no self-respect, little or no confidence, and he was so lacking in ambition that he found it difficult to get out of bed in the morning, every morning. He, however, loved her dearly because she gave him reasons to get out of bed in the morning.

"Mr Benson asks if Mrs Benson can join him when convenient", Mottram tried to sound off-hand because both the women intimidated him. Mrs Benson, like her husband, was ruddy-faced and her hair was cut much like the headgear of a medieval pikeman. Also like her husband, she was muscular and had what she called "a healthy dose of good, honest countryside vitality". As usual she had squeezed all that vitality into one of the spectacularly colourful dresses that she had made for herself by a French woman in Porthampton. This one was white with open and closed red roses, three-quarter sleeves and a jewel neckline. She wore kitten heels that matched her tiger print handbag which had brass studs and dual handles made in the same twisted, plaited way as the handle of a good bullwhip. Mottram looked at it out of the corner of his eye, one day soon he was certain that he would feel it slamming into the side of his head.

Mrs Benson left the bar, Meredith Brewster crossed to the public side and told Mottram, "Enough crawling, H', do some work. Get the bar cleaned, check the optics, then get rid of Old Man Granger from the Snug, he's fallen asleep again, and clean up the gents, and serve that gentleman". She indicated the confused tourist who had given up and was reading a map, "He's been waiting a dog's age".

Harry tried a smile, then poured a pint of bitter beer, plonked it in front of the bewildered tourist, snatched a pound note from his hand, wiped the bar-top and sighed. The tourist took a sip, looked even more confused, stood up and walked out without saying a word. Harry finished the pint and pondered his good luck. Sarson-Taylor banged his glass on the bar, "Ho there Harry, a refill if you would".

Over at the table, the Bensons were discussing options for the big meeting to announce the birth of the British Freedom and Democracy Party next month.

Mrs Benson cut through the burble, "We need more women there. Not one of you has considered that fact".

"In all good faith, Edith, we really need to be concentrating on the youth", replied Jarvis, who was unsure about the advantage of the ladies in most areas of life.

He continued, "One of the failings of the National Front, one of the directions we're attempting to steer a true course away from, is a reliance on older folk. Youth is the way ahead".

Mrs Benson looked at her husband and then back at Jarvis. Her husband shrugged. She turned back to Don.

"Donnie, you're a clever man, a good-hearted man, a man who is important to our Party but Don", she leaned forward across the table, "you don't know what the fuck you are talking about a lot of the time. The Front, The British National Party, The British Union of Fascists, The British Movement, all of them, they were all desperate to capture 'The Youth'. And they ended up with football hooligans, queers, and the sort of easily lead yobbos who spent more time in Borstal than they did convincing other people of the righteousness of the cause.

"I don't even think much of your wonderful new politics but at least I do my fucking homework, Don. So, do yours or the whole fucking shebang will be stillborn.

"Who do you think has the most influence over the Youth? Politicians? Pop Stars? Sportsmen? No, you dinlo, it's their Mums. Get the mums onside and you've got the children. Not just the young-uns of today but going ahead into our history. A beautiful, healthy, lingering history long into the future. Women, Donald, women are central so buck your ideas up", she drained her port and lemon and looked to her husband for support.

"To be fair, Don, she's got a point. You've also got to think about the kids, obviously but she does have a good point".

Ever the reasoned compromiser, Eric Benson, smiled at his wife, "Edith does have a point, we must ensure that we steer British ladies in the direction of our fresh, new vision for their children".

He stood up, put his thumbs behind his braces and he was off, "Remember the War, Donald. Remember those GIs coming over here, flashing their white teeth and fat wallets. Remember them making rubbish of our ladies only to leave them behind with their fuzzy-haired bastard broods. Well, you go to Leicester or Ladbroke Grove or Manchester or even Stilbury, Candover Sands, Alesford in our great county and see what's happening today! See how those bastards have had their own and their population is…" He stood up.

"Sit down, Eric my love", whispered Mrs Benson, "don't make a spectacle… not yet".

"You're right, my love. We must all keep our powder dry before the big day", Eric took a sip from his rum and coke and lit a cigarette. His wife's advice was always on the button. She had been right about his investment in Australian emu farming (a mistake, he hadn't listened), she had been right about not taking on his old airforce pal as his company accountant (he had defrauded the company sending it into liquidation) and she had been right about him needing to do something positive with his energies after the liquidation had sent his mood spiralling down into the depths. He had spent months unable to leave the house. He drank heavily and refused even to play golf. The British Democratic Freedom Party was his outlet. It was effectively her idea in fact.

"Look, love, you're banned from being a company director and let's be frank here, you're not very good at business anyway. So, why are you interested?", she'd asked as they sat in the garden on a summer evening sipping Pimm's and lemonade with slices of cucumber sticking out of their glasses. She didn't give him time to shrug, "Politics, love. Our countryside. Our land".

She had been thinking about how to get him out of the house but not spending any money or failing dismally in yet another business venture. She could set him up in one of her own businesses for pin money. Even he couldn't fuck up working at the small Post Office cum General Store in Shalford; and money that would flow back into the house anyway – so that was covered. However, she realised that this would still give him a lot of time during the day to think, and unless that thought was channelled properly, they'd both be buggered again. He had been a dashing pilot when they'd first met in late 1945. Brutally young and devilishly handsome with piercing blue eyes, slicked back blond hair, and a swagger that gave his beautiful, tight arse all the gifts she was craving. Her love for him was buried in all of that and she still loved him, and she couldn't help that. He had charisma, lots of it. He had the self-confidence and ego of a single male child, and he had the ability to make other men doubt themselves if they didn't look too closely. A part of her hoped that he would mature and become the man that her first impressions had promised.

She had realised that politics was the obvious outlet for him after he returned drunk and happy from a squadron reunion. He had fallen on the bed talking about how they'd won the war but were losing the peace as the country was slipping into the hands of queers and Irish and blacks and Communists. Politics was about raising money.

Finding like-minded men to turn into a debating club was easy given the people she met every day in her various operations around the town. Eric had then really picked up the ball and was running hard with it, building a network of other men who felt let down, and forming a new political party with them. She had been amazed at how many of these brand new parties had formed and melted away bleeding members into each new incarnation so that after a while all these organisations came to look the same but still managed to fight among themselves anyway. She expected The British Democratic Freedom Party to go the same way after a time but hoped that time would be long enough to lift Eric out of his malaise. As far as she was concerned he could have taken up water colours, snooker or even transvestism as long as it kept him happy and out of trouble. She adored him and wanted to keep him safe while she got on with the job of bringing in the money.

Mr Eric Benson took his seat once again. Sarson-Taylor was lurking.

The front door of The Green Man opened and closed downstairs as Harry Mottram ejected Old Mr Granger into the night.

CHAPTER 9

LUNSFORD AT HOME

1978

One thing that could be said in favour of working for the City Council was that it looked after its people. Everybody at the CC who was concerned with the matter of Mr Martin Lunsford's working life was very happy with the way he had been treated as they waved him goodbye on his early retirement.

At 50 years old he had a healthy pension, a whip-around that had raised £101.22p, a payment from the Injury While in Service insurance run by the council, all this plus his navy pension. As far as his colleagues and managers were concerned, and they were all a bit envious but only in a good natured way, that Mark Lumpston was set up for a long, happy life ahead of him.

Indeed, Don Jarvis, by now deputy managing executive duty officer at the Office of Architectural Planning and Design, reinforced this point when he telephoned a week after Lunsford had moved back to his cottage. "You are set for life now Martin, mate. Set for life. Lots to look forward to, world's your royster-oyster – within limits, after all you're not a millionaire Nothing to worry about for you from now until Doomsday.

"The government, Her Majesty's Royal Navy, and the City Council have you safe and sound now. All you have to do is get well, old man. And don't forget to pop in and see your old mates. Don't be a stranger chappie". Jarvis hung up the phone feeling generally very good, and off he went to greet the new recruit, a young lady of all things. Lunsford returned the telephone to its cradle and decided not to pick it up again ever. He went into the sitting room at the front of Oak Cottage, next to the road where all the tanks and armoured cars were driven down to Porthampton for military festivals and possible invasions. At least he would never have to work in the same place as Don Jarvis. "That Odious man", Chloé had called him.

"At least you and Mick made something of his daft plan, sweet man", dead Chloé told him.

We did, we did. We made something, we worked so hard on that place. I hope it was worth it.

"And we've still never seen it because you won't visit", said Mick.

I can't visit. I can't go into the town. Too many people, too many things to remember. Too many new things. I can't go in without you Chloé.

"Oh, you cowardly little bastard. Your mother would be ashamed. We're all ashamed", said his father, Frank.

"I can't go into town. It's too far away. It's too hard to reach"

"Don't you want to see our building? Don't you want to see all the work we did?"

I can't. I can't. I can't go out. I can't see or be seen. I can't talk. I can't think about Mick. Maybe he'd be here to see it with me if I'd moved faster. Like that lad on the ship, like those lads in the water.

"Oh, you cowardly little bastard. How did you ever survive in the navy? Probably hid away in the heads", Frank's voice was loud.

"Just go and look, mate", Mick's voice was fading.

Rather than live in the city itself, the Lunsfords had set up home in the village of Shalford about eight miles south across The Water Meadows. Oak Cottage overlooked The Fleet Road that ran from Porthampton to the south and Crosschester. Heavy traffic: lorries, tractors and the occasional military vehicle full of squaddies heading into the barracks rumbled past and blackened the front of the cottage.

The Lunsfords bought Oak Cottage in the same year that they married. They had done very little to it other than to look after it and bring love to it. It was around 250 years old and had been painted so many times that it never looked out of place over the centuries it had been built around. Its original purpose was to house the village brewery manager. The Elders brewery was a square Georgian Building with a low pitch roof with wide flat eaves.

Until the start of the 1970s the brewery business had been a huge success serving three kinds of ale and beer to Crosschester and surrounding towns and villages. This ended when the eldest brother in the founding family had closed the brewery, taken the money and moved to New York City to work in advertising. Ale was not the way forward. His little brother thought differently and began to make small batches of a beer he named Elders Finest in a large shed in a forest. He prospered, locally.

People who knew the Lunsfords rarely entered Oak Cottage through the front door; instead they'd be welcomed through a back door that opened into a large square room. That beautifully proportioned and beloved room was an uncluttered and perfectly working kitchen with everything in its place if you knew where that place was, which Chloé did. It took up an entire side of the house and had a small patch of garden running under its long window. The kitchen, with its long, scarred and polished oak table, made from a slab of oak that had been seasoned by salt water and holystones, was where the Lunsfords spent most of their time.

Visitors who knocked on the front door from the slim strip of pavement between the house and the busily dangerous Fleet Road stepped through it into a short hallway. From there, if they turned to their left, they faced the stairs that lead to two bedrooms, one bathroom, one lavatory and then further up into the loft full of insulation, Christmas decorations and forgotten boxes. They would not be taken into the kitchen but to the sparse, formal front parlour. This was the room that Lunsford had taken himself into, and where he stood looking blankly into space.

In front of him was a door that led into the cosier, more private back room, which the Lunsford's called the Lounge Room, with its fat old sofa, its TV in a wooden cabinet, and its photographs of friends and family; the Lounge was for Sunday afternoons and summer evenings with the doors open. Unlike the always loudly busy kitchen, and despite its drinks cabinet, bookshelves and hi-fi stereo, the Lounge Room was usually the reserve of peaceful relaxation. It even had a set of sliding glass double doors giving a view out over the Water Meadows towards St Eade the Virgin's Church on the rise. In the summer they'd slide the doors open and breathe in the mix of grasses and fresh, chalk-running water that blew in with the southerly breezes. Sitting on, or rather in, the fat sofa together they could hear Sedge Warblers, Whitethroats, and Skylarks over the gentle flows of the chalk streams that threaded the meadows connecting and reconnecting with their mother, The River Icene.

There was a harmony in the gentle folds and flows and rivulets of the Water Meadows that had taken centuries to orchestrate with saturation and drought, growth, death; with men digging and channelling, and the cattle who grazed there. Other people came to the meadows to paddle, play games and eat picnics before packing up and walking home in the sunset. The Lunsfords had the pleasure of seeing the meadows every day, as if it was their garden.

Lunsford had avoided the lounge since he got back from hospital. When even the simplest of things seemed insurmountable he would retreat to the austerity of the wooden chairs in the parlour, but for the most part he spent his time in warm neutrality of the spare bedroom.

Oak Cottage sat quietly in Shalford, a village nestling in a shallow dip at the foot of chalk hills. If you were going to walk then the route to Crosschester would take you across the Water Meadows, across the Great London Road, under the railway viaduct, up and down Mizmazz Hill and on through the suburbs. To the east of the cottage stood St Eade's Church as it had done for a thousand years or more in one form or another. Beyond that was the relative poverty and cheap housing of the Churchfields housing estate, a place that the nicer people of

Shalford avoided talking about let alone visiting. To the west was Hunters Wood, a dark green, untidy, oversized copse that was home to badgers, owls and rats. It was also the setting for many of the terror-tales that the local kids used to pass down to each other for thrills and dares.

Before it was called The Hunters Wood it was 'The Hunters Forest', a vast and favourite royal chase for Saxon higher-ups and their hangers-on. Back then the River Icene flowed through the forest. It was in full, vigorous flow, straight as common sense, deep enough to be the keeper of secrets. It was the colour of Citrine or the colour of nothing depending on the run-off from Mizmazz Hill after a heavy rain.

Legend had it that a massive, yellow and white fish lived in a pool in the Icene back then. Huge, vicious and as ancient as the landscape. A Pike, an animal named after a simple, brutal and effective weapon. It was as old as the water. It was yellow like sickness, mottled like a slug, white like death. It could change instantly to soul black to hide in the depths.

Its teeth were honed by taking the arms and legs from children who dived into its pool or swam through the reeds and water weeds that filled the river in the summer. No one kept count on the number of children that the fish, known as 'Ancasta', had maimed and then consumed over the centuries. Of course, no one had even got close to catching it although many people had claimed to have had epic fights before Ancasta bit the line and disappeared. All of this held true in Lunsford's childhood. By that time the dark pool was outside Hunters Forest, which had contracted due to what were generally referred to as "Works". By 1934 due to the canal and railway Ancasta's dark pool was now on its border.

As a child living in Churchfields in the 1930s Lunsford knew all about the legendary pike, every single possible detail no matter how gruesome was part of the kids' language. The bottomless pool was where the brave and the stupid dived.

Every inch of the Icene along the stretch from Shalford to Crosschester was so clear that you would have been confused as to whether the caddisfly larvae were skitting on the surface hunting for flesh or were on the riverbed contemplating another kind of savagery. The kids of three villages, Shalford, Commiton and Bursley used the grassy area around the pool as a demilitarised zone during the spring and summer. No one ever fished there. No one threw stones or bottles. Up and down the river people played and laid in the hair weeded clear cool of the Icene being nibbled gently by tadpoles. Not in the Pool though. Never there, never except for one kid.

Lunsford had heard of one kid though. A kid from the Glenmore children's home that overlooked the Fleet Road. Everybody knew this kid, he was called Terry Timmons and he was a wiry boy of about 13 with spiky, ice blond hair, blue eyes, a sharp nose and lips so thin they could never smile. Terry spoke fast and filled his short sentences with "fucks" and "cunts" and "twats" and "wankers", and he didn't care who heard him. You kept away from Terry unless you were his brother, Keith, or unless he took to you. If that happened there was no getting away from him until he decided to fuck you around because you'd fucking pissed him off, you bastard.

At the end of one particularly long, sweltering day deep into the sunset Keith Timmons – so the story went – goaded his little brother into diving to the bottom of the Pool to retrieve a watch or a cigarette lighter or a bike light, no one was sure. Only Keith could have got away with this. Terry had no respect or fear for anybody else. At 15 years old. Keith was two years older than his brother and two foot taller, but even he wasn't a big lad. He was wide and he was muscular, thick necked but he wasn't tall. Both Keith and Terry were awash with aggression and broad South London accents. The boys had been transported to the backwoods of Shalford in the van a few years before. No one could deal with them in Streatham, so they were bundled down to stew in boredom until their violence cooked out and they decided to countrify and calm down a bit. Then they were off to the army or the navy. Years of bad diet and smoking the tobacco they could steal or find had meant that when they got out of the van, they were grey as chalk dust mixed with funeral ashes. Bags looped hung under their eyes, and their walk was stooped and shuffling. No one knew if they had parents and it didn't matter anyway.

On the hot evening of the goad (it wasn't a dare, both lads knew that Terry would do it, there was no way out of it, it was when that was in question), and after some months in the Water Meadows during their constant escape attempts, both boys had some colour on them. Because of the salads and other foods, they managed to steal from people's picnics and other places, and the sweet, fizzy cider they drank, they were also carrying a little weight. As soon as they began to bicker, anybody who'd known them for more than fifteen hellish minutes began to drift home, looking back occasionally in case something exciting was happening to someone else. The less well informed, or bruised, gathered around to watch. In hindsight Lunsford thought he may have seen the start of a fight between the boys but as ever with memory it didn't really matter because he felt sure he had seen something. Maybe he'd just heard Keith yelling at Terry, and Terry screaming back. It was a long time ago after all.

The day after as he walked from Churchfields down past St Eade's, into the Water Meadows to school in the village each boy and girl along the way had news.

"I heard the police were up Glenmore, taking kids away or something", said one girl called Tracy.

"No, those lads never got back from the Pool I heard, the coppers was asking questions all over our street all night, I heard them when they were in our kitchen late", said a ten year old called Martin.

"I heard that Ancasta got him", said Michael Barnes, the kid with the snotty nose who no one ever believed any way.

"Got who?"

No one believed Michael Barnes. Of the poor folk who lived in the Churchfields estate, the Barnes family were the poorest. Michael always had a snotty nose and was constantly looking to pick up scraps of other people's food.

"Got that kid from Glenmore, dragged him down, you could see the blood and guts on the surface later. I went down there last night, there were police all over and ambulances not just bobbies either, proper private eyes and all that".

"Fuck off Barnsey!" yelled the other kids and Michael stood back, wiped his snot encrusted nose, put his hands in the pockets of his short trousers and waited for them to move off.

A few weeks later the story he'd told stopped being a story and became news instead. This was when Tim Roach, the captain of the Shalford Preparatory School football team began to share the story using roughly the same details with maybe a little added gore and with the wrong names for the boys. Everybody believed Tim Roach. Over time, the fact of the Timmonses themselves faded into the legend where it grew in anger and gore until the legend itself was forgotten.

Forty years later, sitting in the parlour trying not to face other histories, his memory threw up the names of the boys. Unlike Chloé and Mick, the faces and the voices of Keith and Terry were clear as the air on a cold, cloudless winter's day. He welcomed the memory, the legend, his feelings about that scorching summer when he was eight or nine or ten because it took up valuable space. He began to wonder what had happened to Keith and Terry in reality, and with that thread he was taken to London and in his memory of London he was taken for tea and cake on the Charing Cross Road with his mother and on and on deeper into any thought that wasn't a thought of today.

An hour or so later and hunger forced him out of his revery. He had to venture out into the village to the post office that also served as a general store where he would pick up essentials for living because something in him still refused to die. He went in just before closing time when he knew that Mr Benson the storekeeper and postmaster would be eager to shut the place up and drive back to Crosschester so there would be a minimum of chatter. He bought some eggs, a jar of strawberry jam, two tins of Heinz baked beans, a loaf of white bread, a pack of pork sausages and a copy of The Chronicle for the crossword. He said a hello and a goodbye and then walked the half mile past The Volunteer pub and the Primary School, past the old forge that was now a sweet shop run by two elderly brothers, passed the florist and the butchers, all closed and back to Oak Cottage. By the time he closed the back door he was shaking and close to tears. The voices in his head, his chorus, were silent. He made himself a cup of tea with four sugars to try and calm the shock, and spent as little time as possible in the kitchen as he could. He took his mug into the parlour and resumed his seat after taking one of Chloé's weird books from the small white painted, pine free standing shelf.

Chloé hadn't been born in Shalford or even Crosschester, and this made her interested in finding out more about the area. To this end she collected books and pamphlets by local authors, the kind of work that is produced by enthusiasts and sold from churches, museums and general stores.

Lunsford had picked out a copy of *Legends and Folk Monsters of the County* written by Dr Alice Wilson (PhD) in 1968. It was a substantial book, 400 pages, case-bound with flimsy hard covers and low-grade paper, with black and white illustrations by the author.

The book contained mentions of creatures including The Shalford Ancasta. It also contained The Sea Calamities, which devoured sailors and passengers whose ships were wrecked off Porthampton and Henton-on-Sea. The Batsford Dragon, a creature that fed on cattle, pigs and the unfaithful was there. So was the dragon who was said to be the consort of Witch Sybil, the crazily wild and wise (according to Alice Wilson) woman burnt at the stake by Judge Henry Pollexfen in Crosschester in 1673. Her dragon had swooped to collect her burning body from the flames and they both flew over the crowd declaring revenge on the entire county.

He looked over at the door into the lounge and thought again about going in there. Instead, he stood up, turned off the table lamp and made his way upstairs to the spare bedroom with its single bed. He turned off the main light, got undressed and got into bed, before long he was asleep, and smells of The Water Meadows were inside his dreams

Lunsford woke at 6am and tried to go back to sleep. The room was dark, the heavy curtains closed, and he saw no good reason to leave this bed let alone the room. He wasn't hungry. He had no one to see. He had no one he wanted to see. He rolled over, face to the wall and closed his eyes. Neither sleep nor his bladder were sympathetic to his growing depression, however.

Eventually, and with no joy at all, he turfed himself out of the bed, into his clothes and along the corridor to the lavatory. He finished his business, washed his hands and cleaned his teeth and wished his mind would stop churning through his pasts. He just wanted to empty out. He made his way downstairs to the kitchen where he put on the kettle, dropped a teabag in his blue and white football team mug, took the milk out of the fridge, sniffed at it, and became aware of a scratching sound coming from somewhere in the house. The kettle shrilled and at the same time there was a knock at the front door. Lunsford took the kettle off the stove before it had time to fully come to the boil. He ignored the knock on the door. He ignored it again as he poured the milk into the tea.

He ignored a further knock on the front door, it was 8:30am, and with a mug in hand he walked into the parlour to sit down and finish the crossword he'd begun the previous night. Again, the scratching sound came, this time he felt certain that it was coming from the outside, on the Water Meadows side of the house.

Again the knocking came at the front door. Two sharp taps, then a beat, then one more sharp tap.

"Hello, Mr Lunsford!" he didn't recognise the voice.

He still refused to go to the front door. He didn't even remember if he knew where the key to that door was kept.

Another set of three knocks.

"Mr Lunsford!" it was a woman's voice, and an assured one.

Another pause. Another three sharp raps.

He could also hear the steady scratching from the other side of the house. It was a patient sound. Not a big creature but not a rodent. Certainly not a human being.

"Mr Lunsford! Let me in! My name is Helen Cousins, I'm your health visitor, let me in. Mr Lunsford are you all right?" the woman's voice didn't sound at all concerned, it sounded annoyed.

Then he remembered the woman from his last week on Ward 12. She was thin lipped, tall, all high cheekbones and small eyes. She had looked him over, said things in a voice like wire mesh and had promised to visit him, "with great regularity" until he was "back on his pegs and ready to go". He had taken a dislike to her immediately.

Still, she pounded on the front door using the same rhythm, with the same cadence, like a machine. Still the scratching noise came, and Lunsford now thought that must be coming from inside his lounge room.

"Mr Lunsford, this is extraordinarily bad form of you. If you are in there you need to answer this door, if you are not in there, you should not waste the time of professional people!".

Lunsford stood up from his chair, then bent over to ensure that he could not be seen through the parlour window, and in this posture he made his way to the lounge door, he pressed his ear against it, still bent nearly double, and listened.

"Mr Lunsford! Open this door! I will give you one more minute!" another triple rap, he thought he could hear her sighing in the way a cobra might sigh when faced with yet another recalcitrant mongoose.

Lunsford opened the door to the lounge, and still bent over he faced into the room he'd not been able to face for so long.

CHAPTER 10

THEIR OLD ROOM

1978

Lunsford stood up and looked into the lounge room. Its old floor made of heavily polished jigsaw pieces of golden brown parquet, second hand from a cold school up north. He and Mick had spent a week fitting it. It should have been a comforting sight. It wasn't. It was as solid as memory.

He felt it with his right hand and then his left, it had a warmth that was familiar. The messy bulk of the massive old sofa was sitting against the long side wall facing the fireplace, which he could smell from where he knelt – a gentle smell that evoked Christmas ashes and first thing in the winter mornings. The wall behind the sofa was painted a light beige colour, the one surrounding the deep set fireplace was stone, blackened by years then growing golden pale almost as sandstone as it grew away from the smoke and flames.

To the left of the fireplace as he faced it from the sofa was a cabinet with a hi-fi stack of amplifier, record player, and cassette recorder; expensive stuff, a gift to Lunsford and Chloé from Lunsford and Chloé. Music had been far more common in their house than talking or television. Next to that was an ornate lamp masquerading as a melting candle in a gold candle holder. The lampshade was a taut white-gone-cream cloth stretched over wire with an open square top and a tasselled, fluted bottom. He'd taken an electric shock from the brass switch fitting on that lamp just after they'd moved in, and so was always a little nervous of it. Behind the lamp and record player were shelves of records, his and hers, mostly hers, all mixed together. Lots of jazz (New Orleans, his. Bebop, hers. Big Band, theirs), English folk rock (hers), Elvis and Jerry Lee (his), and a variety of classical music, jostled each other in no particular order because they knew where each record was by sight and repetition.

He preferred the classics to the all-over-the-place jazz that Chloé tried to explain to him. The big band stuff, Benny Goodman, Tommy Dorsey, Glen Miller, that was fine and understandable, you could tap along to that. That was enjoyable but not the modern jazz business, the John Coltranes and Thelonius Monks and the Miles Davis's, that seemed far too hard to listen to, to be soaked up in, to enjoy.

"If you need to explain it, it's not really music is it? It's more like an exam", he'd said to Chloé after she had tried and failed to steer him through A Love Supreme or Brilliant Corners.

She had sighed and stroked his face with the back of her hand because she loved him. After many years of marriage there were many things that each of them realised they did not love about each other, and they were thankful for that. Their house and their life together were settled but not stultifying, small shards of emotional grit still made it into their loving shell. After the first five years of living in wedded collusion it became clear that certain understandings had been assumed that did not stand up to the simple complexities of everyday life.

Struggle and skirmish took over from early and unalloyed romantic love. These skirmishes played out in the bloody theatres of cleaning the house, choosing a record to listen to, getting a dog or not getting a dog, the colour of the bedroom walls, toothpaste tube squeezing. Finally, they argued about kissing: too hard or too wet or too short or too long was just not good enough. This revelation was shocking as both of them had convinced themselves that their kiss was the sure proof of their immediate and eternal connection. This led to all kinds of self-consciousness, anger, doubt, shame, further clumsy exchanges, despair and hope. All silent. All internal. Chloé discussed it with Mick's wife Jeanne. Lunsford discussed it with no one.

For a while as they went about life hour by hour and day by day until it seemed as if they would just have to settle for dry, limited touch. Then, one night looking into the Water Meadows from their sofa breathing in the late summer evening air, after a long day doing not very much by the river, and after months and months of not wanting to lose each other, they kissed. It was the reminder of the small perfection that had been their coupling and it happened as the sun came down. It wasn't a long or short kiss, it was flavoured with grass cuttings, running water, clear and cool over chalk, a small white wine, and a half-pint of beer. What followed was shock in silence as they held each other's hands and smiled, were relieved, energised with love, and knew that they could go on.

The kiss came after negations and screaming matches had exhausted themselves. Both Chloé and Lunsford pushed and levered each other into and out of various positions, meant and performed in the hope of retrieving the meaning of themselves individually within the relationship and of the relationship itself. After the kiss Lunsford remembered to vacuum the house and dust in the parlour without being asked (eventually he took pleasure in seeing the house clean).

Eventually Chloé remembered to consider his responses when choosing new things for the house. Eventually they both agreed to move quietly around the other things that could have broken them. This was their marriage. Moving from moments where they thought that they'd never known each other to moments when all they wanted to know was each other.

Lunsford sat down on the sofa in front of which was a low, octagonal table with a glass top and on top of that were some old newspapers and a tea mug. It was Chloé's choice of table, some designer or other she'd read about in a magazine and then found someone in Crosschester who could do a decent copy for half the price. It wasn't to Lunsford's taste.

The last time he'd used that table he had promised himself that the mug would get removed to the kitchen and the newspaper taken to the garage and added to the pile. Instead, he had left the crossword unfinished and the mug where it was and walked into town to meet Mick for the final drink of their lives.

To the right of the fireplace was a cabinet with two sliding doors that incarcerated the bloated television that they'd bought in 1970 and then mostly forgotten about. On top of it was a large, clean glass ashtray for guests. Also, mostly for guests, was a glass drinks cabinet next to the sofa.

Lunsford pulled his head up and looked at the glass double doors with their view into the Water Meadows. He saw a dog pawing at them. Its mass of shaggy fur was every autumnal shade imaginable. Its paws worked in a steady rhythm. Its brown eyes stared into the room. Its jaws were closed. It was the height of his knee. There was no rush or panic to get into the house, just a clear and particular design. It had no collar, so there was nothing to identify it.

"It could be rabid", he thought.

"Don't be silly, love, there aren't any wild, rabid dogs around here, we would have been told, we would have been advised", said Chloé.

Lunsford said, "Sit. Sit down", and then for some reason he would never fathom, he waved at it. The dog stopped scratching and sat down, setting its head to an angle that indicated curiosity and a little impatience as if to say, "Hurry up then, it's been ages, let me in".

There was little Lunsford could do in the light of the dog's expression than to make his way to the doors and, with some hesitation and gentle force – the lock hadn't been used in a year or more – slide them apart. The dog sat, looking up at the man, a smile on its face, and waited to be asked in.

"Like a vampire", said his dad's voice.

"Come in then", said Lunsford and in it came trotting muddy, Water Meadow paw prints over the wooden floor. He noticed immediately that the dog wasn't sniffing anything. It was as it was already familiar with the room, with the house, with Chloé and

Lunsford's smells. As it walked its claws made tapping sounds like beads thrown onto marble. Lunsford closed the doors and returned to the sofa. The dog climbed up and settled into Chloé's spot at the meadows end. The dog looked over at Lunsford, blinked her eyes once before closing them and shortly afterwards she began to snore.

He got up and stood in the middle of the room looking at the dog and feeling entirely unsure about the situation. First things first though, he walked over to the doors and reached out to shut them. He was hit by the smells of the Water Meadows. Such a resonant attack. Such a beatifying beating. He breathed in deeply and took long ago summers and winters inside him. There was the smell of the giant sycamore tree that had been felled by lightning and hollowed out over the years, so it was as a castle or a spaceship for the children. There was the smell of the smoke from recently extinguished candles at St Eade's church. There was the smell of under-age fag smoke from the weir side. There were the smells of a half-sunken boat, of bullies and of bicycle chain oil. There were the smells of lightning and cheap, fizzy cider. There was the smell of Chloé and Lunsford out in the world together again. Then the wind whipped the tears on his face, drying it clean with its splintering cold. He shut the doors and turned around to find the dog lying on its back, all four legs in the air, paws flopping at acute angles. She was still snoring. Lunsford thought about lighting the fire but all of a sudden he felt incredibly tired and decided instead to sit himself in the padded sofa and rest.

He fell into a nap, then quickly into a deep sleep, and soon the room was full of the sounds of a man and a dog. Both were dreaming. Both jerked their limbs then settled then moved jaggedly again. Both sputtered and moaned in their respective languages but brokenly. The only ones who could have heard them were the spiders of the house, maybe the spirits of the meadows but who knew if they existed? As the day wore on, so the pair slept on. As the weak heat and the light of the day faded, they wriggled gently against each other until the dog's head was resting on the man's lap, and the man's hand lay on the dog's head; their body heat circulated and mixed. His head was thrown back and snoring in a guttering way as his dream life body interacted with his physical body. He was having the same dreams as usual but with the slight addition of the new dog.

In his dreams he called her 'Adelaide' and she responded to him quite often. The dreams covered several years during which they walked a lot. They made trips to the pebbled beaches of the south coast and to the Isle of Sands with its granular snobbery: even the poor people (the extremely poor people) looked down on the mainland as unlucky and somehow infected. They visited London and Paris with equal bemusement at the language and customs. They set sail for New York City and explored its valleys. For the most part they walked through Crosschester, Bursley and Commiton back to Shalford, never the other way around. In Crosschester they inevitably began their walks at The Market Cross. This dominated the streets around it. They began to walk from what his dream life had realised as The Wulfric Hall, which Adelaide used as a pissing post. Looking down on her from each face were several grotesques and gargoyles: angry, sarcastic, bitter faces; strange, violent acts in wearying detail.

The pair walked through sickly sweet Doric columns at the front and through the double doors with their door knockers in the form of

Winston Churchill's cigar-smoking skull. Entering the building they were shattered by yells and howls from bullet-headed giant grey men. Half of them were standing still, saluting and watching as the others beat each other. Suddenly they all stopped and began scourging their own backs with bicycle chains and sprigs of holly.

When Lunsford woke it was dark. He stretched his limbs and felt the dog's head under his hand. He smiled. He had enjoyed her company during their dream travels. She growled a low growl, unhappy that her sleep had been interrupted. When she finally recognised him she licked his hand and jumped off the sofa.

She walked over to the door to the parlour, which Lunsford had closed, and she sat down, looking over her shoulder at him quizzically. Seeing that the man wasn't moving, she barked at him to hurry up. This did the trick, and he opened the door. The same process happened again to get the pair from the parlour into the kitchen and there they stood staring at each other. She barked once again.

"Quiet now Adelaide, no need for that", the dog quietened down, and looked at him with an expectation of a momentous event such as the arrival of food.

Outside the nightbirds were singing, they were all unsettled, uncertain of their notes and sequences so that their songs became confused and intersected with each other producing a new and frightening song. The other animals in the meadows and further into Hunters Wood stopped what they were doing and began to growl or whimper.

Lunsford had never owned a dog. He didn't know the first thing about dogs except that they needed feeding and they shat all over the place. This was exactly the sort of thing that Chloé would have excelled at. He looked at Adelaide, she looked up at him. He went through all the cupboards in the kitchen, slowly one by one to find anything that might be suitable for a dog to eat. Eventually he settled on the contents of a tinned Fray Bentos steak and kidney pie. Fortunately, the tin doubled as a dog bowl. He placed it with its dark brown, cold congealed contents on the doormat and looked at her. If a dog could shrug, then Adelaide shrugged. She sniffed the food and then ate it methodically from outside in, tipping the dish forward with her paw as necessary.

Once she'd finished, she looked up at him expectantly. He didn't understand at first, there were so many things the look could mean, the dog was confusing him.

Just like the fucking country used to be, son. Now look at it. Fucking chaos. Foreigners everywhere. Smelly, garlic curry and crap. It's all changing, son. All fucking changing. And not for the best. What's wrong with things like what they were?

His dad had been drunk, violent, absent, needy surely yes, but not political. Also, given he didn't believe in ghosts or the voices of ghosts, the words he was attributing to his father must be coming from him he realised. He'd never even thought about foreigners or the state of the country. He left politics to other people. He left that line of thought lie and tried to imagine what Adelaide might want to eat after the cold filling from a cheap steak and kidney pie.

Lunsford looked down at the dog. She looked back up at him. She licked her black liquorice shoelace lips. He licked his dry, red lips. She nodded. He stroked her. She rested against his legs. He thought more deeply about the problem at hand before deciding that she needed a drink.

He picked up her improvised bowl and took it to the sink where he filled it with cold water. She wagged her tail. She returned to her station in front of the door and placed the water-filled bowl in front of her. Without a second look she nosed down and drank. He patted her head. She growled quietly but continued to drink. When she'd finished the bowl, she looked up again and he reached down, picked it up and repeated the act. This time Adelaide didn't growl when he ruffled the tangle of fur on her head. She drank and, when she was finally satisfied, she lay down next to the kitchen door and closed her eyes. It felt late. Lunsford and the dog had been in the lounge for hours. He was very, very tired. He looked back at the dog guarding the door and he went upstairs to the spare bedroom.

Outside, snow clouds were building up, the temperature was dropping, and the light was unsure how to behave. There was no wind, not yet but it was brewing in the trees in The Hunters Forest.

CHAPTER 11

LUNSFORD MUST GO OUTSIDE

1978

Lunsford woke at 7:30am still very much in the dark. Adelaide was curled comfortably at the end of the bed so that he nearly kicked her out of the door while he stretched to wake up. She growled but seemed to give the man the benefit of the doubt.

He looked at this watch and thought, "This means there's a lot of the day to get through. A lot of day to drag on before bed again. I wish I drank. I wish I had a hobby. I wish they weren't dead. I wish we had kids. I miss them. All day left. I wish I had courage. I wish. All day to go".

He sat up in bed and switched on his bedside lamp. "You're still here then?" she growled gently in response. I'm hungry.

She must be hungry, he thought. She wagged her tail.

"When are you going to be leaving then, Adelaide? When do you head off home?" he said out loud.

She stood up and jumped off the bed. She headed downstairs where she scratched at the kitchen door. She then investigated the blue Fray Bentos dog bowl. Empty, thoroughly empty. She kicked it and went back to trying to force the door.

Lunsford hauled himself out of bed, slipped his feet into his tatty slippers and trudged up the hall to the bathroom where he did the necessary before emptying his overnight water glass. He washed his face and hands, brushed his teeth and examined himself in the mirror. He was thin. Thinner, probably thinner than he should be but there was no Chloé to tell him.

You need to eat more, my love. You're wasting away.

The lines on his face and forehead were ingrained, his grandfather had the same plough lined skin. He passed his hand over his stubbled chin and discounted shaving and then picked up the hairbrush and passed it through his greying hair. He looked in the mirror again expecting a change, he had very few memories of his own face. He was ageing like his grandad had aged: gradually and by the book. His grey-blue eyes were fading to milk. He promised himself a visit to the public library in Crosschester to find out if this was a bad thing or whether it would just pass – he knew he wouldn't go. Downstairs in the kitchen, Adelaide kicked the blue bowl across the floor again and returned to the door in quiet desperation.

Lunsford jumped at her noise then padded back to his bedroom where he changed out of his pyjamas. He put on a thick, brown, cable-knit shirt with short sleeves and a stag motif on the left breast, a pair of dark blue slacks that used to have beautifully ironed seams like the backs of swordfish. He put old his brown brogues that were now on their third sole.

A clatter came from downstairs. Lunsford girded himself to face whatever it was down there destroying the house but then remembered Adelaide the dog.

"She's going to need feeding again if she's staying. I'd like her to stay but that means going out to get food. I hope the Post Office sells dog food. What if it doesn't? Get some more pie? Do dogs eat Corn Flakes?", he said out loud to himself.

Downstairs Adelaide kicked the bowl again.

This time in his own head he said:

"I need to go out to the shop. Go to the shop, then back home. Open the door and walk to the shop. It's not hard. I probably won't have to meet anybody if I go early. Only Mr Eric Benson. Do I need a bag? Have I got enough money? What if somebody stops me for a chat? Where is my wallet? She is hungry. I am hungry. If I didn't feel hungry, I wouldn't need to go out again. But she is hungry".

"How did you get so weak? Not from my side of the family. Must be from your mother", back came his father, Frank, as if he'd never been dead.

Leaving the house to go to the shop was terrifying. People might try and help, and that would be shattering. However, the trip had a defined start and end. He could do that. He looked at his watch, it was still more than an hour before Eric Benson would open the shop. He folded his discarded pyjamas, put them under his pillow, pulled the counterpane over the bed and headed to the kitchen where Adelaide rushed to him, barked and then rushed back to the door.

"Come along Adelaide. You can't want to leave so soon. You've not even eaten", he looked at her bowl which was in the middle of the room, "and you've had nothing to drink, you must be parched".

She barked and scratched in what seemed to him to be fierce panic. He felt terrible. He didn't want to lose her company. Her novelty didn't scare him.

She barked and scratched and lifted her muzzle to the sky and she howled. Lunsford quivered. She was obviously in distress. He needed her to stay, and he could make that happen simply by refusing to turn the handle and push on the door a little. He stood firm. She jumped at the handle. He closed his eyes and she howled louder and more plaintively.

"No, Adelaide. Just wait. Wait for food. You'll be happy here, I promise".

"You don't know that. You've never had a pet. All the pets we had as a family I had to fucking slop out and exercise. Let the poor little fucker out, it wants to get back home. Jesus, you're a fucking disgrace".

"Shut up dad! Please, please stop". Lunsford walked to the door, knelt down and gave Adelaide a final scratch under her chin, and opened the door. She rushed out and he watched her go. He stood and closed the door.

"That's more like it. That's my son. Couldn't be bothered to look after a fucking stray dog. Too much of a responsibility for you was it? Like looking after your wife and friend and your own dad? Prick".

As usual his mother was nowhere to be heard.

Lunsford decided to concentrate on the everyday. The cupboards, as he'd feared, were bereft of any kind of food for dogs or men. He checked the fridge: some eggs that were as light as water when he shook the box. A half bottle of milk, some cheese, some cottage cheese and a carrot, all ancient and nasty. There was no bread in the bread bin. Not much to go on. He decided against visiting the white battleship of a chest freezer that Chloé had insisted on buying. It sat at the side of the concrete and pebbledash garage that he and Mick had built just after the married couple moved in.

"I'll have to make a shopping list. I wish we'd had kids, they could have done all this. Why didn't we have kids?" he thought.

"I'll have to go outside. There's nothing I can do here. I don't want to talk to people. I don't want to answer their questions about how I'm feeling and isn't it a shame? How does anybody get over a tragedy let alone a double tragedy? Aren't I brave? And they're sure they could never get through like me. Brave. Yes, brave. So brave.

"But of course, during the war we all managed to get through, didn't we? Having so much death around you that must be horrible mustn't it? If there is anything they can do? Just ask. Just ask.

"What did he need? What can they do? What did he want? What? What? What? Would he like a pound of tea? Or a visit? Or a quiet afternoon? Or his wife and best friend back? Or to be dead himself? Would he like to go to the pictures? Or the football? Or the bingo?

"Would he like to have people round for tea? Or would he hate that?

"Did he think the weather was going to get any wetter? Lovely for ducks and what was he going to do with himself today? Lovely for ducks?

"How did he think he had recovered after the accident? He

shouldn't blame himself of course and does he have enough soap at home? And what was he eating? Did he have an iron? Would he like to buy one? They were electric these days, so easy! Did he have someone to come and do for him because, and no one was judging of course but it's easy to let it all go isn't it?"

He had no idea what he wanted any more or if he wanted anything anymore.

"I must go and put some flowers on Chloé's grave next week. What kind would she have liked? Should I get lilies? Would she have liked that?" he didn't know, he didn't know at all.

He looked out of the window, it was raining. He was crying. Adelaide was scratching at his door. She was, he was sure of it. He opened it and she came in, soaking and far from happy. As he closed the door against the weather, he saw a pile of dogshit and piss near the wall.

"I am so sorry Adelaide. I am so sorry, love. What an idiot I am", he said out loud.

She shook herself, spattering the room with warmed, muddy rainwater. Then she wandered over to her blue, metal bowl and nudged it with her nose. Still empty. If a dog could shrug and look disappointed, Adelaide was that dog. Lunsford grabbed some old cornflakes and added them to the bowl with a little water and looked at the dog. She went to the bowl, shoved her nose in, then shoved her entire face in and started to eat greedily.

The front door letterbox opened and slammed shut. Lunsford ignored the post and instead grabbed his jacket from the hook on the kitchen door. He put it on and found his wallet in an outside pocket. He picked up his keys from the bowl by the door and looked up at the clock over the sink, it was still too early. He had to waste some time. He made himself a cup of tea and picked up an old copy of The Chronicle that Joan must have dropped there when she was cleaning the place up.

The headline declared, "Free Speech Champion Begins Hunger Strike Today!". A lead story about a chap called Rafe Roberts from somewhere in the Midlands who had gone on hunger strike in Crosschester Prison. He had been arrested and convicted under the new Race Relations Act after posting an advert to sell his house that read:

"To avoid animosity all round positively no coloureds need apply"

He had fought by defending himself. His supporters loved this decision. The legal profession was confounded. Less confounding to all concerned, save Mr Roberts himself, was his sentence of six months in prison for Contempt of Court due to one too many splenetic outbursts at the judge. The tabloid newspapers and the people in the pubs and the old ladies and gents sitting at home decided that this term went against all the values that the country held dear.

Most of them remained of this view despite photographs of Mr Roberts dressed in a white sheet, standing in front of a burning cross on a piece of industrial wasteland and published in The News of the World. He was holding up a photograph of a young, white man called Kevin Gately who had been killed during an anti-Fascist demonstration. Roberts had added to the photograph in red felt pen the words:

"YOUR NEXT IF YOU DONT LOVE YOUR COUNTRY BE WARNED!"

On the day Roberts was sent down, the National Front and a ragtag of other like-minded groups handed out leaflets outside Crosschester Crown Court. One of these, emblazoned with an upside-down Union Jack had been slipped into The Chronicle and fell onto Lunsford's floor. He picked it up and put it on the table and turned to the old sports pages where Crosschester Rovers FC had drawn at home again.

Lunsford read on, moving back through the newspaper from the sport via the small ads, the TV listings and the puzzle pages, and onto to the letters page. The letters were comfortingly familiar, dealing as they did in outrage about dog fouling (Lunsford had not considered this, and made a mental note), the price of bread ("disgusting"), the new one-way system ("designed by an intellectual type who must never have visited our beautiful City!").

Adelaide scratched at the door and barked.

He looked down at the leaflet. He wasn't a political man. He voted because voting was a civic duty and he'd fought for it. He always voted the same way. Crosschester, despite its two large council housing areas and the poverty in many of the outlying villages was calmly and confidently, occasionally aggressively, big and small C Conservative.

Keep BRITON British! NEVER EVER to be SLAVES!
Enough is ENOUGH!!
We Want Are Country Back!!

March for White Rights!

March fo Peace!

FREE RAFE ROBERTS!

Great Britain what a joke. YOU HAVE BEEN WARNED! Britain will not be GREAT again until the following happens!

- Get Britain out of the Common Market
- Stop ALL immigration
- Start repatriation
- Stop the Jewish Internationalists!
- Stop inflation by keeping proper control over our monetary system
- Sack all Communist School Teachers
- Crack down hard on Distrupters in industry
- Stop property speculators
- Housing for British people
- Get tough with criminals
- Ban the I.R.A.
- Fight corruption in government
- Raise pensions to two thirds average wage
- Repeal Abortion Act
- Out, out out! with Asians, Queers, Niggers and Jew Usurers!!

ENOCH WAS RIGHT! FREE RAFE!

Lunsford thought about what he'd read. Asians? Aside from The Emerald Dragon take-away on the High Street in town he'd never seen an Asian anywhere in Crosschester, but maybe he hadn't been looking at them. As for Jews and queers, he wouldn't even know where to start. That said, there had been rumours about Ben Novak from work for a while until he relocated.

"I don't even know what an Internationalist is, and surely the IRA are already banned? How could you spot a Communist? What is the Abortion Act? Who are the Distrupters? When did all of this start? Must have been when I was in hospital? Are all these people coming into the country? When are they coming?" he asked Adelaide.

His heart was racing and his head was aching. He balled up the leaflet and made to toss it into the bin by the door and closed his eyes.

"This is why I steer clear of politics, you see. This is why I steer clear. There's nothing I can do. There's nothing I understand", he said to her.

A high pitched tone had begun in his head, travelling from left ear to right and back again. He opened his eyes, the leaflet was unfolding on the table where apparently he'd dropped it. Thick lips, hooked noses, IRA, promises, warnings, red ink and black skin, Queers and Teachers all roared up at him as the paper spread out like the fungus blooming. He closed his eyes, the tone ricocheted across his skull. He couldn't catch his breath.

"What is happening out in the world?", he said.

Adelaide came towards him and took his sleeve in her teeth, she was growling a low growl and madly wagging her tail. He could feel her soft mouth on his arm, no biting but guiding. He realised that he was looking down on himself. From his vantage point, numbly near the ceiling he could see Adelaide trying to unlock him from himself. He could see his head flung back, eyes tight shut, and he could hear himself moaning. Adelaide kept pulling and growling. He tried to breathe. Overhead he was confused and angry at himself.

Someone was yelling now and banging on the front door "Mr

Lunsford, let me in", he covered his ears and stood up, "Let me in!"
Huge thudding tolls came through the house as the black iron Lion-
headed clapper was smashed into its door plate. The tone in Lunsford's
head harmonised with the resonating bass of the thumps.

Adelaide kept pulling and growling, and finally Lunsford
unwrapped himself and stood up. Adelaide let go of him and ran out of
the kitchen. Half blind and deafened Lunsford followed her. She ran
past the front door, which was bulging with the massive shocks it was
receiving, she ran into the parlour, he followed.

"When did I get so weak? How did I get so weak? Why didn't we
have children?" he thought and waited for Frank to pile in.

"You need to answer this door. Answer this door if you please!"
the voice came again. Louder. More authoritarian. No one who came to
the front door of Oak Cottage ever yelled. Adelaide ran through the
parlour and into the lounge where she stood at the double doors
shaking, full of angry excitement and cornflakes.

Lunsford opened the doors, quietly, and they both bounded
through, over the low wall and into the Water Meadows. Lunsford
hadn't run anywhere in decades and his legs were not up to it, so he
stumbled forward at slightly more than walking speed, Adelaide
sprinted ahead, jumping with joy. The morning air was crisp and
beautiful, filling their lungs with the outside world. There were no
other people to be seen.

He looked over his shoulder and saw that the house was no longer
in sight. He stopped. Adelaide ran a loop, leaping over streams and
finally settling at his side, looking up, wagging her tail, licking his
hand, so much energy. Lunsford looked around him. He loved the

Meadows and the memory of that love overwhelmed him, but Adelaide wouldn't let him settle.

"I'm all over the bloody place, aren't I? When did I get so bad? All the things that have happened should have made me stronger. Loss makes other men stronger. How did I get so weak?", he asked the Meadows.

He decided that he wasn't impressing the Meadows nor its birds or the hidden animals, so he stood straight, breathed in and out, and pointed himself in the direction of the Post Office to face Mr Eric Benson. Adelaide definitely needed proper food. It would be unfair on her or she might leave again in search of someone who would take care of her. After all she had only appeared in his life because she was hungry and needed somewhere safe to rest.

His floating, disengaged and seceded self, neither dead nor alive, hungry nor satiated, neither pained nor assuaged considered the situation and agreed.

"At least she's honest. There's no side to Adelaide. At least we can trust her. She doesn't lie. Anybody will leave if their needs aren't met. That's simple and understandable. She's not yours, it's more like you're hers. Stop crying now, you poor old sod. Let's walk".

Adelaide joined earthbound Lunsford and they all headed off across the Meadows in the direction of the Post Office and the ministrations of Mr Eric Benson, Postmaster, and centre of village communications.

CHAPTER 12

HE CARED DEEPLY FOR EVERYBODY IN THE VILLAGE

1978

Mr Eric Benson looked like he should have been running the butcher's shop or sitting on the board of a brewery. He was a large man, full of fat and energy, red ruddy faced, thick lipped and thicker fingered. Owing to a weak knee he stood slightly lopsidedly behind the counter, occasionally passing his hands through his thick clump of black hair and sighing. Eric Benson cared deeply for everybody in the village and couldn't bear the idea that anybody might have a problem, a trial or a tribulation that he might not be able to help with.

As a one-time prime mover on the Parish Council, Mr Eric Benson had been responsible for pushing through several bylaws that ensure peace and quiet for every upstanding citizen of the village. He was proudest of his bylaw that meant any musician who hadn't already played in the village and wanting to perform in any of its four pubs had to be sponsored at a cost of £20. The money had to be paid by the relevant landlord. Any rowdies, Punk Rockers or god forbid, minstrel types who wanted to play at The Bugle, The Dolphin, The Volunteer or The Bridge Inn was effectively barred. No one was certain that the Parish Council had the statutory powers necessary to pass bylaws, nevertheless the elderly inhabitants of Shalford could not have been happier.

The Bensons were a respectable family that took pride in the village, the city, their county, the crown and their country. There had been Bensons in Crosschester and Shalford going all the way back to the Doomsday Books, so they thought. Solid upper-working class stock, not so highly educated as to be distanced from the land; not so uneducated as to have the wool pulled over their eyes. Mrs Eric Benson's maiden name was Edith Cousens, her family had been shop owners for generations.

Mr Eric Benson described her as, "Feisty".

"She doesn't suffer fools".

"She calls a spade a spade if you get my drift".

She was a brick wall of a woman who had produced three strapping boys, two of whom were happily married and living in the USA and Canada. The third boy, her youngest, Arthur, had yet to marry or even to find the right girl. He'd moved to Australia the day after his eighteenth birthday and had disappeared into the Northern Territory somewhere. His parents learned this from Andrew, their eldest.

"He's finding his own way, love", Mr Eric Benson had told his wife.

"He's a wild-minded boy. Maybe he's learning a trade? He'll find his feet soon enough", Mrs Eric Benson replied to her husband before finishing drying the dishes.

"And Australia is a fine country full of healthy, Christian people. Plenty of good, strong sunlight and the outdoor life. It'll be good for Gerald", she said.

"He'll settle down", said Mr Eric Benson as he poured himself a scotch and a gin and tonic for his wife.

With that they put Gerald to the back of their minds. They were slightly relieved that they didn't have to put up with any more of his open disdain for their beliefs and values. They could never admit to feeling a little ill at ease about the way he spoke and the way that he carried himself. He was camp though. He was fey. They knew it. They saw it when he was very young, they thought they could sport it out of him. They would never admit this to anybody else because Gerald was family, and family was the keystone of everything they felt deeply about. However, after he disappeared into the Northern Territory his name just slipped out of use.

The Bensons were committed Christians. A smart, red, leather-bound copy of the King James Bible lay on their coffee table in the parlour. Another large family Bible took pride of place on the shelf in the dining room beneath an expensive and hazy colour photograph of the Bensons holding a large Union Flag with the romantic landscape of the Lake District in the background.

Mr Benson's family tree, dating back to 1830, was inscribed on the inside cover of the book, and was waiting for the first grandchild to take his place. The Bensons considered themselves to be, for the most part, happy with their lot. But that lot was being chipped away at on a daily basis. The country, which had stood alone with enormous success, pride and honour, was now looking shabby, a little unclean even. Unpleasant smells and sounds were emerging from some of the bigger cities and infesting the wider country. Even a staunch and copper-bottomed old place like Crosschester might soon become somewhat disagreeable to visit during the evening they imagined.

Having taken stock and talked to the newspaper boy about his round, Mr Eric Benson opened the Post Office to the public on the dot of nine. He limped and lolloped back to his perch behind the counter and waited for the arrival of the elderly folks. They used the Post Office, as it was generally known, for all their daily needs from toilet paper and newspaper to sharing their woes and fears. Eric Benson knew what the village was thinking and feeling. The elders discussed what their grandchildren were saying. The parents complained and worried about their children. If there was one thing Mr Eric Benson could not bear it was people who didn't talk about their lives and the lives around them. Without knowing everything he couldn't help with anything. He needed to bring people together, to fix fences and examine wounds, to ensure the safety of the whole against the encroachments of the few, the new few.

Lunsford approached the Post Office, his body shaking with the thought that the stranger had got into Oak Cottage and was at this moment going through his belongings, turning things over, stealing Chloé's jewellery and her clothes that he'd still not been able to throw out. Someone was touching his mug and plate, knife and fork.

120

Someone was going into the lounge room and rifling through their records taking what shouldn't be taking. Taking what he had left.

He dried his eyes and mopped his face with his handkerchief, he buttoned his shirt up to the neck, he would have loved to have disappeared inside his jacket. Adelaide was at his side. He walked up the white painted steps, five of them, to the front double door of the Post Office and, breathing in deeply, he stepped over the threshold.

"Good morning Mr Lunsford, so good to see you. How on earth are you this morning?" Mr Eric Benson stood up gingerly from the stool where he spent the day like a corpulent Val Doonican with one foot on the footrest and the other on the floor. He had heard all the news about Lunsford's accident, his current condition, and of Mick's death.

"All of us in the Benson clan were terribly upset to hear the sad news about Mr Downes. What a terrible, terrible loss to the county. A remarkable man so I understand despite some of his choices, if you see what I mean".

Lunsford didn't. Lunsford was doing his best not to listen to anything Benson had to say. The tone in his head wasn't abating but instead was ringing from left to right and back again. Instead of responding to Mr Benson, he headed to the left of the shop where he hoped to find dog food or pies or something.

"Getting back on your feet I hope Mr Lunsford. And you've got a lovely new dog. What's his name then? Come here boy, come to Uncle Eric".

Adelaide gave out a low growl and Mr Benson smiled because he didn't want to back down.

Lunsford scoured the shelves for washing powder, packets of soap, and a bottle of bleach. He patted Adelaide on her head. She grabbed his arm and led him away from the cleaning products over to the rack of closed boxes, each of which had a scoop on top attached by string. The boxes contained anything and everything from dried apricots to plain flour. In the middle was something called "Kibble". Adelaide was wagging her tail madly so that Lunsford took that as a pointer. He looked over at Mr Eric Benson and asked, "Kibble?".

Happy at the interaction, Mr Eric Benson nodded with vigour and replied, "Dog food". Lunsford found a large, brown paper bag and using the scoop filled it with the pellets of the kibble. He then gathered several tinned steak and kidney pies, a bag of teabags and other bits and bobs that struck him as useful and went to the counter.

"Well, then Mr Lunsford what do we have here?" Eric Benson processed Lunsford's purchases, "Two pounds and twelve new pence please. I'll just pop one of these into your bag too, it might be interesting for you. I certainly hope so" he dropped a leaflet on top of the dog food, took Lunsford's money and counted out Lunsford's change, which he slid it into a tin with The British Democratic Freedom Party logo Sellotaped onto it. "We'll just pop that in, all for a worthy cause". Lunsford nodded, collected his goods and prepared to leave as quickly as he could.

"Before you go Mr Lunsford, can I interest you in coming to an important meeting? All the details are on the leaflet I popped into your bag. It really will be a thoroughly enlightening and invigorating event. We have guest speakers coming from all over the country to talk to us about the place of free speech and honest values in today's changing world. I myself will be speaking about our young people and how they can be effectively involved in the process of maintaining the moral and patriotic balance that we, their elders, fought so hard to maintain in the face of foreign aggressions. There'll be free beer for the first hour or so, and also sandwiches. You should come, a man of your standing would be highly valued and it would take you out of yourself".

Lunsford shrugged and shook his head. He turned around and with Adelaide at his heels he left. The question now was what to do? Where to go? He had no idea if it was safe to go home.

"Maybe those people have broken in? Maybe they're hiding in the house waiting for me. Where can I go? Why won't I fight them? Why didn't we have children? She didn't want children. No, I didn't want children. After the miscarriage. We should have had children", he thought.

Adelaide barked as they stood in front of the new Pelican crossing waiting for the lights to change. Adelaide barked again at the total lack of traffic stopping their progress. The little man turned green, the electric lamp post made a chirruping noise so Lunsford and Adelaide crossed the road. The greyness of the morning had been blown off course, the mist had passed, all overhead was blue, the air was crisp and pleasantly cold. Lunsford's head was empty of noise and the walk was clearing his mind.

"No point in wandering the streets with a bag full of kibble. Time to face what needs to be faced at home", he told Adelaide.

He shuddered. She wagged her tail.

"It's my house. My home. Has been for years. I will not be frightened out of my own home", he continued trying to impress her.

"You're a coward though. Always have been. Cried your eyes out at the sight of some blood and brains. Run away like you ran away and left your pal Mick there to die. Run away little boy", said his father.

It was 09:30.

"A lot of the day to go. I can't be wandering around like some old tramp. I have to go home and face what has to be faced", he told Adelaide.

"Whoever it was is probably gone. Walk a little. Get your confidence back", Chloé told him.

"Nonce", said his father.

Lunsford looked down at Adelaide who returned his look and wagged her tail again. He realised that she probably wouldn't be much help in a fight. Then he remembered the leaflet that had been included in his newspaper. It seemed out of place. So overtly political.

He couldn't understand how Bill Simmonds the editor of The Chronicle could have let that sort of thing into his newspaper. Lunsford and Mick had played dominoes and darts with him quite regularly, and he couldn't remember Simmonds ever talking about politics. In fact, as far as he recalled, the chap never talked about much more than horse racing and the British Army. For a newspaper editor he'd always seemed rather incurious.

Memories of his navy days in the North Atlantic and then the Pacific returned to him: far, far more terrifying than anything a bunch of hooligans might be able to offer up. A lad standing next to him had been cut in half by the wing tip of a Japanese Zero. He'd had to jump and sink through thick engine oil down, he survived. He'd brawled with Yanks in New York bars, and fought with the RAF in Port Said.

He looked at Adelaide, "I'm in my fifties for Christ's sake. I'm not that old. It's my bloody house. My house!"

He was scared. Adelaide nuzzled his leg. It was time to go home and face whoever it was who was invading.

Chapter 13

Oak Cottage under attack!

1978

Adelaide crossed straight over the road and headed back up the hill to Oak Cottage. Lunsford followed her lead and soon they were both cresting the hill by the large mounting stone.

"I'll see if they're still waiting outside. It's been half an hour. What do they want? What could they want? Who invades your house at eight thirty in the morning? What did they say? I can't remember what they said. Why didn't we have kids? Kids could have helped", he asked her.

Adelaide looked up at him and growled gently but supportively he thought.

"Madness setting in. First sign", he said out loud.

They turned the corner and saw the front of Oak Cottage where someone, maybe a gang, was waiting inside the house having entered through a window or the back door.

Or down the chimney? Seriously, did the voice sound angry? Think back. The voice did sound angry, yes, yes angry. Did the voice sound violent?

He thought hard. He cast his mind back. He dug deep but climbed out quickly before his memories dragged him further down. The voice that had scared him out of his own house had sounded angry but not violent. It was a woman's voice. A sharp one, hard one, insistent and not used to being ignored.

Lunsford and Adelaide went around the house checking all the downstairs windows: all closed. They circled back to the kitchen door and found it locked.

"Send the dog in first, if it barks…", urged his father.

He unlocked the door, told Adelaide to stay, and walked into the kitchen. Adelaide ignored him and went straight over to her Fray Bentos bowl. She looked up at Lunsford.

He told Adelaide, "Best thing to do is stay here in the kitchen. We've got everything we need here for now. Food, tea, a paper. Wait for whoever it is to come to us if she's still here. She'll have to make a move before we do".

"Send the fucking dog through the house", his father yelled.

Lunsford was very much against sacrificing Adelaide to the insanity of a knife-wielding she-maniac. Instead, he put the kettle on and poured the dog some kibble – she sniffed at it, tilted her head in query and then began to eat. He unpacked the rest of his shopping and put each item in the places that Chloé would have put them.

"She's up there somewhere and you're too shit to go after her. Wait until you're asleep. Frail old man like you, easy pickings even for a woman", his father chipped in.

Lunsford shrugged and took his tea to the table where he sat down and began to read the leaflet that Eric Benson had dropped into the white plastic bag at the Post Office. It was a piece of A4 cartridge paper folded vertically down its centre line, with a logo that included the image of Britannia sitting on a rock that had initials 'BDFP' chiselled into it. Beneath her was the phrase, "Yesterday's Proud Values for Today's New Britain!". On the back was a map with a list of buses that stopped at the meeting location, The Wulfric Hall. There was also the telephone number for "Mumford's - Proud to be a British Taxi Company". The front of the leaflet read as follows.

Public Meeting - All Welcome

7:30pm OCTOBER 23RD

NATIONAL SPEAKERS

SANDWICHES AND BEER!

Dear Fellow Briton,

You are welcome to a public meeting of The British Democratic Freedom Party (BDFP). Our Party wants to hear what you think about the situation in our beautiful country is in under the current Political conditions.

The BDFP is a patriotic and democratic party that believes in Britain, its people and its future as a great and energetic power for good in the modern world.

• We Believe in the free discussion of ALL ideas and beliefs

• We Believe in the rule of law

• We Believe Progressive Traditionalism

• We Believe in one Christian God

• We Believe that the current crop of politicians are ALL out of touch.

• We Believe that a British Government must never commit British troops to any conflict which does not directly advance British interests – ever!

• We beleive in effective border controls

• We Believe in Patriotism

• We Believe in Political Democracy

• We Believe in Economic Democracy

WE BELIEVE IN BRITAIN!

Lunsford put the leaflet down and looked around for Adelaide who was asleep by the door, untroubled.

It seemed sensible enough although he couldn't see himself attending, thought Lunsford.

There was still no sign of the invader. If there was anybody hiding with murderous intent, they were doing so with fabulous stealth and monkish patience. The silence was oppressive. Lunsford's skin was pricking, he was caught in a now resident fear of going outside entangled by being equally scared to remain in his own home. Uncertainty was wrenching his sinews, which felt as if they were pulling away from his muscles and bones, turning him into a broken doll of a man. He was a straightforward man, used to a contented life.

But here he was, sitting alone – aside from a dog he didn't choose – at the kitchen table that Chloé had got him to build from the railway sleepers thrown aside when Shalford Station was terminated. Alone and shaking, talking to himself out loud or in his head, he couldn't tell.

I can't do this anymore. I can't. I can't. I can't. No one's coming to help. I don't want anybody to come. I want everybody to go away. I want everybody to leave me alone. I want to be dead but not like this, not in my own home, alone, robbed, mugged, left for dead, left to rot.

Adelaide yawned loudly from her place under the table, and that raw sound in the silence shook Lunsford out of himself.

He wanted Chloé back. He wanted Mick to talk to. He wanted all his confusion gone and he wanted to want his heart to beat again. He wanted his house back so he could drink tea and eat toast and pat the dog and read the paper and listen to the record player and he wanted the voices out of his head.

He stood up, breathed in, straightened his shoulders. He meant to stride purposely into the hallway but he walked slowly. He looked up the stairs and yelled:

"Is there anybody up there?! Sing out! Come on!" His own voice was shattering as it careened around the house ricocheting off every surface, crashing into itself and back into him.

"Come out! Let's be having you!!" he shouted.

On the doormat behind him was a pile of leaflets and flyers from the council, the local teashop, the local football team and the Parish jumble sale committee, there was also a single letter.

He walked into the parlour where he shouted again before making his way into the sitting room. No one was there. He turned around and returned to the hallway.

He stopped, balled-up his fists hoping for more strength to come. His new, dank fears, his loneliness and his rising anger all fermented into an inebriating fuel that propelled him up the stairs and into his bedroom. He looked for whoever it was who had slipped into his house. Sick with fear he looked behind the door, under the bed, into the wardrobe: no one was there.

Into the spare room: no one there.

The bathroom: empty.

He shouted with fearful anger as each place was cleared. By time he pulled down the ladder and climbed up into the tiny, memory-stuffed loft he was screaming in lonely agony.

"You can't scare me! You don't scare me! This is my place! This is my house! My house! Our house!"

He sat in the loft hemmed in by boxed evocations for an hour. There was obviously nobody in the house. Never had been. He climbed down the ladder to the hallway, he went into their bedroom and sat on their bed and sobbed. His crying was dangerous, it split his face and skull like the dripping of rainwater on rock over a million years compressed into a split second. The elemental pain spread through him shutting him down to silence. He fell back on the bed trying to find any breath of Chloé. Still crying deep and dreadfully he wrapped himself in the counterpane and eventually fell into a barren asleep.

CHAPTER 14

INTO THE HUNTER'S WOOD

1978

He had slept for 24 hours. Straight through, no movement, no dreams, and now he felt stiff and starving. He took a rushed and cold bath. He washed his hair with a bar of soap that made his eyes sting.

He went downstairs, fed the dog, had a mug of tea and two soft old digestive biscuits he'd discovered in a cupboard he never even realised they had. He wanted to sleep again or at least he went back to his dark bedroom. But Adelaide had other ideas. She was insistent, nuzzling him, jumping up at him. He gave up and half an hour later the pair were walking across the Water Meadows, Adelaide leading the way, stopping to make sure he was following as she led them to Hunters Wood.

Lunsford hadn't been back to the Wood since his early days courting Chloé. She didn't like the place at all. She loved beaches and open fields, hill walking: she hated forests. The trees didn't reveal

anything to her, they hid lives and occluded views and seemed to
encourage and amplify the winds.

One night, laying out in the Water Meadows on a blanket, she'd
told him "It's always dark in the woods, don't you notice it? Always
dark. I don't imagine anything in there I'd want to meet. It's damp, it
rustles and the smells are of decay. All the undergrowth. It's all so
chaotic in there", she paused and lay her hand on his chest. Nothing
alive should be as old as some of those trees, she'd told him. Some of
them were there during the Civil War, longer, further away in time.
Like that Yew tree at the church, horrible. Alive before we were alive,
and alive after we're gone. He had taken her hand and thought about
the sky and her and football and her.

He didn't understand because to him those woods were touchable,
explorable, climbable, even a little mysterious. The smells - even the
damp - intrigued and excited him. She read Alice Wilson's books on
myth, legend, monsters and strange beasts and took them all a bit too
seriously. He'd laughed at her, which was of course unfair. Chloé was
the clever one, the intelligent one. She had a degree in chemistry. He
had some O'Levels, and training in drawing other people's designs.

But he loved Chloé, so they steered clear of the woods and kept to
the meadows and the town.

"So, we never went into these woods, she and I. We never shared
any time in the dark, mouldy, quiet. I liked those woods too", he told
Adelaide.

"So, why didn't you visit them on your own? Chloé did things on
her own. She was her own woman. You sat at home and did fuck all",
said his father.

He often mistook her fears for lack of realism or over-imagination. Since her death, however, he missed that imagination more than he could express. She was the reason that the television remained off. Every evening she would read and read out loud when she came to passages that fascinated her or made her laugh, or which she thought would interest him.

Her unfounded fears frustrated him though because back then he didn't have any of them himself. Events unfolded as they would.

He stopped, Adelaide stopped and sat down, "Think of all the things I could have done but didn't. Think of all the things she did. Despite all her anxieties and her fears about what terrible things were going to happen all the time. Despite all of that, she got on with life. She didn't rest unless she needed rest. She kept you alive with her love and life", he said to her. She wagged her tail.

"Whatever did she see in you? What are you going to do now?", his father said.

"It's unhealthy is what it is", he'd told Chloé once during an argument about the speed he drove their car. "You need to trust me. It's insulting, it really is the way you go on. I've never been close to having an accident", he'd said.

"That's not helpful, Martin. Calling me unhealthy because I worry that we might crash into a tractor or an animal around the next bend".

"I know these roads. I know the bends. You need to trust me".

She looked sadly at him, "It's not about trust, it's about that next bend. You can't know what's around it. No matter how well we both know the roads. It's not that I don't trust you, I don't trust what's next". She smiled at him and then her anger came up and out.

"Seriously, Martin. When I ask you to slow down or take care, I'm not questioning your fucking skills. I'm questioning whether bravado will get us and someone else injured or killed. Driving from home to town isn't a race. You don't need skills. It's a journey. It's a bloody journey from our house to the shops", she could feel herself getting angrier, "it's an everyday act of... shopping for god's sake. When I drive, we get there about two minutes later than when you do. Grow up and take my feelings seriously".

"Feelings", he huffed as the next bend curved into sight, and he slowed down.

"Yes, my feelings", she said as they closed in on the rear of a tractor dragging hay bales, and he braked.

He'd thought about that conversation a lot after her death. She wasn't proud of her anxiousness nor was she so disgusted by it that she tried to hide it.

He treasured what he and his mates called Common Sense. He tried to express this to her many times leading to the great mistake when he had accused her of being irrational. She'd told him to stop being so bloody arrogant.

"Let's talk about what you think is irrational shall we?" she'd asked.

"Voting for someone because you've always voted that way. Choosing to buy one pair of boots over another pair of boots because the first pair are a nicer colour even if they're not as hardwearing. Choosing the hurtful word when the context is about feelings, friendship or the end of a friendship. Taking the pretty route not the direct route. Being scared about something that you can't describe accurately. Waking up in the morning wanting not to be awake ever again. All irrational to you, Martin. But they're all fucking real. Some of them are choices, some are things no one can do anything about. When you say, 'rational, reasonable, logical' or 'common sense' you're talking about yourself, about your choices and your predilections most of the time but you're confusing that with objectivity and eternal fucking truths!"

She'd stormed out that day leaving him angry and betrayed. They'd been married for two years at that time and he thought it must be the end.

She'd been cold in her anger, unflinching, certainly not open to discussion, not open to, "Calm down honey", or "you're shouting, people might hear". She wasn't going to calm down, she'd told him later in their fat, saggy beautiful sofa. Sometimes there was a need to get heated. Other people could mind their own business. This was their marriage, she said, not other people's. She called him a name, the name of a brute, a codeword between them ever since, and she kissed him, and then they listened to music.

Lunsford thought about this as he walked behind Adelaide, and he missed Chloé very much.

"She had a life and she brought it to the house and now it's all gone. She invited Mick's wife Jeanne over", he told Adelaide.

She stopped and looked back at him, checking in, making sure he was still progressing into the heart of the woods but he'd stopped on its fringes and was shaking a little. The dog tracked back and looked up at the man quizzically. She barked because she needed to be in there amongst the smells, the damp leaves and other animals.

"Quiet now Adelaide. Quiet. I'm coming". He pushed open the kissing gate, letting the dog through first before passing over into the woods.

The narrow, stone-paved track in front of him soon disappeared as the holly bushes, bracken and brambles and guelder rose encroached and then engulfed it. Lunsford and Adelaide made their way further and further into the interior not seeing the badger setts low down or the tangles of mistletoe high in the branches of dying trees.

The smells of the mulching earth, the bones, pelts and animal remains that made it brought him back to Churchfields and the sight of his father, dead rabbit in hand, blood down his shirt, beer on his breath, pain in his plans.

Adelaide barked at a squirrel. Lunsford shook himself clean of that past. He'd know these woods so well into his young life when he climbed the trees and hid in castles made with the fallen branches. In the autumn and early winter months he and his friend Mick, would search out mushrooms and berries to eat or sell. There were only a few kinds of both known to the boys with the knowledge passed down to the other kids.

Lunsford looked around and realised that he could no longer even identify the trees around him. Decades of adult work had washed away that unnecessary knowledge. He stopped, stood still as a peacock and listened. Despite the lateness of the year, there were still birds singing. Most of them were singing warnings to each other about Adelaide.

Lunsford couldn't name a single song and this saddened him. He crouched down and picked up a handful of the rotting leaves and soil that made the forest floor and moved it from hand to hand. He breathed it in hoping to be informed and transported by it. He longed to be brought back to a time when its smell and texture were as familiar to him as his own house. Nothing of the sort came. All he sensed was decay, damp, grit, shame, his hideous father, and the blood and fear of those creatures that hadn't been successful in their flights. Prey and praying.

He stood up and looked for Adelaide who was looking back at him, her front paws resting on the flank of a massive fallen tree. She was panting, having sprinted left, right, centre and back, looping around the man, chasing smells and shadows. She looked as if she was smiling at him, beckoning him on, telling him to be less worried about things. It was mad fun, all of it. Forget the memories that weren't coming back or were coming back broken. Her experience of memory was different, much less importance was laid at symbols and altars. The tears and sacrifices that people drenched their lives in meant less than a nearly caught pigeon to Adelaide. She wanted to go deeper. She wanted a drink of water, she could smell it somewhere, but it wasn't close, so it was time to move on.

Lunsford tried to pat her on the head but she was too quick for him. She was happy. Simply happy, excited and at the same time at ease. His own descent into the guts and entrails of his loss fought back. Loss of memory and not being able to move on from memory, what a bind to be in.

She barked again. She was insistent. She was thirsty. She turned her back on him and trotted on, further into the woods, deeper under its interlocking branches and winter bird songs. As he walked, the ground became a bed of soft, brown pine needles. The trees shot up around him, straight as an old woman's fingers. He didn't remember pine trees in any part of the woods. These were strange, unnatural, recognisable, almost manmade compared to the other natural, twisting grotesques. The more he looked at the pine trees, the more he saw architecture more than nature. These had been planted in rows, in ranks, in files and not by the hands of a million pagan gods – more like one tractor going back and forward all day.

He looked for Adelaide, but she was nowhere to be seen. This worried him. By now he was deep in Hunters Wood and not only was the light thinning, so it seemed was the air. He called her name and waited.

He called her name, this time with more urgency.

Nothing. Not even leaves rustling. No sound.

Half an hour passed, during which he became unfamiliar and uncomfortable with his own voice, which gradually sounded like a recording played back to a room full of strangers. Each time he asked her to come back he could also hear his aloneness.

Nothing. Not even rustling. Even the birds are silent.

He stood in the quiet hoping for her return. Then he started yelling to himself in anger and disappointment. Where was she? Out of the quiet he thought he heard talking. He heard the leaves falling, as badgers and the other evening creatures began to move in the undergrowth.

Again, he called for her and again he waited and again she didn't come. He felt foolish. He'd known the animal for less than a week. She was a stray after all. An all autumn coloured shaggy stray dog who had wandered into his house. He had given her a name for no other reason than that was the first name that came into his head. He had started to imbue her with magical powers of thoughtfulness and insight. He'd started to imagine that she had a voice to speak to him with. But she was a stray dog. Just a stray dog. Of course, she'd wandered off, just as she'd wandered in.

He stood by the husk of a fallen tree that lay on the dampening forest floor like the massive arm of an ancient woman, severed from her body and left to rot on the ground. He picked his way through brambles and dead, yellow bracken, his boots sank to their laces into the black mud, so he imagined himself becoming part of the place. As he moved in what he hoped was her direction he was misdirected by streams of brackish water so dark that anything, even a savage pike could be lurking there. As he moved in what he hoped was her direction he questioned why he was even doing this. He could be at home in the parlour, reading a book, drinking some tea, enclosed, not fearful. He knew his fear wasn't of animals or wood ghosts or county monsters though, it was that he might not see the dog again.

He reached a wide, flat, circular clearing surrounded by malformed oaks and beech trees and those pines. A truly terrible yew tree stood to the west of the circle, casting its shadow onto a twisted Ash with its old man's skin. There was no Shalford in sight. Crosschester was lost.

"Adelaide!" he called again, elongating her name like a child lost in a fairground calling for his mother. "Adelaide!"

The darkness in the branches was hard, not a soft evening shade, not a shade at all. Here in the woods, the darkness crackled with the remains of the day's light.

"Adelaide!", he thought he cried out loud but realised that he was only calling for her inside himself.

An owl called to her partner across the clearing with no reply. Lunsford was cold, his old boots were leaking.

"Not the best, are they?" a voice low-down to his left said in a matter of fact way.

For a moment Lunsford was certain that Adelaide was finally talking to him. Either his mind had finally given in to a year of opiates and confusion or the dog was magic and everything he'd ever known was broken. What surprised him most about either of these probabilities was that neither of them bothered him too much. He was surprised that Adelaide's voice was so mellow and male. He'd imagined that she would sound like a rather scruffy but ultimately able and energetic young woman. Certainly not an estuary drawl. Lunsford had visited London twice in his life for a total of 16 hours and all the accents had jostled together, sharp elbowed and lump hammer jawed shouting and carping. He looked down at the voice.

"Afternoon sir", said a very tall young man with cropped, red hair. He was wearing light green overalls and builders' tan boots, and he was making up a small fire from sticks and dried moss.

Lunsford hadn't seen him when he walked into the clearing.

"Good afternoon, Mr?" he said.

"Just call me Fawley", said the young man standing up and proffering his long-fingered, badly manicured left hand to be shaken.

"Good afternoon, Mr Fawley", Lunsford replied, trying to work out how to make a left-handed greeting.

"Just Fawley. Want a smoke?"

"No thank you, I don't", Lunsford thought too much about his handshake and not having touched another human being for months or not wanting to be seen as an easy mark – the young man looked hungry, maybe even desperate – he applied too much pressure.

Fawley released Lunsford's hand, "Bloody hell, there's no need for that. It's supposed to be a greeting not an arm wrestle. Calm down".

"Sorry, sorry", Lunsford was embarrassed, he dropped both arms to his side. "I don't suppose you've seen a shaggy brown dog have you?"

"First thing's first", said Fawley, returning to his fire lighting and looking up at Lunsford with beautifully clear, grey eyes, "What do I call you? What's your name? I can't keep calling you sir, can I?"

"Lunsford", said Lunsford, crouching down next to Fawley.

"Mr Lunsford? Bob Lunsford? Lunsford St John-Stevas?" The fire had taken on life, and Fawley was adding fuel. He reached into a heavy cloth bag and took out a tin of sausages and beans. This surprised Lunsford who had assumed that the young man would have foraged some food or, more likely, would have no food at all.

"Martin Lunsford".

"Do you want some sausage and beans Martin?"

"People just usually call me Lunsford".

"I can see that, no worries, Lunsford. As it goes, I have seen your dog, just a few moments ago actually. Happy thing isn't she? Up to her ears in vim."

Lunsford grinned despite himself. "Oh, she's not my dog really. She just turned up and hasn't left yet. She probably likes the food and warmth".

"And the company?" Fawley was stoking the small fire, adding twigs and dry leaves.

Lunsford looked at the ground, shook his head, "I'm not good company".

Fawley opened the tin with a small knife that he'd also taken from the bag. "Sure you don't want some scran, Lunsford?"

"No, I'm fine really. I just want to find the dog and to get home", he paused, he was hungry. He looked around and saw a lean-to made from fallen branches and topped with interlaced bracken that surely hadn't been there when he arrived. It had a wide mouth facing east, and a floor covered in more of the bracken.

"Do you live here, Fawley?"

"No", he chuckled. "I stay here every so often but I don't really live anywhere much. I travel around doing odd jobs. I like forests and woods, and this one's a corker during the colder months. Lots of cover. Don't know if you've noticed but the deeper in you come, the warmer it is too. Bloody useful that. Are you sure about the food?"

Lunsford stood up. No matter how hungry he was he still didn't quite trust this Fawley character. He really needed to get back to his home but he was still unable to think about being there without the dog.

Fawley placed the tin of beans and sausages into the fire and called out, "Adelaide". Two minutes passed during which time Fawley took a billycan, an old green glass bottle of liquid and two teabags from his bag.

"Adelaide", he said, softly. He added the teabags to the billycan and poured clear liquid from the bottle on top, then he balanced it precariously on top of the tin of sausages and beans.

"Nice name, how did you come up with it?" asked Fawley.

Lunsford thought for a few seconds, looking into the fire and then into the forest, then back at Fawley. For the first time it occurred to him that Fawley knew the dog's name. How on earth was that the case unless he also knew the dog?

"I don't know. I suppose she just looked like an Adelaide, and she answered to it", he replied.

Adelaide came in from the north, head-up, tail wagging, tongue lolling, twigs and leaves sticking out every which way. She trotted over to Fawley, licked his hand, and sat down looking at him and then at the fire. He reached out his left hand and pushed his long fingers through the fur on her head, she vibrated and leant against him making a low, peaceful growling noise.

Lunsford was certain that the two of them knew each other, it was no coincidence that the dog had led him to this spot and to this man. He re-examined Mr One-Name Fawley.

Tall, thin, everything about him was thin, from his nose to his fingers. Weirdly thin, as if he could turn to one side and be only a slit in the air. His hair was straight and short. Lunsford looked more closely while trying to hide this fact. There were silver-grey threads running through the young man's hair, the firelight and low evening light also suggested that these same threads ran through this skin like another circulatory system. Absurd. What was less absurd, however, was that for some reason this Fawley had managed to lure Lunsford into this strange circular clearing. He'd heard of this kind of crusty, homeless people with their trained dogs. He had seen one of them begging near the Market Cross in town before they were moved on.

How easy would it be to rob someone out here, deep in the wood? Murder them. Then leave them to rot into the mulch. Lunsford wanted to run but this Fawley character obviously knew the blasted forest so well that that there would no point in it. He would only get more lost, more exhausted, colder. That dog, that fucking dog, it looked up at Fawley, then wandered over to where Lunsford was crouching down like a frog.

It was wagging its tail, looking friendly, looking like calm company. But no. Everything was falling into place now. The trees around him closed in, the brush and bushes appeared to grow thicker. One of the owls called to its mate but received nothing in reply, just a silence like its own flight.

Everything around Lunsford was wrong. He could feel his bones growing heavier, and his head was starting to ache as if there was a beast in his skull slowly opening its jaws. He stood up and steeled himself or tried to. He felt such pressure on his skin that he was sure it would soon fall from his skeleton. Nothing was right. He was wrong. He was in the wrong place. The fire was too yellow. The air was too yellow. The treetops started shrieking as the wind accelerated overhead. All the birds were dead. His eyes were as dry as twigs. His mouth was full of terror. It wasn't just the man now, not just Fawley and that dog, it was everything, the entire world was rejecting him.

He looked to the ground but he had no connection to it, never had, never could have. This world was escaping him, leaving him floating just above the dirt and the tiny bones of dead birds, the rotting pinecones and the blood from millennia of constant hunting and killing, hunting and killing, by men and animals, hunting and killing and he wasn't there, he was disappearing fast, he had no connections.

There was so much silence though, rushing through his head. The only piece of him that remained was to that of a victim. He could do nothing. All things were to be done to him. All bad, all violence, all humiliation. There was nothing he could do to intervene in his own life.

Go home Mr Lunsford.

We don't need you here.

You can't ease the pain

"Sausages and beans, very sugary, all I've got though", said Fawley. Adelaide walked back over to him, shrugged and lay down. She looked up at Lunsford who was now standing, floating, still and moving fast, open mouthed. She was Fawley's dog. It was obvious. He was alone, floating, waiting for it to come so he could be left alone here to be sucked into the ground and forgotten. His voice was stilled somewhere. His memory was shaking. His memories were an avalanche.

Go home Mr Lunsford.

You can do nothing here.

You can't ease the pain.

There is nothing you can do.

Go home

Far below, Fawley was eating his meal.

"I've got nothing you know. Maybe about two pounds and some

change", blurted Lunsford, almost relieved that he'd managed to piece together the mystery of the over-friendly dog, the visit to the wood, the sudden appearance of this young man.

"Pardon?" replied Fawley, obviously surprised.

"I don't really have anything worth taking", he took his wallet from his pocket and threw it at Fawley's feet. Adelaide picked it up and wagged her tail.

"It's been quite a lot of effort for not much return I'm afraid. I should really get going now", he didn't know how to move. He'd never been robbed before. He had expected it to happen during his London visits, or maybe in Crosschester after a particularly nasty home game against Waterville United, but not here and not in such a diabolical way.

God knows what else was in that bag, he thought. A gun? Knives? Black magic? An axe?

"Seriously, what are you going on about, Mr Lunsford?"

Fawley finished his meal, drank his tea and put out the fire with the dregs. Adelaide stood up and wandered over the Lunsford, when she reached him, she leant against his legs, looked up, and started that panting, smiling effort he'd become quite used to. She dropped his wallet at his feet.

"You're going to rob me and kill me", out it came. Stupid, showing his hand, making it plain to this man who could be a lunatic that he knew what was going on.

"I'm not, you know", Fawley prodded the can of food. "Why would I?"

Adelaide placed her head under Lunsford's right hand and

demanded a stroke.

"You know this dog. You called her by name. She led me here. She led me to you. Why would she do that? She's enchanted or you've trained her as a lure for marks like me", Lunsford was sobbing now. Floating and sobbing and looking down on himself.

"I thought she was your dog though, brother. You said you were looking for her". Fawley stood up. He took a pair of thick gloves out of his bag, reached down and removed the billycan and the tin of food from the remains of the fire.

"How did you know her name!?" screamed Lunsford, as angry and upset that he had lost his companion to this wood sprite or street thug, or whatever he was. "How did you know her name?"

"You were calling her name all over the woods at the top of your voice, for god's sake", Fawley looked sad but not shocked at the turn of events.

He smiled, "Lunsford, the quickest way out of here is that way", he pointed towards the large oak using the long, slender index finger of his left hand. "Keep the central cathedral tower on your left. Keep St Eade's steeple on your right. It's not far and you'll be on the paved path again. Home safe, and don't stop along the way. It's been interesting meeting you. See you again maybe?"

Fawley put his various bits and bobs back in his bag, which he slung over his shoulder and across his body. Lunsford saw that it had words and phrases written on it in what looked like felt pen. He couldn't make them out. Fawley turned on his heel, checked back to ensure the fire was out and stalked off into Hunters Wood and the darkness.

Adelaide followed him.

CHAPTER 15

THE TROUBLE WITH SPEAKERS

1978

Don Jarvis had some terrible news for the steering committee: neither Reg Fountaine nor A.K. Jordan had agreed to speak at the opening of the Wulfric Hall. As he walked to The Green Man he tried to work out exactly how to deliver it. He had been given the job of confirming the attendance of the two most important speakers at the first public meeting of the British Freedom and Democracy Party in The Wulfric Hall. He had not come up trumps, and so was spinning the message frantically in rehearsal.

"It's quite the coup for you Eric, you get all the limelight, you get to stamp your authority. I'd say that we can put this down to a win".

That might work. He could try that.

He wouldn't try that.

"Eric, we paid our respects and they were thrown back at us. We're better off without those dinosaurs. Forward, full steam ahead!"

Nope.

"Eric, we have a clean slate!"

Not a chance.

"Eric, I couldn't get hold of Alfred or Reg. I'll try again through the week, now let's get down to business".

Weak but it might give him some time.

Inside the pub the evening drinkers were trying to relax in the face of another week's work. To a stranger coming in from the street the place would have seemed brutal. To the regulars washing down Sunday lunch, The Green Man offered a place to chat about the weekend's fun or chores. Fishing, rugby, football, cricket in the summer; how the van or car was faring, how the world was getting on with itself – badly as always. On the bar were several tins full of charity monies. The tins would be filled before the evening was out as the drink brought on sentimentality. The regulars in The Green Man, for the most part working men, who played at least one charity game of something or other each year, sending all proceeds to war widows or veterans, and in one never to repeated case to Oxfam.

They looked after each other too. When old Mr Granger had been found sitting near at a small, lonely table nursing the only half-pint of beer he could afford because he'd gambled his pension away on a tip from Pete the bricklayer, they all got him pissed and made sure he had enough for chips and fish on his way home.

When Mrs Harper's husband Colin had passed away, of course the wake had been hosted in The Green Man and paid for by subscription, as had the uproarious party after the funeral. Colin Harper was a popular bloke, all opinions and back-slapping, stood his round and could bowl a tasty spin when called for. He worked at the prison. He was hard but fair, everybody said so even some of the just released inmates who popped in for their first taste of freedom after every sentence served.

Don despised The Green Man. It made him scared. It made him doubt. Why the Party chose here to meet was an anathema to him. Something about being among the people. Something about Meredith Brewer's pockets more like. He reached the front doors, breathed in, loosened his collar by running his finger around it and realised quite how sweaty he was. He hated confrontation. Hated it because he inevitably came off worst.

He pushed hard because you had to so the door could move over the sticky carpet and walked through the crowd. They were all full of earlier overdone beef and cabbage and underdone potatoes. They were thick with powdered gravy. They were red faced. They were all well soused. The atmosphere was rancid with twenty Brylcreemed heads, and pockmarked with violently bulky gold signet rings on hard, fat fingers. Eventually old friends were sure to round on old friends as old grudges rose from poisoned recollections.

Don hated the jukebox that cranked out distorted rock'n'roll because its speaker had been kicked in one night and no one had got around to mending it. He hated rock'n'roll, it came from the blacks, from America, it was too raucous and rude. At least it wasn't jazz. He hated the terrible beer, sour and thin with poor keeping. He hated the watery whisky served in greasy tumblers. He hated the way they all loved it. He hated the stink of shit and bleach that blew in from the Ladies and Gents. He hated the imminent violence. He hated the thick, filthy patrons who inhabited it day in and night out. Bellicose, belligerent, confident because they knew no better.

Prison Officers, dustbin men, policemen, van drivers, builders, gamblers, rough sorts all. Sometimes the wives and girlfriends would join their men in a foetid evening of sentimental songs, and chants against the IRA or the Jews or opposing sports teams. Never for anything. The harridan women would be bawling along, pissed on gin or Babycham or both, their make-up dripping off their haggard or bloated faces. There were no in-betweens with these harpies, they were either skinny to the point of emaciation or they were jellied, wobbling masses of flesh and cheap, synthetic printed coverall smock dresses that stuck sopping with sweet to their mountainous thighs and stomachs. They reeked of cigarette smoke, foul shampoo, chip grease, rough sex, and sickly children.

He had his doubts about what exactly the Party's plan for a whites-only nation was if this crowd was going to be the result. For all their talk of Britons never being enslaved, and of an England being a Jew-free Jerusalem, this herd of sheep were never actually going to do anything about it.

Most of all, today he really hated the sticky carpet that caught his shined shoes as he tried to make his way across it. It stuck him in a place like a fly in a trap. He struggled against it and made it to the door to the upstairs bar, the private bar. As he walked upstairs, Mr Eric Benson's words came back to him.

"They're our people, Don, but they don't know it yet. And they don't know any better. They can't and it's not their fault. The education system is run by the elites and their queer, liberal socialist lackey schoolteachers – they make sure of it. It's in their best interests. It's up to blokes like us to lead them out of their ignorance and into a country where they, the salt of the earth, the workers and their families can grow strong and white and fair".

Don held his breath against the stench of the Gents downstairs as it wafted up behind him, catching him in a foul airlock between the closed door head of him, and the recently closed on behind. He really did not want to go in and deliver the bad news, but this was forcing him on.

Eric Bentley, Vyvian Sarson-Taylor and Bill Symonds were at their usual table by the window overlooking the street. Mrs Benson was at the bar talking to Meredith Brewer who was never downstairs. Harry Mottram was nowhere to be seen. Don walked over to the bar, first a good scotch whisky to settle the nerves, that'd do it.

"A large whisky please, Meredith", he paused, "and some ice". He wanted a good single malt. She poured him a cheap Teachers without breaking her thread with Mrs Edith Benson – something about a Greek singer – except to say, "55p" which he paid in exact change. He drank the whisky as fast as he could, which wasn't fast because his hands were trembling. He could feel Eric Benson's eyes burning into his neck.

Eric was discussing strategy with Bill Symonds, editor of The Chronicle. This waiting patiently for a response that might or might not come. As far as Bill was concerned, if he thought an idea was bad, poorly crafted, daft or in any other way worthless he simply wouldn't bother responding, assuming that the speaker was too stupid to understand any constructive criticism. If, on the other hand, he considered a point to be constructive, well founded, intelligent or useful he would refrain from wasting time confirming it. He would assume that the speaker knew it was a solid idea. Bill would often simply write a person off completely based on his own highly complex and intensely personal set of criteria. In that case not only would he not respond, he wouldn't even listen. He never responded to Sarson-Taylor.

He saved his remarks for when they would have maximum devastation, the only impact that really mattered. He specialised in setting traps for his staff, for anybody he encountered really. Most people expected conversations to be conversations: exchanges of views, of pleasantries, ideas tossed up and batted around. Traps being traps were always surprising. Bill's traps were always dispiriting too.

For example, a young reporter had come to him with a feature idea about comparing the summer fete on Chibelton Avenue with the one on Sebastopol Road. Bill listened patiently, it was a great idea for a local newspaper. It publicised two occasions so there could be some advertising sales revenue to be had, but as importantly it pitted one group of readers against another. This ensured sales. Bill told the young man to go away, do the interviews, take the photographer, do the interviews but only if he went to the places mentioned in the brief, otherwise he'd hand the writing and the by-line to a senior reporter.

"You're sure about everything?" he asked, smiling.

"I, I think so yes, sir", said the cub, dreaming of his name in print for the first time.

"Positive. Being positive is a good thing. You must have confidence in yourself", Bill was mentoring.

155

"Yes, sir, positive!"

Bill picked up the phone and commanded his secretary to ask the senior local reporter in.

"David", he said when the scruffy older journalist had taken a seat. The cub was still standing. "David, I want you to take Phil the Lens to Chibelton Lane", he emphasised 'Lane'. "Take this brief. Have the feature back to me for Monday. You can both leave now".

That was Bill all over. Any other editor would have corrected the youngster over Lane versus Avenue. Not Bill Symonds. Facts were Facts for Bill. Facts were Truth. Truth was Objective. Truth was Beauty and Beauty was Truth.

This attitude also fulfilled and maintained his view that most people were too thick to be anything other than recipients of the objective facts that he was assiduous in parsing from the mess of the world. He liked to think that he wasn't so arrogant to believe that he was the sole arbiter of facts and truth, those two things being synonymous. He readily deferred to folk who were obviously specialists in their fields, also to people who had climbed to positions of power. Power was directly equatable to ability, that was a straightforward equation too. If you were capable enough, you succeeded, he was proof of this.

Although individuals were generally dull, stupid or naive (synonyms as far as Bill was concerned), gullible, even iniquitous, as a mass, as the Public and The People they were powerful and to be feared and respected. The mob, to Bill, was a noble singularity, an entity made of truth. However, if your group had been at the bottom of the heap for centuries, the equation was equally valid. Groups without power did not generally deserve power.

Bill also had a seething reserve about people who had not acquired their own wealth. Bill hated people who had money, land, power passed down to them. Folk whose ancestors had fought the battles, built the land, but who did nothing themselves except live off reputation and interest, he despised them. As far as he was concerned if the entire British landed class departed to their true homes in Europe, the country would be a better place.

Don tossed up whether to go straight over and confess to his incompetence and lack of initiative, or to stay at the bar drinking heavily. Stephen Hedges was at the bar, sipping rum and apparently not breathing or respirating in any way. Don noticed the other man's hands, which were beautiful.

He wished he'd gone to Leicester instead of just phoning. He sipped another whisky and grimaced as he always did. Stephen Hedges looked at him, and Don looked down at his own stubs of fingers attached as they were to child's palms. He looked back but Hedges had disappeared, then Mr Eric Benson called out.

"Don! Fella! Come over here with the good news mate!" Eric had obviously been on the sauce and was even more red in the face and urgent than usual.

Don picked up his glass, clutched the black slipcase he always carried and, with a fall in his step, made his way to the table. He sat down and opened his mouth, and Stephen Hedges sat next to him so close he could feel his breath.

"How fares the war then, Donald?" said Mr Eric Benson jovially.

"To come straight to the point, Eric. To clear the decks and set fair for the way forward. To put none too finer point on matters. Eric, to be clear…"

Stephen Hedges put his hand on the back of Don's neck, just left it there. It was strong and cold. Don shuddered and smiled weakly.

"What is your report?" Bill Symonds asked.

"Bill, you know these chaps, you know Alfred and Reg of old. You know what they can be like", Bill did, so this assertion didn't merit a response.

"Eric, I want you to think about what I'm going to say as a blessing in disguise, it's a chance for us to make our own mark, for you to forge your identity as the leader of a great new party. What I'm pleased to report is a silver lining, Eric. A great big silver lining".

Mr Eric Bentley looked confused. He enjoyed having his ego buffed but he wasn't sure where this one was going. Bill Symonds did.

"Which one of them isn't coming, Don?" he asked, his voice as crisp as old paper.

Don knew he had no way out and it was time to give up. "Neither one is coming. Reg won't come if Alfred comes, and vice versa".

"What?" Mr Eric Benson was perplexed.

"They've fallen out with each other. Badly".

"Again, predictably", said Bill.

"What?"

"Reg said that Alfred called him a snivelling queer at the Union of British Truth meeting in Walsall…"

"Well, did he?"

"I don't think that's really the point, Eric. The point is that Reginald understood that Alfred called him a queer. As Reginald is in fact a queer, this barb would most definitely have struck home".

"What else did Alfred have to say?" Eric turned to Jarvis who had finally finished his scotch and with trembling hands was lighting a Dunhill king-sized cigarette. He coughed long and hard.

"He said he wouldn't share a stage with a bender for fear of his arse being touched up".

Mr Eric Benson slammed both fists into the tabletop, "They've shared platforms with each for fucking decades all over the shitting country! What in fuck's earth is going on?"

"They've shared more than platforms", said Bill Symonds to himself. He then spoke directly to Eric.

"It's obvious what's going on. Both of them want to lead the new party. Neither of them can bear to see the other getting any spotlight. At heart they're both weak men who doubt themselves and who let their relationship dynamic compromise their political vision and ergo, ours too. Their weaknesses have infected their respective parties. So, to an extent, Don has a point. Their refusal can be seen as a positive benefit to our endeavour".

Don looked relieved.

Stephen Hedges breathed, "We have to shape this story".

Eric and Bill nodded. Bill continued, "Yes, we're still left with a problem. Because of Don's abject failure to convince either Reg or Alfred that the best interests of a resurgent British Nationalism should override their petty sexual squabbles, we have no guest speaker. No guest speaker makes us look parochial and limits our appeal. We must remedy this".

Gene Vincent's fabulously crippled, black leather voice drifted up the chimney from the public bar below. The men at the table looked at each other, looked at their drinks, Gene sang on. Don was too nervous to say anything. Bill was Bill, waiting for someone to say something stupid. Mr Eric Benson was wracking his brains for any kind of answer. Stephen Hedges had nothing more to say.

Harry had replaced Meredith behind the bar, so she had decided to join the gentlemen at their stalled think tank. Mrs Eric Benson joined her to see what the idiots had concocted.

Out of the grimy windows Crosschester was in darkness and the week was grinding to a halt. Church goers were leaving their worship and their Good News bibles on their pews and were wandering home for supper and bad television. Snow had started to glide onto the cracked paving stones and medieval roofs of the city. In the Cathedral grounds the bones of a man who had died of drink split with the cold, and the last leaves of autumn finally degraded beyond recognition on their journey to dirt. Up in the prison a man who had served 25 years for a murder he may or may not have committed prepared for his last night of sleep in a gaol hard bunk while the prison officers slowly and quietly beat a new inmate convicted of fiddling with small boys in the football team he coached. Still the men in The Green Man thought on.

CHAPTER 16

THE GREAT SURVEY

1978

Sister Helen Cousins was in a terrible mood. She was a tall, thin woman, touching six feet and, like most tall women, she had adopted a very slight stoop. Her black hair had flecks of grey and was always in a tight bob held together with pins and lacquer. She always wore hard wearing, black slacks. Her black brogues were always polished. Her blouse was white with small, jet buttons, her jacket was dark, dark grey. Her face was pale, her grey eyes were sunk back into her skull. She looked older than forty. Her skin was like softened cardboard scarred by soft lines of age and experience. Her thin lips were tightly pressed and bloodless even during her rare, and always performative bouts of smiling.

Mr Martin Lunsford did not instigate a smile. She hadn't taken to him at first meeting in the Royal County Hospital when she'd stood over his bed watching him. Even in his sleep he appeared to be a shifty character: too still, too… asleep. When she woke him up to question him, he definitely was not concentrating on her good offices. In fact, he seemed not to be concentrating on anything at all. Glassy eyes, blank expression, he provided dull, mumbled answers to simple, direct questions. She'd keep a watch on this one, she'd told herself, this one would be trouble.

She was right, of course. Today he had barricaded himself into this little house and was refusing to take further advice from a trained professional. However, Helen Cousins wanted to make things better for this Lunsford. She wanted to make things better for everybody.

Every household in the tight-knit community of extended, interconnected families who inhabited the Churchfields had been paid a visit by 'Sister Helen'. She was inevitable. She was carrying out her Great Survey. No one was sure what the Great Survey (their name not hers) was about, but everybody knew that the questions just kept coming and coming. Every door was knocked on, every bell rung, and those doors that were not immediately answered were revisited until they were opened.

The Great Survey made people uncomfortable in their own homes. It, seemingly with a life of its own, asked for their views on violence on television, the theatres and in the cinema. It asked about their favourite and least favourite foods. It demanded information about how often they washed, bathed, ate, urinated, exercised. Everybody assumed that this was all official National Health Service business. Everybody was wrong.

The Great Survey was not exclusive to Shalford. Sister Helen would bicycle to all the other villages that crowded Crosschester like piglets to a sow. She planned to use the collated data as the basis of her manuscript on the Smaller Settlements of England and the English.

She was not a native of the village, and that at least gave her a sense of pride. She had first leant her bicycle against the front wall of the detached council house that was Number 31, The Circle, Churchfields, Shalford on the dusty afternoon of Wednesday, May 15th, 1946. All the other properties in Churchfields were semi-detached and had been given nicknames. The house that overlooked the Icene and was called 'Riverview'. Another was called 'Newlyweds', yet another went by 'BarbRich'. Sister Helen called her residence, "Number 31, The Circle, Churchfields, Shalford". It was a grey, pebble-dashed, lowly thing. Its concreted walls wept. It had two rooms upstairs and three downstairs including the loveless kitchen. It had an outside lavatory that sat at the end of the scruffy garden overlooking the graveyard of St Eade's.

Helen lived there on her own and in her own contentment. In her mind she kept herself very much to herself. She spent her time reading, writing reports and eating vegetarian food, which she hated but which did her good. She spent her week cycling the eight miles or so to and from the Royal County Hospital's district nursing centre. She was: professional, didactic, waiting. She had retired three years previously, in 1975 but she continued to monitor the situation even as she prepared her manuscript.

Her view of the world was that it was a looming catastrophe brought on by incompetence. Since the end of the war, it felt to her as if everybody had relaxed and stopped noticing the endemic threats to their own civilisation. People had stopped caring and everybody's motivations were dubious. Everybody except Mr Francis Galton and the Dean William Inge. The former because of his views on work in the development of science of Eugenics, his intellectual martyrdom in fact. The latter for his views on the absurdly over-praised behaviours of Democracy. Helen found it difficult to tell the rule of the mob from that of the vote.

Sitting at her escritoire, the host of her favourite reading material kept watch over her from a shelf above her head. A small collection of journals and extracts critiquing Mary Ainsworth's Strange Situation Procedure sat at one end bookending Galton's Inquiries into Human Faculty and Its Development, and The Minutes of Third International Eugenics Congress (1932), at the other end was Dean Inge's Our Present Discontents, Outspoken Essays: First Series (1919). All were well-thumbed with multiple bookmarks shark finning from their sensible pages. She looked up at them with the kind of warmth that would only make a difference if you were freezing to death and alone.

The small settlements of England were the foundations, the keystones of civilisation for Helen Cousins. The people were more interesting to her than the mulatto masses who littered the cities and their suburbs. The fabric of any city was always going to be stretched tight enough to be torn by unrest. Big cities - metropolises – rose and fell. This was not true of the hamlets and villages or some of the smaller towns. Small places, linked by mutual suspicion and rough roads, were eternal. Each one only required a single point of cohesion to function: a pub, someone important, a church, a statue, a sports team. Sometimes these could be combined with a point in time, a festival, a commemoration, a communion. The time had to be compact and to offer a culmination. Sister Helen was fascinated by the power of these combinations of time and place to organise people and strengthen them into a purpose.

St Eade's Church was her current obsession with place. She spent a great deal of her time there and in Crosschester's extensive public library immersed in research. The church was built over a ring of twelve huge druidic Stones. A thirteenth stone was discovered down near the small, wide bridge that carried mourners and wedding guests across the River Icene to and from the Water Meadows.

That stone was called the Mounting Stone by the locals, but Helen had discovered in a charter from 972AD that it was properly called Ssægdnestán or, roughly translated, "The Mystery Stone". The charter was vague as to why this stone had been given any name at all. So, Helen dug further and discovered the reason in an obscure work on myths and legends in the county, written by a historian called Dr Alice Wilson. According to Dr Wilson, the Ssægdnestán was more likely to mean, "Sacrifice Stone" and had extraordinarily little mystery about it.

Helen finished her report on Lunsford, promising herself that she would revisit that situation the next day. Her report was terse, efficient and highly confidential, and one day soon someone in authority would read it, she hoped. She closed her files and finished her black tea. Then she stood up, smoothed down her slacks, she filed her reports in the tall, iron, lockable filing cabinet standing olive drab like a silence in a battle. She locked the cabinet. She was dissatisfied. She was highly dissatisfied. She needed more tea.

CHAPTER 17

LUNSFORD LEAVES THE HUNTERS WOOD

1978

Lunsford watched as Fawley and Adelaide left him. His demolishing fear turned to astonishment and then to embarrassment. He was still floating just above himself, just above a life of mud and numbness, the life that was left to him. He looked up at himself looking down and neither one had an answer for the other.

He was cold, old, thirsty, and hungry. He wasn't lonely, he was bereft. He had no desire at all for the company of other people. The only reason, he realised, that he wanted to reunite with Adelaide was that when he talked out loud to her, he didn't feel quite so odd. The dog helped. Even though he understood she could leave at any time with the certainty that she had arrived.

His parents had warned him about people who talked out loud when there was no one there who cared to listen.

"The bitch was playing you. Taking you for a fool and you can't see that you're better off. Fucking idiot", his father piped up.

His body felt like the ash tree: fissured, broken skin, eaten from the inside. He wanted to be at home with the curtains closed, cold and dead on his bed with Mick standing there making the necessary arrangements for a respectable and dignified funeral. With Chloé mourning downstairs.

It made Lunsford think. Even as he was hanging in space not wanting to return to that old, cold lump on the ground, it was making him think. He thought about how he missed them both. He was floating and he was sitting on a log, his trousers were damp and so were his face and hair. He tried to stand up. He tried again. He was too heavy. All the weight he ever been was now centred on his spine and forcing it down; glass boulders full of foetid, fatty water, tied to each vertebrae chaining him in place. He slumped over, head in hands, the destitution of his heart loud in his ears: rushing and pulsing like traffic driving past a tramp in the rain and never stopping, coming and going and coming and going, overlapping and fading only to roar and fade again into the tramp's empty, sighing hope.

He jerked his head up so he was looking at a yew tree. He could feel the edge of the log he was sitting on. It was jagged, not sawn but split. Blown over in some storm or corrupted from inside. Again, he tried to stand up. The sound in his ears, which he realised was blood pulsing, nothing more complex or mysterious, had subsided. There was nothing complex or mysterious about his current situation all in fact.

"Bloody cold. Bloody hungry. Bloody Old", he said to himself from on high.

His ill treatment of Fawley came back to him. How had he been so rude to someone who, when all was said and done, had been nothing other than friendly? Why his madness had made him insult Fawley? Why had he even considered robbery and murder? How absurd. How childish. What the bloody hell had happened in his head since leaving hospital? Was he heading for a breakdown? He asked his floating self. If he was, who was there to help? The life he'd lived with Chloé had been wonderful but he realised it had also been circumscribed by their contentment in each other.

"That's not true is it? Chloé had lots of friends, she had a lovely big funeral. She had birthday parties, people came round every week to see her, she had hobbies, she went out. She liked to be around people", Mick popped in.

"It was you who didn't like to mix. Never have. So, let's stop on with this whining about who's going to take care of you. No fucker is. Why should they? Reap what you sow, son", said his dad.

He knew his internal voice well because he'd spent his life working in concentrated silence with it. These other voices were not his.

"Not you, not us", said floating Lunsford.

That voice was steady, always the same. It could badger and criticise, that was often its job but he had learned to trust it. Its tone and timbre had remained the same since his childhood. He'd never thought of that before. The voice had never aged or changed. Lunsford assumed that everybody had their own voice if for nothing else than to pass the time at a bus stop or to decide what film to watch at the cinema or to swear at the idiot who had drenched you with filthy puddle water as they drove past the bus stop.

The man who drove too fast, skidding and aquaplaning heading into a wall. Lazy death bringer. Lunsford was still shouting at him. Screaming. Not loud enough that other voice though. Lost in time. Lost time.

Now he was lost in a wood like some fay child from a fairy tale. He was out of context, out of Oak Cottage and away from work – he'd never go back to work. He needed to move, to walk home. It had been ages since he'd been at home. He wanted bed and blankets and silence and Adelaide at the door.

His guiding voice, the one that had been with him since he first took a step was quiet, split between heaven and earth. The voices advising and kicking him were a jumble of familiar people. Chloé's voice, in the background someone else's, another woman's, maybe his mother or grandma, maybe a schoolteacher, definitely a woman, definitely dead. His father was in there too. Talking to him more than ever he had in life. Words, phrases, intercessions in a flat but at the same time furious tone. Those other voices were certainly growing louder and more frequent.

"So, why did I come the giddy goose and think, no believe, that the young man was going to rob me and then murder me?" he asked himself out loud to be sure. He was still unable to make any purposeful movement.

Mick asked, "How incredible would the training have been to ensure that she would find you (for some reason you, out of everybody else in the county), then wheedle her way into your confidence and affection only to lead you to robbery and death? Where did all that come from?

"Since when were you so important? You've never been important", said Frank, lazily, out of habit, as if he was doing something else.

"You've prided yourself on your unimportance", said Chloé with no malice.

"Broke your mother's heart. No fucking ambition", said his father who was an expert in both of those things. "Broke it into pieces and didn't care".

Lunsford was shaking. His whole body. Cold or scared. Vibrating like a wren. He wanted so much to be at home, in bed, hidden in blankets, in the dark, with Adelaide at the door to ward off strangers and welcome in death.

"Maybe it was the chap's age?" he, floating, thought. "Youth and violence always go together".

"Didn't we throw stones down from the trees at the tourists? Didn't we nick sweets from the Sweete Shoppe? Weren't we hellish ourselves sometimes?" asked Mick.

"Fucking funny though", said Frank.

"But why did I think he was going to murder me, steal from me?"

"It could have been his weird clothes?" said Mick.

"Since when were a set of overalls and a pair of boots weird?"

"Maybe his hair? His accent? His confidence?"

"He was so much more confident than I am that's for sure, than I've ever been".

"Maybe you made assumptions about Fawley based on where he'd found him? Hunters Wood?", suggested Chloé.

She was wrong though.

He had spent hours and days and ages in Hunters Wood as a boy and a teenager. Even when he was trying on adulthood with regular Saturday bus rides into Crosschester to try and hang out with bigger lads. When he and Mick attempted to be cool with slicked back hair, secondhand suites and shined up scuffed brown boots, smoking hack-up-your lungs fags, one between the pair of them. Even then when they grew a little and sat on the bottom step of the Market Cross trying to get the attention of girls. Even then there was no fear of Hunters Wood. As boys, they'd go into the Water Meadows to net minnows, and then into Hunters Wood to smoke roll-ups and drink cheap cider. High up in the trees they pretended to be Mowgli or Tarzan or someone exciting and exotic from the books and films. Shouting down at the tourists and pretty girls. Even then. Especially then, the woods were home.

But what had happened? He tried to stand. He realised that it wasn't Chloé's fault at all. Hunters Wood was dull when it had to compete with music and fags and imagined sex and cars. It faded from memory as adulthood drowned it out. The war killed its memory. Then at home on dry land, with mundane and safe work, there wasn't time for its reality.

Lunsford on the ground breathed in deeply: dank, cold air filled with animal shit and rotting wood. He desperately needed so much to be at home, in bed, hidden in blankets, curtains pulled together tight, shutters locked, eyes closed, inside himself.

"Well, move then. Stop thinking. You're not going to die here unless you decide to", urged Mick.

"Coward. Puff. Nobody cares but you, and if you don't care then end it here you fucking burden", said Frank predictably. That predictability, like the sea hammering a coastline, just added to the demolishing force.

The moon was up and bright. It reflected light into the circle highlighting stones and small bones. The air was growing colder. There was no birdsong, no owl or nightjar or nightingale, no robin or song thrush, no singing, no screaming foxes, certainly no human voices. The quiet was astounding, nothing touched him, not even the ground.

Floating Lunsford said, "How on earth am I remembering the names of birds I've not thought about in decades? Where is this information coming from? Where is the plan for this?"

Landlocked Lunsford breathed in hard. He still had strength in his body. His brain still worked, if only to provide him with strange sensations. He forced himself down and demanded that he re-enter himself and stop being an observer. He re-joined himself.

"Wake up. Get out of this place", he demanded of himself.

He closed his eyes again. He saw a kind of darkness that he would have loved to have climbed into and stayed forever. His own darkness. He opened his eyes. The moon was so bright it illuminated roots rising out of the ground like dinosaur bones from dry tar.

"A Hunter's Moon. You know that. You can use that. It's a fine, good sign", said a woman's voice.

He looked at his hands. He looked at his watch, it was 6pm, only 6pm, it felt like midnight a hundred years ago.

Memories, false and true, came into him like stones thrown by children at the already shattered windows of an old house: Mick and the car. Lunsford and the car. Chloé in her last second.

"I wasn't there".

"You were there for me. I held you there in my heart".

The still-birth of their daughter.

"You couldn't even breed. Good decision. Good decision for the rest of us", Unlike in life, Frank was showing quite some tenacity.

Memories floated up from the earth and hit him. The squaddies by The Green Man pub yelling abuse, tensing their muscles and comparing tattoos. That day in London. Carving his name high up in an oak tree. The kiss with Liz Unsworth under the cathedral arch near the College. Falling out with Mick. Not getting on that plane to America. Adelaide's soft bark. Fawley's directions.

"Fawley's directions. Helpful Fawley. Someone's helped you out for no reason, in the face of your mistrust and anger. Fawley's directions, now there's some hope for you", said the woman's voice.

Lunsford felt even worse about the way he'd treated the young man. No wonder Adelaide had followed him.

Keep the central cathedral tower on your left. Keep St Eade's steeple on your right. Couple of steps and you'll be on the paved path again.

Lunsford stood up. The moonlight came down and down and down, heatless light, false light. Reflection and illumination. The dinosaur bone roots became serpents arching out of a dead sea and receded as a thin strip of cloud passed over the face of the moon. Lunsford walked over to the oak tree that was his first waypoint. He looked left through a gap in the treetops. He looked right. Through a gap in the treetops.

Both the cathedral's central tower and the steeple of St Eade's were in plain sight. The moonlight pin-lighting each of them in the surrounding darkness, both beautifully visible briefly before the wind blew the treetops back and the cloud returned to ruin the face of the moon. The brief visibility was enough for Lunsford. Right enough in no time he was back on the paved path, which he followed until he could see the Water Meadows. In all, the trudge from what he was certain was the heart of the wood to the fringe of the meadow had taken him ten minutes. His face was damp when stepped out of Hunters Wood and into the Water Meadows.

He began the walk home, the Hunters Moon providing enough light to steer him clear of rivulets, molehills and a badger that had ventured out hungry and angry. His floating self wanted to break free but couldn't.

CHAPTER 18

ANSWER THIS DOOR IF YOU PLEASE!

1978

At the same time Lunsford and Adelaide were venturing into Hunters
Wood, Helen Cousins mounted her bike and headed out of
Churchfields to the High Street. Then towards Oak Cottage to finally
beard Mr Martin Lunsford in his den. Her black, leather satchel was
secured in the basket that was welded to the front of her blue bicycle. It
was filled with survey forms, pens, a copy of George Bourne's 1912
Change in the Village, a Polaroid camera for instant results, and a letter
sealed up in a brown envelope.

This Lunsford situation was untenable. Mr Martin Lunsford had,
to the best of her knowledge, supplied no information since he had left
hospital. How on earth could this benefit the wider community in the
future? What a selfish man. What a selfish, selfish man.

She powered up the high street, overtaking another damned farmer
on what may as well have been a steam driven tractor. She hated the

countryside. She wanted this Lunsford situation over with quickly, before lunchtime because she needed to visit the public library in Crosschester. She needed to investigate a new line of research for what she had started on The Psychodynamics of Village Life in the Evolution of Nationhood. She had ordered a collection called India's Villages edited by a Mr M.N. Srinivas, she had also (finally!) insisted that the librarians source a translation of Gemeinschaft and Gesellschaft by Ferdinand Tönnies. Ronald Frankenberg's Communities in Britain was finally available for her to check out. She detested going to the public library with its coughing and sneezing and the old tramps slumped into newspapers, and young children buzzing about, but needs must. Due to the unfair unpleasantness in Oxford, she could no longer visit the Bodleian and maybe this was adding to her distaste for Crosschester's offering, but frankly the latter wasn't fit to lick the boots of the former.

On she cycled, past the primary school, made of flint, and overlooked by a giant Scot's Pine. Down Berry Lane by Latimer's the butchers and under the railway bridge with its green mould and echoes of trains long gone to more interesting places. Had it been open to her she would have kept on cycling all the way back to when she was at her happiest. But she had important work to do and, like the pioneers who came before her, she knew that loneliness and sadness, misunderstanding and exclusion were her lot.

Finally, she stopped and leaned her bicycle against the flint wall that separated Mr Martin Lunsford's house from the Fleet Road. She straightened her skirt, checked that her short, bobbed hair was all in place, tightened her leather gloves to her wrists, collected her satchel from the basket and strode through the gate, ensuring it slammed shut with an almighty crack behind her.

Fortunately for her purposes Mr Martin Lunsford's house was not fitted with one of those new doorbells that you couldn't hear if you were standing outside. Instead it had a large, glossy black door knocker in the shape of a lion's head, which had managed to make quite an impression on the thick metal plated set into the door to save its blue painted wood. She pulled the lion's head back as far as it would go and using both hands and a will to victory, slammed it back into place. She did this three times then stood expectantly.

"Mr Lunsford! Mr Martin Lunsford. It is Helen Cousins. You need to answer this door. Answer this door if you please!" she called through the letterbox.

An elderly gentleman passing by with his ancient, black Labrador coughed loudly.

"What!?", she spat.

"They never answer that door", said the elderly gentleman.

"What do you mean?"

"That door's not been opened in years. They never open it. You'll need to go round the side", he indicated with his walking stick, "to the kitchen door".

She shrugged her shoulder, sighed and went round the side of the small, rather shaggy house to find herself standing outside another red door. This one had no knocker nor a bell, but it did have a glass panel that enabled her to see into the empty kitchen.

"That's if he's in of course, which he isn't", the old man said to this dog, who sniffed and dribbled a little.

Helen pressed her face to the glass, both hands shielding her view from the intercession of any interfering light. What she saw didn't surprise her at all.

A cup was piled up in the sink. The floor looked as if it hadn't been swept let alone mopped in months. There was a Fray Bentos pie tin sitting on it. On it! There were dying flowers in a chipped vase on the table. This person was not looking after himself. He was also quite obviously not in the kitchen. She knocked on the door, it made a frustratingly tiny sound, a dull 'tink'. So, she took a coin from her purse and ticked-and-tacked that against the glass panel. Then she yelled.

"Mr Lunsford! Answer this door! It is an important visit. It is about your health. Answer this door now please".

She waited, maybe he was upstairs. She checked her watch, 8:55am, maybe he was still in bed. She could certainly imagine a man who could leave a kitchen in that state would still be in bed at what was essentially 9am. She knocked again with fist and coin. The coin left a scratch on the glass but that would make little difference to the shabby little house. She called again, attempting to moderate her tone while still getting her message into every room in Oak Cottage.

"Mr Lunsford, please let me in. This is for your good and for the good of the community. Let me in! We need to assess how you are progressing or whether you are not. Your... " she consulted her notebook, "accident was a serious one and who knows what the long term effects might be? Please open this door", there was venom in the word "please".

It was becoming obvious that even with her best efforts Mr Martin

Lunsford was going to continue not answering his door. She consulted her notebook once again and read a note regarding his next appointment at the Royal County: no date, no time, just an exclamation mark. She withdrew a fountain pen and the letter from her satchel, she removed the letter from its envelope, placed it on the door and prepared to sign it. It read:

To: Mr Martin Lunsford

From: Helen Cousins (GNC 297422)

Telephone: 715565

November 29th, 1978

Dear, Mr Lunsford,

This is the third time I have tried to complete your health check following your discharge from the Royal County Hospital in Crosschester. I am sure that you will agree with me, that this is not fair to yourself, or, to the wider community. You should, at your earliest opportunity, telephone me, to confirm a date and time for me to visit you at your home. My telephone number is clearly written at the top, and foot of this official note.

Sincerely, yours,

H.M. Cousins (GNC 297422)

Telephone: 725565

She signed the letter, replaced it in the envelope and sealed it with spit on her right index finger. Of course, there was no letterbox on this door, of course there wasn't. Clutching the letter, her irritation reaching peak level, she stalked back to the front door.

"Was he in then?", the old man, pipe in hand, dog at heel had waited exactly to ask this question.

"No. He was not. Do you know when he will be back?", she replied as she slipped the letter into the house. It floated onto the doormat.

He thought for a moment, looked down at the dog, took a draw on his pipe.

"Well?" every single thing was annoying her.

"I've no idea missus, no idea. Good morning. Come on then Sambo, time for your walk", and off they went. She thought she could see his shoulders shaking slightly but no mind, she had bigger things to be getting on with. She took out her notebook and added the date and the time of her visit and replaced it in her satchel, placed her satchel back into its rack. Then as she began the ride into Crosschester the rain started thin and soaking.

CHAPTER 19

THE PUBLIC LIBRARY AND THE PUBLIC BAR

1978

Helen propped her bike against the wall of the Public Library in Crosschester and took the books for return from the basket. She brushed her skirt down, straightened her hair and walked through the back door, up the rising corridor with its parquet flooring and paintings of forgotten city worthies, through the reading rooms and up to the librarian's desk. She placed the books on the table and said a brusque good morning.

"These are coming back then, Miss Cousins. Did you enjoy them?", asked the junior librarian.

"They were not for enjoyment thank you, Miss Finch".

She withdrew a typed list of the books she wanted to take home and passed it over to the younger woman. Rather than read it, however, Miss Finch stood up on her toes and leaned closer to Helen Cousins.

She whispered, "I've seen you've been reading a lot of Dr Alice

Wilson's work. Well..." she paused like someone about to give their child a huge birthday surprise, "she's over there by the dictionaries".

She flicked her head with the subtlety of a horse in heat, in the direction of a woman dressed in what appeared to be a wide selection of long, brightly coloured scarves, with brown, leather jackboots on her feet, and a knitted hat crowning her salt and pepper hair.

Miss Finch returned to the list of books she'd been presented with, licked her pencil's nib and said, "These will take me an hour to rustle up, we're a bit short-staffed today and there's a party due in from Commiton Primary School, I hope that's not too much bother".

It was too much bother, it was a great deal of bother, a very great deal of bother indeed, thought Sister Helen, but there was no point in making a fuss. Making fusses was unedifying, patience was a virtue, and she would write a letter to the authorities about the under-staffing and the over familiarity of the staff who had bothered to turn up for work when she got home with her books. She turned away from the counter and headed off in the direction of Dr Alice Wilson, who had moved on from the dictionaries and was currently examining a copy of *The Anglo-Saxon Chronicle* as translated from the original by the Reverend James Ingram in 1823.

Sister Helen coughed and Dr Wilson looked up.

"Excuse me for interrupting your researches", began Helen, "but I had to come over and tell you how good your work is. I've just finished your book about Shalford. I wonder, are you thinking of continuing that line?"

Dr Wilson closed the book and looked worried, "Thank you very much for your kind words", she spoke quietly and deliberately, so quietly that Sister Helen had to lean closer. She smelt alcohol on the other woman. It was 11:30 in the morning. She leaned back in mild disgust and great disappointment.

"I rarely get to meet any of my readers. If I'm honest with myself, I doubt that I have many", Dr Wilson smiled. "As for my next book, I have decided to spread my intellectual wings a little and I will be looking at witches and witchcraft in France in the 14th Century. It's all very intriguing".

Sister Helen was taken aback. Dr Wilson's work had, as far as she was aware, concentrated on the wealth of histories right here on her own doorstop. The county was her stamping ground. This county and this country.

"France? Why France"

Dr Wilson took a step back and stumbled onto a child's chair that had been lurking behind her. She fell to the floor with her skirts and scarves flying around her.

"Drunk!" thought Sister Helen.

"I am not drunk", said Dr Wilson as a matter of course because more often than not she was. She reached out for some help. "I've not touched a drop".

She was possibly even injured given that the chair had shattered beneath her weight, but she was not at all flustered. Helen took her hand and pulled her up. The doctor rose slowly and when upright, tidied herself and finally responded to the question.

"Don't you feel that the links and connections between our own country and others across the Channel, our fellow Europeans, are often fascinating and inform us about ourselves? In a sense, studying our neighbours is studying ourselves but from contrasting perspectives".

As she spoke about the direction her work was taking, her voice grew louder, clearer, more confident and her expression became intense.

"Well, I imagine that there might be something to be said for contrasting our Englishness with the ways in which other people behave in their own countries", Sister Helen offered. "Do you need to sit down?" she had noticed that the other woman was swaying a little.

"That would be terrific, yes, yes I think I would, will you join me in my reading room?" She headed off to the librarian's desk.

Sister Helen consulted her watch, she had time to fritter, and she was intrigued by the obviously highly educated woman who was also quite plainly an alcoholic, so she followed.

"Daphne, dear girl, we're going across the road to The Crown and Anchor for a confab, be a darling and pop over when my books are ready could you?", Miss Finch stuttered, "I...I...I'll do my best Doctor Wilson but we're very understaffed today".

"You'll be gone moments dearest girl, no one will miss you", she patted the young woman on the hand and glowed with good will.

Sister Helen was mightily impressed, but less so when Miss Finch turned to her, "Miss Cousins, I'm afraid that someone has already taken out Inquiries into Human Faculty and its Development and it's not due back 'til next Tuesday but on the good news side, Pearson's Scope and Importance to the State of the Science of National Eugenics was returned just this morning, and we're checking it in so it should be ready for you at the same time as Dr Wilson's".

"What about Terman's *Measurement of Intelligence*, and also Mr

Webb's *The Decline in the Birth Rate?*", she snapped.

"We're getting those ready for your Miss Cousins, quick as quick can be". The reading public were nothing like she'd been led to believe during her training.

"Come along dear lady, to the reading room! We've lots to discuss, I've not had a good tete a tete for quite some time. Hurry!", Dr Wilson exited the library from its ornate double doors and stepped onto the street. Sister Helen shot Miss Finch a final scowl and turned on her heel to follow.

Minutes later both women were sitting at a small, round table in the downstairs lounge bar of The Crown and Anchor pub with two soda waters in front of them. The Crown was a pub more usually at home with drunk soldiers and even more drunk local youths too young to be drinking what they were trying to drink. Upstairs in another bar, a jukebox was blaring out some form of rock music so loud that it crashed through the walls, down the stairs, through the door and nuzzled up to the open fire. Two lads, scruffy in duffle coats and sneakers, stinking of patchouli oil, and smoking tight, cheapskate roll-ups were sitting by the bay window, sipping pints of snakebite and mumbling about how much they hated sport. Aside from them the pub was desolate for 11:45 on a Friday morning.

Dr Wilson leaned back in her chair, "I love this old place, literally no one I know ever comes in here. It's like a holiday for me away from the formal fuckery of academia. Without one single word of a lie, dear lady, that is a cesspool of politics and plagiarism. Don't be fooled by the elbow patches, pipes and politesse, it's a cannibal festival", she took a sip of her drink and grimaced, "Not dissimilar to publishing".

"I will publish one day soon", said Helen, running her finger around the rim of the glass, preferring not to find it anywhere near her lips, "When I have decided on an appropriate publisher of course".

"You should, my darling, you should! Bring a breath of fresh air to the cess".

She took another sip and changed the subject. "I understand from your conversation with our Miss Finch that you're interested in Eugenics, that's not a popular path to tread, tell me more".

"Popularity is no indication of seriousness, Dr Wilson".

"Please call me Alice".

There was no chance of that. Helen was talking to a doctor, she wanted to be sure that everybody knew that.

"Don't you see that every, single day in the cultural malaise of unthinking, ignoble savagery, and magpicism? The mulatto nature of our artistic, linguistic and educational spheres? All of this is popular but has no quality. It is creating a fractured society that is serving not a single one of its citizens with care or conscience. It's about time we looked a great deal harder to less popular, more strengthening and invigorating ways to build culture otherwise we'll rot, and rightly so".

Sister Helen finally took a sip from her greasily cleaned glass and retched a little.

Alice Wilson looked around the room. The Crown was two hundred and fifty years old and it showed. It had become an army pub because of its proximity to the bus station where squaddies came and went. As a consequence, and as a form of defence when the going got drunk or amphetamine crazy, the pub's walls memorialised the Royal County Regiment – known affectionately as 'The Green Men' – with paintings and photographs of smiling boys in uniforms and civvies, holding up guns, lances and trophies, sitting on tanks, kissing astonished women, standing in cemeteries, or charging moustachioed into impossible cannonades. One wall of the pub, the one behind the knackered piano was reserved for postcards from theatres of war or holiday spots both with roughly the same sentiments about "shit food", "smelly locals", "fit birds" and "having a fucking wonderful time, wish you were here!".

Alice desperately wanted to put vodka in her soda water. She had a quarter bottle in her voluminous carpet bag on the floor by her shaking right leg.

Upstairs the jukebox started a new song and the opening baseline beat down on them. The singer was a woman, she was shouting about not being dictated to.

"I'm so sorry, I've not even asked your name, and I can't just keep calling you 'dear lady', I know I do that. It's because I have a terrible memory for names, I have to write everything down, I really do. What is your name?"

"Helen Cousins, Miss. Miss Helen Cousins", for a reason buried deep inside her she then put her right hand out. Dr Wilson looked at it, and then realised it required her to grip and shake. Neither woman particularly enjoyed this sort of physical contact but both were forced by ingrained courtesy to adhere to the conventions, so a grip and shake broke out, briefly, before they relaxed into their own seats.

Their upbringings were, in fact, not very similar at all. While both had been bright and intelligent girls, one was an only child, the other was one of seven siblings and sat somewhere in the middle. Both girls had been born in the same month of the same year. Both were alienated from the world outside by the formations and formalities of their own families.

Helen was brought up in a coldly passionate, Evangelical household where Christmas was frowned on, and marching was considered excellent exercise. Surrounded by fresh, freezing air and regular doses of prayer to a God so pure that any dialogue was blasphemous. She knew that the world outside the house needed cleaning, cleansing, helping, saving because what was good and true was distant and ungraspable and the path to it was dirty, pitted and falsely signposted. She once knew that the clean, plain, wonderfully essential and ecstatically straight light from Lord God was what would make the world perfect. Cut back, trim down, sort out, burn with holy fire, make sense. Happiness was sense. Happiness was clarity and strength. Soon, though, she had experienced other people, other people who God had apparently also created.

Alice was raised in a Roman Catholic home, soft with incense and Latin incantations, richly stained heavy with symbolic mysteries. Icons and statues removed her imagination from the everyday. Her family's faith was predicated on blood, supported by the gorgeous sacrificial Christ boy and his saintly virgin mother. Saints were sent to guide and guard her with bloody tears, thorns and silent lambs with slitted wounds of beautiful, unknowable depth. Her church was the original church. So, she was told. She was told that the world outside distrusted her family because of their foreign religion. She was told that was how it was meant to be. That was right, they were special.

Both women had lost their God in their twenties. Neither could completely shake off their religions.

The patchouli boys in The Crown had started to yell at each other about science fiction and bus timetables. A song with someone screaming about the modern world collided with the open fire briefly. A bus past outside full of pensioners on the way to the bingo, and children bunking off class.

"Well, Helen, if I may call you that, that's certainly an interesting position to take vis a vis social engineering. Where are you intending to go with your line of investigation into Eugenics?"

Helen was going to reform her environment so that it was controlled and became a gentle, thoughtful and clean place for decent people to inhabit.

"At the moment, Dr Wilson, this is purely to educate myself about a way of thinking that I feel has been unfairly traduced".

"You already feel it has been traduced but you are educating yourself about it?", Alice was already a little bored with the constant use of her title but she had to wait for her books and was enjoying the warmth of The Crown, so she took another sip of soda water, and leaned in.

Dr Wilson's soppy use of "dear" and "dearest" grated on Helen but she'd had no one to discuss her work with for an age, and her books were still not available so she continued, "Eugenics is a straightforward route to diminish the unhappiness of civilised cultures…"

Dr Wilson interrupted, "You say, 'civilised' and I'm not sure I understand what you mean by that word. Might you explain your thinking" she paused, "dear?"

You patronising bitch, thought Sister Helen, shocking herself. She was not used to being challenged, especially not about simple facts. She assumed that everybody understood what was meant by civilisation, especially a published academic. Investigating such a commonsense term appeared to be a waste of talent, so she began to surmise that the Doctor had none after all. She was a scruffy alcoholic. Her work was probably overrated. Helen made a mental note to read more critically.

She dismissed the question, "Dr Wilson, I'm sure we don't need to split hairs over the meaning of commonly understood words. The more pressing question, I'm sure you'll agree, is that a healthy mind reaches its full potential without the body being in accordance with that enterprise. This is true not only for the human body but also for the body of a civilised and civilising society. Eugenics is a laudable, but misinterpreted, methodology for ensuring the health of the whole. For example, it can and should be reinterpreted to benefit our creaking health system". She made a mental note to write this down as soon as possible.

One of the scruffy lads said, "Seriously, Batman would beat Superman? Batman couldn't even beat Popeye the fucking sailor man". His mate stood up and headed upstairs to the loud bar, which Dr Wilson would inevitably visit later in the day. The music from the upstairs bar had calmed a little, another woman was singing, with the door open her words slunk in.

"Jesus died for somebody's sins but not mine"

Both women winced. The door to the upstairs bar slammed shut, the other lad stole a long draught from his mate's glass and winked at the two women before turning to the window on which Daphne Finch was tapping frantically and pointing at Dr Wilson and Miss Cousins. He waved back at her, made a face and called to them, "I think this one's for you, ladies", in an accent so cut glass that it would have graced a Cathedral window. He was a student at the famous Crosschester College school, slumming it on a school day.

"Our books are here thank goodness", Helen went to stand up.

"Actually, I disagree with you Miss Cousins", there was no movement from Alice Wilson. Helen sat down hard but rather up for a fight.

"I beg your pardon?", she said.

"Firstly, you're confusing 'culture' with 'civilisation'. Aside from that, Eugenics is flawed from first principles because it relies on an impossible predicate. It relies on the subjective judgement of a self-appointed superior group".

Oh, you bitch. You smarmy, wordy bitch, thought Helen.

"One group judging the fitness of all every other person, and not only that but feeling deep in their emotional cores that what they're doing is scientific, objective, practical and worst of all, right.

You're drunk. You filthy waste of learning, you harridan.

"All judgement comes to us not from an unambiguous realm of objective fact, instead it comes from human beings and we are temperamental, mercurial and prone to influence", Dr Alice Wilson stopped, her breathing was steady. Her hands were steady.

Sister Helen could no longer be calm, "What waffle! Words on words. Do you realise how much a single person suffering from a hereditary defect costs the community during his lifetime? Do you not realise that to aid the damaged is to multiply it? It is the same as maliciously providing future generations with a multitude of unnecessary battles to fight. The aim of Eugenics is to represent each class or section of society by its very best constituents. Once that is achieved we can leave them to work out their common civilisation in their own way and in their own place".

She was shouting now, standing up and shouting. "You obviously think I am a stupid woman, unpublished and dilettante amateur, well let me tell you that I know", she spat the word, "I know what I believe to be true. I can see and understand. I am not stupid. You must not patronise me with your messy, jumble, your high and mighty excuses for analysis! You are no better than I am. Facts are facts".

Alice finally took a quarter bottle of vodka from her bag, and poured a wonderful slug of it into her nearly empty glass. She drank.

"You have simply regurgitated verbatim Herbert Spencer, Francis Galton and Margaret Sanger at me. That's not understanding or analysing, there is no room for discussion in that, dear, dear Miss Cousins. That is simply reading out loud like a child with their ABC".

"This public house is disgusting! You stink of cheap alcohol, you filthy drunk charlatan!" Sister Helen rose from her seat, took up her briefcase and walked out.

Alice Wilson stood and walked up the stairs to the bar with the loud music and young people.

Miss Finch knew the score with this one, she returned to her post and began applying for Civil Service jobs.

CHAPTER 20

HE CAME OUT OF THE DARKNESS

1978

Head down with striding intent through the fading evening light and the Water Meadows came a short, stout man in his late twenties with a frog-like face and a loud voice. He stepped through the chalk streams, a fishing rod in his right hand, a large, khaki tackle bag strapped right to left across his body, a flat cap, riddled with salmon lures on his head.

He was dressed head to knee in a suit of thick yellow corduroy, with tan leather rider's gaiters wrapping his knees and lipping over expensive but well worn, brown brogue boots. He wore a bright red tie with a small crest, a wide checked green and white woollen shirt and a tweedy waistcoat as yellow as his suit jacket with stains that spoke of years of good living, fishing, shooting and riding to hounds. Topping the whole expensive and deliberately weathered look was a ruined waxed Barbour jacket with innumerable pockets.

"Good evening to you! Great good evening to you sir!" the man exclaimed as he strode straight up to Lunsford and stood so close that his breath was warm on Lunsford's cheek. He had the smell of country houses that their owners called stately homes, of prep and public schools and of aimless living. He took a step back, looked Lunsford up and down, nodded, smiled a hint of a smile and stuck out his right hand.

"Good evening", replied Lunsford, taking a weaker handshake than he'd expected. The man placed his left hand over Lunsford's right and shook it as vigorously as waves in a paper cup.

"The name's Thomas Vyvian Sarson-Taylor", he said, releasing his watery grip. "Friends call me Tom. Call me what you like just don't call me late to dinner!" he snorted at his own tired joke. He took out a silver hip flask, took a swig, and jiggled it at Lunsford who demurred.

"Take a sip, take a sip! It's a 12-year old, single malt, family owns the distillery I think, lovely nip. What's your name?"

Sarson-Taylor's mouth never seemed to open or close more than a slit. It was as if the man was both his own ventriloquist and dummy.

Having grown up in Shalford with its preparatory school that fed young boys to the ancient, public school of Crosschester College, Lunsford had seen this kind of man before. His entire demeanour spoke of ancient, engrained wealth.

The College educated its students in the ways of the legal industry, and Parliament, of farming and stocks and bonds, of the army, the navy and the High Church. The boys were taught Latin, rugby and self-reliance. Loneliness and camaraderie were dealt with as equals. The truly intelligent were weeded out and groomed for long lives of academic security. Happiness was taught as something that happened after lights out. The outside world was a possession.

Lunsford listened closely to make sense of what Sarson-Taylor was saying as the words and pauses of common speech blurred into an estimation of English. Sarson-Taylor took another swig from his hip flask and replaced it in one of his many waxed pockets.

"Are you sure you don't want a sip?" he said, flipping the lid of his hip flask and pushing it at Lunsford who once again shook his head. Sarson-Taylor took another swig and dropped the flask into yet another pocket.

Lunsford asked, "I wonder, have you seen a dog, about this high?", he gestured just above his knee.

Sarson-Taylor thought for a moment before consulting the evening mist. He looked back at Lunsford, "Do you know, I have. A dog, yes, yes I have! Yes! About this high?" he flapped his hand around vaguely. He was triumphant. "Yes, yes and yes. I saw just the beast trotting off towards the pub just before we met".

"Was she alone or with a young man, tall, very short hair, dressed in green?"

Sarson-Taylor took out his flask and took a thoughtful drink. Lunsford waited. "Tall fellow. Young, you say?"

"Yes", said Lunsford.

"By God, it was with a tall young man!".

Then a thought occurred, one that appealed to him greatly. "Fawley, that's the name".

He offered the flask, once again Lunsford refused it.

"Yes, that's what he told me his name was", Sarson-Taylor

confirmed.

"Fawley, yes. Terrible boy. Be wary of him. Consummate liar. Not to be trusted. Wanders around the countryside. Goodness knows where he's actually from. I've heard it might be Northern Ireland. IRA or some such". He took another sip. "Or he might be a gypsy or the son of Lord Fitzwallace on the run.

"All I know is that he's a chap who does not understand the rules of pub nor club. He holds one to the flimsiest of debts", he paused, "He steals too. It would not surprise me if he slurped milk straight from the udder rather than paying for it. It's well known that he's a poacher, a thief, and a burglar. Not our sort, not at all".

Lunsford was rooted to the spot watching the man talk, and slowly growing used to his accent. He was genuinely concerned about Adelaide though.

"Would he do something to the dog?"

He imagined Adelaide being forced to fight other, bigger dogs in an out of the way barn surrounded by screaming drunks baying for her blood and their money.

Sarson-Taylor thought for a second before replying, "Gosh, yes he would. I would not put that past him. Terrible, terrible chap. It would not surprise me if he's put your dog under some gypsy curse and is training it up to do his dirty work". He took out another, slightly more ornate flask from yet another pocket and proffered it. He didn't wait for a response and took a nip himself.

"You say you saw them heading towards a pub? Which one The Bridge? The Volunteer? The Dolphin?" Lunsford asked.

"No, no, no not those. To The Phoenix", Sarson-Taylor gestured towards Churchfields, "It's just up the rise, near St Eade's".

Lunsford was genuinely confused, "I've lived in Shalford all my life and I've never heard of The Phoenix".

"Terribly small", said Sarson-Taylor, already marching off in the direction of the mystery pub, "very quiet. One has to know it to know it if you get my drift".

Lunsford followed along, "Is it very new?" he asked.

"Ancient place. Doomsday Book I would have thought. My family owns it I think. Wonderful place, marvellous people, salt of the earth".

Lunsford struggled to keep up, and Sarson-Taylor wasn't slowing down, he was intent on getting to the pub.

Sarson-Taylor turned his head slightly and called out, "Buck up! Buck up! We're nearly there. You're going to love this place. Love it".

Sarson-Taylor continued to talk but Lunsford had stopped listening. The two men walked out of the Water Meadows, over the small iron and wood bridge that crossed the Icene, and up the short rise towards St Eade's church.

CHAPTER 21

THE PHOENIX INN

1978

Instead of turning left off Church Lane and into St Eade's, Sarson-Taylor marched through a narrow, chalk-floored path, a path that Lunsford vaguely remembered seeing but had never used.

"Hare Rise", said Sarson-Taylor looking over his shoulder, "I think the family owns it". He sped up.

There were high, dark hawthorn hedges on each side of the Hare Rise as it wound on and on. Finally it opened out onto a wide village green with no village surrounding it. In the centre of the green was a sizeable pond. Around the green were twelve small, grey stones, roughly shaped with a single, sturdy metal chain passing through a hole in each, linking them together.

The only building that Lunsford could perceive was a two-storied, jettied pub, its hanging sign declaring it to be "The Phoenix". It looked warm, welcoming, it was as familiar as a taste or a smell from many years ago. It had a gabled door with leaded windows each side, each of which had a wide, gloss black sill, perfect for holding drinks, smoking harsh tobacco, watching cricket and chatting during the summer. There was a patch of gravelled ground with a wooden bench and some old wooden chairs edging onto the green. The roof of The Phoenix was heavily mottled with moss and lichen. The whole scene was familiar and utterly alien. The disconnection was not abstract, it was the only reality.

While Lunsford was trying to understand this entirely new part of his village, Sarson-Taylor had already opened the door to The Phoenix and was ushering him in.

"Come on! Come on! You must meet everybody!" yelled Sarson-Taylor, heading to the bar, fist in the air waving a ten pound note. "The usual! The usual! And make it a large one, and a pint of Elder's Darkest for this gentleman".

"I don't, I mean I haven't eaten" Lunsford was standing beside Sarson-Taylor at the bar, and he was being given a once over by a tall, thin lady in her sixties or twenties. Her hair was grey and outrageously glamorous. She wore a white blouse, or possibly a man's shirt, over which was a light green linen suit. She moved like Katherine Hepburn. Beside her was a small man who was pulling a pint, having already handed Sarson-Taylor an enormous, heavy crystal glass of dark, caramel and heather-smelling whisky.

"A hot beef sandwich for you", he told Lunsford, "and another of the usual for me, thank you very much Robert".

The diminutive barman took down the bottle of scotch from the shelf, refilled Sarson-Taylor's glass and put it on the bar top. He placed

Sarson-Taylor's change on the bar top without saying a word. He looked at Lunsford and explained in a salt-flecked, copper voice, "I'll bring your sandwich over to your table, sir."

"Over here, over here", Sarson-Taylor had taken a seat at a battered, oak table by the window. He pulled out a seat to Lunsford who sat down, still feeling a little bewildered.

"We didn't ask about the dog", he said, looking into the pint glass and the almost black liquid that sat staring back.

"Oh, the dog! Yes, my fault, my fault entirely. I'll ask Robert when he brings your sandwich over. Wonderful beef, local herd I believe. My family probably owns it".

"Drink up, drink up!", he took a packet of greasy, bent playing cards out of one of his numerous pockets and began to shuffle them.

Lunsford examined the pub. The low ceiling featured intricate, yellowed plasterwork images depicting hunting with dogs, a ring of stones, what must have been Hunters Wood, the church of St Eade's and a series of knights or kings with their feet pointing down and their arms crossed over their chests, looking pissed off at the sheer tedium of it all. The half-wooded walls of the pub were covered with paintings of all sizes depicting Shalford village and Crosschester: familiar places in both peopled by unfamiliar figures. Lunsford noticed that over the fireplace was a large street scene. It showed the Guildhall with Kings Gate Row running in front of it as it reached out towards the King Egbert roundabout. It was snowing. There were streetlights, which seemed to flicker. A man was standing in front of the guildhall, he was bent over slightly lighting a cigarette in cupped hands.

"Here's your sandwich, sir", the diminutive barman presented the sandwich on a thick white china plate before placing it on the table. He put a large glass of whisky in front of Sarson-Taylor without a word.

"Welcome to The Phoenix, sir", he said to Lunsford. "I, Robert Gumm, and Mrs Werldinham, our lady of cheer, hope all is well with you and that you will enjoy your visit. Please do try the beer, you will find it hard going at first you will grow into it. Is there anything else I can get for you?"

Lunsford nodded, said thank you and couldn't think of anything else he wanted. Robert Gumm waited patiently.

"No thank you, Mr Gumm", Lunsford said.

Gumm nodded and smiled, then frowning at Sarson-Taylor, he returned to his station behind the bar.

"Oh, for god's sake, man, have a drink! It won't kill you", Sarson-Taylor sipped his whisky and placed his cards on the table.

Lunsford took a speculative mouthful of Elder's Darkest. Robert Gumm was right, the first sip verged on self-harm. The beer was bitter with a deeply unsettling flavour that was a mix of the inside of a very sour old man's briefcase and a damp early evening at the football in winter. He winced and wanted to spit it directly into the fire. The beer sat in his mouth, the bitterness subsided and the flavours changed into oranges roasted with almonds, of dark chocolate and apples fried in rich butter. He swallowed. It went down like it was already part of him. He had never tasted anything like it, he took another mouthful. More flavours, less desire for death.

"My god this is good", he felt his body warming from the inside, and for the first time in quite a while he thought he might grin. He sipped some more and then remembered something.

"You didn't ask about Adelaide", despite the pleasure he was taking in his pint, Lunsford was slightly annoyed.

"Adelaide? Oh god, yes, that dog. So sorry. Look when you go to the bar, you can ask Bob Gumm, he'll know what I'm having".

Sarson-Taylor leant over and collected one half of the sandwich. He bit into it, and gravy dribbled down his chin and onto his tie. With his mouthful, he waggled his glass at Lunsford and winked. Lunsford, leaving his unfinished pint, walked over to the bar.

Robert Gumm had the whisky ready, "What's it to be for you sir?"

"I'll have a half of that lovely beer please Mr Gumm. You haven't seen a shaggy brown dog, about yay high, no collar recently have you?" Gumm thought for a second or two, pulling the pint using a mahogany pump handle that looked as if it had been cleaned and polished tens of thousands of times.

"I'm afraid I've not, sir. How was your sandwich?"

"I've not started it yet, but it looks beautiful. A local herd I hear", Lunsford handed over the money. "If anybody mentions the dog, you will let me know, keep the change".

"I most certainly will, and the beef is from Scotland I'm afraid. It's all dairy around here", replied Robert Gumm casting his eye over the fresh clientele who were slowly filling the room. They were, for the most part, men, of unknowable ages between eighteen and eighty, all of whom looked as if they inhabited The Phoenix rather than just drank there, none of whom Lunsford had ever seen before. Cards and cribbage boards, newspapers and packets of fags, dominoes and darts were withdrawn from pockets and placed on tables. The bar was lined with calm ranks of drinkers waiting their turns before peeling away like bombers after a successful drop.

Gumm handled every request and transaction effortlessly. He chatted with each patron, nodding to the next in line, he was less a barman and more a machine of the public house trade. Dressed in dark blue canvas trousers and sixteen-eye, cherry red Dr Marten boots, he wore a u-necked, short sleeved, white cotton shirt. He was not a tall man, five foot four, maybe a hint more but he exuded incredible strength. He was sturdy and there wasn't a single piece of fat on him, he was all muscle.

A very great deal of Robert Gumm was made of tattoos. There were two swallows in flight holding an anchor and chain, a compass with North, South, East and West replaced with Margot, Elaine, Tatsuo and Chuck. Black and white Tally bands with HMS Goliath, HMS Vanguard, HMS Swiftsure and HMS Theseus flecked both arms. Two signal flags, a blue cross on a white background stacked on another of three horizontal stripes of blue, white and red stood out on his thick, heavily veined neck.

There was a mermaid sitting on a rock, there was a five pointed, two toned star. Several highly decorated ship's wheels jostled with a drunken girl in a red dress laying in a champagne saucer shouting, "Sailor Beware" on his left forearm. The words "Eric and England" stood large on his right hand next to a punctured, red heart. Lunsford was surprised that Gumm's bald head wasn't also covered but there it was weathered like a boulder and bare of illustration. His blue eyes were the least interesting part of his face, which was completely hairless. His nose had been broken and badly reset, his mouth was full and sensual, with incredibly white teeth that appeared every time he smiled, which was often.

A low hum of conversation and cursing smoked around Lunsford as he walked back to the table where Sarson-Taylor had finished off the sandwich and was eagerly awaiting his drink. Sitting next to him was the grey haired lady and astonishingly glamorous Mrs Werldinham. Lunsford sat down, handed Sarson-Taylor his drink, poured the half pint into his pint glass and took a long draught and said, "Good evening, Mrs Wer…" he tailed off, unable to pronounce her name.

"Mrs Werldinham", she laughed gently because this was a problem she'd faced a hundred thousand times before.

Lunsford looked embarrassed and was relieved at her gracious approach, "Well, Mrs Werldinham, you have a very nice pub here, very nice indeed".

"Oh, Mr Lunsford, it is all very much Mr Gumm's work. I simply float about the place getting in the way. Mr Gumm has been a singular boon both to me and to The Phoenix ever since he joined us from the Royal and Merchant navies many years ago. He's a dab-hand at all sorts of useful matters". Mr Werldinham lit a cigarette and inhaled, "I hope you don't mind?"

"Certainly not" replied Lunsford.

"Are you enjoying the beer?" asked Sarson-Taylor, who had just stifled a belch and was wiping his mouth with a yellow spotted handkerchief.

"It's remarkable stuff", Lunsford replied, taking another sip of what was by then, from start to finish, one of the most delicious things he'd ever tasted. "A local beer you say?"

"Did I?" asked Sarson-Taylor, looking a little shocked at the idea he might have divulged any such information. He looked to Mrs Werldinham, "I don't believe I did but who can say, madam?"

She frowned and put her hand over the crook of his arm as he was starting to raise his drink to his lips. She pushed down. Sarson-Taylor attempted to exert some opposition but failed.

"Well, that's just not fair, madam. Here I am, helping a stranger to reunite with a loved one of an evening and I can't even have a small drink to warm me through. Not fair, not fair at all". With no fight in him, he left the whisky on the table and took out a long-stemmed pipe and a tobacco pouch and went about packing the rank smelling shag into the bowl.

"If you're going to smoke that thing, then please take it outside", Mrs Werldinham glowered at him, then lit a fresh cigarette from the dying heat of the one between her slender fingers. Lunsford hadn't noticed her exhale the first one.

"Well, I say, madam. I say. It is minus 40 degrees outside and you expect…" at that moment, Robert Gumm, having served and satisfied every patron in the pub, walked up to the table and looked at Sarson-Taylor. That's all. He just looked at the other man who was sitting with his back to the wall with the window on this right. Gumm showed his white teeth and the cold of his eyes. Sarson-Taylor huffed and replaced his pipe and pouch in another pocket.

"Same again all round if you would please Gumm", he said, making as if to take out his wallet.

"It's past eight o'clock…", Gumm paused for longer than required to remember a familiar word, "…sir. There is no longer any table service".

Sarson-Taylor looked downhearted but cheered a little as he noticed Lunsford, "I don't suppose you might see your way, as a newcomer as it were to…"

Robert Gumm put his left hand on Lunsford's left shoulder in kindness and comfort. "You sit comfortable now, Mr Lunsford", he said.

Mrs Werldinham coughed as delicately as a cough could be, loaded as it was with full authority to stop all other sound, and beckoned Gumm to her side. She whispered something to him. He frowned. She put her hand on his forearm, covering an incredibly happy looking naked man who was also heavily tattooed with a swallow on each of his open hands, and she whispered again. This time Gumm glared at Sarson-Taylor who was doing his best to shrink into the wood panelling. Gumm nodded his immense head, tapped his nose, pointed at Sarson-Taylor, and then returned to the bar, tossing Sarson-Taylor's heavy glass from hand to hand like a Ping-Pong ball as he walked.

Mrs Werldinham spoke to Lunsford who had nearly finished his pint, "Vyvian tells me that you've lost your dog or she's run away. What a terrible shame, were you close? I mean are you close?". She tapped the cigarette into a plastic ashtray that Lunsford hadn't noticed before. Her fingers were long, strong and precise, her face was beautiful in a way that only living in many fascinating ways and places could explain. Her skin was pale, the crow's feet around her green-grey eyes, the laughter lines around her mouth and the fine, almost invisible furrows on her forehead would only have been notable by their absence. Her cheekbones were high but not sculptural or composed by any trick of makeup or design. Her mouth, its lower lip slightly fuller than the top, was painted with an intense shade of red that reminded Lunsford of sweet and poisonous Yew tree berries. He was slightly in love with Mrs Werldinham, maybe he was a little drunk. He finished his pint and replied.

"She's not so much lost as she went off with this young chap in the Hunters Wood. Just trotted off after him this afternoon. I'm not entirely sure if we're close or not if I'm honest or if they are. I've not known her long, she adopted me", he smiled at the memory of the dog, "but she's been good company and I live on my own so…" he tailed off, unsure how much more to say, unhappy and unpractised at talking about himself, certainly unsure about talking to other people at all.

"Fawley", hissed Sarson-Taylor, bearing the expression of the thirstiest most hard done by man in the world, ever.

Mrs Werldinham looked puzzled.

"Fawley stole the bitch, I am sure of it. It is exactly the sort of thing he'd do. He is forever running off with other people's stuff. You know he is. Everybody does. Someone should have some control over him, it is quite an impossible way to live".

Mrs Werldinham shook her head at his petulance, then stood and walked to the middle of the room to a table of four farmers or stonemasons, all of whom stood up from their seats to greet her. Two of them, each one taking one of her hands, helped her first onto a chair and then onto the table. She coughed into her clenched right fist, waited for a few seconds and then in a voice that reached all the corners of The Phoenix, announced, "This gentleman, Mr Lunsford he's called, has lost his companion. She is a brown, shaggy dog, she is yay high", she indicated the top of her tight, "and she answers to the name Adelaide. If you can be of any assistance, please feel free to come to my table this evening where a pint of your choice will be available. Thank you".

It was as if Elizabeth the First had just delivered a speech about victory against astonishing odds. The room fell silent while she spoke and then erupted with shouts of, "Hear! Hear!", "Find the dog!" and "Hurrah!" as pint jugs and tankards were waved in the air. Shortly afterwards the room fell back to a hum and a hush threaded with clinking, laughing, hurumphing and swearing of oaths.

Lunsford was astonished. Mrs Werldinham returned to the table through the settling throng with a tray on which were a pint of Elders, and Sarson-Taylor's glass full of whisky. She placed it on the table and sat down next to Lunsford, who immediately took a drink.

"I don't think this Fawley he stole Adelaide, I think she may just have preferred his company to mine" he explained.

"Rubbish, that boy is a terrible thief. One never knows where he is going to appear next but one can be sure that he will cause chaos when he does. He cannot be trusted. Not one single jot. God knows what he is going to do with your poor, poor defenceless Adelaide". Sarson-Taylor toyed with his whisky and tunnelled deep into his dank mood.

One or two men bumbled or sidled over to the table with stories about how they'd seen a dog that day that could well have been brown but now they thought about it was probably too tall or small or smooth haired or maybe it was a fox.

Mrs Werldinham nodded and sent them away to the bar for their free pint.

"So, Mr Lunsford if it's not too rude a question, do you live alone through choice or tragedy?" asked Mrs Werldinham.

Lunsford thought for a moment, took another drink of Elders and replied, "That's a strange way to put it, choice or tragedy".

"We are not meant to be alone, no matter what the songs say. We are social creations taken as a whole. We may drink alone or work alone, or even feel alone but we'd prefer not to be alone. Now, I understand that there are honourable exceptions to this rule, noble hermits, archivists, pole sitters.

"Our marvellous Fawley likes to travel by himself. But even Fawley loves to meet new people along the way, and one day when he has somewhere to call his home I think he would like it to be a place where he is not alone", she paused, "at least in the spirit of that matter".

Sarson-Taylor huffed and hissed at the sound of the name.

Lunsford relaxed a little.

"Mr Lunsford, you've avoided my question. How enormously well-mannered of you", said Mrs Werldinham. "Please do go on though".

Lunsford looked into his glass and realised that there was maybe one small mouthful left, so he drank it. He was definitely drunk by now. He wanted to smoke. He didn't care. It also struck him that mentioning Chloé's name, Mick's name, Chloé's and Mick's name, their words, saying them out loud into the air could be a good fine wonderful act.

He stood up, "Excuse me, I need some air", he said.

CHAPTER 22

A VISIT TO ST EADE'S

1978

Mrs Werldinham stood up, giving way for Lunsford to move toward the door. "Should you need some company Mr Lunsford please do let me know", she said to the departing figure who was being gently bounced from person to person like a slow, deliberate pinball until he disappeared out of the door and onto the Green. The shock of the cold, clean air hit him like a policeman's words to a mother at three in the morning.

At first he couldn't breathe. Then he grew used to the change and his lungs finished screaming. He was drunk. He'd not been drunk for years. After decades of learning the skills of a drunkard from watching his parents, he swayed and looked for something to steady himself with.

He remembered the bench outside The Phoenix and headed for it. He sat down, nearly slipping off onto the gravel that glistened like fossilised tears in the moonlight. He had no idea what time it was. He had little idea where he was. He felt untethered but not scared. He let out a long, satisfying belch and sniggered like a child. He felt intolerably sad. This neck-breaking change of mood struck him as absurdly dramatic and so he mocked himself with a set of noises that could have become words but never quite made it. He looked back into the window of The Phoenix and saw golden light from electric bulbs all flickery and low. The pub was full but he could hear none of the usual pub noises. The windows were fogged in condensation and spidered with ice.

It's a strange place, a very strange place, a very strange place indeed, strange. I like it. What do they put in that beer though? I've not been this pissed in donkey's years. I feel sick.

"You feel fine. Drink more. Always drink more", said his dad in his head.

I feel pissed drunk.

"You are pissed drunk. Drink more. Always drink more".

I feel alone.

"You are alone. You deserve it. Learn to deal with it. It's the only thing you can be sure of", his long-dead dad said.

He looked up to the sky for some help, from God or a Guardian angel, or a meteor or a monstrous claw or himself.

I'm no help! I'm drunk, drunk as a skunk lord. Drunk as Christmas Eve, he thought out loud.

He hadn't thought about God in so long. Not since he had been demobbed and married his Chloé. The war had taken God away, sunk him to the bottom of the North Atlantic, weighted down with his own words. The War couldn't destroy God of course, nothing could, but fathoms of ice cold salt water could obscure him.

Chloé was not as she put it, "A godly woman". The only reason they were married at St Eade's and not in the register office on Crosschester's Courthouse Lane was to keep his mother happy. Mother was the kind of Catholic who fell in and out of compliance with her faith depending on the time of year or the amount of unpleasantness going on at home or in the wider world.

No help came from God. The sky was mute. It was a shade of deepest blue, slit with thin chiffon clouds. There were so many stars that he thought he might cry at the sight of them. His grandmother had told him on the night that his grandfather had died that if you look up into the night of a funeral, the first star you saw clearly was your loved one looking back down at you. He'd wanted to do this, to look up, on the night of his grandfather's death. Surely, he'd demanded, he should be able to go outside and look up and see his grandad freed from his sick and broken body looking back down.

"It has to be the night of the funeral, there must be time for your spirit to move from your body into purgatory and then to heaven", he was told.

"What's purgatory?" he asked.

"It is a place where you purified, cleaned of all the sinful things. You can only be in heaven if you are pure you see, if the terrible things you've done aren't washed away and cleaned you can't enter heaven".

"What if I can't be cleaned?" asked Lunsford remembering the time he had marked the wall of his bedroom with a picture of a white horse done in penknife and crayon when he was five years old. You could still see the marks for months and months and ages afterwards. He remembered that his dad had shouted at him about ruining the things he had, about destroying their house.

"Not our home though. That was already ruined", said a voice he struggled to recognise.

Dad had yelled about respect. He had been angry with Lunsford for ages. He wondered if that was like Purgatory, he hoped it wasn't because it had been a terrible time.

Lunsford stumbled up from the bench with the immunity from damage that only comes to drunks who make decisions. He brushed himself down, drew in a deep, freezing breath, staggered and sat back with a crunch on the bench. He was going to Church. He hadn't been for years, not since his wedding. This was the right time. He stood up, fell forward on his hands and knees. He really wanted a smoke. Third time lucky he rose.

"All seeing, all knowing. You're slurring. In your head. Talking to yourself and you're slurring like your dad. Time for church. Time to go", he told himself.

What remained of his father's body had been buried with no fuss and no headstone in the churchyard of St Eade's the Virgin. His mother's funeral, on the other hand, had been well-attended with a sweet sadness and most of Churchfields present. There had been a soft rendition of *All Things Bright and Beautiful* by the kids from the primary school where she'd been a dinner lady. In direct contradiction of her husband's will she had demanded not to be buried with him or even near him. Instead she was laid to rest close to a slender ash tree in the churchyard. You could see the Water Meadows down the hill and across the River Icene from the foot of her grave.

Swaying like a sailor he crossed the green to Hare Rise. He looked down to pat Adelaide. He felt sad. There was no reason not to feel good. Stones colds sobers he was. Stones. Colds. This being untethered from the old world was paying off after all. No connection. It was beginning to feel a lot like Christmas.

"She's gone. She came. She went. No time at all. Couldn't hold onto her. Taken away", thought Lunsford, slurring in his head from the Elder's.

"Fucking hell! Stop fucking whining! Stop moaning. It's a fucking dog fuck's sake a dog. You've lost your mind. A fucking mongrel dog" either him or his dad yelled.

"Why did she come in the first place? Why did she even have to turn up with her wagging tail and brown eyes and her stupid face", he said as he walked.

"Time to buck up your ideas Martin" said the mystery voice.

Lunsford was halfway down Hare Rise when he stopped dead.

"What I need is a purpose. I need a purpose yes I do. Or being dead. A purpose or being dead. If we don't find a purpose by next week then dead. A purpose in life. A hobby? No. I've never had a hobby why would I start now? Something bigger a big purpose. Rob a bank? Don't need the money. Sail a boat to Africa. Don't like the heat. Be dead?", he said out loud.

He laughed a laugh that was soaked up by the hedges on either side.

He shut his eyes and had no answer. Eyes shut he continued to walk until he felt the ground under his feet change from frosty mud to gravel and he was at the border of the graveyard in front of his family and friend.

"Well, here we are then", he said again out loud, trying to test his own resolve. He pushed through the metal kissing gate that separated the field of the dead from the world of the living.

He walked up to the unlocked front doors of flint-skinned church. Lunsford's marriage, the marriages of his parents and their parents, of christenings, funerals, confirmations, harvest festivals and school Christmas Carolling going back, as far as he knew, to the start of Lunsford time.

The place of worship had been here in one form or another for thousands of years with various additions and the odd deletion in more puritanical times. Its foundations were pre-Christian, its floor of Saxon stones was overlaid with mosaic, its most recent ceiling was held there by Norman columns, its walls were decorated with Queen Anne murals. Its Georgian altar was covered in an altar cloth sent from Kenya in 1971. The hymns and carols sung from the Regency stalls were accompanied by its sonorous Victorian organ. The stained glass in the West window managed somehow to hang together without impinging on its quiet importance and had been restored (badly and with no grace) in 1887. It was a beautiful mess of faith, ambitions and time.

Lunsford went in, splashed some Holy Water on his face from the small pool by the door, and walked to a pew at the front directly opposite the towering pulpit. Up in the rafters among the cobwebs he floated and sang *All Things Bright and Beautiful.*

The sound of his own footsteps reinforced his sense of being alone, and the residual smell of incense built up over centuries made him pine for his childhood when the church had been a mysterious excitement. He genuflected, something built into him by his mother, his father never went to church.

"Can't be doing with it. If there is a God, he's not spending his time in Shalford bloody church is he? No idea what your mother sees in it. Mad", his father had said every Sunday.

It got us all out of the house on a Sunday morning so you could deal with your hangover, Dad.

He crossed himself – again Mother – and sat down.

"I love this church. It's solid. It's seen a lot. There's a lot of life been had in this church", he said from on high.

Down on the pew he felt sick.

"Why am I here? Why did we all come here at all? Why am I sitting in a cold church feeling sorry for myself? I shouldn't drink. It's down to the drink. It isn't. This place has our roots more than anywhere else. This place can help".

"Bollocks", said a familiar voice, said Frank.

He looked to the statue of St Eade the Virgin. She was smiling despite the nails that had been hammered into her feet, the boulders tied to her arms, and despite her weeping eyes that had been extinguished with burning switches. When he was little and at the funeral of some uncle or other, he had soaked up so much incense and the service had droned on for so long that he had spent half an hour looking into the face of St Eade. He swore that she had winked a blind eye at him. He told his mother who wiped his face with a spit-fuelled handkerchief that smelled of handbag perfumes. She had told him what a blessed boy he must be, but he must promise not to tell his dad. He promised and it became the first thing in his life, the first of many things, that he kept from his father. St Eade wasn't winking tonight. Despite her smile, Lunsford could see her pain, not her physical pain but the pain of her doubt.

St Eade was the virginal daughter of the leading family of Crosschester in 951 or thereabouts, details were scant. Until the age of 16 she had been a devout maiden who had been taught to read and to write to better study the words of the Saints and the teachings of The Bible. Rather than keep this wisdom to herself, however, she began trying to educate the local children into Christ and those Saints. This was generally frowned upon but due to her family's standing, and wealth, a blind eye was turned by the church officers. That was until she took this process of education too far.

She began to translate the work of St Bartleby of Bute into English and to use her translation to teach the good working people of Crosschester and its surrounding villages how to read and write. She did this by walking from village to village, hamlet to town and sitting in town squares and on village greens. Her father and brothers pleaded with her to stop but she couldn't.

She once saved a girl from drowning in a well by praying for the waters to rise and to raise the lass to the top, it was said. She had healed an old lady of several horrible diseases by speaking the words of Saint Bartleby (who had himself been martyred by having his ears punctured by daggers, his hands scalded in boiling oil, and his chest crushed with boulders). Eventually, her family despaired of stopping her in her pedagogical crime spree. They called for the sheriff to intercede, which he did and within the week St Eade was standing before the Hundred Court offering no other defence than silence.

Shrift was short and she was put to the ordeal so she might recant. She retained her silence, "Growing more holier and in the peace of the Lord as each ordeal and trial failed to shake her faith", her beatification document stated in 1919. She was finally canonised in 1928.

Aside from some of the goriest details, Lunsford knew little of her story. He had spent his childhood imagining what awful things his saint – his personal saint – must have done to deserve so many different terrible tortures. He also worried about St Eade.

After his time away from the county fighting a war against the Nazis and their Japanese allies, after he'd seen what God's creatures could do to each other, those sights had encrusted his soul and turned his face away from St Eade's. After he came back, he rarely visited the church and largely lost any memory of her statue and the way in which he had been comforted, moved, made to feel like a very special boy by its humanity.

Neither he nor Chloé was religious, so this compounded his drift from his saint. Now Chloé was gone, but St Eade's stood in front of him. He picked up a hymn book that was stored on the pew and flicked through it, he stopped halfway.

> I vow to thee, my country, all earthly things above,
> Entire and whole and perfect, the service of my love.
> The love that asks no question, the love that stands the test,
> That lays upon the altar the dearest and the best.
> The love that never falters, the love that pays the price,
> The love that makes undaunted the final sacrifice.

He tried to hum the tune, and was surprised how quickly and easily it came back to him. Behind him someone else began to sing the hymn. He stood up and turned around and saw Fawley standing at the back of the church.

"Hello there Lunsford".

Fawley walked slowly towards him. "It's a great hymn that one. Holst. Great stuff. Are you going to sing some more?" He smiled.

Lunsford walked towards Fawley. He was unsurprised to see him because he was not surprised by anything now. He was pleased to see him though.

"What do they put in that beer?" he asked, already sure that Fawley would know exactly what he was talking about.

He put out his hand and Fawley took it and shook it. "Good isn't it?", Fawley smiled brightly.

"I have an apology to make to you Mr Fawley".

"Just Fawley, no mister, please", he replied, walking down the aisle.

They stood facing each other, Lunsford looked up into the face of the younger, taller man.

"Well, Fawley, I have an apology that I hope you'll accept. I was rude. Very rude but I've not been myself lately. You see I've not been out of hospital for long, after an accident, my friend, you see, he died, I survived. I dream about it a lot. I dream about saving him, I..." Lunsford stopped talking. He was shocked at his own outpouring.

"What are you doing, man?! No one wants to hear about your problems, pissed or not. Wind your neck in. Christ, alive!" said the familiar voice of his father.

"That's such sad, sad news, Lunsford?" said Fawley.

Lunsford let go of Fawley's hand, coughed to clear some time, and drew his coat more tightly around him.

"As I say, I'm really sorry for having been so rude, Fawley", he walked past Fawley towards the doors.

"And I accept your apology. So, how should we celebrate?", Fawley followed.

Lunsford stepped through the doors into the night and was met with a huge welcome. Barking, jumping, panting, tail wagging and all sorts of joy.

"Adelaide!" Lunsford's smile lit up the night. Fawley closed the church doors and clapped at the sight of the man and the dog reunited.

"She's a strange one, Adelaide. Lovely dog but she's got her own mind. I thought cats were the curious ones but this one here, she puts them to shame, puts her nose in anywhere and everywhere doesn't she?" Fawley's smile matched Lunsford's.

"How about a pint in The Phoenix?" he asked.

"On me, of course", replied Lunsford, overwhelmed with the happiness being fed into him by the dog.

"Of course, let's go".

CHAPTER 23

BACK TO THE PHOENIX

1978

As Lunsford, Fawley and Adelaide walked through the doors, Robert Gumm was standing in the middle of the bar of The Phoenix, nose to nose with Thomas Vyvian Sarson-Taylor.

"What", yelled Gumm, "Did you say?" He had balled his fists.

"I said that you should be more polite", replied Sarson-Taylor, shrinking into this Barbour jacket.

"You said something else. Repeat it", Gumm was in no mood to fuck around. Not in his pub. Not on his watch, not from this little shitfucker.

"I don't remember", stuttered Sarson-Taylor backing away straight into a table, spilling pints and fags and ashtrays and shorts.

"Oh no son, I think you do. I just think you're too much of a coward to repeat it, isn't that right?" Gumm may not have been a tall man but he was towering over Sarson-Taylor.

Sarson-Taylor saw a path to the door as the locals moved away in case Gumm decided to reduce the other man to flecks of dust. He turned tail and ran as fast as his stubby legs would allow him, fishing tackle flying as he flicked his bag open. Hooks and lures exploded about like shrapnel. He stood at the doorway, prodding the air with the bottle opener from a Swiss Army knife and screamed, "You're not even a pure Englishman! You're not even a pure man! My family owns you! It owns all of you!"

He spat into the crowd whose laughter and jeers spurred him out onto the gravel. He crawled over to the green, stood up, and screamed again, "Your time is coming you queers! You Jews! You... you... you... Your time is coming soon, you mulatto herd!

"As for you Gumm, as for you..." someone threw a pint jug at him, narrowly missing his head. He ran across the green and down Hare Rise.

"Man can't take his drink", said Gumm gently picking a hook from the hat of Gentle Dominic, one of his regulars.

"Bloody hell, Gumm what did he say?" asked Fawley, shaking him firmly by the hand.

"Doesn't matter Fawley. He's gone now. He'll be back tomorrow or the next day sober and he'll apologise and then we'll go through the same thing. He's a harmless little shitfucker but indeed he is a shitfucker. Two pints is it? Usual table?"

Fawley nodded and led Lunsford to the table near the fire. Robert Gumm arrived with two full glasses and a smile, then returned to the bar.

"Lovely bloke, Gumm. Ex-navy, goodness knows where he's from originally, and that's what niggles at Master Sarson-Taylor. Bob Gumm finds it hard to make enemies no matter where he is in the world. I was in a bar with him in Singapore a few years ago and a fight was brewing, you could smell it in the humidity. This American bloke bumped – I say 'bumped', I mean 'barged' into Bob, you could see his pals shaking their shoulders and stretching their necks getting ready for a ruck. Well, ten minutes later they were all drinking together, laughing and talking about baseball. You wouldn't credit it, you really wouldn't. I didn't even know he knew anything about baseball but apparently he'd played a few games for a minor league team in Philadelphia. Amazing man, I love him to bits".

Lunsford had visited Philly when he was in the navy. He'd even watched the Phillies play at Shibe Park. He didn't understand a thing that was going on in front of him but he'd enjoyed the long day and the beers and hotdogs. He wondered what had happened to the friends he was with, the ones he'd made that day.

"You could try and get back in touch", said the mystery voice.

I don't know their addresses. Chloé did that sort of thing. I left that sort of thing up to her. Yet another thing. Yet another part of life I lived through her.

"Maybe you can find the address book?"

"Have a drink. Have another drink", said his dad.

He downed a half pint of the Elders Darkest Ale.

"You ok, Lunsford?" Fawley could see the drink slurring around behind Lunsford's eyes making a queer mess of his head. He was well aware of the effects of Elders on someone unaccustomed to it.

"I think so Fawley. I was just thinking…" he drifted off.

"What about?"

"About Philadelphia and friends of mine", he started thinking about Mick.

"You've been to Philly?"

"Many years ago, yes. I was in the navy. In the Royal Navy. Years ago, years and years. The USA was amazing not like here in England in Shalford. I think I'm a bit pissed Mr Fawley".

"Just Fawley", Fawley leaned back on his chair against the wall. "Being a bit pissed is fine. Is Mick that friend of yours you were talking about in the temple?"

"He is, he was, my best mate. Known him ever since Little School down there on Queen Street", he gestured vaguely towards Shalford but he really was lost.

"He was better than me", he took another drink.

"What do you mean, better?" Fawley nodded to Robert Gumm for the same again. It was very close to Last Orders. This meant that it was very close to a lock-in, a safe, peaceful lock-in. This entailed Gumm kicking everybody out, and everybody walked around the pub to the backdoor and filtered back in picking up where they'd left off. There were no police for miles to stop this, and even if one did chance by, they usually turned a blind eye.

Robert Gumm had been invited in by Fawley. Fawley had been invited in by a tall lady who spoke in songs and swore in dazzling, audacious, foul volleys. Her name was his memory. Lord knows who invited her, maybe she'd been there from the start. Maybe it was her pub or at least her ground.

"Last Orderrrrrrrrrs at the bar ladies and germs!!" Gumm yelled at the bar full of people who already knew.

Lunsford considered Fawley's question.

"Why was Mick better"? As usual he wanted very much to keep the answer – and his workings out – to himself for as long as possible but the Elders Darkest was mediating against this. So, out came the explanation. His words flopped and flipped out over the table, all unbalanced and vulnerable like elvers blindly seeking food and safety.

"Better, Fawley, better. Better than me, all round nicer bloke. Thoughtful like. Good to his wife. Thoughtful to his wife. Made friends easily went out of his way. Not a bad word for him or from him. Better. Better at work. Better", he laughed and picked up the new glass of Elders. "Better at cricket and gardens and better at telling jokes and stories. Outgoing. Interested in other people. Better".

"He sounds like a saint", Fawley said.

"He was a saint", Lunsford took a drink, past caring now about appearances.

"Was he really though, Mr Lunsford?"

"You're a boy, a boy you're as old as we were when we joined up you... boy", another sip.

"You'd be surprised", whispered Fawley then lifted his voice, "In my experience, saints are often a waste product of grief".

"Or politics", said Bob Gumm who was collecting glasses.

"Or politics", agreed Fawley, touching Gumm lightly on his bare forearm. "But I'm not referring to the church here but to actual people".

Lunsford had seen death, "I've seen more deaths than you could cope with my boy. More grief than I can cope with".

Fawley nodded, "War grief, Mr Lunsford, when you had to move on quickly and you were in the company of other men who had experienced the same deaths. When you had no time to think until much, much later. Maybe decades later".

"What do you know?" said Lunsford, drinking again.

"Time at the bar please ladies and germs!! Rush home to your loved ones! Be quick before they've gone for good and taken all the silverplate and memories!"

Everybody put their glasses down and observed the usual ritual.

"Fawley, you two stay here and help me clean up", Gumm was playing his part in the age-old pub drama.

Lunsford, his head in his hands, "Saints! Saints?"

"Have you ever heard the phrase, 'you mustn't speak ill of the dead?" asked Fawley.

"Of course I have, everybody has. It's respect that's all".

Gumm locked and bolted the front doors. Then walked over to the backdoor and unlocked it. Gentle Dominic was there, ready, breathing out smoke and condensation.

People started returning to their seats and the glasses of booze they'd left behind. They resumed half-finished conversations. The buzz of The Phoenix was returning but, out of respect for the law of the land, at a slightly less volume.

"It's not respect. It's fear and it goes back to the start of fear. Absolutely nobody sane, including Saint Mick, would be comfortable if in life you only ever said wonderful things about them or to them. Just imagine.

"It doesn't honour the dead, not one bit of it. The opposite in fact.

It insults the lives they lived, the connections they made, the mistakes they made. No one has a life without bad behaviour. This saintliness isn't for the dead, it's about keeping angry spirits at bay. People don't want to die, Mr Lunsford. It makes them angry".

"This isn't life, it's death. He's gone. Mick's gone and gone for good. Jeanne's gone too".

"Jeanne?"

"Wonderful girl. Mick's wife. Suffered lots, Jeanne. Gone now".

"Dead?"

"To Birmingham".

Fawley laughed, he couldn't help it, he enjoyed Birmingham and always had. His eyes twinkled and he relaxed a little as he waited for Lunsford to join him in laughter. Instead Lunsford slid from morose to mad-angry.

Adelaide whined from beneath the table at the prickling atmosphere.

"Funny is it? I don't think so. I think it's respectful. And this hocus pocus about 'angry spirits', what's that all about? Mick's dead. His memory isn't. He's not coming back. Spirits? Bollocks. Rot and bollocks. Rot. Let's have another one of these beers. Let's have a drink to Mick!" Lunsford stood up, steady as a sapling, and started a perilous journey to the bar, "To Mick!" he yelled over his shoulder.

Several drinkers in the vicinity responded, "To Mick! To Mick!" because it felt like the right and friendly thing to do.

Adelaide was out from under the table and wandering in a repetitive circle making low noises.

Fawley patted her and stopped her circling, "Time for you to come outside then lovely hound, before you burst. Good girl" and the pair exited by the back door.

"Who's Mick?" asked Gentle Dominic who was standing at the bar all dressed in secondhand army camouflage with a green beanie on his head and a roll-up burning his yellow stubs of fingers.

"Fine fellow from what I know", said Craig the builder who honestly had no idea.

"Mick, you know, Mick. Here's to him! To Mick!" said Annie from the allotments.

Lunsford was making gestures at Robert Gumm that indicated he wanted another round. Gumm came around to him with a packed and bone-dry drinks tray.

"Are you sure you want this? You've been putting it away tonight Mr Lunsford and you're not used to Elders, it's not to be taken lightly".

"Got to toast Mick. Go to shut this talk of disrespect and dead spirits. You know what Bob, can I call you Bob? Bob, you've seen the world, you've got some age behind you. You know what I mean. You know about people who you miss and how they never come back no matter how much you can't bear them to be gone".

"To Mick!" said a voice over by the front door.

Robert Gumm smiled and said, "Let's get back to your table, I'll bring the drinks". He lifted the bar flap with one hand, keeping the tray high up with the other. On it were six glasses. Three pints and three heavy tumblers two half-filled with dark rum, one of a lucent green liquid that Lunsford didn't recognise.

Mrs Werldinham was sitting at the table when the pair of old sailors arrived. She took a glass of rum from the tray and nodded to

Gumm. She seemed angry to Lunsford but then again, the whole world seemed angry.

"I'm drunk", he said and plonked down in his seat.

"I know", she replied.

"I'm talking bollocks I think".

"You're slurring nonsense that's for certain, I could hear you from over there. What is the matter Mr Lunsford?" she emphasised 'is'.

"I'm drunk is the matter. I don't get drunk. I don't even like drinking, it's this beer", he looked at the glass, "it's too good".

"It is rather wonderful".

"Magical", he took a swig, "What do you do? You're very tall. You're unbelievably beautiful. What do you do?"

"I don't know how I'm supposed to respond to a drunken man's drunken complements so let's move past those. I run The Phoenix among other things. It's a family trade going back many centuries. I enjoy it. I have no problems to speak of. I have a happy childhood. I have a contented life. I like people. Why are you so unhappy?"

Lunsford's inner voices were outraged at this directness. They were cowed by it and attracted to it. Too shy to do anything useful and too angry.

"My wife and best friend died within no time of each other. I loved them. My other friend, I think she is, I don't know, well she's gone north, long, long way. It's not difficult. I'm unhappy and that's why, it's easy to understand. I think I can drink this stuff for ever", he took another swig and eyed up Fawley's pint. "And don't tell me it's better out than in, and I should talk about it and…"

"Far from it, Mr Lunsford. Bottle it all up, and never open the bottle again. Indulge your silence and reserve if that's your way to happiness", she sipped her drink and lit a cigarette.

"Can I have a smoke? I mean I may as well. What's to stop me? Who's to stop me? Stink up the house. Stink up the bedroom and kitchen and the drawing room and the lounge, stink the whole house up".

She handed him a cigarette, black, slim, long, elegant.

"Enjoy yourself. Let yourself go. Now, Mr Lunsford, what are you going to do tomorrow? What are you going to do next year?"

He lit the cigarette using a matchbook from the table. The question sank in.

"To Mick!" said Angela from the monumental masons.

"To Mick!" said Lunsford, avoiding any thoughts of the future.

"Mr Lunsford, what are your plans for the future?"

Mrs Werldinham wasn't letting go. Lunsford finished his pint and reached for Fawley's, expecting to be stopped. He wasn't. He drank. Mrs Werldinham pushed a whisky towards him. The pub hubbub melted and liquified around him and filled his ears with other people's conversations. He felt Robert Gumm's hand on his shoulder as if it had reached through opaque bathwater. Gumm was leaning into the table and exchanging full glasses for empty ones.

"You're all right, matey. You're all right. You're welcome in The Phoenix", and off he went back to the bar through the crowd of busy drinkers.

"Tell me about your wife", Mrs Werldinham took another sip, exhaled a ghost of smoke, smiled amiably.

"Chloé, saved my life. Made everything worth it. Happiest girl I ever met. Beautiful too. Life saver. Would do anything for me. Couldn't do", he paused, "can't do anything without her. Anything. Nothing". He sipped the whisky and thought for a while.

"Clever too. Chemist. Not at Boots", his words dried up. He'd said everything about Chloé that he had to say. He was stumped. He didn't want to think any more deeply about her, especially not the end.

"To Mick!", a drinker pressed his face up to Lunsford, grinning genuinely in what he hoped was a friendly way.

"To Chloé", he whispered.

"Is that it, Mr Lunsford? All those years of marriage and you've consigned Chloé to sanctified helpmate?"

He struggled to understand what the woman meant, why she sounded so critical, so vinegary.

"She was wonderful. Chloé. Wonderful woman, wonderful woman", he waited for some profound memories, or a sympathetic look, maybe a touch on his arm from the woman. He craved her understanding. She was silent, just smoking calmly, she took a sip from her drink.

"She was more than a helpmate", he said.

"Go on", she exhaled, and he remembered his cigarette, which he had yet to drag on, protruding from this right hand and dying a death.

He tried to smoke and the memories of a clean house, clean air, clean lungs free of salt water and the never-ending fear of torpedoes, and sobbing mates cascaded into him. He stubbed the fag out, took another hit of the whisky and looked at her.

"I don't know what you mean", he said, "I mean, I don't know what to do, I have no one to turn to".

"That's the way", she replied", that's the start of it".

"I don't understand. I don't understand. You can be as mysterious as you like, but I just miss her. She was the love of my life and I miss her".

"Were you there when she died?"

He stood up, pointed his finger at her, staggered and sat down again, his backside thumping into his chair like an old fighter's split boxing glove smacking futile into a wall.

"What kind of question is that!?" he yelled, or he thought he yelled when he was whispering, choking on the fact that he had not been there when Chloé had died. He'd taken hours to get to her.

"Not that I knew she was gone. I should have known. Something should have told me surely if I loved her?", he slumped back into his chair.

Mrs Werldinham said nothing. She smoked and smiled, and he faded out into Elders Darkest Ale and rough whisky. The Phoenix was a soft pillow to pass out onto. Its fire was no longer stoked nor fed but it was still warming as it went into hibernation, its beautiful, safe wintering perfume was a cushion and a comfort. The conversations around Lunsford, the debates and arguments, bad jokes, great jokes, filthy jokes, admissions, discussions, offers, demands and counteroffers soaked into one to create a delightful blanket over him smothering his own thoughts in a cosy safety as he passed out.

Mrs Werldinham got up, finished her drink and walked over to where Robert Gumm was polishing the bar top and wishing more drinkers a "good morning" or "safe home, princess" or "don't blame me when she cracks you with a pan!".

"I'll be back for him later, Robert".

"No, you won't, Ma'am. You know you won't. I'll keep an eye. Don't fret. Why have you taken to him though? He's one of many and that little rat Master Vyvian Sarson-Taylor introduced him in, so he's a potential problem if you ask me".

"I would ask you Robert. You know I would. But you also know that the only reason that Sarson-Taylor brought him into The Phoenix was to scrounge drinks from him and hide behind a guest knowing of your impeccable behaviour as a host".

Gumm was unconvinced. Sarson-Taylor got under his skin, always had. The man couldn't stick at anything and worse, he didn't need to stick at anything. He drifted from idea to idea whenever one blew in, no matter where from. You couldn't trust that kind of a person.

He'd come in the previous day with talk about England this and Britain that. Our people this, and Outsiders that. For some god-knows-what reason he'd started talking to Gumm about how they both knew the score, how they'd travelled the world and seen how that world looked to England for guidance. How it was "our duty" to do the right thing and the right thing was keeping this great England pure. English land, English children, English blood and English culture. Sarson-Taylor had never once in all the years Gumm had tolerated him ever given a thought to culture. He'd take a drink from anybody at any time for any reason. But last week in the lunchtime Phoenix bar, scant of drinkers and other good company, he'd told Gumm, "I drink to be sociable, you know that Robert, you know that well. But I tell you this, old man, you'd never catch me drinking with one of our swarthy cousins or our fuzzy headed friends or…"

"Shut up, drink up and fuck off Viv-Ian", Gumm had been polishing glasses at the other end of the bar and trying not to listen.

"I shalln't, Gumm. My family…"

Gumm interrupted, "…owns this pub and has done for ever, I know. Because of that, I don't need your money. You can drink for free. Drink it all up you spoilt boy. As I say, you can fuck off, I'm not serving you", Gumm continued to polish beautifully clean glasses, but arched his back and cricked his neck as was his way.

"Are you a Jew, Mr Gumm, I've never asked, Mr Gumm, are you a Jew or an Englishman, Mr Gumm? Because Gumm does not sound like an English name. Gumm. Gummerman? Gumberg? Gummerick? Gumfeld? Are you an Englishman, Mr Gumm Gumm Guminsky?"

Sarson-Taylor reached over the bar to the bottle of scotch that had been sitting just out of his reach. He filled his glass and put the bottle down in front of him. "And I don't need you to serve me", he drank the glass down and filled it again.

"My mother was a Jewess from Russia. My father was a Catholic boy, an Irishman, an Irish Free Man, a Free Stater. Or the other way around. I forget because, as you know Viv-Ian, I was brought up by the love of England's church and charity and then by her navies. The Royal Navy, the Merchant Navy. For all I know I'm as Jewish as Solly Kasman from Crosschester market, why?"

"It's just the way you come across", he took the bottle, put it in his bag of tackle and shotgun shells and walked to the backdoor. "A little grasping. Ungenerous. Dark and scabrous… and that nose of yours", and with that he ran.

Gumm continued to clean the glasses. He whistled a tune.

CHAPTER 24

THE HANGOVER FROM HEL'

1978

Lunsford woke up with a fragmentation hangover and hands that felt and looked as if they'd been dragged through gritty barbed wire. He knew it was daytime because the sunlight showed him the blood in his eyelids. He refused to open his eyes in case he had gone blind. He felt that he had gone blind. He hoped he had.

He refused even to attempt to open his mouth in case it had filled up with the moulting pelts from his teeth. He refused to move in case every bone had calcified and was powder. He lay still. His head was marble and was fracturing with anxiety about the night before. His bladder was having none of it though. While every single other part of his body was busy changing its form and purpose to torture him for poisoning it, his bladder remained unwavering in its duty, and it was not open to discussion.

"I could just lie here in my own mess. There's no one to notice.

Just lie here until the sun goes down and then lie here some more until I die. Unless I'm already dead. What was that noise?" he thought quietly.

His ears, full of the machine sound of his own pumping blood had picked something else, maybe human, here.

"Where is here? I don't care. It doesn't matter. I can't move. Where am I?"

He could smell tobacco and wet dog. His face was pressed into something soft. He remembered snow but the air around him was warm. He felt sweaty.

"Where am I? If they come and kill me that'll be a mercy. Why did you drink so much? What did I do? What did I say? What did you say? Who was I with? There's that noise again. Let them come".

His bladder screamed its simple demand. Lunsford, who was still fully dressed, opened one eye. It hurt because molten lead was being channelled through its vortex veins. He tried to open the other eye but gravity was acting so freakishly against the lid that there was no way it was going to part from the rest of his face without denuding his skull completely. He turned over onto his back. What vision he did have was as blurred as St Joan's on the pyre seeing her accusing bishops through the smoke and flames. He heard the noise again, it was definitely speech.

"No, no, no you don't. It's not for you!"

Lunsford realised he was inside a house. Looking more closely at the light fitting over his head – thankfully not switched on – he realised that he was in his own house. Stomach and bladder, working together, managed to slide Lunsford from the bed to his knees.

"Oh God, please, although I have never believed in you, please say this is the end".

A part of him was laughing.

"You did some living last night then? You got drunk for the first time since... you met some people".

He crawled to the door but this didn't help either of the parts of him that were urging him to more immediate action, so he stood to a crouch and managed to relocate himself to the lavatory. Through the sounds of his own expulsions he was able to make out the voice again from downstairs. Two voices in fact: one barking and the other singing although he was unable to make out the song. Switching position from supplication to sitting he imagined how satisfying death would be now that he was filled from stomach to throat with acid. Then he heard a thumping walk, double stepping up the stairs.

"Lunsford, you're awake! We thought we'd lost you", it was Fawley. Fawley was in his house. "Come downstairs when you feel able, we got breakfast on for you".

"Oh God. No. Not breakfast!" he moaned.

An hour later Lunsford was sitting on his bed wearing an eccentric collection of clothes. Fawley had the good grace not to have bothered him again. Downstairs he heard banging at his front door, followed by the sound of Adelaide's claws ticky-tacking from the kitchen's tiled floor and across the hallway. The door resonated again and to his astonishment he heard it opening. Fawley had opened the front door.

"What on earth? What is he doing? He's letting the people in from last time. Or he was the people from last time and they're his gang!"

"Oh, for goodness sake Martin. For goodness sake. This behaviour has got to stop. Take a hold of yourself, stir your stumps, do something positive. Enough", it was Chloé in his head. Or it was him doing an impersonation of Chloé.

He stood up and walked to the landing, carpeted, quiet, hidden from the front door, and he listened.

"Mr Martin Lunsford? I am Sister Helen Cousins, from the Health Service. I demand that…", a sharp voice stabbed out.

Adelaide barked, more in query than valour.

Fawley replied, "I'm afraid Mr Lunsford is away at his house in Florence, Italy for the next month. He is exploring his inner landscape with a view to publication".

"He's in Italy?" asked the lady somewhat surprised.

"He is. For a month, maybe more depending on his self-exploration".

"He has a house in Florence?"

"He does. A small place, more of an apartment really on the Piazza Vittorio Veneto. I know for a fact that he welcomes visitors. May I take a message?"

There was silence. A good silence.

"Florence? Why Florence? I'll have to ask him", he thought.

"Well, that's not really good enough. I'm not likely to trek to Italy to discover the state of Mr Lunsford's health. I am not even certain that he should be travelling that far…"

"By boat too. He loves to sail", Fawley interrupted, "adores it. All the fresh sea air and the challenge of the waves. He has a tidal birth down on the Humble River, easy access to the Channel. He's a remarkable sailor", Adelaide barked as Fawley concluded.

"Yes, I understood he was in the navy", Sister Helen attempted to claw back some authority.

"Very much so. He was involved heavily in the hunt and destruction of the Bismarck in '41. That was before his move into Naval Intelligence but he never talks about that for obvious reasons".

"Yes, indeed", the woman's voice softened slightly. "Would you mind telling me your relationship with Mr Lunsford?"

"I would, but it's hush-hush you see", Fawley was obviously enjoying himself immensely.

"I left Mr Lunsford some correspondence on my previous visit, I wonder if you can tell me if he has read it?"

There was a pause. What Lunsford was unable to see as he crouched at the top of the stairs just out of view of the sharp-voiced woman was that Fawley had bent down and collected the small pile of letters that had mounted up on the doormat. He fanned them out and gestured with his eyes towards them. "Is it here?"

Sister Helen saw her letter immediately, "Yes, yes it most certainly is", she plucked it from the fan and waved it in front of him. "And it's not even opened!" she said in astonishment.

"What does it allude to? How can I help?" Fawley's voice was soft and genuinely seemed to offer help to Sister Hel's project.

"Do you live in the village?"

"I do. I am. Here I am."

"Would you mind answering this questionnaire? It would be immensely useful in enabling the most accurate collation of health data in this area. I, we, the Health Service, are collecting and tabulating statistics you see. To better understand the changing fitness of the nation to operate for the good and indeed the betterment of the nation. It won't take more than five minutes", she had taken a clipboard onto which was held several sheets of paper: her questionnaire.

"Madam", said Fawley, "I would be honoured to contribute".

Sister Helen made as if to come into the house, maybe to sit at the kitchen table, drinking tea, discussing her ideas with the tall, grey-eyed, red haired, high cheekboned, young man. He made no movement to suggest that he was inviting her in. Instead he said, "I am so sorry to seem oafish but I'm afraid the rest of the house is closed to the public for reasons of safety and security. I'm sure that someone in your position can understand".

"Indeed Mr…"

"Horace Johnstone. Mr Horace Johnstone of this manor. You may know of my family?"

"I am sure I must Mr Johnstone", she smiled and took the top off her Parker pen.

"Call me Horo, all my friends do. Now, shall we begin?"

Lunsford sat down, straining to hear every detail.

"Question 1: Mother's Maiden Name?"

"Helena Pisula, God rest her soul".

"Question 2: Father's Full Name?"

"Brenton Fitzwilliam, damn his eyes to hell".

"You didn't get on with your father?" She sounded to Lunsford as if she wanted to comfort Fawley.

"He was a vicious swine, a drunk and a philanderer, but let us go on with the next question".

"Date of birth?"

"I wish I knew".

"I beg your pardon, Mr... Horo".

"I wish I could tell you. You see shortly after I came into the world, my father murdered my mother in a sotted fit of jealousy. He gave himself up to the police and put me into the care of the state who then put me into the care of two cruel aunts who never told me my true age. Instead they made me sleep in the attic and tend to their garden. Thankfully I was able to make my escape with the help of my only friend, Mr William Wonklestein. To this day I am unable to say if I am twenty or twenty-thousand years of age".

Sister Helen felt that somehow something was wrong, "Please Mr Johnstone, I believe that you're not taking this process seriously, surely a man like you know how old he is", this was not a question.

"Sister, may I call you Sister, not everything in this new age we inhabit is as simple as one might hope. Let's say that my birthday was September 25th, 1957 would that help your survey?"

"Please call me Miss Cousins, and yes thank you", she felt certain that he had provided her with the correct information, after all why wouldn't he? "Now, if we may move along".

"We may. What is your next question?"

"Question 5: where was your place of birth?"

He answered quickly, Adelaide was clawing at his leg, and the game was getting boring, "Crosschester, the Royal County Hospital".

"Excellent, excellent. Next question", what followed were a series of questions about which diseases, illnesses, breaks, sprains and fractures Fawley had suffered from since childhood. He answered with random yeses and nos as the fancy took him. Sister Helen prepared to finish, turning to a new set of questions she explained, "These data are aimed at getting a more national picture of what people want from the National Health Service. Please answer honestly", he nodded. She began.

"Does the National Health Service do enough for British natives? Yes, No or Don't Know?"

"I don't know", said Fawley, who didn't care.

"Are hearing aids luxury items or should they be funded at the expense of taxpayers?"

"I think they should be tax funded, same as spectacles, callipers all that sort of thing".

She frowned and made a note.

"Would you be in favour of State funding to remove the threat of hereditary disease and ease the burden on families? Yes or No?"

"Could you explain a little more about what you mean?" Upstairs, Lunsford was keen to hear the answer.

"It's good that you asked, many people don't show an interest. What we mean in the case of this questionnaire is that if it was possible for the Health Service to ease the pain of families afflicted by crippling or otherwise preventably damaging issues would you be in favour of this?" Her pen was poised over the tickboxes.

"That sounds like a wonderful idea", Fawley nodded.

Sister Helen smiled and nodded.

"Last question, and think deeply please before you answer. This is not simply about your own family but the nation as a whole and, of course, the happiness of our children specifically, do you understand?"

"I think so, yes", said Fawley who was bored.

Lunsford was leaning comfortably against the wall, his hangover marginalised by the fact that he wouldn't have to deal with this woman and all these questions.

Sister Helen said, "If you were to be told that a child of yours was going to be born a cripple, in such pain as to make it incapable of contribution to the wider society when it reached the age of majority, and of such a diversion of valuable resources prior to this age that it would threaten the care of happier and healthier children, would you consider a termination of the pregnancy to ensure the greater good?" she took a breath.

Fawley thought about the question. Lunsford considered it.

"That's an exceptionally long question, Miss Cousins. Very lengthy. If I'm being honest with you, I went into it with the full expectation of coming out the other end with an answer but I have to admit that I got lost halfway through. And now I don't quite know where I am".

He put his index finger to his bottom lip because, as far as he was aware, that's what people did when they were thinking deeply about something and he didn't want there to be any confusion. He didn't want her to think he was being rude or simply drifting off to think about something else.

"Could you simplify it for me?"

"I'm afraid not, no Mr Johnstone. After a great deal of thought, and considering all the possible interpretations, it was decided that this was the optimum way of describing the question and reaching a reasonable set of answers".

Sister Helen wanted this question answered because it went to the heart of the petition that she was hoping to send to the government in Westminster. It was the key to her endeavours.

"Oh, I see, I think. What was the question again?" Fawley always thought the absolute best in people. In his experience of travelling the world, it took a great deal more effort and commitment to be rotten than it did just to get on with things. So, he had honestly not understood the question, which appeared to have very many cracks in its foundations. Maybe he was wrong.

Sister Helen had considered the gentleman to be of above average intelligence at the start of this questionnaire. She had a niggling feeling that something was up. However, the statistics were hungry for data rather than specific people, so nothing lost there. She tried to imagine how she could simplify the question, maybe that was all to the good in fact. Maybe it would help harvest more potent data because, if she was honest, the low quality of interviewees she'd had to contend with hadn't inspired her.

"I will try, Horo. Would you terminate the result of a successful copulation if you knew that the issue would be unable to contribute to the wider society? That it would in fact be a drain not only on your family but on normal children?"

Fawley was still flummoxed but he didn't want to disappoint the woman who appeared from the look in her eyes and the deepening colour of her cheeks to be greatly concerned with his answer.

"How do you mean?" he asked.

Upstairs Lunsford had nodded off. Adelaide had gone back into the kitchen and was curled up, dreaming of fields and running.

Sister Helen looked at Fawley in disbelief, raising one eyebrow.

"Do you mind me asking you something", Fawley felt stupid, he felt awful. He'd been so concerned with himself and his thoughts that he'd totally forgotten about the woman.

"Please", she was exasperated, "do. What would you like to know?"

"Is there something wrong with your child?", he held out his hand to hold hers and then thought better of it. Just touching people like that was often not very appreciated especially not in England.

"I, you, I… what? I don't have any children", she was stunned.

"Oh. I don't understand the question then. Do you mean if there was some magical way we could see into the future of our child and see for certain that they were going to do harm to people, would we stop them being born? I'd have to see the magic really. I'd also have to see why my child did the harm in the first place and try to stop it".

"No. No, I do not mean any such thing. There is no magic here!"

Fawley tilted his head slightly and pursed his lips.

She continued, "I am talking about science. Science!"

"Oh", he felt foolish but relieved, "I'd like to see the science then".

"There is no science yet!" she seethed. "We are imagining it!" Lunsford woke up with a jerk and his head spun.

Fawley smiled, and skipped very slightly on one leg, "Then I will imagine that all the kids are happy then".

Sister Helen looked at him the same way she looked at all idiots, with anger.

"Please pass my card to Mr Lunsford on his return and tell him he needs to make an urgent appointment", she handed him a card that she'd had printed some months before at her own expense, one of 20.

"He's a very busy man", Fawley assumed a faux serious tone, and held out the letters. Look, according to this postmark this letter is from one of his Naval Intelligence contacts in Birmingham. And this one", he examined a letter from an insurance company in Rhyl, "looks as if it's from a government.

"Can you please ensure that Mr Lunsford reads my letter as soon as he returns from Italy. It is imperative that I am able to assess his fitness and complete the valuable work of public health currently being carried out for this area".

"Madam", Fawley sounded steely for the first time, "what is your name? Who are you working for? What is your angle?"

"My angle?"

"Your angle" he interrupted before she could build up a head of self-righteousness. "I don't see any official looking imprimatur on this letter. There is no seal, no notification, there is nothing at all to tell anybody that it comes from The Health Service. It is hand-addressed. It is in a white envelope. All official documentation in this Great Britain of ours is, proudly ours I may say, are always enveloped in beige or brown. I demand sight of your credentials and the title and name of your chief of staff immediately madam. As a citizen of this nation of free people I have that right as stated in Magna Carta, ratified in the Enclosures Act, and re-ratified in The EEC and the Single European Act of 1973".

Sister Hel was aghast. Nobody in this benighted village had ever had the temerity to question her authority. Yet here she stood in front of this young man – although his darkening eyes suggested he should be much, much older – in her freshly ironed uniform and notes obviously with both inherent status and natural authority, only to be questioned and arrogantly so. She wasn't standing for it but as she was about to speak the tall man indicated the door.

Sister Hel's sighed one of the long, frustrated sighs that she'd been deploying since she began her great project. She put her clipboard back in her bag. Fawley put his hand out to shake hers but his fingertips only touched the back of her coat as she turned and walked up the path and away from Oak Cottage.

As soon as he heard the door slam shut, Lunsford made his way downstairs and into the kitchen. Fawley was standing at the counter near the oven, mixing eggs to accompany the deep, dark smells of frying bacon and black pudding.

"Fried bread or toast, Mr Lunsford?" asked Fawley as Adelaide sauntered over and barked once in salute.

Before he'd had the time to think he replied, "Fried bread please, Fawley".

"Yes, yes, that's the stuff".

"What are you doing in my house?" Lunsford sat down at the kitchen table and looked at the clock, it was twelve thirty. Fawley had tuned the radio to a pop music station that was quietly punching out a song about Baker Street in London.

"Someone had to get you home last night, or rather this morning. You'd made quite the night of it. How's your first Elder's hangover?"

Lunsford took the mug of dark, wonderful tea that Fawley offered him and tried to construct any sort of description of exactly how awful the hangover had been at the beginning, fortunately the memory was passing. He sipped the tea.

"I'm scrambling these eggs; I hope that's good for you. I like mine like they make them in Auxerre", Lunsford made the expression of someone who had no idea what or where Auxerre was and was entirely unsure of his stomach cared to find out".

"Don't worry, Mr Lunsford".

"Please call me Martin or Lunsford".

"Ok, don't worry Lunsford, breakfast will make you feel one hundred percent better, and then maybe a walk?"

"What did I do last night?"

"Do you really want to know, Lunsford", Fawley poured more tea.

"I think I do".

"To start with, you did nothing that won't see you welcomed back to The Phoenix, so you can relax".

Lunsford drank his tea and pushed the food on his plate around, "That's not answered my question".

"You did nothing to embarrass yourself. Would you like some ketchup?" Fawley sat down opposite and chewed on some toast and marmalade. Adelaide twitched in her sleep.

"Still not telling me what I did".

Lunsford took a forkful of the scrambled eggs along with some cracking bacon, looked at it and put it in his mouth. What a wonderful sensation. He was expecting it to come straight back up.

"Christ this is the best thing I've ever eaten in my life. It's egg and bacon but blimey, I feel better already".

He took more forkfuls, more swallows, more life-urging sensations until he'd finished the plate and soaked up the deeply satisfyingly salty, savoury mess with fried bread before finishing his tea and, for some reason he couldn't imagine, holding his mug out and nodding at it for more. Fawley smiled, laughed with a little joy and did the job.

"Please Fawley, aside from the drinking, what else did I do?"

"Well, to be honest, Lunsford, me and Adelaide were outside for a lot of it so I can only cast secondhand daylight on it but suffice to say…"

"No, suffice to say, mate, none of that please, what happened?" had he not eaten so well, Lunsford would have been deep in hangover dread.

"Do you usually get up on tables?"

"No", his heart sank.

"OK, fair enough then, so that was a one-off. To be honest it was the last thing you did, and it was to say thank you to everybody in the pub, which by that time was me, Adelaide and Bob Gumm. Even Gentle Dominic and Old Mr Granger had left by then".

"What was I thanking people for? Seriously, Fawley, I blacked out. I've never done that before".

"Your memory may have done but you were good company on the stagger home. All songs and stories. A joy to be with".

"Yes, but before that?" he gulped down hot tea and tried to remember and not to remember at the same time as is the way with hangovers.

"Before that you talked a lot to Mrs Werldinham about Chloé. About how you hadn't talked about Chloé because you felt that you'd let her down and you didn't want to recall her spirit by saying her name out loud".

For the first time a new voice that was an old voice spoke up.

"There was nothing you could have done, Lunsford. Nothing, my sweet man".

Lunsford sat bolt upright.

"Is that you Chloé? Are you there? Sweet man you called me".

"You are my sweet man", she insisted.

"Lunsford, are you ok? Would you like more tea?"

"What else did I say, Fawley. What else did I do?"

CHAPTER 25

IT HAPPENED LAST NIGHT?

1978

Fawley poured the tea and cleared away the dirty plates and cutlery to the sink where he began washing up. Lunsford walked to the drainer and began drying. Adelaide barked in her sleep. She twitched. She kicked. The clouds over the house were thickening with snow and were ready to split themselves into the dark afternoon. Neither man said a word, and Adelaide slept in fields and rivers, across the Water Meadows, through Hunters Wood and into an evil, stinking, colossal city, under an old car with sirens blaring around her and other dogs snarling and snapping at her face.

Fawley knelt down and scratched her head, bringing her back through the city and the woods to her new home. She made a low grunting noise, licked vaguely at his hand and slept on. Fawley went back to his chair and began constructing a cigarette. The snow started to fall.

"Do you mind if I smoke this in here?"

"I'd prefer it if you didn't. Chloé hated it", his throat was hurting and the smell and sensation of his smoked cigarettes from the night before rushed back at him mercilessly.

"What about these Fawley? What the bloody hell happened here?" He held up his fists, showing the younger man the raked skin of his knuckles, "What did I do?"

Fawley looked crestfallen.

"Ah, that. Well, as I said, you did nothing to get you barred or embarrass yourself but you may have had a bit of a tussle".

"A tussle, it feels like I killed someone! I don't have a bruise on me as far as I can see".

The snow was falling hard, mixing with bird calls and the black ashes from the hearth fires in the houses of the village. There was no clear view out of the kitchen window, everything outside had disappeared.

"Oh, for goodness sake", said Lunsford, "Who did I have this tussle with?"

Fawley's mood picked up.

"A fellow called Harry Mottram. Nasty piece of work. He turns up every so often spoiling for a fight with Bob Gumm, some old grudge or an old friendship gone sour. Sarson-Taylor invited him in years ago, and once you're invited it's exceedingly difficult to get uninvited. I keep pointing this out to Mrs Werldinham but she's a stickler for some traditions".

"What the bloody hell happened then? Why did I get into a fight with him?"

"You were talking about your friend Mick by that point. In tears so you were. It was very moving, so I was told".

"I was not in tears", he had no memory other than the memory of how he saw himself.

"Crying? You sweet man. I knew I married a good one. Mick cried. He cried when our baby died. Sweet man you're only remembering what you think you need to remember. Why are you hurting yourself?

"Mick never cried. I never cried. Never", he answered her.

"Sweet man, you did. You both did".

"Never".

Fawley, oblivious to the other conversation, continued, "As I say, this is all hearsay, me and Adelaide were out and about. But Bob Gumm and Mrs W told me, Bob was in the cellar and Mottram had come in and was ranting away about a family who had taken over the Craven's sweetshop in town".

"What did I do? I've never been violent", Lunsford asked.

"Except on occasion, my sweet man. Let's not skate over matters. Let's be honest. You were always honest at least", whispered Chloé.

Lunsford flinched. She was right. He had a past.

Fawley went over to Adelaide.

"Mottram put a pile of leaflets on the counter and was making as if to head off back to The Green Man. But he spotted Mrs Werldinham and you. From what she tells me, he ran over to you both, scattering empties, and demanded that you took a bunch of his flyers. Mrs Werldinham took one, read it, balled it up, and threw it into the fire".

Fawley stood up and began pacing around the table, head down.

"Mottram was incandescent", he said with some sadness.

"So, when did I hit him? How did that happen? For God's sake sit down".

"Well, Mrs Werldinham hurt his pride. Pride means a lot to these people, it's part of a code or something".

"I never hit women", he screamed at you. "But you, mate, you, you're like a fucking dog, a lapdog, a mongrel dog, just sat there letting her do your fighting for you. Fucking coward you, aren't you?".

"You said, "Eh? You what mate?"

Mottram said, "You're a fucking lapdog mate. Be a fucking man. A proper man, able to take care of your women".

Bob told me later that even downstairs he could hear Mottram yelling and ranting about how, "You're the reason that England is failing, it's your fault. Your fucking fault!"

At this point Bob Gumm came up the stairs.

Mottram was in full flow though, "Enoch said, he said, a nation heaping up its own funeral pyre. The whole place will be overrun, is being overrun. Nothing left for us, and half-men like you are going to let it happen".

"What are you going on about though, mate?"

"Mottram with his bitten lips, crushed yellow teeth, screaming veins standing out on his neck, flowing with bad ideas", said Fawley.

"What I am on about is the fact that our country is disappearing, mate?", Mottram yelled.

"What's that all got to do with me?", asked Lunsford, sobering slightly.

"You're a fucking cowardly bastard!" Mottram spat at you, full in your face. "You look like a fucking Jew too".

Then he picked up a chair and he swung it at your head. Bob Gumm told me that you went into decent defence, fist up over your face, forearms covering your heart. Not bad for a man as pissed as you were.

"The chair smashed into your fists, and you were knocked clean onto the stone floor. Mrs Werldinham had to lay Mottram out and bar him from The Phoenix. A first as far as anybody remembers.

"She barred him straight out of the door and onto the green, she continued to bar him all the way down Hare Rise. You could hear her barring him by the grunts and groans. It was then that I walked in the back door. Bob had picked you up and sat you down, and we decided it would be the best thing all round if me and Adelaide took you home and here we are. I don't much like conflict though, so can we move on?"

Lunsford laughed. "So, my fists were bruised by a chair?", he was slightly relieved.

"Tell me about Mick", that came out suddenly as if Fawley had been holding it in for a long time. "Tell me about Mick".

"I'm tired and hungover Fawley, can it wait?"

"I don't think it can really, Lunsford. I think you need to get some things out of yourself before they do you harm", Fawley was serious, and Lunsford wanted to fight his new friend's certainty with his own trepidation.

"Talking cures? Just not my way, Fawley. I wasn't brought up like that, quite the opposite in fact".

"Mate, if you can do it drunk, not only can you do it sober but even your drunk self knows that you need to do it in. Your drunk self's usually a good guide to what's buried inside. But he gets confused and then angry. So, it's down to you to do good for you".

Lunsford looked out of the window at the snow and the gales of wind that controlled it. It was chaos. Everything was chaos.

I hardly know this boy. I can't just talk about Mick.

"Sweet man, why not?" her voice again.

Why can't I? Why on earth not? It's like I'm burying him twice.

"You hardly know this boy. Showing a weakness like this when you don't have the excuse of drink!", his father. His father who constantly talked about himself, drunk and sober.

"Lunsford don't bury me in silence. We're still pals", Mick.

"Don't be so sentimental boy. Don't be so weak. Mick's dead. He's not coming back no matter how much you witter on to some hare-brained tramp. Be a man. Leave the dead in their place", yelled his long-dead dad. "You're using too much imagination as usual. Get a hobby. Get a drink. Get some sleep. Get an allotment. There's no need for all this soft bollocks. Mick's dead. Chloé's dead. We're all dead. You'll be dead soon. Dirt and gone".

"Don't forget us", Chloé said gently.

"Old pal. Don't kill us again with forgetting. Say our names aloud. On the hills and in the woods and on the land and at the football". Mick, exalting.

"Yes, my love, talk to me in the kitchen and on the road and doing the shopping and laying quietly in our bed. Don't take leave by silence. We haven't stopped loving you", Chloé, holding her tears.

"They're just ghosts, boy. Just dead weights. Be a grown-up", father dear father.

The wind outside was forcing the powdery snow to compact itself, making thick but fragile shapes in the air that resembled living things dancing with the dead, the one leading the other, the lead changing second by second.

"Cup of tea? That always helps", asked Fawley.

Lunsford looked at him, and he saw a tall, thin, pleasant young man who he had quite taken to. Fawley asked again, "Tea?"

Both men knew that this was code, and both men laughed. Fawley began to make a brew, and Lunsford talked.

"Mick and I were friends. Best friends I suppose you'd call it. We only ever fell out badly once and we got over that. War will do that; help you get over things I mean".

"You worked together after the war? You were saying last night", Fawley brought over the tea and sat down to listen.

Sipping and blowing on the mug of tea, Lunsford replied, "Yes, we did. Sat in the same office for years. The last thing we worked on was that new hall in town. We bloody made that work too, from scraps and bits and bobs. Madness how that thing ever got the go ahead".

"The Wulfric Hall?"

"That's the one. What kind of name is that?"

"It's the name of an Anglo Saxon king who was executed by the Normans and whose lands – including this village actually – were confiscated by the church".

"How on earth did you know that?"

"The longer you live, the more you pick up", both men sipped their tea. Adelaide got up and walked under the table to nestle at

Lunsford's feet where life was generally warmer. She fell back to sleep quickly and dreamt on.

"Well, Mick and I were given a proper hodgepodge of stuff. We both drew up the plans and tried to add some, I dunno, some humanity to the bloody thing".

"What do you mean?"

"The place was mostly poured concrete, ugly, plain, no light. All straight lines, with four smallish windows all pointing light down at a wooden dais. Everybody else is in the dark except for the, and this is a strange one, except for the torch light".

"Torch light?"

"Yes. Actual flaming torches mounted on the walls. Weird. The thing is that there was only room for about nine of the things. You see, the hall isn't that big. It's got all the airs and graces of a monumental great thing but it's all packed into the size of a three-bed detached house".

"So, how did you humanise it?"

"Well, Mick is, was, mates with the carpenter they got in to make that dais and the lectern so... do you know what a Misericord is?"

"Like a gargoyle?"

"Not really, no".

"What then?" Fawley felt put in his place but he also felt that Lunsford was showing confidence, happy once again to have returned to the solid ground of his own expertise even fleetingly.

Lunsford was getting into his stride, his pleasure in the work he used to do was flooding through him again. He'd been good at his job but together he and Mick had been excellent. They'd jostled each other long, picking up bits and bobs of knowledge along the way, a longstanding and friendly competition.

"Gargoyles have two purposes, to direct water away from the outside of a building and…" Lunsford began to lecture, feeling comfortable.

"To protect against evil spirits", Fawley interjected eagerly, and Adelaide whined quietly.

"Well, a Misericord has nothing to do with water or evil spirits. They're carved scenes or images in little tableaux on the underside of pews or seats. There's a long and quite respectable history to them but what we, me and Mick, found out was that because many of them were rarely seen, some of them were quite rude. Two fingers up at the people who didn't pay or were too pompous.

"Mick had been reading about them and drew up two of them: one of me and one of him. He had his tongue out and I was, well, I had my arse out. Just little carved jokes. Small things, no bigger than your hand. The carpenter was happy enough to do the job for a few pints and a bottle of Bells. None of the bigwigs could be bothered to come down during the building process. But I never got to see if the two of us, me and Mick, were popped up there. I hope we did. I'd love to see us".

Lunsford leant back on his chair and closed his eyes. He felt terribly sad, but for the first time in a terrible, long while he didn't feel stupid, he felt that he had something to be sad about.

"Look, if you don't mind me staying here for the night, maybe we can go for a walk and have a chat tomorrow, maybe we could visit the Wulfric Hall?" Fawley had an idea.

They both looked out of the window into the snow. Adelaide looked up, saw what she saw, and covered her head with her paws and returned to sleep.

"That weather's not changing any time soon, so yes, please stay. Thank you for breakfast", Lunsford went back upstairs. It was three in the afternoon. Fawley walked through the parlour and into the lounge room where he looked through the books. He selected a large one by Dr Alice Wilson PhD and sat down to spend an afternoon in comfort, reading.

CHAPTER 26

ERIC BENSON AND SISTER HEL'

1978

Sister Helen woke up and sighed again. Overnight she'd been troubled by the idea that the people she was battling to improve didn't, in fact, want improvement. As she mounted her bicycle, she knew for certain that his rejection was exactly the reason that improvements were absolutely necessary. The Salt of the Earth, the good folk, the capital 'P' People, the citizens of the oldest democracy in the world, the bosses of the foundation Parliament had all been consigned to educational dustbins long ago. They didn't know what they wanted. She needed more than ever to make them aware of their best interests.

This reassertion of belief in her cause, and in herself, meant that she could throw off the incident with Mr Horace Johnstone. She would deal with Mr Lunsford in good time. This was no time for fatigue or delay. Now was the time, as Mr Churchill had famously said, to go forward with Britain. But first it was time to post a letter, an important letter. One of the most important letters she'd ever posted. A letter to the Prime Minister.

She was soon standing at the counter of Shalford Post Office looking over the leaflets as she waited for service behind a queue of tiny but extremely voluble old aged pensioners.

"Yes, the sweet shop, Mr and Mrs Craven's one, yes, changed hands last week. Sold to a foreign pair".

"They never got over Darren's death".

"How could you though? You couldn't".

"You wouldn't".

"You wouldn't dare".

"Well, at least they'll get a retirement, they always worked so hard in that shop".

"Well, I hope the new ones are too foreign if you get my meaning".

"Why's that then, love?" Mr Eric Benson prepared to serve the next tiny woman.

"Well, you don't know what you're getting otherwise do you? You can't be certain, and everything will smell of their food. I've a sister who lives up north and she says that her town stinks of curried this and curried that. Didn't use to. Mill town, it smelt of cotton, so she says. Two First Class stamps and a packet of Bensons love, please".

Mr Eric Benson served the woman and then looked around the shop to see how many more customers were going to take up his time. He saw six regulars and that Nurse Cousins who used to have *The Times* and *The Telegraph*. He saw that she was immersed in the latest BFDP leaflet. He completed the transaction and moved on to the pensioner.

Sister Helen was oblivious to anything except the leaflet. This was her prized faculty: she was able to concentrate to the exclusion of all else no matter where she was or who she was with. The flyer was fresh, and like nothing she'd seen in the village.

The British Democratic Freedom Party

PUBLIC MEETING

Tuesday September 26th

Wulfric Hall, Crosschester

7:30pm

ALL WELCOME

GUEST SPEAKERS

FREE FOOD AND DRINK

PUTTING GREAT BRITISH VALUES FIRST

We are the Party that Remembers

• You and your family

• Our brave armed forces

• Our police, fire and ambulance men

• All the sacrifices that made Britain Great

• Without our glorious past we have NO FUTURE

On the reverse of the leaflet was an advertisement for a gymnasium.

COME TO GRANTS GYM

The SLEEPERS HILL, CROSSCHESTER

(Next to The Green Man pub)

FOR THE HEALTH & FITNESS OF ALL BRITISH PEOPLES

GRANTS GYM OFFERS SPECAILIST TRAINING IN:

BOXING (inc sparring)

WIEGHTS

ROWING

MILITARY CALISTHENICS

Also Advice on what to eat and drink to keep fit once you've got fit.

And more

All at reasonable prices

Open Monday to Saturday 08:00 - 22:00

FOR THE SURVIVAL OF THE FITTEST!

No Timewasters!

(Ask in the pub for more details if we're shut)

There were so many Union Jacks that it was difficult to read but… but… but it was at least a start. Grant's Gymnasium. There were like-minds there.

"Can I help you Miss Cousins?" she looked up and into the too-close, round red face of Mr Eric Benson who had been tapping her on the shoulder and putting that same question to her in a rising voice for what seemed to him like five minutes.

"Can you tell me about this?" Sister Helen snapped out of it.

Mr Eric Benson returned to his position behind the counter. "I certainly can. We were having a meeting…"

She cut him off and flipped the leaflet over, "This. The gymnasium. Mr Grant and his goal to make the country fitter and healthier".

There was no Mr Grant. The gym was owned by Miss Meredith Brewer who also ran The Green Man pub. Miss Brewer had realised that if men exercised for a while they'd build up a thirst, so why not cash-in on both ends of that deal. Most of the time the gym was full of paying customers and no staff. This was because after their first visit, none of the men thought they needed any instruction. Every so often Meredith would send Harry Mottram in to lift some weights, spar with the fattest looking gym member, punch him in all the wrong places and call that training. No one questioned the set-up because they all liked having a glorified tree house with a boxing ring and some heavy objects to lift. As for dietary advice, this usually consisted of a sheet of paper with tailored information along the lines of:

Monday:
Breakfast: Porridge. Fruit Juice.
Dinner: Bread (Brown. No butter). Tea (No milk). Apple
Tea: Egg Salad. Water.
Evening: 3 glass of Guinness or 4 glass of Ale (No spirits). Beef or Pork sandwich.

So, on and so forth with various caveats regarding the amount of exercise per sandwich or pint, something about calories and burning candles, and warnings about sweeties. All of this had been cribbed from magazines that Meredith had seen in the hairdressers or the waiting room at her local surgery. No one at the gym was going to compare notes and even if they did Meredith had told H' to christen them 'Brothers-in-Arms' to keep them content. Brothers-in-Arms worked a treat.

Mr Eric Benson was aware of all this, and also of the fiction that was Regimental Sergeant Major Glen Grant of the Royal Country regiment.

Injured on active service, S'arnt Major Grant was not going to let the amputation of a leg below the knee, and a shard of German shrapnel over his heart, stop him from reaching the peak of fitness. Returning to England, to his wife and his multitude of healthy children in 1919, the giant of a man had used his pay to build the gym for all the People. So, the story went.

S'arnt Major Grant had passed away at the ripe old age of 96. That shard of Hun lead had sliced into his aorta or something and he'd died on active duty with that sniper's round killing him decades on. His funeral had been a hugely moving and significant occasion. The streets lined with grief-stricken women waving Union flags, sobbing men holding their caps to their hearts, and awe-struck children, silent, heartbroken but inspired. The specially routed train from Crosschester station to Grant's birthplace in the Scottish borders was swathed in black cloth, with black ostrich feathers adorning its smokestack. It was waved off with more yet flags, more tears of gratitude for a job well done, a 21-gun salute from the barracks.

Mr Eric Benson regaled this fiction to Miss Cousins, who nodded and sighed at the appropriately tragic and/or sad moments.

"So, who is responsible for carrying the Sergeant Major's vision forward, for maintaining his legacy?"

That one stumped Eric. No one had planned for someone with genuine curiosity so, as a leader, he improvised.

"We, members of the British Democratic Freedom Party are the keepers of Grant's vision. Why, may I ask, are you, a very feminine lady, interested in such a masculine endeavour, Miss Cousins?"

Had Mr Eric Benson not been such an unhealthily fat lump, Sister Helen might have felt slightly complimented. However, he was quite definitely not breeding material and therefore she was revolted at his attempted flirtation. She stepped back and crossed her arms before responding.

"I would be extremely interested in hearing more about your party and its plans Mr Benson. You see I have quite a substantial body of work ongoing regarding the continuing weakening of the nation. Certainly, if Great Britain is to end its time at the foot of the evolutionary tree by dint of laziness, gluttony, complacency and downright devaluation of its own common stock then so be it. That is nature. That is science. That is our fate.

"However, I feel – and I'm sure you agree – that with suitable rigour, the correct intellectual, physical and educational underpinning, with the odd sting of stick rather than the constant indulgence of the welfare state's never-ending supply of carrot".

"The Nanny State as we call it", Mr Benson interjected.

"Yes, certainly. With all of this we can at least return the nation to some semblance of its former vigour. The entire world and not simply these islands would benefit of course".

The Post Office became a silent place, a shrine to the ideas of this wonderful woman. Mr Eric Benson was in awe, maybe a little smitten. He'd never heard anything so beautifully clean and strong coming out of the mouth of anybody quite so female. He coughed. He nearly spluttered. He had to sit down. He nodded violently as he regained his position on the stool behind the counter where he sat, vibrating with newfound energy.

Mrs Farger came through the door in her fur hat and her coat made from what looked like green and brown woven armour, her brown stockinged legs bulging down into her red plastic sandals. Her yappy dog called Carlos accompanied her as always. She'd come in for fags, bread, dog food, gossip and to complain about things. Behind her came the Misses Charlton. Tall, and silent as secret vows. It was rumoured that they had been nuns who had left St Florin's Convent in Commiton in the 1950s. In the village their silence was as legendary as their lemon drizzle cake, which they delivered to the Shalford fête every year without fail before fading back into wherever it was they lived.

Mr Eric Benson's disappointment at the unwanted incursion of the women, one of whom bored him, while the two others scared the hell out of him, was palpable.

Sister Helen didn't make it to the counter in time and, cursing her lassitude, she put the leaflet in her pocket and went to the newspaper rack to wait it out.

"A second class stamp, some biscuits for Carlos, a tin of peas… two tins of peas, a Mothers Pride, a packet of Rothmans, a bottle of lemon barley water, a feather duster, a tin of furniture polish and a packet of Fisherman's Friends please Mr Benson, I feel a cold coming on, Mr Benson". Mrs Farger never visited the shelves herself. Her husband had been someone in the Colonial Service, she had once had command of several servants in the Tropics. She was prepared to let the large man who ran the shop do his work. While huffing and puffing his way from peas to the Fisherman's Friends Eric kept a close eye on Miss Cousins, just in case she left without going more deeply into her ideas.

"Mr Benson, did you see that Mr and Mrs Craven's shop in Crosschester has been sold to an Indian gentleman?", Mrs Farger watched as Mr Eric Benson packed her trolley.

"The Asian family? Yes, I'm aware of that, Mrs Farger. Will this be all?"

The Misses Charlton glid over to the section of the shop that displayed bleaches, vermin traps and drain cleaners, and ran their long, delicate but incredibly strong fingers over the products as if reading the labels in Braille. Dorothy, the slightly younger, blond Miss Charlton with the postbox red lipstick and plunging neckline, and Sigrid the red-haired Miss Charlton with eyes of catastrophic depth, dark green and never wavering occasionally glanced at each other. They never spoke to each other, there was no need. When one of them did speak, it was usually Sigrid. She spoke in an unplaceable accent that shuddered with chill in such a poetic tonality that people never wanted her to stop. When Dorothy, never "Dot", spoke it was with such gravitas and authority that people were often moved to bow slightly without knowing exactly why.

Mrs Farger hadn't finished yet. This place was her temple of tittle-tattle and she was devout.

"So, not Indian then? From Asia are they? What else do you know, Mr Benson? I heard that the Craven's sold up because their son Darren had been beaten to death outside the Guildhall in Crosschester by a gang of", she paused, "Asians, that's what I heard".

It began to dawn on Sister Helen that she could bicycle into Bursley or Commiton and buy a stamp and it would probably be quicker. She made to walk towards the door. Mr Eric Benson panicked. He knew that the BDFP needed intellectual mettle, some brainy heft and he knew that he was looking right at it if only Mrs Farger would move out of the way.

"Yes, that's right. Beaten to death. Asians. Will that be all Mrs Farger? Excellent. Please say hello to your husband", Mr Farger had been dead for a decade.

He almost threw her change at her before pushing past her, "Ms Cousins how may I assist you!?"

The Misses Charlton, who were standing at the counter with bleach, dog food, caustic soda, a hammer, nails and some vanilla ice cream vibrated but said nothing. They were, in point of fact, desperate to scream their anger at once again being overlooked but being pathologically shy and only ever safe and comfortable in each other's company they remained as silent as the nuns they'd once been. Seething, hurt, terrified of the wider world.

Sister Helen, being a courteous and correct citizen – and British to the core in her queuing habits – was having none of it. "Mr Benson, these ladies were here before me".

Mr Eric Benson, who was always unnerved by the Misses Charlton, served them quickly with a fixed smile. As they departed the Post Office, the pair nodded gratitude to the other woman with slight inclinations of their foreheads. Both of their faces were blushed pink, and they were shaking with anxiety as they headed home to clean and mend the house and garden shed, and to walk their cats, Harvey and

Jemma.

"Now then, Miss Cousins, how may I assist you finally?" Mr Benson bowed as far as was possible without all the buttons on his red waistcoat popping off. She realised at once that for a large man who apparently exerted some influence in his locality. Mr Eric Benson could be entirely small and obsequious when confronted by someone he assumed was his superior. Which she was.

"Two First Class stamps please Mr Benson".

He picked two from a roll and handed them over, taking the money and putting it into the huge and ancient till. She turned to leave, already deep in thought about the gym. She was rapidly reaching the conclusion that she had been wasting time building up statistics to present to a government that was patently obviously unconcerned with the fitness of its own citizens. It was time for action. It was time she took that action.

"Miss Cousins, I wonder, would you like to visit Grants?" The word punctured her protective bubble. "I beg your pardon, Mr Benson?".

"I was wondering... given what you said... if it's convenient... whether you might like to visit Grants Gym? Maybe I could be your guide?"

She didn't need to think, she'd done too much thinking.

"Yes, Mr Benson, I would like that very much indeed".

"You might also like to join us next door in The Green Man for an informal chat about our new political organisation. We are seeking to improve the lot of the Anglo Saxon peoples, beginning with our own nation. I believe that your ideas and your energy align themselves with our now in many areas, and it would be good if we could pool our resources".

Sister Helen was used to working alone, she wasn't a 'team player'. She didn't disdain group endeavours, certainly not, people should work together. Failure to do so had brought the country to its current, supine position on the world stage. It was a simple fact, however, that outstanding individuals worked more quickly and efficiently outside of the group environment, their contributions to the greater good were made with the personal sacrifice of self. People like her ploughed a lonely furrow with little or no thanks but gratitude had never been a reason to work. She straightened her back and shot her cuffs.

"I don't drink alcohol, Mr Benson", she said.

"A wise decision I'm sure, Miss Cousins. I can assure you that you'll find the members of the BDFP to be a sober group of men in all senses of the word".

Sister Helen seemed appeased.

"So, shall we say eight o'clock tomorrow night upstairs in The Green Man on Sleepers Hill?"

"And the Gym?"

"As I say, the governing council of the Party has oversight of the gym, I'm sure we can arrange your tour there and then". The party didn't have any oversight, Meredith did, but this was a wrinkle.

"I will see you at eight then, and thank you Mr Benson".

CHAPTER 27

A WALK THROUGH THE WATER MEADOWS

1978

Lunsford, Fawley and the foundling dog woke up early and refreshed on Sunday morning. The powdery snowfall of the previous day had firmed to a pleasing crunch outside, the sky had regained its sun and was as pale blue as Adelaide's eyes. They men drank dark tea and ate a large, greasily fabulous breakfast over which they discussed working. Fawley had worked in so many countries and in so many jobs that Lunsford was baffled that he looked to be only in his early twenties.

"You know what we should do?", Fawley wiped his plate clean with the last slice of white bread in the house.

"Buy more food?"

"Well, that yes. I'll get the supplies in."

"No roadkill?"

"No roadkill, but you really should give it a try one day soon".

"No roadkill", Lunsford was not moving on this one. "What else should we do then?"

"We should pay a visit to your building, Lunsford. We should visit the Wulfric Hall. After all it was the last thing that you and Mick combined your talents on. I think it's only fitting that we at least see how it turned out".

This was unusual for Fawley who had a lasting and deep distaste for Crosschester, a city he would avoid the bricks of if it was at all possible. However, as far as he could see to get Lunsford out of himself and back into some semblance of happiness, they would have to go to town. Lunsford was feeling guilt over the death of his friend. This guilt was taking him away from the world and making his memories sour. Much as Fawley would have relished buying both Mick and Lunsford one more pint to delay the encounter with Darren Craven's car, that option wasn't currently available to him.

"Fawley?"

"Yes?"

"Why do you care? Why are you doing this?"

Fawley didn't bother to think, "Because I like to see happiness more than sadness I suppose, and let's face it you're not happy".

Lunsford went to the sink and began washing up. Fawley started drying. Neither man said anything for a while. Outside the house, in the Water Meadows nothing moved, the wind was elsewhere, and even the plants had slowed their growth to near death. A plane passed overhead on its way to Europe. In front of the house, traffic slushed past itself going to and from Porthampton.

"I still don't think I understand", said Lunsford.

"Well, it's like this: we all live in different worlds but on an average day those worlds overlap..."

"No not that sort of thing, which frankly is a bit too weird for my thinking. I mean, why are you bothering? If you think about it, we don't know each other and there's no..."

Fawley interrupted, quite sharply too, "Weird? What I was going to say is that sometimes a person's own little world overlaps with another person's and it's ideal in that situation for both to come away with something that makes each one more happy than unhappy. You know the difference it makes to your mood if, after you accidentally bump into someone on a busy street, both of you just nod, accept there was no malice, and walk on? Maybe even smile?"

"I suppose, yes", replied Lunsford, washing a mug so ringed with tea stains that it could have been built that way.

"Well, that's what I mean but on a slightly grander scale. Do you know about Karma?"

"Sort of. More superstitious nonsense though, really isn't it?" said Lunsford not remembering his recent trip to St Eade's.

"Never mind", if he was honest with himself, Fawley had a problem understanding Karma, and he'd been to Tibet and talked with holy men for days on end.

"How about, 'What Goes Around Comes Around'?"

"Yes, but it doesn't does it? That's soft-boiled thinking. It's just not true. I've seen perfectly nice lads, not a bad bone in their bodies, drown in front of me, engine oil burning out their lungs, blinded, freezing. I saw Mick destroyed for no reason at all. My Chloé", he was shouting now "My Chloé, a clever, beautiful, lovely woman. Hard worker, sociable, eaten out by cancer. What goes around comes around, what utter bloody bollocks. Here I am, standing in the kitchen that she made, washing up bloody teacups and plates, ready to go for a walk in the fresh air, in the meadows she loved, ready for a walk to a place that Mick made, here I am. Here I am. Here's me. I've barely had a good word to say about anybody in my entire life. The only reason we ever saw anybody outside of Mick and his wife was the Chloé organised it. People loved her. Other people".

Fawley dried a dry plate, "Yes, that's what I mean".

"What the bloody hell? What?" Lunsford was close to tears of anger, confusion and grief.

"What goes around comes around. Lazy fucking nonsense. You make your own luck as much as you can and all the rest is what you're born into", his father was back. "Family is family. People are people. Country is country. Things are as they are with no fucking magic fairies in the sky making it all better. Fucking priests and vicars and hippies and, shit gets shovelled and one day you're holding the shovel and the next day you're taking the shit".

"Frank, Frank, calm down. You'll do yourself a damage". His mother was there.

"I'm dead you mad whore".

"Oh, Frank. You're such a nasty piece of work. Even in the serenity of death, you're a pub bore and a bully", said Chloé.

"Fuck off, he should never have married you. Made him a weakling".

"Frank, he's not the one who died of drink and hatred. Now shush", she replied.

Adelaide was scratching at the door. She needed to get out and about because she didn't appreciate the shouting and anyway there were things to be getting on with. The people noises seemed to be leading nowhere in particular. She could smell the air outside the house and it was delicious. She could hear the world outside that the men couldn't, and it sounded exciting. Even the cold coming in from under the door was giving her more life generally than the stuffy, greasy, drowsy shambles that was going on around her. Her senses were firing. She barked loudly. She scratched at the door. She demanded that action was taken.

"Calm down Lunsford, look we're upsetting Adelaide with this arguing and the tone. We've made her fearful. We should go for a walk. We should visit your building if for nothing else for you to see it".

Lunsford could see that Adelaide wasn't happy and this made him feel guilty. There was no need for her to feel the way, all she wanted was a piss and some exercise. Simple as that.

"Alright, the dog needs to go for a walk", he told Fawley who already knew.

The two men dressed in warm winter clothes and left the house via the kitchen door to walk into Crosschester through the Water Meadows and over Mizmazz Hill, a hill that looked as if it must have been an Iron Age fort but wasn't. Once up and down there was a straightforward trudge along the metalled road, via The Sleepers Hill, through the grounds of the Monks Chapel and into the main part of the town. Then finally they would be at The Wulfric Hall and, hoped Fawley, Lunsford might meet Mick in peace.

Adelaide took the front position in their file with Lunsford in the middle still not sure why he was doing what he was doing and still angry.

In Crosschester, Sunday was dragging along with all the vim and vigour of a vacuum cleaner emptying ceremony. The Little Sweet Shoppe in Jewry Passage should have been open to sell cigarettes and the Sunday papers, baked beans, eggs and bacon, plastic children's toys, and all kinds of magazines. It would have been had somebody not thrown bricks through the wide front windows early that morning. The windows had been glazed into place in 1876.

Some of the bricks had human shit on them. One of the bricks was wrapped in notepaper. The bricks had woken Mr and Mrs Aditya Kharbanda and their children at five in the morning, half an hour before the adults would normally have pushed themselves out of bed to begin opening the shop. The shit smelled bad and had spattered everywhere like the dead blood it was. Both Mr and Mrs Aditya Kharbanda had comforted each other, told their children to go back to bed, explained that some stonework had fallen from the roof of the Woolworths that nosed over them across the tight medieval passage, and then got on with clearing up.

Mrs Kharbanda's mother had told her years before, "Never read the notes that come, darling. Just throw them out with all the other garbage. Anything that comes tied to a rock or brick is definitely not worth your notice, there are more constructive things to do with your time".

Mr Kharbanda's father had told his son, "Work, that is all we can do. Work harder than them. Work with greater integrity and better business sense. Keep your head down and work until you can buy all their bricks and all their paper and all of their ink. Use every bit of anger and hurt, and remember you have family. All these bastards with their bricks and their messages have shitty hands and hearts".

So, the Kharbandas cleaned the shop that was also their home, and boarded up the smashed windows until they could call a glazier on Monday. Then they put signs that their children had made with glitter and paint on the boards saying, "STILL OPEN WELCOME ALL TO COME IN". Then they stood behind the counter of their revamped and reinvigorated shop and waited for customers as the icy wind blew down Jewry Passage and carried the smell of shit out and into the Guildhall and onto the Market Cross.

Adelaide soon disappeared and had her head into a hole in the ground. She tried to squeeze her entire body in, to no avail. Had she reached the badger asleep inside she would almost certainly have lost the fight. Badgers, at least Shalford badgers, were famous for fighting dirty. They took joy in slashing and clawing their opponent. They showed no remorse. As Fawley and Lunsford approached they saw her tail wagging frantically and heard her barking like a hysterical Victorian poet at the sight of naked ankles. Fawley tapped her lightly on the back with a hawthorn stick he carried with him and she reversed, saw it was only him, and went back down the hole. The badger inside was awake and as usual it was angry. Adelaide stopped wriggling at the sight of the size of the thing. It was huge. She struggled to remove herself as it turned and began to move towards her. The badger began its slow turn as Adelaide scrambled for to get her head out of the sett. The badger seethed and made a chittering sound that turned rapidly to an irate keckering and finally to the snarl that meant it was fully turned about and ready.

The two men kept walking and talking. The badger moved fast. Adelaide unplugged herself and made to run into Hunters Wood.

"Not the wood Adelaide, there's a good dog", shouted Fawley as the two men walked on towards the rising, soft, dark mass of Mizmazz Hill. Adelaide turned in mid-air and seeing that the badger had retreated, strutted past the entrance to the sett and ran to lead the way to the hill.

Mizmazz Hill had a maze on top, carved into the ground. Legend had it that a schoolboy from Crosschester College, driven insane by the weight of expectation and sheer cruelty of his surroundings, had carved the maze out using just a silver soup spoon. The carving had continued year after year for centuries. It had become a ritual for scared and lonely boys to dig a few feet down into the chalky earth before hanging themselves from the oak tree that provided no shade in the summer and no protection from the southerly winds that swept over Mizmazz for the rest of the year.

Also up there on the hill was a cottage. A pretty house thing with three rooms downstairs and two up, with a hilarious mockery of a wooden garage leaning, clinging to its south side. There was a scrubby yard at the front and a pretence of a kitchen garden at the back. Inside the garage was a bicycle and an ancient, slapstick Austin Healey sports car that had given up any intention to motor let alone sport decades ago. Inside the house were books, pile upon pile, shelf upon shelf, bags and boxes of books. The only things that were even close to the number of books were the bottles of vodka, mostly empty, some with small measures waiting at the bottom. Some throttled dry of their liquor and then left – always standing up.

This cottage was two hundred and fifty years old or more, it had been built by the College to house a happily wedded couple whose job it was to stop terrified and depressed pupils of important families from digging the maze and hanging themselves from the oak tree.

Tragically of course, the truly suicidal carry out their last moments quietly without wishing to draw the kind of attention that even the most well-meaning or politically expedient guardian might use as alarm and stop them. This meant that the first, and in most cases last, job that the people who lived in the cottage did was to take down the corpse of a dead boy from the tree. Given that no matter how hard an era they lived in, how inured to pain they thought they were, this harrowing task was enough to finish even the happiest of happy couple's employment.

So it was that after two hundred years of insanity, fear, sadness and zero rental income, the College authorities decided to take real action on behalf of students and their families. Following a cost-benefit analysis that led on from the risk analysis, the oak tree was cut down, the maze was filled in, and it was decided to rent the cottage to whoever would take it with the proviso that if possible the occupant would keep an ear out for possible distress. This was part of the rental contract, and it enabled the College to assure parents and guardians that a watch was still kept on the now denuded hilltop. Every few months or so, a junior member of the college staff accompanied by a workman would climb the hill and fill in any new maze work.

For the last ten years Dr Alice Wilson (PhD) had rented the cottage. It suited her. On this Sunday morning she was reading *The*

Sunday Times and drinking very, very sweet, black coffee. Her breakfast was usually two tumblers of Smirnoff vodka that would fortify her until her lunchtime drink but this morning, as happened every so often, she'd not felt the need. Every time she finished an article she would sit up a little straighter in her high-backed chair and look out of her window onto the hill and out over the city. She had got up early, her hangover, mild, had been forgiving, almost friendly. As usual she had thanked herself for getting the Sunday paper delivered rather than having to trudge down to town and back up the hill.

"Well done, well done. Remember, a daily affirmation is always helpful and all that bollocks", she said out loud.

Walking through the meadows towards the hill neither Fawley nor Lunsford had broached the subject that had divided them earlier. They walked a steady pace, side by side now, taking in the weak sunlight. The more they walked, the less angry and the more upset Lunsford became. In fact, he was enjoying the icy, fresh air.

"Best turn around and go home again before it's too late. Stay in the house, you don't want to go up that hill, nothing good's going to come from this walk with this bastard", said his father.

Then they heard Adelaide shrieking in obvious pain. They turned to each other, said nothing then and headed off to find her. What they found instead was Thomas Vyvian Sarson-Taylor standing over Adelaide whose head and upper torso were already deep inside another hole. Both of his hands were on her back pushing hard. He was yelling and laughing, "Go on in my girl. Go on! Go on! You savage! You beast! Go on you bitch! Have old Brock before he has you! You savage! You beast! Damn you!"

Her head and most of her body were wedged down in the badger's sett. They heard her shrieking again, muffled, harrowing, because the dog was fighting back but it only had its teeth free versus the badger's claws. Fawley, hawthorn stick ready in his fist, ran yelling, "Let her go! Let her go now!" and barged Sarson-Taylor out of the way. Lunsford, who hadn't seen rage like it in anybody let alone Fawley, pulled the dog away, the badger snarled and reversed into its peace.

Fawley was transformed, his willowy body was just muscle. His long, thin face had become a stark facade behind which was hatred burning visible through the black holes of his eyes. His mouth was agonisingly wide open showing sharp, sharp teeth and he was spitting blood because he had bitten down on his own tongue. He was screaming. Lunsford was astonished. The badger that had carved into Adelaide's face and chest with its filthy jaws that had only recently finished gnawing on a rat.

"Fawley! Stop! Stop! She's alive, she's breathing!", Lunsford made a grab for Fawley's upraised arm before the younger man could bring the hawthorn club down on Sarson-Taylor, who was cowering and trying to make himself heard.

"Don't! Don't! I was saving it! I was saving her! I was saving the bitch. Don't hit me! You mustn't!"

Sarson-Taylor was on his back in the stinging nettles and dock leaves, in the mud and melting snow clutching his bag, which had spilt its contents around him. Quarter bottles of booze, barbed fishing hooks, shotgun cartridges, playing cards and letters in slit-open envelopes, boxes of matches and feathers scattered on him and around him. He was sobbing and pointing at Adelaide.

"I was saving her! Kill the badger! Kill it. Kill the fucking beast!" he screamed.

Fawley stopped and brought his stick to his side. He held out his hand to take the other man's. He helped him up still saying nothing, still seething. Once Sarson-Taylor was on his feet, Fawley knelt to deal with Adelaide. Lunsford joined him while Sarson-Taylor collected his detritus and drank his whiskey.

"We need to get her some help", said Fawley. Lunsford nodded and picked up the dog who whimpered quietly. She was badly gashed, she was bleeding, her eyes were clawed closed and her breathing was shallow.

"This way", Fawley moved off towards Mizmazz Hill.

"Where are we going, Fawley?" asked Lunsford.

"Into town, to a vet, we can't deal with this, look at her!"

"On a Sunday?"

Sarson-Taylor spoke up, "No, wait. I know someone. I know someone who can help. She lives on the hill, she lives in Watchman's Cottage. She's got a telephone, she's closer, we can call. This way".

Fawley looked at Lunsford who nodded an agreement. Much as they distrusted and were disgusted by the other man, this was the best plan.

"What if he's lying?" asked Lunsford?

"He probably is".

"I'm not lying. I saved your bitch from that vicious beast. I've risked rabies! I could have died. I am a good man. I am. Why on earth would I lie?"

"There's a drink in this somewhere for you?" Fawley shrugged.

Sarson-Taylor looked sheepish and then switched to outraged and hurt, "What if there is? What difference would that make to you? It's the hound that should be the worry".

Now snow was falling, and it was difficult to know if Adelaide was shaking with shock or with cold. Fawley shrugged again and started walking up the path that led to the top of Mizmazz Hill. Nobody said a word until they reached the summit past the stump of the oak tree, which stood by some freshly scratched markings on the wet ground. They went through the front gate of Watchman's Cottage behind Sarson-Taylor.

CHAPTER 28

A MEETING ON MIZMAZZ HILL

1978

Sarson-Taylor beat his fist on the front door of Watchman's Cottage and was preparing to do so again as he waited for Alice Wilson to rouse herself from what he imagined was a mighty Saturday night binge. He just wanted to offload the dog and have a drink. Helen was always good company, or at least she could be relied on to have a bottle on the go, which amounted to the same thing.

He hadn't the faintest idea if she had a working telephone, but he was absolutely certain that she'd have booze in, and fags and maybe cheese and bread for toasted cheese with Worcester sauce. He'd met her at an Alcoholics Anonymous meeting years before. He'd been forced to go by his siblings, "or no more moolah for you, Tumbledown Tom". So, he went for a few meetings until the whole thing blew over. He'd sat next to Alice and he could smell how much she wanted to commit to all the hustle and the rules. She reeked of booze but not of any desperation to go clean, a desperation he'd also lost a long time before. She wanted to go clean, but she didn't seem to need to.

He liked being pissed. Every time his kidneys ached or his piss turned the colour of old treacle, or his face felt like it must surely slip off the front of his skull down into the lavatory bowl or the gutter; every time these things happened it was because he was sobering up not because he was drunk. Drunk was normal, everything else was terrifying.

He wanted to die of drink because that's what the best of the Sarson-Taylors had done down the centuries. It was a romantic way to end and, anyway. No one would mind.

Not a single person in his family that's for certain. Maybe the members of the BDFP would, they had taken him to their hearts. Good, solid, English stock. Salt of the Earth types. They respected his family name and its history more than the actual family did. With all its overseas investments and divestments and foreign deals; with Europe this and Europe that, and no time for Thomas Vyvian Sarson-Taylor, the family had lost its way.

"Yes, what?" Alice was at the open door and she was annoyed at being torn away from her reading and her cup of coffee and her fag.

"Alice! Professor Wilson! Good Day! I found myself passing and I thought I'd pop in. I've brought some good friends. May we come in?"

Fawley, with Adelaide in his arms, didn't bother with a response and barged through into the main room of the house. "Vyvian here tells that you're good with dogs".

"I did not. I said that the prof might have a working telephone. You are still connected are you not professor?"

Dr Alice Wilson looked at Fawley and then looked again. She thought she recognised him but she had no idea where from. A pub? Probably. Some awful academic conference? Quite likely. From university? She looked again but couldn't quite remember.

Then she saw that the dog was dripping blood onto her floor and realised that, as usual, Sarson was telling lies. Par for the course. It wasn't as if the uncarpeted floor hadn't seen worse than dog's blood. She picked up the papers and laid them under the flow. Then she grabbed a cushion from the sofa, put it on a clean part of the floor and covered that too.

"Put him down there, and we'll see what we can do".

"Thank you... Miss?" Lunsford asked.

"Alice, for goodness sake call me Alice", she replied.

"She's a professor, you know", said Sarson-Taylor looking at the bottles on the shelves.

She glowered at him, before replying to Fawley, "I'm merely a PhD, I'm afraid. A doctor but not the useful kind. Have we met?"

"Not really time for that, can we use your telephone? Do you have a phone book? You don't know any vets do you?" Fawley asked.

"It's over there, the book is in the same cabinet. And no, I'm afraid I don't".

"Lunsford can you make the call please? I don't get on with those things", asked Fawley who looked genuinely concerned.

Happy that he had something useful to do, Lunsford walked past Sarson-Taylor, who was eying up a nearly full bottle of vodka that was sitting between copies of *Folk Heroes and Village Villains* and *Crosschester's Ghostly Visitors: Migratory Spirits Then and Now.*

He found a suitable telephone number and dialled it and waited.

"No answer. Told you, it's Sunday", Lunsford was panicking.

Sarson-Taylor snapped at him, "It's Crosschester for Christ's sake, the only things more numerous than veterinarians are pubs and farmers! Here, give me that thing".

He took a notebook from one of the numerous pockets in his waxed jacket, dialled and spoke to the person at the other end with a surprising authority.

"Well, I don't care I say! Get someone over to the Watchman's Cottage on the hill, fast as you like. The bitch doesn't have long and she's a prize hunter of the Dad. You mustn't want to let him down I'm certain. Good. Good. Be quick, post-haste and all that guff", unnecessarily he slammed the phone down.

He then turned to the room and waited for the effusive thanks he so richly deserved. There was silence. Very cold, very definite, very much a 'you horrible little bastard' sort of silence. Sarson-Taylor was honestly and obviously shocked by the reaction. He was hurt and the hurt burrowed in and down as it always did, joining all the other hurts and slights and unfairnesses he'd swallowed since he was old enough to understand.

"What? I've got you a vet haven't I? So bloody ungrateful. Your type always are though.

"Alice, may I have a stiffener please?" He found a tumbler in the old glass fronted cabinet and poured himself a shot that Stalin would have baulked at.

"We'll all believe that when we see it. For all we know you were talking to the Speaking Clock. And no, you may not have a snifter",

Alice took the glass from Sarson-Taylor and swallowed the vodka.

Fawley checked Adelaide, there were several nasty cuts to the face, her chest was heavily wounded but she was breathing, in fact she was nodding off.

"So, gentlemen", Dr Wilson determinedly looked at Lunsford and Fawley, "would you like a drink?"

"Is there any chance of a cup of tea?" asked Fawley.

"Absolutely, there is", she replied.

"But first, what in fact are you doing with an injured dog on Mizmazz Hill on a Sunday morning?"

Lunsford spoke up, "Just a walk, just to clear the cobwebs".

"That's not strictly true is it Lunsford?", said Fawley. "My friend here has been going through a pretty rough time and is quite low". Lunsford flinched at such a personal revelation.

"He was involved in a hit and run in Crosschester. His close friend from school, from the Navy, from his work was killed, right before his eyes. He spent time in hospital", it was Alice Wilson and Fawley's turn to flinch. "And this was after his wife died", he paused, "of cancer".

Alice looked at Lunsford and made the face that English people make in the face of desolating tragedy: an amalgam of between smiling of embarrassment and a frowning with sympathy, all eyebrows and lips.

"That all sounds absolutely awful for you, awful", she said.

Fawley continued, "My good friend Lunsford here with his friend Mick had produced plans for a grand new building in the city. We thought it might be a good idea to go and see it. To give him a sense of achievement".

"Why today?"

"Why not today?"

"Which building is it? Would I know it?" asked Dr Wilson genuinely interested.

"It's The Wulfric Hall up the hill from the Market Cross where Taylor Street meets The Porthampton Road".

Sarson-Taylor looked confused, "The new hall? The Wulfric? It does look grand!", he took a bottle from one of his pockets and sipped.

"Not enough windows. Not enough windows by far", said Lunsford, remembering when Jarvis had drawn thick red lines through their banks of beautiful, simple, elegant windows along the west and east sides of the building.

"Light must come from the words, from the truths that are spoken in this hall. Too many windows interfere. Remove them", Jarvis had declaimed as if he had originated this idea. Under duress and feeling a strange loss for the first time on the project, Mick and Lunsford deleted the light.

"Oh god, that thing", said Alice before realising how hurtful that probably sounded. "Why don't I go and get the tea?" and off she went into the barely used kitchen.

Sarson-Taylor took up a tumbler and a bottle of vodka he'd found and poured some in, then added some more for a good measure.

"I know that building. I think it's wonderful. I've been in it. In fact, I've been invited to speak there at an especially important meeting to be held for the city, the county, maybe even for the country and our people". He was beaming with self-importance.

"For the country? For our people? What do you mean?", asked

Fawley, looking at Adelaide who had drifted into sleep.

"We've had enough. It's time we took a stand", said Sarson.

"Who's "we"?" asked Fawley.

Alice had returned to the sitting room with a tray on which were tea things and some revered looking chocolate digestive biscuits, "Had enough of what? What on earth do you have to complain about?"

"It's time we took a stand against the invaders to our land, our culture, our history!" said Sarson-Taylor, hiding the tumbler underneath his seat and parroting what he'd heard at several British Democratic Freedom Party meetings recently.

"Help yourselves to mugs, I'm sorry I have no sugar or honey… or milk". Alice sat down on the baggy sofa next to Lunsford and turned her face to Sarson-Taylor.

"Vyvian, the last time we spoke at any length you were going to write a monograph on freshwater fish and the tactics required to hunt and catch them over changing seasons. Now it's Invaders and History and Our Culture?" She took a sip of black tea but thought about vodka and to be free of company.

Sarson-Taylor dug into the patchwork of polemic that had been spoken at him by the members of the BDFP.

"I come from an ancient family, an ancient English family with a heritage and a history dating back before the Norman Conquests. We are in the Doomsday Book".

"Domesday", corrected Alice and Fawley in unison.

Sarson-Taylor spat back, "No matter. No matter. Nitpicking, nitpicking. Exactly the type of behaviour I would expect from your type of person".

"My type of person?" Fawley sat up straight.

"Yes, the traveller type, the tinker. The eternal wanderer. The cosmopolitan. No roots and no loyalties except to your own kind. No culture. No blood of your own".

Fawley shrugged. He'd tried to like the bloke since they'd first met in The Phoenix on a day in May with horses grazing on the Green, and men discussing cricket, smoking pipes and warming their ale. He wasn't somebody who usually gave up but this time there was no point continuing. Sarson-Taylor was boiling for a fight, which he would lose because Fawley could easily snap him in two, and they both knew it.

"Do shut up Thomas, you silly little man", snapped Alice. Sarson-Taylor deflated mainly because he wanted to stay on with the warmth, the booze and some company that made him believe he wasn't drinking alone.

"You shut up", he mumbled at Fawley, who shrugged again.

Lunsford said his thanks for the tea, and bit into a pallid looking chocolate biscuit that bent but refused to break in his mouth.

"What's going on? Where's the vet? What are these people talking about? Why don't I just leave here? Go home? The dog. Adelaide. Never a bloody word of judgement. Never a look of doubt. I love that stupid dog", he thought.

"Queer bastard", Frank was still in his head.

"Oh Frank, let it all go. You're dead. Can't you relax? You've got all eternity to be in. Can't you see hope? Change? Even a little pleasantry? Oh Frank, sometimes I wonder how you managed to produce my sweet man", Chloé sounded a little annoyed.

Fawley stroked Adelaide. Alice opened a book about Palaeolithic structures in the local area and paged through it with little attention. Outside the snow was melting and Mizmazz Hill was soaking up the thaw-water as it did with all the liquid that fell on it. Sarson-Taylor couldn't stand silence because in it were the secrets of other people's unspoken but mutually recognised judgements of him. He knew what everybody else thought about him. He knew that people were constantly saying terrible things about him. Of course he knew, he wasn't insensitive or stupid. The Party was there to support him, the Party didn't judge him. The Party respected his family name, his heritage.

Now he had pride. One day. One day. One day. One day soon, he'd show Fawley. But this silence. Horrible. He wasn't stupid and they weren't clever. He had a cause and they had nothing at all. Nothing whatsoever.

"Listen to me. You must come to the meeting. It will open your eyes", he pointed at Lunsford and Dr Wilson. "It will make you see all the things you don't want to see about what's happening to our country and our race, our Christian religion, our blood", he paused and remembered what he'd been told about not-alienating the bourgeoisie or somesuch political cleverness.

"I have only the greatest respect for the other races, of course. After all, we here in Albion, and our great Empire dragged many of these races into the light of reason and civilisation. They need to stay in their own countries and in their places... in order to bring those places on. Our country is full. Although powerful and generous we are only a small nation with limited lands, an island race that's what we are".

Dr Wilson stood up straight and laughed, "When is this meeting? I can't wait to come and take it all in. Really, it sounds like great fun. Will you be taking questions? Are there more speakers?"

Sarson-Taylor rummaged around in his bag and brought out a leaflet which he handed over.

"There will be other speakers. Mr A.K. Jordan, a close friend of Mr Enoch Powell, he will be speaking. As will Mr Reginald Fountaine, a comrade in arms with Sir Oswald himself. We are expecting speakers from Spain or Portugal as well. The whole event has been precisely and brilliantly planned and arranged. You must all come along. Even you", he nodded at Fawley, "might learn a thing or two about truth. God's honest truth.

"And you, Mr Lunsford, you're a man who has fought for his country. You're a man who has lost friends. I understand that your best friend was run over by a car driven by a young man driven to hopelessness and suicide by the sale of his birthright to a family of Asian immigrants. Surely you can appreciate the importance?"

Frank Lunsford, dear old dad, was enthralled, "He's got a point. The town is changing. The country isn't the one you and I fought for, son. Remember when you knew everybody and the ones you didn't know, you knew about. You knew what kind they were. Remember when peace came, son, when we had beaten them all after standing alone for so long? How lucky were you to come home? How welcomed and beloved?"

Chloé said, "Frank, you never stop moaning".

"Shut your mouth woman", said Frank, "It is all different from what I can see. The blacks come in from Jamaica and other African places to eat us out of house and home and do no work. The Asians come flooding in taking all the little shops. And as for his kind, that Fawley, his lot never settle; locusts, rats. I know son. I know".

Mick was silent as Frank Lunsford raged on inside his son, but Lunsford could feel him seething.

"Vyvian, what about the past is that you most miss?" asked Dr Wilson.

"Before England withered? Before they started to bury her in the unusual and the abnormal you mean?"

"If you like, yes".

He wasn't a clever man, he'd never wanted to be but Sarson-Taylor could see a trap when one was laid for him. He'd had enough of this, people picking on him. Anyway, the pubs would be open by the time he made it into town. He could drink in a quiet Sunday snug with the escaped husbands and professional drinkers, where nobody ever tried to be clever.

"Come to the meeting, that's all I can say. Come to the meeting. Now I must leave as I have important matters to attend to elsewhere".

He opened the front door to leave and bumped into the vet who he had completely forgotten about. The pair had a brief discussion about horses, fathers, ongoing business before Sarson-Taylor swept out of the cottage yelling, "Tally fucking ho!" as he went.

The vet was a pleasant enough chap who gave Adelaide the once and then twice over, pronounced her years from death and quite the fantastic specimen of canine vigour. He cleaned up her wounds and told the humans in the room that the best thing for her was to rest for a day with minimal movement.

"Can we take her back down the hill and home?" asked Lunsford.

"Do you have a car?" asked the vet.

Lunsford twitched and said, "No, no, neither of us does". He hadn't been in a car since the hit and run. The thought of it shook him cold. Alice, remembering her battered, rattled old motor, shook her head.

"Then I'd suggest that she rests here until at least tomorrow. You don't want to take a chance with one of Sir Philip's favourite hounds. Although, I must say I'm surprised that such a, well, if you don't mind me saying, such a mongrel is so highly valued".

"Oh, she's a pure-bred Australian Drop Bear Hound. Thrives on the chase. She's savage and ruthless when she wants to be. You're lucky she didn't take your hand off actually", said Fawley.

The vet shook everybody's hands in a perfunctory but friendly way and left. Everybody looked at everybody else. Adelaide went back to sleep.

"You don't have to stay, you know. If all she's going to do is sleep I can cope with that. Why don't you go and see what you were planning to see before all the light's gone?", asked Alice.

"Can I ask you something first? Mr Fawley?"

Lunsford excused himself.

"Of course, off you go" said Fawley.

"You're much older than you look, aren't you? You're very much older".

Fawley smiled.

"I'd love to sit down and talk to you about your life. Would that be possible?"

"For one of your books?" Fawley stroked Adelaide and stood up, stretching so that his palms were flat on the ceiling of the old cottage.

"Ideally yes. That would be quite a thing wouldn't it?"

"I don't think so, no, Dr Wilson. I've no real desire to be recorded for posterity. Please don't mistake that for any judgement on your work. I've read everything you've written and there are few other people I would like to have document my life. I'm just not the sort of person who wants to be chained to documentation".

"Well, I can't say that I'm not downhearted Mr Fawley but I understand your position".

"Please just call me Fawley", he touched her hand with his and they were both contented for that moment.

"Although there are other names I could use, aren't there, Fawley? Older names?"

Fawley smiled, put his hands by his sides and said, "Time moves on, leaving some things to fall to earth, shatter and disperse".

"What's going on?", asked Lunsford back in the room, actively trying to ignore his relatives arguing in his imagination.

"I'm ready to go, are you ready to go?" asked Fawley.

"Not really, no."

Lunsford would have been perfectly happy to sit in the saggy, comfortable armchair reading a book, sipping a cup of tea or two as the morning gave up its rights to the afternoon. He felt that he'd probably got over as much grieving as he was likely to do for now.

"Come on man, get your coat on. We're interfering with Dr Wilson's work".

She coughed and nodded gently.

298

"What are you working on by the way?" asked Fawley.

"A book on the legends and myths surrounding a healing character called, among other names, Hāzeni, Chagren, Kanashimi, Mina Amaiera, and Kipu Loppuu depending on where you find him", she paused, "or her, or it.

"She travels in the company of a companion spirit, a silent wild creature who provides succour and devours terrors and sadnesses. In these islands he has been known as Gefyllan Gyrn and Róf Hárasteorra.

"In this county I've discovered a gent called John Foeglere who goes way back past the Conquests. He shares many of the attributes associated with the global traveller myth. For the purposes of the sales, I'm going to call the book, *The Legend of the Grief Taker*. Good, don't you think? Catchy. Sticks in the mind?".

"It all sounds fascinating. I look forward to reading it", said Fawley, blinking as if caught in a searchlight briefly.

"I'll be sure to send you a copy, if you care to give me your address", she smiled.

"Time to go, Lunsford. While there's still light in the world. Let's go and see your work. Goodbye Doctor Wilson. A pleasure to meet you at last".

"Goodbye Fawley, call me Alice, and don't be a stranger".

Fawley stroked Adelaide and whispered something in her ear. Lunsford made all the courtesies required in order to leave someone else's home. Five minutes later they were both out in the face of the biting wind and making their way over the brow of Mizmazz Hill and down along the pre-Roman path to the city of Crosschester.

CHAPTER 29

THE MARKET CROSS & REASSURANCES

1978

They made their way down Mizmazz Hill and along the pre-Roman Road into Crosschester without much conversation. They'd grown quite comfortable in each other's company, and Lunsford even felt a little fond of the gangly young man. They rounded the corner and paused before taking on the road up The Sleeper's Hill.

"Do you wish Adelaide was here?" Fawley asked, maintaining his stride.

"You know what, I do, and I was never much of a man or a boy for pets, but she's had quite the effect on me".

On they walked through the snow on the pavement.

"She does seem to be able to take yourself out of yourself", Fawley said.

"She scared the life out of me the first time we met; did you know that? I was in all sorts of strange thoughts then. I thought the dead were coming back for me. I don't know what I thought".

They trudged up to the summit of the hill and looked out over the city. Fawley, full of trepidation because of everything that Crosschester had done in its past. Lunsford, in shock that he was standing so close to it, less than ten minutes' walk from where his best friend had died, and he had done nothing to stop it happening. He looked to the west and saw the grim, black brick stack of The Royal County Hospital's chimney contrasted against the almost white sky.

"I don't want to go down there, Fawley. What good will it do me?"

"You don't have to, Lunsford. I wouldn't dream of forcing you to. I've no idea whether seeing your building will do any good at all. I just thought it would be an idea to get you to stretch your legs, get out a bit. Look around, get the lay of the land", but he kept walking and Lunsford kept walking with him. Each had his own reason not to. They walked down into the town where the weathered, bronze statue of the Saxon Queen Eadburh stood high on her plinth, goblet in hand, looking at the Guildhall.

"I want to see those gargoyles that you told me about", said Fawley feeling the cold for the first time in ages.

"Misericords", said Lunsford. He smiled at the memory of the mucky wooden figures. He realised that he'd never seen the finished articles either. Not Mick's protruding tongue nor his bare arse. In all probability they'd never made it into the final, awful, humourless structure.

"Yes, I think I'd like to see those too. I just don't think I'm up to it today that's all. I think we should get back to Adelaide".

"Not a problem at all. Maybe we can try again tomorrow?"

The continued their walk down onto Montgomery Street past Pete Pyke's the baker, Daltrey's The Butchers, Pitkeathey and Adcock's bicycle and toyshop, the enormous place stocked with meticulous attention to the children's needs, and finally past the florist owned by the Sarson-Taylor family. They walked past Woolworths, Boots the chemist and the Wimpy Burger bar which was next door to the shabby-fronted but incredibly fashionable Hole in the Wall restaurant. Kings Row and the Guildhall were in front of them, the football ground was away to their left if they turned down, the Westgate and city museum were to their right.

"I can't walk by the Guildhall. I can't see that wall. I can't see him go again", thought Lunsford.

"Oh, you are such a fucking coward. Face up to it. Face up to what you didn't do. You basically killed Mick, your best mate", said Frank.

"Quiet Frank", said Chloé, angry again, thought Lunsford.

"Yes, shut your mouth, Frank. On and on you go, don't you? Just shut up. Leave him alone. Leave him think. Leave him feel something good. I'm here because someone in a car killed me. That's all', said Mick.

"It's true. It was my fault. I'm really sorry", said Darren Craven.

Lunsford heard Mick breathe in sharply. He heard him growl like an angry hound, and then he heard Mick let rip but not at the driver of the car. Mick's ire went straight into Frank Lunsford.

"Frank, you're dead because you killed yourself. By accident. You blew your head off didn't you? Left your kid to find you, didn't you Frank?

"Didn't you? You left your boy to walk through your blood and brains didn't you? You left your wife to deal with your debts because you got pissed one night and started playing cowboys and Indians with your own gun, didn't you Frank?

"You weren't even a suicide, were you Frank? Not even a desperate man. You didn't even have that much heart and soul. You were an accident, weren't you, Frank? You're a fucking idiot, Frank.

"You didn't even check your own gun, did you Frank? The accident of a pissed-up idiot and you think you can give advice to anybody? You're a bloody chancer.

"You know why your own wife isn't here, Frank? She can't bear you even now. She can't bear to be in your own son's head, helping him out because you're here, Frank. Go away, Frank. Die for good. Stop hanging around".

Lunsford said out loud, "Yes, Frank. Please go. Go away. Fuck off. I don't need you, there's nothing you can do here, go home, Frank, go to wherever you call home".

"There! That's my dear, sweet man, there you are! It's so good to see you again, Lunsford", shouted Chloé.

"I love you Chloé. But I can't go near the Guildhall today. I just can't face it".

"I'm so sorry Mick. Dad's right, he's right about me not facing up to things".

"See!!? See!!?" screamed Frank like a child.

"Go away quietly now, Frank", said Chloé and Mick in chorus, like parents.

"I don't want to. I can't go. I want to be here. I can't go to the next place", Frank paused and the next words he spoke were washed in tears, "I'm scared. I want a drink. I need a drink, you're all cunts, cunts!", his voice faded away to nothing and left nothing behind except memories that were already fading.

Lunsford couldn't help it. He laughed.

"What's so funny? You OK Lunsford?" Fawley tapped his friend on the shoulder.

"Yes, yes thanks but I need to get back to Dr Wilson and Adelaide now. Can we do this tomorrow?"

"Of course we can, of course. Clear your head, eh? Get some space in there for your own thoughts, then come back fresh. We can go and see those misericords. I'll come to your house tomorrow morning and we can see what's what then".

"Thank you, Fawley", he took the younger man's hand and shook it. It was the first time he'd touched another human being in so long. Fawley's skin was rough, warm and dry. Lunsford held on for dear life, memories of Chloé and love, and Mick and playing the fool moved gently from the back of his mind to the front and his heart began to heal.

"Where are you off to now?" he asked.

"I've got someone to meet, she might be able to arrange for a lift up north. I got to think about moving on again you see. I don't like to spend too much time in one place if I can help it. I get itchy feet. I'll see you tomorrow, okay? Be ready for nine, have the tea on. Give me love to Adelaide?".

Fawley headed off in the direction of The Market Cross leaving Lunsford alone on the street with the winter darkness highlighted by the streetlamps as they flicked on one after another. Fawley was leaving. Lunsford was shaken by the news.

"Who else do I know in this place now?" he thought.

CHAPTER 30

SISTER HELEN & THE GREEN MAN

1978

Sister Helen walked into The Green Man pub and looked around, and as she did, she felt sadness and pity. She had never seen, let alone been inside, such a noisome place. The amount of grease dripping down the foreheads of the men who were just standing up defied her comprehension. It was going to take a great deal of persuading for her to have anything whatsoever to do with this so-called political party. The patrons all looked as if they'd just come out of prison that morning, a lot of them were old school Teddy Boys and the pub had a sourly violent nostalgic undertow, a very dark drag.

The Teds were slick, greasy creations of a past they couldn't remember. Born too late to actually fight battles but too early to become part of a new wave, they stood around looking behind themselves for the inspiration that even their parents had moved on from.

Violence over style, she thought. Their style reeked of mothballs, stale ale, Brylcreem, sweaty fists and an England she knew she should love but appalled her. She passed through the mass relatively unscathed and made her sticky treaded way up the stairs. On each side of her were pictures of sporting heroes: jockeys, footballers, cricketers, a large, bald gentlemen of advancing years who was holding a bowls bowl and not smiling.

There were faded cloth Union Flags stuck to the dark wood panelled walls with drawing pins and brittle, yellow Sellotape, and there were bleached out photographs of Winston Churchill, Queen Elizabeth II, King George VI and Enoch Powell. She opened the door to the upstairs room expecting to be met with the same ear shattering caveman music, and grease drenched, smoke poisoned atmosphere, what she found was more like a library full of particularly studious readers. Save for the women at the bar. Horribly over-dressed. Horribly unfit, bloated and horribly vacuous, thought Helen as she stood in the doorway waiting for attention. No one looked up. She coughed. Still no one. She coughed again, more loudly. One of the men sitting at a table over by the window looked up. Such an unpleasant looking individual, he was grey in every aspect except for his eyes which, occluded by thick-lensed, black rimmed spectacles, still appeared to be a dull yellow. He nudged Mr Eric Benson who was sitting with his head in hands.

"Helen! Please come in", she remained where she was until the gentlemen had the courtesy to stand, and Mr Benson had the good grace to walk over to her.

"Would you like a drink?" he asked in a tone more suited to a boy speaking to his headmaster.

"A soda water with a dash of lemon please Mr Benson".

"Most certainly, would you do us the great honour of joining us?"

She nodded and let him guide her to the table where she sat, bag in lap, trying only to breathe through her nose.

"Harry, a soda water and lime for the Doctor Helen Cousins", Mr Benson yelled as he took his seat.

Sister Helen had only one correction for Mr Benson, "Lemon", she snapped.

Benson offered copious and oleaginous apologies, corrected the order and grew even more red faced than usual. He introduced the other men around the table. He was explaining the appearance of this newcomer, a woman to boot, when the door opened and an expressively drunk Teddy Boy in his late thirties fell into the room. He looked up from the floor in astonishment and announced, "This ain't the fucking bog for fuck's sake" before throwing up anyway. Harry Mottram was ordered to deal with it.

"This, this sort of behaviour is why the country and the Anglo-Saxon, race has fallen into such decline", said Sister Helen at the same time noticing with further disgust the selection of fingerprints on her glass.

"I couldn't agree more, dear lady", Vyvian Sarson-Taylor piped up. He very much wanted to be heard today. He'd been thinking about how he really ought to make some sort of a mark on this world, gain some respect, make the most of his potential. Or at least this is what he had been told that he must do, and for the very last time. This time his brothers and sisters had laid it out for him. Variously scattered around the managerial ranks of the armed forces, the Church, and into good, solid, advantageous marriages they were all sick of Vyvian's lack of contribution. Letters had been written and received, read and thrown down in pointless anger. When brother Jo, the blond, blue-eyed perfection of the family phoned Vyvian to demand that his younger brother actually got his bloody life sorted out, "before daddy finally melts".

He knew that the jig was up and work was required. So, with the imminent danger of having his allowance cut to the bone, he had settled on rising through the ranks until he finally sat in the House of Commons in the wake of his dear old pa, grandpa, great-great grandpa and so on and so forth.

He'd briefly discussed his plan with Don Jarvis, and Jarvis was very supportive indeed. Surprisingly so was Stephen Hedges.

"Yes, that sounds about right for you Vyvian", he had hissed when presented with the idea. "You should do that".

Stephen Hedges had seen atrocity from all sides, and he knew which side he wanted to be on. He would side with civilised savagery, with democracy managed in a sensible manner for the greater good, which meant the white good because when was the last time a blacky or slant-eye did anything to improve the world? As for the Jews. He'd seen what they really were, and it had been revelatory. Stephen's road to Damascus had taken him to Lower Saxony in Germany.

Today, and every day since, he was driven by the memory of that one day at the liberated Bergen-Belsen concentration camp. He'd seen the creatures fighting each other for clothes or food, or just standing and gawping, slack jawed, no fight in them. He'd asked a superior officer, "What the hell did this lot do to deserve this?". The officer had replied with tears streaming down his stupidly young face, "Christ I don't know Hedges, I just can't imagine". But corporal Hedges had meant something entirely different. He was trying to fathom what must have driven Germany, a proud, sensible, cultured state to mechanise the destruction of these Jews and Slavs and queers and Reds and in so doing sacrifice itself? Logic dictated that there must have been a reason for an entire country to join in one voice and commit itself to such an inevitably suicidal cause. Such a sacrifice. Such a sacrifice.

The sight, the smell and especially the touch of the inmates at the camp filled him with revulsion and anger. These creatures had lacked the courage both moral and physical to fight back. He had never forgotten about it. Every night his dreams were of going back to that Camp, being mixed in with those half-people, being mistaken for one of them. Of starving with them and eating of them, of turning into one of them with no hope of rescue.

He would wake up screaming for help alone in his bed with the light on. Some nights he would dream of being one of the camp guards he had deloused and debriefed, he spoke German having taught himself from records and books. They were hollow-eyed and cliff-cheeked, they were too old or too young, they were beaten but inside they were still proud, he was sure of it. He could hear that in the disciplined responses to his questions. Proud men overtaken by the mislead and the misguided. In his dream he would try to rally his fellow officers, he would run and run with them all the way to England, to home, to Crosschester where he would be met by wave after wave of laughter from his own people who would strip him of his uniform and fire him at the stake in front of the Cathedral to the music of drums and chanting.

"Bill! Bill! Drink? Come on old man! Wakey woos!", Eric was rattling Bill's bones at the elbow.

"What is this woman doing at our table?" asked Bill, "And get me a scotch".

Mrs Benson was also interested in the answer to that question. She had stopped her conversation with Meredith and had got off her high stool at the bar to make her way to stand behind her husband who coughed and began to speak.

"I was invited here by Mr Benson", Helen Cousins wasn't going to be spoken for by anybody. Apparently I have some ideas that will go some way to rejuvenate your project.

"What ideas?" Bill took his drink from Jarvis and sipped, loudly. A woman with ideas was unlikely and possibly as dangerous as a monkey with a machine gun; scattered, chaotic, unsound. But occasionally, by accident, hitting the target. Stephen Hedges leant back on his chair so that his face disappeared into the gloom.

Helen continued, "I believe that if we are going to achieve anything as a group, as a race, then we have not only to do so now but we must continue our achievements into the future. While educating the mind, the heart and the soul are all well and good, there is nothing more likely to stifle the work at birth than a generation of unfit, weak people taking it forward. The mind and the body are interlinked. So", she stared at Bill, "what is the progress of your gymnasium?"

Bill looked back with absolutely nothing in his eyes or face, "I have absolutely no idea what you're talking about madame".

Mr Eric Benson snorted a little beer and rushed to fill the chasm in conversation that had opened up. However, before he could get a single moist, pork pie-crumbed word out, his wife made her substantial presence felt.

"Do we know you? Do we know her Eric, Bill, Don? I don't think we do. Who is she? What's she after? Have you seen her before Meredith? Harry?" she yelled to the bar. All heads shook.

"So, Eric, introduce me", she pulled up a stool and settled on it.

"Doctor Helen Cousins please meet my better half, my constant companion and advisor in all things, my darling wifey, Edith, the missus.

"Edith, this is Doctor Helen Cousins, an intellectual tour de force and somebody who is aligned directly with our unitary beliefs regarding bringing hope, strength and mastery back to our great nation".

"Oh, do fuck off, Eric", Edith laughed without engaging with Helen.

Helen engaged though, "Hello Edith. Yes, I am a professional woman who earns her own money. I'm more than capable of looking after myself, and I take no nonsense. Pleased to meet you".

Eric was hopeful, this kind of blunt honesty would surely appeal to his straight-talking wife. He could see his new ally and his beloved wifey getting along like two, impressive semi-detached houses on fire. There was a bond, he was certain.

Helen stood up and pistoned out her right hand at the other woman who refused to acknowledge it. If Edith Benson had any spit in her dry mouth she would have aimed directly into this woman's eyes. Instead, she simply stood up, turned her back, and returned to the bar leaving the words, "Snobby bitch needs a length if you ask me", hanging like volcanic ash in the air.

Eric's head dropped and not for the first time that day.

"Well, that's a good start", said Bill, happily.

"I have invited Doctor Cousins to ask her to speak at our meeting. As my wife pointed out a few days back, we can benefit from the voices of a woman supporting our endeavours. Doctor Cousins is not only a woman, she is also a lady, and if I might say so, a bright and feisty one".

"And because we've been let down, we'll take anybody as a speaker otherwise we'll look like another pathetic bunch of yokels baying for the past", said Bill, idly.

"Bill, please. We've got two ways of dealing with this. We can either be downhearted, or we can use this as an opportunity for us to take control and widen our support base", said Eric.

Vyvian, who had been quietly chugging back bad scotch from a bottle he'd taken from behind the bar, stood up.

"Let me speak. Gentlemen, I will speak. I have a lineage, a history, roots deep in the soil. The blood of my family goes deep in the soil here with its legacy and traditions in soil! Here in Crosschester! In England my heritage and the line, the line from, of my family. Before Doomsday. I am a true Englishman, a man of this soil and blood and soil and of this land of ours. I shall speak and the people will know the truth". He stood as unsteadily as he sounded. He was sobbing gently, tears rolling down his cheeks as his flat cap slid off the back of his head.

"Gentlemen and ladies! Especially the ladies. The streets are wet with the rivers of blood", he paused to let that sink in. "This cannot stand!". He took a scrap of paper from one of his many pockets. He had written up speech in pencil, with lots of crossings-out. He coughed to clear his throat.

"Ladies and gentlemen of the proud BDFP. The supreme function of statesmanship is to provide against preventable evils. In seeking to do so, this supreme function encounters obstacles which are deeply rooted in human nature. Human. Nature. Nature not nurture. You can't make a savage into a human. I digress. Above all, people, humans, human beings, us, we often mistake the prediction of troubles with the causing of troubles and even for desiring of troubles: 'If only', people love to think, 'if only people wouldn't talk about it, it would probably all just go away'.

"It won't go away. No. It won't. They will not go away with their food stink and crime and children and Jewing. We may have saved them from Hitler and Stalin and given them freedom but they just keep coming. Inter-breeding! Taking over! And I for one simply do not have the right to shrug my shoulders and think about something else. What Enoch said, what Rafe Roberts says! Thousands and hundreds of thousands of us are saying: there is a total transformation of our beloved land by the niggers, jews, spics and frogs and nignogs and pakis and queers and peasants and gypsies and thieves! There is no parallel in a thousand years of English history!"

"Prick", whispered Don to Bill.

"Is he? Oh dear, never mind, let him blow himself out. He's useful, or rather his family is useful", replied Bill.

"Fucking bellend", Edith said to Harry Mottram and Meredith with no mind to her volume. They nodded, as they always did.

"As time goes on, the proportion of the total population of England, of Great England, of Britain, which we love, the population who are immigrant descendants, those born in Britain will rapidly increase. It is this fact which creates the extreme urgency of action now, of just that kind of action, which is hardest for politicians to take, action where the difficulties lie in the present but the evils to be prevented or minimised lie several parliaments ahead!" he dried his tears with his sleeve, took another swig from the bottle of scotch, and continued.

"We have seen what the coloureds have done in the United States with the riots and destruction of their great cities. We have seen what the Asians do in their own countries after we leave with corruption and with burning their own wives and with homosexuality and with ingratitude to the civilisation that we bestowed on them and with all that, how could they? How can they, with all that, everything we gave them". He stopped dead and thought for a second.

"Cricket! Cricket!" he yelled.

Then he continued in more measured tones, "We have seen what the students, ravaged by Communism, have done in France! So-called intellectuals throwing paving stones at the Arc de Triomphe! Do we want to see this repeated here on our sacred soil? In our jewels of the crown? No! Not in our England by the grace of the one Christian God. Our God? No! We have seen what the Christ killers have done to Russia and elsewhere with their rootless, money grubbing schemes. We have seen in our very Crosschester what those Pakis have done to a once wonderful shop, a memory of sweets and lovely times from our childhoods", he hammered his hand on the table.

"We have seen all of this and yet we are doing nothing!! Nothing! We are letting our culture die! Be murdered dead. It's committing suicide in front of all of us, everyone. Death. Oh, death! Death of our Past! Of our future! Of our future's future murdered!! Oh vile, vile murder! Oh, suicide of the pure at heart! Oh death!

Stephen Hedges, out of sight in the dark, nodded. Everybody else cringed and then cried for more.

Vyvian lowered his tone, "Our country in her death throes in front of our eyes. She needs us! This country that made us from babes to warriors – but noooo, not warriors any longer! – This, our country, is in dire and dangerous straits! We are losing control of, of our past. And past is history! History gentlemen! Thomas Hardy! Elgar! Sherlock Holmes! The Light Brigade! Mr Churchill!

He was shouting again, "We must take back our past because our Past is Our Future! And it is white like we are!" He slumped down on his chair and leant back against the wall, wet eyes closed awaiting the applause.

Gene Vincent snuck up the stairwell from the jukebox downstairs.

"Perhaps upon this Lonely Street there's someone such as I, who came to bury broken dreams and watch an old love die…"

"Anyway, what kind of thing were you thinking she should talk about?" Bill asked Mr Eric Benson, while studiously ignoring both Vyvian and Sister Helen.

"Over to you Helen, if I might call you that".

"Mr Symonds, I believe that's who you are, although an

introduction would have been at least courteous. Mr Symonds if I am to speak it would be about how, for all races in the world, the physical and the mental are in lock-step, both faculties require honing, improving, trained-evolution otherwise they will become corrupted and useless and we will, rightfully, be overtaken and supplanted by races more fit to take on the sacred task of leadership and civilisation".

"Eugenics?" said Bill.

"Yes of course Eugenics. But a perfected form of Eugenics".

"Oh, for goodness sake, I was hoping that you would bring something new. The British people do not understand Eugenics and what they don't understand, they don't like, and what they don't like they either ignore or they fight and destroy. How do you mean to perfect it this time?"

"I have compiled statistics".

"The average British person doesn't like statistics. Doesn't understand statistics one little bit. Why should they? What else have you got?"

"You are very rude, Mr Symonds".

"You confuse directness with rudeness, Doctor Cousins. What else have you got? Eugenics will not fly. Most people do not like to think that they or their families are weak and pathetic and not worthy of breeding. Most people are three meals from poverty. You cannot tell the people we need that they are unfit for their own country. Most people want a pint and a pie and a laugh with their friends, with friends of their own culture and religion. The people who do care about breeding stock and bloodlines will take care of their own. Eugenics is a busted flush and if that is all you have to offer, if all you can do is lecture white, British families on why they are lazy, ineffective, unhealthy and weak, then you're worse than dangerous to our cause".

"What exactly is your cause?" Sister Helen stood up, collected her bag and leant with both hands on the table. Bill Symonds seemed almost to have colour in his face. He also stood and pushed his face close into Helen's.

"Our cause is simple: a decent, safe, clean country for our own people", he snarled. "We are founded as a non-racist, democratic party. We have always held true to those principles and we always will. Patriotism. National Democracy. Political Democracy. Economic Democracy. Liberalism and Traditionalism. Simplicity. We want out of Europe. We want out of the Empire..."

"Commonwealth", hissed Stephen Hedges.

"We want away from the ingratitude of the peoples of our former Empire. We certainly do not want all their problems being shipped over here. We want to be left in peace, the peace we fought for and saved for the rest of the world. We want an end to endless change and pointless modernism. We want jobs and food on the table. We want the right to live in our country in our way without being swamped".

"The fact that you need to point out that you're not a racist party says quite a lot".

"What's wrong with racism!? Everybody is racist! It's nature. Dogs are for dogs not cats! What's the problem?" yelped Sarson-Taylor from his position in an old, velveteen covered chair.

Harry Mottram was up and ready. He'd previously been warned for sounding "too racist" in public, so he couldn't see why the little Toff should be able to get away with it. "Shut up Vyvian, you pointless, pointless twat, or I'll break you. The only reason any of us put up with you is because of your family for fuck's sake".

Downstairs the 1950s were in full swing with Elvis crooning sentimentally about now or never. The men and women who had to be up for work the next day in bakeries and post offices, to deliver the milk, work on the farms and in the garages were all easing their ways out of the weekend. Nothing monumental or world changing was in anybody's minds; as usual Sunday night telly was shit, the weekend was too short, outside it was cold and although going back to work was a pain, at least they had jobs to go to. The evening was unfussed and was going to be done within another four hours anyway. One bloke asked another bloke what he thought about the Pakis moving into Jewry Street. The other bloke said, "Not bad is it. They got some good stuff in there, and they're always bloody open too. Them Cravens never seemed to change a thing and only seemed to be open for about three hours a day".

"And never on Sunday".

"Yup. Never on a Sunday".

"Have you tried them onion badger things?"

"Christ yes, bloody nice or what?"

"I don't really like spicy food see, but those hit the spot".

And once again, once again like clockwork Elvis was replaced by Jerry Lee Lewis and his Great Balls of Fire and the night moved on.

Back upstairs the night had stalled. A tableau of desecrating ambitions was laid out for the world to see if it had been bothered to look. Across the tableau, painted in watery greys and thick reds, yellows and off-whites, was some partially cleaned vomit on a dirty, half-polished old oak floor. Scanning back was the long table by the window. Mr Eric Benson, face red as a Muscovite May Day parade, head in hands attempting to have an out of body experience brought on by frustration and the death of hope. His nearly bald head was shaking back and forth. If you'd leant in close enough to his tear stained lips you would have been able to hear him moaning, "No, no, no".

Towards the window, Bill Symonds and Sister Helen Cousins were frozen in rage and certainty, unable to see each other's humanity let alone their point of view. Right as rain. Correct as soap bars. Unable to retreat. Incandescent face to face with grey, bloodless fury.

The tableau, maybe a painting hung over a never-again-used fireplace in a room with a door that never opened, maybe a Polaroid photograph at the bottom of the sea, depicted Don Jarvis, lanky, flaccid, unmemorable, ambitious within a square yard of imagination, as he walked from the table to the telephone behind the bar. In the centre of the picture, with the moonlight coming through the window framing his wet face, Thomas Sarson-Taylor was ready to go again.

Sister Helen wasn't finished and nor was Bill Symonds.

Bill shouted, "We are not a racist party. We are a party for decent Christian British people who want to be free of the storms of the world and its politics. We are for peace. We are for quiet. We are for the way things were when people were polite to each other. We are for the values that the modern world sees as old fashioned. We want nothing to do with Race".

Stephen Hedges spoke, quietly but everybody listened as soon as his icicles of words touched their ears.

"Race is only a factor when one invades another and reduces it to savagery and brutality. I have seen this. I have experienced what happens when a race brings brutality and savagery onto itself by its greed for the world, its need to be involved in everything, sticking its nose in, touching everything and spoiling everything it touches. I have seen what happens when that race, through its own complacency and inaction in its own defence against peoples it has wronged is brought down to the level of rats, animals, vermin. We do not want that for Britain. We are a civilised and civilising breed of men. We have brought civilisation to the uncivilised world, and it has thrown it back into our faces.

Bill took up the theme, "But they still want all the benefits, so despite having ejected us from countries they continue to flood into ours, they're pouring in like sewage everywhere you look. Damn them. Damn their ingratitude. We want plain, simple, Peace. Peace. Peace and to be left alone", Bill sat down and slumped in his seat exhausted by words.

"It sounds to me as if you're a party not of politics but just of mourning, of grief for some lost place in the world. Pathetic. Life does not go backwards. Life moves on and leaves the weak and those who give into grief, such a pitiable emotionality, behind. We must be strong, and not just strong now but strong all the way down the generations to come. If we are not then we will go under. Thank you gentlemen. I have seen quite enough of your mother's meeting of a political party. You are not worthy of my time and effort", she stood and kicked her chair away so that it skidded into a pile of leftover vomit, and she walked out.

Vyvian stood up, his frog-like face was wide-eyed, what passed for his jaw was clenched. "Gentlemen, I will speak at our meeting tomorrow. My family, as you are all aware, goes back…"

"Shut up Vyvian. Just shut up for God's sake", Mr Eric Benson had seen the future and it was a mess, and Sarson-Taylor was only making it messier. "There isn't going to be a fucking meeting. Look at us. Look at the state of us. You're a drunk who bends whichever way the wind blows because you've never had to stand up for yourself. Look at Bill". Symonds was almost crouching in his chair he was so balled up with tension.

"As for Don, where is Don?", Jarvis had put the telephone back in its cradle and left the pub a few minutes earlier.

"As for Don, he's got as much life as a party balloon the day after the fucking party".

"I'm here guv!" Harry yelled from the bar. "Always will be, just like always".

"I know H'. I know. But you're not much of a speaker are you, mate? More of a doer".

"What about you Stephen?"

Hedges had gone.

Harry looked pleased with this summation of his character and continued drying glasses he'd not yet washed. He held them up to the flyblown lightbulb to see them shine. He started whistling a tuneless, arrhythmic song until both Meredith and Mrs Eric Benson looked death upon him.

As for herself, Edith Benson couldn't care less about the apparent destruction of her husband's latest hobby horse. It had kept him occupied for a year or so, given him a sense of importance after he'd lost his management job at the City Council because the silly old darling wasn't the brightest of buttons. This political thing had meant he was happy to plough away at the Post Office while she got the other businesses into high gear so they could sell up and move to South Africa or Australia or somewhere hot and white before they got too old. She'd find something else to keep him occupied in the intervening months, golf maybe, or a seat on the Parish Council. Maybe he could learn a language. She drifted off into her favourite place: planning other people's lives.

Meredith Brewer just thought of herself as an innocent bystander just watching the world get on with screwing itself. People made too much of a fuss about things as far as she could see. Life was simply too short to be bothered with all this nonsense. She'd never trusted a politician and she never would because, and she couldn't fault them for this, they were out for what they could get. As long as people continued buying beer, eating the stodgy food she so prided herself on, and handing over the cash, she wasn't bothered with anything much else. Let the blacks in, kick them out, cover the town in Jewish Pakistani Dago queers, put them on boats and tow them out to sea, it was all the same to her. She was intending to fuck off to Spain with the lunk that was Harry Mottram.

Out in Crosschester and its suckling villages that Sunday evening, people were watching the television or playing Scrabble, drinking tea and thinking about Guy Fawkes, bonfires, fireworks, and who'd win the league, their holidays and work tomorrow. Mr and Mrs Kharbanda had taken stock and were in the upstairs flat over the Shoppe. She was reading fairy tales to the kids, and he was reading books about the local area.

"I will be heard!" yelled Vyvian, "I will be! I own this pub. My family owns this city! I will be heard at last. I have things to say. I deserve your respect. I want to contribute!"

"Fuck off now", Edith Benson motioned to Harry Mottram to eject Sarson-Taylor, and H' was all too happy to comply.

"Out. You, out", Harry was seething with gleeful rage. He loved this sort of thing.

"I will have you all sacked!", screamed Sarson-Taylor.

Meredith Brewer, ever for the easy life, spoke up, "No you won't little lad. No, you won't. We've talked to your father and he's given us a freehand here, especially with you. Or should I quote verbatim, 'Especially with that useless little tick if he starts to behave like a spoilt brat'.

Harry shouted, "According to your dad who was in here last week, he used to lock you in a priesthole when you were a naughty boy if you'd pissed the bed again or refused your dinner. Lock you in and walk away until you'd calmed down and learnt how to behave. We don't have a priesthole, so out in the street you go".

Rather than put up a fight that he knew he would lose, Vyvian moved to the door as swiftly as he could, turned and gave a weak two-fingered reverse Churchill to the assembled company, and left vowing all sorts of revenge.

Harry was hyper, "We can go after him and teach him a lesson! Get back on track. Make an example". He didn't understand what the lesson would be about, but he knew it would be swift and harsh.

"Do as you feel H'. Just make sure not to bring anything back to here", said Meredith.

CHAPTER 31

A DEATH IN THE GREEN MAN

1978

Eric Benson was politically dead and he knew it. Everybody upstairs in The Green Man knew it. "So, what's next?" Stephen Hedges knew what was next. The entire project was going to die on its arse because it had no foundation in anything other than unharmonised ideas and inaction. Leaders like Moseley, Franco, Hitler, Mussolini, Enoch were all direct, to the point, simple to understand. They understood their people and the needs of their people. They *were* the will of their people: peace, security, clarity, purity.

The people didn't look to them for philosophy, they wanted the opposite. The people looked for iron willed certainties with a bit of mythic backstory thrown in for good value. Bill knew that what happened next was the search for a leader, again. He didn't want the job itself. He did want the cause to go forward.

Hedges spoke, "Nothing is going to happen. This entire thing is a parochial farce. You're a weak man, Benson. Weak and too full of yourself ever to understand what is needed to raise this country up, to defend it. You've never grasped the very heart of what it is we were trying to achieve. All the people want is peace to get on with their lives. Peace and certainty".

Mrs Eric Benson, who had been observing from her stool by the bar, climbed down and strode over, a heavy bottomed, empty glass pint glass dangling by her side. She stood in front of the table and lit the cigarette that was wedged on the corner of her mouth. Took a drag. Held it. Exhaled it.

"With all due respect, Stevie, fuck you. The people – whoever the fuck they are – don't want peace. They want uproar. Then they want everybody as they were, in their own places, in their own countries", she looked to the bar and ordered another drink with a flex of the eyelid to Meredith who jumped to it. Another one of the downstairs denizens had wandered upstairs and pushed through the door looking for a cigarette machine.

"Here, let's see what this gentleman wants for his country shall we? Come over here, mate!", she yelled at the bewildered looking Ted. He was wearing an electric blue drape jacket with black velvet lapels. His trousers were extreme drainpipes, with a long chain hanging from his belt down his right leg, looping back into his thigh pocket. On his feet he wore electric blue brothel-creepers with black crepe soles.

"Fags?" he said in an accent bred from deep farmland and an imagined version of Memphis, Tennessee.

"Meredith, bring us a packet of Number Six along with my drink", she looked at the newcomer, "Filterless?"

"Yeah", he replied.

Meredith took a pack from under the bar and brought them to the table where the Ted sat down and accepted them. "Bitter, pint", he looked at Mrs Edith Benson, "and a scotch?" Edith nodded and Meredith did the honours, returning to her station through the tension and gloomy silence.

"What's your name?" Edith asked, lighting the man's smoke.

"Eddie, Eddie Craven".

"And what do you do, Eddie?" asked Edith.

"Garage mechanic", Eddie was drunk and a bit freaked out at being in the upstairs bar. He took a sip of the scotch, which made him wince. The stuff sold in the downstairs bar was obviously watered down. He tried to make a mental note.

"You're a good one too, I bet".

"Yeah, I think so. I like my job, it's a decent job, I like it", he finished the scotch and took a swig of the bitter to clean his mouth and throat. His whisky glass was refilled.

"What about the football?"

"Yeah, I like the football".

"Born and bred in Crosschester?"

"Thereabouts, Commiton, I'm local yeah. My boys are downstairs as it goes".

The sounds of people singing drunkenly along to Gene Vincent and The Blue Caps grinding out *The Day the World Turned Blue* mixed with breaking glass and cheering came up the chimney stack and into the room.

"It's good to have a gang of your mates. Like-minded folks.

People who know where you're from, what you're about. Same in the town as it is in a country don't you reckon Eddie?"

Eric Benson sat back down and looked at this wife interrogating the young lad. She was calm and seemed gentle, friendly like she wanted to make Eddie the Ted her new best friend. Eric had no idea where she was going with this, but he was transfixed because he remembered that look, the demeanour in both his wife and her target. It was completely familiar, he'd played his part in it.

"I suppose so", Eddie took a sip of the ale and thought about leaving. Only courtesy kept him there, after all he had a scored a packet of fags and some drinks, and he was a gent he liked to think.

"Do you have any kids?"

"Nah, not yet. I'm not married. Years left for that".

"Got a sweetheart?"

"Yeah, why shouldn't I have?" Eddie tried to look menacing.

"Of course you have Eddie. Good looking chap like you. You like a bit of fishing? Some fish and chips? Bit of telly?"

"Yeah, look what's all this about. I only came up here for fags", there was only so much politeness in a man, Eddie was ready to leave. Or fight.

"Yes, Edith. What is this all about?" Bill asked.

Don Jarvis had come back from his phone call at the far side of the bar, where he had poured himself a soda water and lemon that could easily be mistaken for something stronger. He slipped into the chair next to Mr Eric Benson. Mrs Edith Benson ignored Bill, and tapped Eddie on the hand in a friendly way,

"Eddie what do you reckon to peace and quiet?"

"Yeah, it's good I suppose", Eddie was itchy, uncertain.

Gene Vincent made way for Dick Dale who plucked out *Let's Go Trippin'*, forever sharp and groovy off the vinyl and into the hips and groins of the dancers downstairs.

"And what about a protectionist policy using non-aggressive yet effective tariffs to control the balance of trade with both Commonwealth, non-aligned, and aligned nations combined with a non-interventionist foreign policy that would effectively see us deploying only defensively following a withdrawal from the North Atlantic Treaty Organisation in order to promote a pax Britannia state at home?"

"You what?", Eddie was nonplussed so he took a drink. Meredith came over and filled his glass with more scotch. Edith laughed in solidarity with Eddie. All the other people around the table were buffoons compared to Eddie and her. They were the honest ones. Speaking their minds. Saying it how they found it.

"Eddie, do you want to join forces with people in France and Italy and Germany and Scandinavia like Sir Oswald wanted? Do you want to be part of a Continental Superstate?"

"Sir who? A Continental what? Fuck that, we beat the Germans twice, so we didn't have to have anything to do with Europe. Now the Germans are rich, and look at us! I don't even want to be in the Common Market. What is this all about?"

"Sorry, Ed. I was just spouting off some nonsense someone told me recently. I couldn't make head nor tail of it either. You're okay though, got a nice drink? Bear with me, love. Meredith, be a love, get Eddie another drink.

This girlfriend of yours, Eddie. She's pretty is she? Doesn't wear glasses or anything? She can hear ok?" Edith kept going in a calm, measured tone.

"She fine. She's a bit short sighted, me too, what of it?", Eddie drank.

"Eddie, how do you fancy being told who you could or couldn't have sex with depending on their eyesight?"

"Bollocks to that, no bastard can do that", said Eddie.

"It's a thing called Eugenics, Ed. Eugenics. It's a theory".

"Fuck it and fuck any bastard who tries it on!".

"Last few questions, Eddie, I promise", she didn't stop to gauge his reaction, "Do you want foreigners telling you what you can or can't do?"

"Fuck off, that's what we fought wars to stop isn't it, fuck's sake? Great Britons will never be slaves! No surrender to the IRA!", Eddie spat viciously as the expensive whisky slapped his brain around like a Special Branch man at an interrogation.

"How about filling up your pub with their curry and garlic smells and how about them not letting you drink your beer or play your music?"

Eddie just shook his head and finished the scotch. Meredith refilled his glass. Eddie picked it up.

"How about moving onto your street, jabbering away so you can't understand a word? On your own street Eddie? Or in your garage? Or into your kids' school, teaching your kids?"

"Fuck that. Not my kids", said Eddie, was irate on behalf of his non-existent children. He fumbled for a cigarette, found one, lit it, breathed in hard.

"What if it meant capital 'P' Peace, Eddie? What then? What if all that meant a quiet life?"

"It won't though will it? I mean, it wouldn't be", he sipped his beer and became thoughtful. His face brightened as he remembered something important. He stood up, "Britons never shall be slaves!", he said, and then dropped back into his seat.

"Eddie have you heard of The British Democratic Freedom Party?"

"Nope", said Eddie with a shrug, "who are they?"

"Oi! Eddie, it's your round son" another man, taller, bald and red in the face and not just from the climb up the stairs, dressed in a brown suit with his shirt hanging out over his belly stood in the doorway gagging for breath.

"Coming dad!", Eddie yelled back. "Thank you for the booze and the fags", he said politely. He got up and joined his dad, showing him the fags and giving him a drink of the scotch, each helping the other back downstairs.

Edith got up from the table and returned to her bar stool, she took a sip of her drink, lit a new cigarette and turned to Eric, Don, Stephen and Bill.

"So, how long have you lot been dropping leaflets about the place? Months? And young Eddie, who drinks right downstairs, hasn't even heard of you. All your complicated theories and bizarre wishes, all your talking shops haven't reached Ed – a prime target. As far as I can see, aside from being scared of foreigners you've got no more than the Front or the National Party of St George or The Britannia Party or any of those thugs and conmen".

Don Jarvis stirred and smiled, "You won't be saying that when that Paki family starts into your shops and your off licenses and the rest of your businesses". His bland face moved into a sort of smile and he moved his box of matches to align precisely with his tin of tobacco.

"You mean Mr and Mrs Kharbanda? That dynamic young couple who have rejuvenated the tawdry old shop in Jewry Passage? The people who have made more of that place in a month than the Cravens managed in half a century? Hard workers? Imaginative? Money makers? Those Pakis?" she took a drink, drew on her cigarette. Exhaled.

"I'm going into business with those Pakis, son".

Don Jarvis was lost, tumbling after himself down into wretched confusion. He couldn't believe what he had just heard, he turned to Eric.

"Is this true, Eric?"

Eric took his head from his hands, grabbed the bottle of scotch that Meredith had left on the table to feed Eddie with, drank long and hard from it, put it down and shrugged.

"If the wife says so", he said before returning his head to his hands, and burping deeply and satisfyingly. He could see the future, it was quiet, which was a comfort.

Edith turned to Jarvis "Don, you did good work getting that building with the fucking weird name put up. The community will be able to use that for Morris Dancing practice, jumble sales, a beer festival, maybe the Women's Institute cake meetings, loads of good things but aside from that you're a blank little man aren't you? Not a leader. Not even a particularly good follower when it comes to it".

Don stood up, angry, his jaw clenched like a half-risen sunlounger, fists balled, eyes red as a decade old traffic light, "You don't have the right to judge me. You're not even on the Party council! You have no idea what I've sacrificed!"

Edith turned back to the bar, took the bottle that Meredith was holding out for her, jumped down from her stool so that her body pulsated from toes to neck, and ran her other hand through her brittle, black, hairspray mounted hair.

"Sit down Don. Sit down before I knock you down".

Jarvis thought about rushing at her, his fists windmilling, maybe a chair ready over his head to bring down on hers. He'd hated her since school he realised. Hated her.

"Shut up woman!" he screamed in his head, while still managing to sound vague even to himself. He knew that he would stop before getting within striking distance. Bill, who he knew hated this bitch as much as he did, would pile in. Yet even in his imagination Bill just sat where he was and laughed his sallow and mocking laugh.

That did it for Don. Don had had quite enough. Don stood up. Don moved fast round the table to head to the bar. Don was clutching a pint glass that he intended to smash on the bar edge to make a sharp, throat-slitting edge. Don was now desperate to slow down. He looked at Bill and in the hope that he could somehow claw a thin sliver of self-respect. Bill looked out of the window into the snow falling into Crosschester. Don's feet hit the patch of vomit that Harry still hadn't started to clean up. Don continued his progress towards Edith. She raised her arm and brought the bottle down on the side of the bar, smashing it to reveal its fracture blades. Don slid and slipped and eventually came to a stop, on his sick-covered back at her feet. She leant down with the bottle neck, sharp as her tongue, less than an inch from his left eye.

"Say sorry for being so insulting, Don. You were very hurtful. Say it very quickly and mean it", she said.

Don, all tears and sweat and sick, looking directly into blindness didn't think twice. "Forgive me, Edith. I'm sorry. Really honest".

"It'll never happen again".

"It will never, ever happen again", he replied.

He'd never been a fighting man. He would get his revenge at some other time. He had that phone call in his back pocket and would use it when he and only he was ready.

"Get up, Don. Go and clean yourself up", she dropped the broken bottle into the metal bin that Meredith was holding out for her, and she jumped back onto her stool.

"Go home, Don, and do try to stop being so piss weak", Bill Symonds had seen all he needed to see, namely that he'd badly underestimated Mrs Edith Benson and needed to make an ally of the woman. He turned to her and did his best impression of a smile, the kind a man gives his wife when their child has had an over-tired tantrum. He put a stop to the smile with efficiency and said, "Don't worry, Edith, I'll deal with him", he paused and palsied his face again. "We're all tired and on edge. I'm prepared to put any arguments we might have had behind us and we can work together", his face returned to its blank resting nature.

She smiled showing her teeth, "Bill, firstly I don't need you to deal with Don. I've already dealt with him as you saw. As for working together. You make your excuse for a newspaper work from day to day, just. It lives on scraps. If it didn't have Sarson-Taylor money backing it, it would have closed years ago. It's not run a story picked up by a national in years. It has no reputation even locally, an achievement I thought was impossible. No one feels one way or another about it. If Eric's hobbyhorse political party burped and farted its way past tonight's first and last gasp, then you might have been useful.

"The only reason you're here is because you've got control of the headlines and letters pages of a local newspaper. With the proper controlling hand – mine probably – on your strings things might, and it's a big, weak, might, have helped get some sort of message out. You're not here to have ideas. You're here to publish them. Talking of weak men, Bill, where's your wife? You don't have one. Where's your kids? You don't have none. Where's your house? You don't own one. You're the editor of a local newspaper who shakes when he hears a baby cry. I saw that, Bill. I saw you do that. All I'm saying, with all due respect Bill, is to look at yourself before you start chucking bricks at other people".

"Good night", Bill was going to save his dignity. Tomorrow was another day. You couldn't argue with a drunken female, everybody knew that. Bill disappeared into his grey Gannex raincoat and then disappeared out of the bar, down the stairs and home to his small, rented flat.

"No, no, no", Mr Eric Benson moaned, took his head from his hands, looked around and saw nothing, took a swig, and buried his face again. Once again he was drunk, one again his plan had come to nothing, and once again his wife was in the room to see it.

Edith turned back to Meredith and they continued drinking.

CHAPTER 32

MR LUNSFORD & DR WILSON

1978

Lunsford returned to Dr Alice Wilson's cottage on top of Mizmazz Hill and found her reading *The Tiger Who Came to Tea* to Adelaide who was next to her on the sofa, laying on her back, eyes closed, legs in the air with her paws drooping.

"Miraculous, this dog. Simply amazing", said Alice.

"How do you mean?", Lunsford sat in the saggy armchair.

"Well, she appears to have healed remarkably swiftly given the mauling she took. Obviously, the deeper wounds will need more time, the ones on her face for example, but still. She demanded to be let outside to have a sniff and a pee earlier. And I can reliably inform you that she is a huge fan of tinned spaghetti hoops. I'm a vegetarian you see, and I've got nothing meaty in the house. She wolfed them down, if you'll pardon the pun, two tins of the stuff".

"She's healed?", Lunsford didn't even bother hiding his surprise.

"Well, obviously not completely but she's more than halfway there I'd say, not that I'm an expert of course, I'm an anthropologist after all" she deadpanned.

Adelaide yawned, opened her eyes and saw Lunsford and jumped off the sofa. Then, seeming to remember her dignity, she meandered over to lean against his legs. Alice closed her book and placed it on the table.

"I've read some of your books, my wife used to be fascinated by them. Oh, I'm sorry I didn't mean that to sound quite so..." said Lunsford, scratching Adelaide's left ear.

"Mr Lunsford, never you mind. Good lord above, each to their own and all that guff. I imagine what you do might bore the pants off me too", she sipped her tea and smiled.

"I've got to own up that I don't really know what an anthropologist does. You seem to write a lot about legends and myths".

"I do that for the money. Myths and legends sell you see. My academic work is a great deal drier, but because of the drinking, I've found it difficult to hold down any sort of teaching post that requires me to arrive and leave on time, let alone talk to older children sensibly. I'm a terrible alcoholic you see", she sipped what he assumed was her tea.

Not for the first time Lunsford was stumped by her directness and stumbled into another question out of deep embarrassment. "What are you working on now?"

"I'm researching the myths surrounding a character called John Foeglere. He's a popular figure – or at least he's globally ubiquitous – he's an idea all over the world. Tremendous fellow, male, female, animal spirit, bringer of happiness, ender of pain, wonderful stuff, don't you think?"

"I suppose so, yes", said Lunsford who was beginning to drowse with Adelaide by his feet.

Yes, many, many cultures have something about her in some form or another. They all have one thing in common, he always comes into unhappiness and leaves when the unhappiness has gone. In one particularly affecting story from Hordaland in Norway, she is said to have visited the parents of a young child who had died in her sleep in the room next to theirs. He remained with them for months, tending to their garden until he could entice them out into the sunshine to do the same. In that story he, or she, is known as Sorgholder, which in English is 'Grief Holder'. In York she is said to have given succour to several Jews during the mass murders of their kind in March 1190, in this case she's known as Rakhmones or Dame Rakhmones, exactitude is both difficult and often misleading in my line. In Japan she was seen in Nagasaki and Hiroshima, and the Esquimaux of Siberia have a snowdog called The Isuani Kitsanik that appeared after first contact with the civilised world", she paused and lit up a new cigarette before continuing.

"Recently cave paintings have been discovered in Ireland of a Grief Holder, and some tremendous oral histories have tracked him in the form of a horse to the Athabaskan tribes of North America. But I've not enough dosh to get over there so I intend to get off to Norway as soon as I can.

"It's a fascinating set of stories to follow, unlike many other of the mythologies I've looked at, you see, John Foeglere comes with happy endings and hardly any gore – very unusual for myths. There's usually a tremendous amount of blood, pain, viscera, incest and whatnot even in fairy tales don't you feel? Mr Lunsford? Mr Lunsford!"

He had drifted off to sleep wrapped up by the warmth of the house and weighed down by the baggage of the day.

"Pardon, yes? What? Yes. So sorry", he woke with a start, realising he hadn't dreamt for the first time in a dog's age. She shook him anyway, if you had to have company in the house, they may as well interact.

"I'm banging on about my own work again! My goodness, it gets worse if I have a drink, it really does. I'm quite the monomaniac, quite the narcissist. Can't apologise enough. Where did you leave your young man?" she asked, changing the subject and taking a deep, satisfying drag of her cigarette. He straightened up in the armchair and took a sip of tepid tea. Groggy with half-digested sleep he refocused on the room and realised that he really needed to be at home. He looked down at Adelaide who was resting peacefully, then he looked at the wristwatch that Chloé had given him on their last Christmas together. Then he realised what Alice had asked.

"My what?"

"Oh, I'm sorry, your young man. Mr Fawley?"

"Mr Fawley stayed in Crosschester, he's got to see somebody about a lift, apparently he's going up North soon".

Alice sat up quickly and very straight, as demurely as she could, "He seemed genuinely nice. Can you tell me more about him?"

"Not very much actually. I've only known him for a short while, we're not that close. To be honest we never really talk about him or what he does. As far as I'm aware he's one of those types who floats from town to town. If he was a bit older I'd say he was like one of those Gentlemen of the Road that my grandad used to talk about".

"Elucidate if you would", she took up a notebook from that was buried in the sofa and withdrew the stub of a pencil from the folds of her clothes. She licked it in readiness.

"Grandad said that after the First World War some of the men came back to Britain but couldn't find their ways home. He meant that when they got to their houses and families, each was unable to recognise the other. So, the men would leave and begin a new search for what they would recognise as home. He said that they slept in barns and hayricks or under hedges but never in towns or cities. Grandad said that he was nearly one of those men but he was saved by the pub."

"The pub?"

"Yes, a local pub in Shalford".

"Which one?"

"Oh, I don't remember. I was too young really, this was a fairy story really. But I remember him saying that the pub calmed him down, he would go there not to drink but to listen to other people's lives. He'd get clues from them, from their everyday lives, he said. How they'd talk about the harvest or becoming an aunty or uncle or how Christmas was going to see their kids come home or how they'd found a new recipe or backed a horse or read a book or how the household chores were tedious but after the Spring clean the house felt new and full of life. Just normal things".

"What about the Gentleman of the Road?", she was making frantic notes, smiling and nodding.

"Gentlemen, there were many of them", he finished his tea and stood up to stretch his muscles.

"Some people called them tramps. Grandad hated that. Other people call them vagabonds. Grandad called them comrades and, if he ever saw one on the side of the road, he'd stop and chat and give him a few bob. I always try to do the same for the Gentlemen who couldn't settle. I was lucky. I had Chloé, and Mick too really".

"I see, I see", she finished her note taking, the notebook disappeared and the stub too. She slid back into the sofa and lit another cigarette. "Well, anyway, what's to do this evening? Will you be staying to make sure that Adelaide is fit for the walk home? I've not got very much to eat in the house, it would be beans on toast, I'm afraid. I should also warn you that I intend to start drinking, quite heavily in fact. Sun's over the yardarm and all that. I can be quite the bloody bore when the drink's running you see. It's an illness so I'm told".

"I don't drink that much myself. I don't get on with the hangovers", was the only thing Lunsford could think of to say.

"Oh, I passed that point yonks ago. I'd like to stop but I just can't do it. So, I try to keep it to after the sun's over the yardarm in which ever country I find myself in. Then I really got into it with some seriousness. I commit to it. I wish I was as assiduous in the rest of life, but so it goes, eh? As I say, I can be an awful bore, just rambling on and on about my work and possibly making a pass at whoever's closest to hand. No need for you to worry though, you're not my type, even when I'm drunk. Too old you see. Apologies, no offence intended".

"None taken. Would it be safe for me to leave Adelaide with you, and pick her up on my way into town in the morning?"

"God lord yes!" she roared with laughter, "I've never hurt a living thing in my life in my cups or out. Are you sure you don't want to stay the night? The sofa's ever so comfortable and it's a long dark walk back to Shalford". She was genuinely and completely happy for him to stay.

Lunsford, however, was exhausted and needed his sleep. Adelaide had moved back to the sofa and was once again looking more comfortable than Lunsford had ever been in his life.

"Thank you, but I really do need my own bed", he said.

"Absolutely, absolutely. I totally understand".

"I think I'd prefer to leave Adelaide here for the evening and pick her up tomorrow? Would that be acceptable? I mean, what with your drinking and all?", that felt like one of the strangest questions he'd ever had to ask.

"She'll be fine, my dear old darling", she stopped, and he stopped and then they smiled at each other.

"OK, well it's getting late and I do need to get off home. It's been good to meet you and thank you for what you've done for Adelaide. I'm meeting Fawley tomorrow morning so we should be here by 10". She stood up and showed him across the room to the front door.

"Wrap up warmly now. Do you need a scarf?"

"I'm fine thank you Dr Wilson".

"Please in Christ call me Alice", she opened the door and without thinking gave him a peck on the cheek. "Run, run dear old thing. I might change my mind about you after all".

He headed out onto Mizmazz Hill and the night air. He felt the place where she had kissed him, and it was warm and was made happy because of it.

CHAPTER 33

A VISIT FROM MRS WERLDINHAM

1978

On his walk back to Oak Cottage, Lunsford had almost expected to see Vyvian Sarson-Taylor weaving along the path wheedling for company so he could drink with less shame, pointing out every tree, house, fence and fox that were owned by his family. As it was, his walk was a solitary one. Even his voices were quiet, asleep maybe. It was the first time in a long time that he'd had a clear head and he decided not to bother doing anything at all with it. He put one foot in front of the other and breathed in the October air.

The night smelled of rotting leaves, it tasted like Greek Retsina wine he'd tried in Cyprus at the end of the war. It smelled of the previous day's bonfire smoke, of football, of gathering snow, and the water running over chalk in the Water Meadows below. It smelled of the apples that had fallen in perfect ripeness from the orchards around his home village. He breathed it all in and didn't feel sad.

He slept well that night in his own bed in their bedroom. He woke early this next morning, just after dawn as the Fieldfares, the Blackbirds, the Waxwings and the other winter birds were making a fuss of the trees. He sat up and felt the lack of weight by his side. Adelaide was not there. But there was something else, something more. Chloé's scent was just still in the room, or a memory of her body. Either way it was the first time he'd thought about her body since she had died. He'd pressed out thoughts like that. He kicked off the bedclothes and put his feet over the side of the bed and into his slippers. Memories of her body had seemed out of place. No, they were profane, sick because the cancer had made her body into a stark, cynical jest, a pathetically malformed clone, a monstrous pastiche of the real Chloé. He didn't want to remember that. But now this, her smell, this was different and brought different, albeit foggy and softened images for her back to him as he walked down the hall to the bathroom.

The slow light of the autumn morning was breaking over the snow that had fallen after Lunsford had fallen into his dreamless sleep. He dressed himself ready for the walk into Crosschester and went downstairs to get the kettle on and prepare some porridge. As he stirred it, he looked out of the kitchen window into the Water Meadows. Lunsford was, as his grandad would say, "away with the fairies", an image that he was very fond of and that his father would use against him again and again.

He put his coat on, found a pair of gloves, picked up his keys and headed out to buy a newspaper and some milk from Mr Eric Benson before heading off to collect Adelaide. He reached the hallway and saw that there was a pile of mail on the doorstep that needed sorting.

"I'll do that when I get back", he said out loud, then unlocked the door, which creaked and complained, and he stepped out onto the path. It felt strange, it gave the house an unusual perspective. Oak Cottage with its front door open was a different proposition to the home he'd been used to. It looked like somebody else's house. He pulled the door shut and made his way through the village.

Despite the previous evening dismantling his dreams of political prominence, Mr Eric Benson had decided to open up the little village shop. In actuality he had been told that he had to open it up because, as his wife rightly if brusquely pointed out, "the stock won't self its fucking self". He stood looking at the door, engulfed in a hangover so utterly filthy that it almost blotted out that old and familiar feeling of desperate failure. But not quite.

"Good morning Mr Lunsford. A fine October morning".

"Yes, lovely", said Lunsford who had looked at the newspapers and concluded that he didn't need any of them. He picked up a bottle of milk, two tins of DeeeLuxe Dog Food: Veal and Gravy, and a packet of loose leaf tea. While he waited for his change, he browsed the various leaflets by the chewing gum and fireworks on the counter.

Through a haze of pink, like the water during a shark attack, Eric noticed what Lunsford was reading. The remarkable speed he grabbed up all the flyers that mentioned that evening's meeting at The Wulfric Hall including the one on Lunsford's hand.

"You don't need to worry about that one, it's been cancelled. Daft".

"Oh, right, thank you", said Lunsford who had no interest in it other than the location. "Were you involved in some way?"

Benson thought for a moment, "Only on the fringes. It all started very well but then, well, you find out things about people you don't like after a while don't you Mr Lunsford".

Lunsford wasn't really listening. He was thinking about how pleased he was going to be to see Adelaide again. He felt more encouraged, and he felt sure that this was down to Fawley and Adelaide getting him out and about. Had she not stuck her snout down to bother the badger, he wouldn't have met Dr Wilson, the first person who had called him "dear" in so, so long. She was an honest drunken mess. He smiled at the thought of her.

Eric the shopkeeper smiled back, "Mr Lunsford, don't you find that the more you see into people, the more you see their failings, their flaws? And the more they let you down? Even people who you trusted to see things your way? Even that sort of people. It's a shame, Mr Lunsford, it's a real shame. I don't know what's happened to this country for this to happen. Where's the honour, where the loyalty? It's all self, self, self nowadays. Don't you find this, a man of your age and experience?"

"No, I don't think that, Mr Benson. I don't think that at all".

"Well, that's good for you, Mr Lunsford", Eric said, with a slouch that suggested that before long Lunsford would learn the same sad lesson.

Lunsford smiled. Eric smiled back.

"How do you do it, Mr Lunsford? How have you got through your life and still retained this outlook?"

Lunsford heard the weariness in Eric's voice. Despite the usual exchange of names, he'd never really taken any notice of the rotund shopkeeper. He looked at Mr Eric Benson and saw a very usual man, the sort who would have been quite out of place on a warship but not in a canteen. A red-faced man with a voice like a teenage boy. He was wearing an off-white apron, Lunsford supposed to make him feel more like the jolly storekeeper he so obviously was not. He wondered how Eric had got to this place in his life.

"Are you alright, Mr Benson?"

Eric was surprised by this question, it was quite definitely not one he was used to hearing without at least a hint of sneer dripping from the dot beneath the question mark.

"What do you mean, Mr Lunsford?"

"I mean, are you happy? You seem unhappy today".

Eric thought about the question, "Well, seeing as you're asking, I don't suppose I am, happy that is. I'll muddle through though. I always have". This wasn't strictly true of course. Most of the time his wife dredged him up, washed him down and given him something he could fix his attention on for a while.

"Well, if you feel like a walk or pint in The Phoenix, just pop over to Oak Cottage and we'll see what we can do. No point in muddling through on your own is there?" said Lunsford.

"The Phoenix?" Mr Eric Benson replied, shocked at the offer of a walk, bemused by the idea of a drink in a pub he'd never heard of.

"Yes, The Phoenix, up near St Eade's, on Hare Rise", Lunsford took his change and put it into the head of the polio child charity figure.

"You've got me there, Mr Lunsford. I've never heard of that pub and I've lived in this village for a few years now. Still, live and learn. I may take you up on your offer, I very well may do that", he put out his hand for Lunsford to shake, which the other man did. They men parted in good spirits.

Lunsford walked home through the slush and considered what the day held for him.

Well, I'm meeting Fawley, collecting Adelaide from Dr Alice and then off to see that building and the Misericords. He was certain the misericords wouldn't be there, that they'd never been there. "After that, I'm not so sure", he said out loud.

He waited for his other voices to intercede but nothing came and before long he was unlocking his front door and collecting the large pile of post that had accumulated on the mat. He took it into the kitchen and put the kettle on. It was 8:45, outside the sky was light blue with flecks of snow cloud, the sun was up, just.

Lunsford put the kettle on and, because Chloé always preferred it that way, he dug out the teapot and tea strainer. He added the tea leaves he'd just bought to the empty teapot and waited for the kettle to boil. He took two blue and white striped mugs from the cupboard and gave them a cursory clean.

"Sorry love but the best china's not right for this", said his wife.

He turned to the pile of post on the table.

Bill. Bill. Final Notice. Flyer from a chain of holiday camps. Flyer from The British Democratic Freedom Party. Parish Newsletter. HMS Renown Crew Newsletter. HMS Nelson Newsletter. HMS Ark Royal Newsletter.

There was also a white envelope addressed in handwriting he

vaguely remembered from Christmas cards and condolences to Mr Martin Lunsford. He put the letter back on the table without opening it.

I can't face that. Not more condolences. Not now.

The front door knocker cracked like a field gun, and Lunsford headed through the hall eager to see Fawley for the last time in who knew how long.

Mrs Werldinham, resplendent in a leaf green trouser suit, worsted coat, and Wellington boots greeted him with a look of concern, "Good morning, Mr Lunsford. I'm afraid I'm something of a stand-in but Fawley, being Fawley, has had something urgent come up at the last minute, so he asked me to fill the breach as it were",

"Come in, come in. Please", said Lunsford, doing his best to cover his disappointment in courtesy. He was still an embarrassed Englishmen at this previous drunkenness. He didn't think of it as being in her company, she was too grand, too distinct. As he ushered her through the hallway to the kitchen, he tried to pick himself up.

"She is just a landlady of a pub. She's no further up the class chain than you are. She might seem serene, grand, proper but that's because she believes she is", he told himself.

"She's just being friendly, Martin. She didn't have to come, she's being nice. Nothing wrong with being nice", said Chloé.

"Shall I make that tea?", said his mother, forgetting her situation.

"You're here mum?" he thought.

"Well, Frank isn't. So, yes, yes I'm here. I know we never really hit it off Martin, but Chloé's got plenty of good things to say about you, and I always liked that girl. So, now, tea".

"But mother…"

"Oh, oh dear", realising that she couldn't make any tea, she grew sad. "Oh dear, Martin. Not much use I am? As usual I suppose. Yes, not much use… I wasn't much use when you were little either was I, Martin? My fault, all my fault. What was it about me? What is it about me? Do you love me, Marty? Do you think I deserve your love? Can you forgive me? Can I? Are you there Marty? Are you going to help me?" her voice quietened and disappeared.

Lunsford hadn't realised just how he had grown so used to this cast of voices. When he was younger, he remembered his own voice, and his mum's and dad's of course but no one else's. Everybody had those though, they were just the product of families and were simply repeating and reinforcing what was already known:

I could climb that tree, easy.

I could throw that stone.

Don't jump out that tree, Martin.

Don't throw that stone, Martin.

Get your homework done, Martin.

Shut up, the cricket's on.

Shut up, the football's on.

Shut up, the telly's on.

Shut up, I'm trying to think.

Don't expect me to visit you in prison you little bastard.

I could slide in that mud.

Don't, you'll get hurt, Martin.

Come to the pub, mate.

Don't be too late, love.

As a man of limited imagination, however, he knew that the recent conversations, the ones that had started after the hospital, couldn't just be him repeating childish ideas and adult statements. What could that mean for the future?

"I'll not be here for long, Martin. None of us will be. It's time you got on with things", said Chloé.

"Listen to her, mate. We're all off out soon. Things to do and all that".

"Goodness I love you sweet man but needs must and you need to move along".

"What a lovely kitchen, so cosy. How wonderful. Is that a teapot I see?" Mrs Werldinham with her usual graceful self-confidence sat down at the table and took out a packet of cigarettes. "Do you mind?"

"No, no, please go ahead. Let me find you an ashtray", he found a saucer. "How do you take your tea?"

"No milk, no sugar, a slice of lemon, please".

"I'm afraid I don't have any lemon. I might have some of that lemon juice that comes in that plastic bottle shaped like a lemon?"

"Don't you fuss, Mr Lunsford. I'll have one sugar please". She paused, she could see he was nervous of her, maybe even a shade embarrassed. "How's your head? Mine felt like a cannonball being rammed into a cannon that was too small for it by a lance-bombardier who just lost his fiancée to a sailor – and I like to think I can drink. What did we get up to?! Oh, a mug for that tea too if you would" she laughed kindly, like a friend.

He relaxed and got on with making the tea.

She took out a short, stubby cigarette from a light blue packet, lit it, drew in and exhaled, and the air smelled like shore leave in France. Burnt rubber and dark spices.

"Bloody hell, Gauloises", he blurted out, putting her mug of tea in front of her.

"Absolutely. Gentle Dominic managed to smuggle a few cartons back in his van from his recent trip to the Continent. Such a rigamarole, had to hide them, some fabulous cheeses and charcuterie, and a few bottles of very decent burgundy in a secret compartment. Have you heard of Stella Artois beer? Pale stuff?"

"I haven't, no", he sat down at the table.

"Well, we'll have several bottles behind the bar soon", she sipped her tea, "Lovely brew, now what are we up to today? Fawley said something about a dog and a building".

"I need to collect Adelaide from Dr Wilson on Mizmazz Hill, and then Fawley thought it would be important for me to go and see this building in town that me and my friend Mick had knocked into shape".

"Important?"

He shrugged.

"Would that be the gentleman you were talking about so fondly and stupidly during our session of psychology via the medium of Elder's Darkest?"

"Stupidly?", he had dreaded this judgement and hoped that she wouldn't be the one who would inevitably deliver it.

"Yes, stupidly. Unless you're some sort of super-man and you've yet to reveal yourself in all your taut muscled torso and iron jawed glory, with super-speed and super-precognition, super-reflexes and the power to stop moving vehicles on ice, I'd say that you had no chance of saving your friend's life again".

Lunsford sat bolt upright, "Again?"

"Yes", she elongated the word from middle to outside, "again. Don't you remember telling me about how you gave him mouth-to-mouth before running off to get the doctor after Mick fell out of that tree in The Hunters Wood when you were boys? When he called you cowardly for fearing the height and the fall?"

"I remember so little from that night. I'm not a big drinker. I don't remember telling anyone that story ever. Christ, I must have been so drunk", but the part about not being superman, that had got through.

"Enough looking back, Mr Lunsford, let's get going. I want to see this building of yours. And you have a dog to make you very happy", she stood up and put her ankle-length, double-breasted worsted coat on. "Aren't you going to open your letter?"

"Not now. Not right now. Shall we get going?"

They left the house via the kitchen door and headed through the Water Meadows to Mizmazz Hill and Adelaide.

CHAPTER 34

TO CROSSCHESTER

1978

Dr Alice Wilson looked dreadful, truly awful in a pink towelling, dressing gown, moccasins and with her spectacles lost somewhere in her hair. She opened the door of Watchman's Cottage to Lunsford and Mrs Werldinham.

"Dr Wilson, good morning to ye", Mrs Werldinham was full of the joys and she knew the effect on Alice was grating.

"Mrs Werldinham, you horrid, horrid cow, morning to you too, may you rot in eternal torment! Where's Fawley?", she asked in a voice like the aftermath of a forest fire.

"He had to see someone about something somewhere, as usual you nosey baggage", said Mrs Werldinham.

They embraced and the doctor ushered them into the main room of the cottage.

Lunsford couldn't wait for any more of the confusing repartee, the two women obviously knew each other.

"Where's Adelaide?", he asked, controlling the fear in his voice.

"Oh, she's outside somewhere. She's been awake since about four this morning, and so have I as a result. Don't misunderstand me, Mr Lunsford, she's an absolute darling but she's your absolute darling and I can't wait to see the back of her for a while. Shall I call her in?"

There was no need, Adelaide had made her way in via the kitchen door, she took a loud and very pleasurable drink of water from the enormous soup bowl left out by Dr Wilson, looked up, wagged her tail and trotted over to Lunsford.

"Hello Adelaide, looks well, I can't see a scar anywhere", he tried to keep his joy in seeing the dog so well, but he hid it from no one. Even Alice, deep in a hangover, smiled.

Lunsford turned to her in some awe if truth be told, "What on earth did you do for her?"

"Me? Nothing whatsoever, she just slept on the sofa and then woke up as I say about four, at which time she woke me up by nuzzling and then barking at me. She apparently wanted to go for a walk and that walk was impossible unless I tagged along. So, we went onto the hill. It was quite, quite beautiful but bloody hell, I am exhausted. I'll be going straight back to bed as soon as you're gone in fact".

Lunsford could see a bottle of vodka on the floor near the sofa, it had about two nips taken out of it. There was an empty glass next to it and next to that a half-full cup of tea. There was a full ashtray, and a packet of cigarettes with one smoke taken out and he supposed, dying a death in the corner of Dr Wilson's mouth. The whole thing had the look of a night of drinking that had never quite got off the ground.

"That's right, I'm kicking you both out. But you", she pointed at Mrs Werldinham, "you come here for another hug and don't you dare stay away again for so long again".

The two women took each other in each other's arms and stayed there for a minute saying nothing, just breathing deeply and contentedly.

"Right ho Mr Lunsford, let's be on our way before this sour hag casts some kind of hex on us". Mrs Werldinham opened the door, "No, no, don't bother seeing us out", she blew a fond kiss to the other woman and walked onto Mizmazz Hill with Lunsford and Adelaide close behind. The door of Watchman's Cottage shut quietly and was locked. Dr Alice Wilson smiled and made her way to bed. It was bright cold outside. She found herself missing the dog a little, "Over-tired", she said to herself as he fell into the bed and crawled under the blankets.

The wind blew up the hill giving both Lunsford and Mrs Werldinham the strange sensation of being held safely inside it as they leant forward and pushed on down the incline. Adelaide was ahead of them, avoiding any badger sets or trenches of any kind. Her nose was in the air and her tail was wagging in a steady rhythm. Below them Crosschester spread out from the curve of the River Icene and its mirror of the main London to Porthampton Road. Monday morning on a non-market day, and people were already in their places of work, education, park bench, bookies or court. The streets around the Cathedral were dotted with winter tourists, religious types mostly, not so much curious as hopeful that they would finally find God in this place.

Adelaide led the way further into town via Sleepers Hill past The Green Man where Meredith was yelling at Harry Mottram about the state of the bogs. Lunsford quickly grew comfortable in her company but he wondered how it was that he'd never noticed somebody quite so striking in the village before. On they walked, chatting about their lives, the lives they'd seen and what might happen in the future.

The ecclesiastical court was sitting and was considering the question of a burial at Bursley Cemetery. One fat lawyer was doing his best to explain the minutiae to some bored onlookers. This was just the first stage of an ancient and labyrinthine process that was to get increasingly expensive and bewildering as it went on and on and on.

Another lawyer, thin and haggard, rose, the change jangling in his pocket, he returned fire. As usual in such cases at this time for the year, the green-painted, iron radiators had been turned up to full, and quite a few members of the court were falling into beautiful, all expenses paid drowse by the heat and the effects of too much fried bread at breakfast.

The members of the court who were awake, nodded mostly without the slightest understanding of what had just been said. It had already been suggested that this case could run for month if they were lucky and nodding or occasionally tut-tutting if the suggestion of opprobrium was hinted at in the tone and form of speech coming from the desks in front of them pointed towards tuts was their all sacred and well paid task.

Half a mile up the Porthampton Road was the Crown Court where less apparently holy cases were tried by the same legal crew. Crosschester was a beautifully inefficient machine for the production of judgements, it ground on and on with centuries behind and in front of it, oiled by chancers, the savagely hopeless, the prodigiously wealthy and the universally bewildered.

A little further up the Porthampton Road stood the Royal County Hospital where the lingua franca of highly trained lawyers was replaced by the straight down the nose patronisation of senior surgeons and specialist doctors. All these professionals, both courters and cutters, were working for the good of the people who were a sniff below them.

Elsewhere in the town, Mrs Edith Benson was doing the rounds of her various businesses. As Lunsford and his company found themselves reaching the foot of the hill, she found herself in Jewry Passage at her stationery supplies shop. The ever-so meek seeming Miss Frances Julia Cadogan ran the day-to-day life of the shop. She ensured that the staff went about her business at tremendous pace and if not were replaced with equal speed.

"Janet has sent her boy over to say that she's sick and won't be in today or tomorrow. I have tomorrow off to see my niece before she leaves for Australia", she told Mrs Edith Benson after a spatter of cold courtesy.

"Can you get out of it?" snapped Edith.

"No. It's been arranged as you know for some time now. All the family will be there. I can't be left out", Miss Cadogan snapped back.

Edith liked Miss Cadogan, in many ways they were similar in their approaches to the world. The only difference was that Miss Cadogan knew that she had money coming to her with the death of her father, whereas Mrs Edith Benson waited on no man.

"I suppose I'll get Eric to come in, tomorrow's Tuesday, it won't be a stretch even for him. Who have you got to replace Janet?"

"Tracy Craven, she'll do".

"Good. Right. Eric will help out. How's the rest of the business?"

"Good. Very good. Courts are both in session and the College has put in a new order for those fancy pens inscribed with their crest and that".

"Excellent. See you next week. I hope the family goes well. How's your Kevin?"

"Still in the bloom of health last I heard, only a year left to serve".

"For a victimless crime", said Edith.

"He gave the money back too but you know how unforgiving those Sarson-Taylors are", said Miss Cadogan.

They both nodded.

"Oh well, patience is a virtue. Give him my best next time you visit", with that she wobbled out onto the street heading off to her next meeting. As she waddled past Mr and Mrs Kharbanda's general store she waved and they waved back, restocking the shelves with plastic toys and Findus Crispy Pancakes.

CHAPTER 35

IN FRONT OF THE GUILDHALL

1978

"Mrs Werldinham?"

"Yes, Lunsford", she strode on with Adelaide at her heel.

"Do you spend much time in the village?"

"Honestly, Mr Lunsford, I don't. I did once, many years ago, maybe before you were born but it all got a little too broken and twitchy for me. More straightforwardly the only shop in the place was taken over by that terrible woman and her husband".

"Before I was born?", he was astonished that she thought he was so young.

"Never question a lady about her age, Mr Lunsford", she smiled and walked on

"The Bensons run the Post Office" said Eric matter of factly.

"That's the mob. Nasty. Well, he is, mind like a blister. She is just too brusque for my liking", she laughed. "He, on the other hand, he oozes the kind of small-minded ambition at the expense of people he doesn't even know and had never even met that I recognise from another group of men".

Adelaide ran on ahead of them.

"Another group of men?"

"Nazis, Lunsford, Brown Shirts, Stalinists, Leninists, Black and Tans, Hawks, Nationalists, Internationalists, the Inquisition, so many different names for the same sludge. Awful shower of terrible shits the lot of them. Grandiose, ugly too. The names might change but the tatty shreds of the same bad ideas, the same ignorance and fear are still in the world ready to weave into something new, more pleasant on the eye but just as likely to murder anybody who encounters it. I won't have that sort of thing in my pubs".

They walked onto one of the many shopping parades that made up the modern life of the city. They walked on past a shop that only sold buttons, a shoe shop full of parents totting up the cost of the next school year, on past a cafe selling delicious grease, tomato sauce in plastic tomato bottles and homemade cakes, run by a man from Greece who had come over after the war. On they went past the musical instrument shop with the silver teardrop electric guitar in the window and a book of the songs of David Bowie, ready to entice the boys, and one very particular girl.

"What do you make of Vyvian Sarson-Taylor?"

"Vyvian is a child. He doesn't even understand any of that sort of pseudo political or philosophical flimflam. He's not got it in him. He'll switch back to fishing or vintage car restoration soon. He's an empty little soul and he waits to be filled up with anything that doesn't judge him or see him for what he really is".

Mrs Werldinham answered Lunsford's question as they turned the corner onto Kings Row with and walked up towards the Market Cross.

She continued, having put a great deal of thought into Vyvian, "He's the kind of comfortable chap who never really has to worry. He thinks he's involved, important, that his family's doubtful history gives him wisdom and power. But he's exactly the type who would let his next door neighbour be taken away in broad daylight because somebody else told him that it was the best thing to do".

"You seem to know him very well".

"I wouldn't say that, Lunsford, he's just one of those types who hides nothing from anybody except himself".

They came to a stop on Kings Row opposite the Guildhall. Lunsford stood stock still and looked at the huge building with its two lateral sets of steps leading up to a wide platform where monarchs and mayors had stood to observe temperance marches, the returns of troops, brass bands and parades of prize-winning pigs.

Its construction, overlaid with its ornate, sentimental Victorian cake decoration dominated his grieving. He looked down at where the red postbox had stood in front of the Guildhall for almost a century before the car hit it. He closed his eyes.

"Why have I come here to this place where my oldest, dearest friend died because I couldn't reach him?" he asked himself.

"Mate don't be daft. It all moved so fast. You weren't driving the car. If I had been able to, I would have got out the way, wouldn't I? Self-pity doesn't sit well with you", said Mick.

"Lovely man, you couldn't have saved Mick", said Chloé.

"Don't take the credit for something you had no part in."

"Mother, I did though".

"Please call me Mum, please Marty".

"I can't".

"Oh Marty, what did I do? What have I done? Can you ever forgive me?"

"This really isn't about you, Teresa", said Mick.

"I know it, I know it", said his mother who continued, "but maybe if I'd paid more attention or if I'd been stronger then Marty might have been able to help and save Michael. This has been playing on my mind a great deal. What if I'd done more? Can you forgive me Marty?" her voice floated like scum on a dying pond.

"You're forgiven, Mother. You're always forgiven. You were born forgiven", said Lunsford with bite.

"Oh Marty, darling how wonderful. How wonderful you are. I know I can do better, I really can. Marty, what can I do to make things even better? What do you want of me, Marty?"

"Stop calling me Marty", said Lunsford with no emotion, still staring at the vacant spot where the red pillar box had been.

"I will. Martin. Can you hear? Can you still hear me, Martin? I called you Martin, did you hear? Martin, did you hear me? Can you hear me?", she was fading in and out.

"Teresa, go away now. For your own happiness. Leave now", Chloé's voice was icy.

"You have no right to tell me anything, young lady. I carried my Marty, Martin. I gave birth to him. I brought him up and loved him and then you come along and warp his mind. But he's forgiven me now for everything, haven't you Marty?"

"Go away now Teresa", repeated Chloé.

"Marty!?" his fading mother cried.

"It's time now", he paused, "mum. Time for you to go and be forgiven", said Lunsford quietly.

"I am your mother! Call me Mother I deserve respect not just forgiveness, I deserve respect..." but she had faded away before Lunsford quite heard what she was saying.

He felt a gentle hand on his shoulder and found that he was looking into Fawley's face? Fawley was crying quietly. Lunsford closed his eyes, feeling safe and sad.

"Time to mourn for Mick. Mourn him but don't make his death yours".

Lunsford started to cry, just quietly, just under his breath, almost delicately but with such growing force inside him that he thought his own skull would crack open and throw up all the grief he had ever felt out into the city, flooding it, washing it away and leaving nothing of it, only the ancient land beneath it, the river and then the trees. Fawley, towering over him, sang words of encouragement and love, and held him gently until the sobbing stopped. Only a few seconds, less than a minute but forever because such sadness for the loss of loved ones never leaves for good. It reaches into time and pulls itself forward leaving you in its wake and wash. Lunsford felt Fawley's embrace loosen and evaporate, releasing the pressure inside Lunsford who continued to stand still with his eyes closed. He relished the cold and the stillness and the smell of impending snow, the sort that allowed you to stay indoors and look out at the beauty of the land.

"See you one day maybe, Lunsford, much love to you and future. Love and future!", he heard Fawley say.

He coughed, rubbed his eyes, opened them and saw that Mrs Werldinham was standing next to him.

"Where's Fawley?"

"Somewhere about town I imagine".

"Where's Adelaide?"

"She's over there", she pointed towards the Guildhall, "Weeing on that new red letterbox they're putting in place, the bad, bad dog. Adelaide! Stop that at once!" Adelaide refused until she was quite done, at which time she crossed back over Kings Row and rejoined the company, tail wagging frantically.

Mrs Werldinham looked at her wristwatch, "Why don't you nip into the bus station loos and clean your face up, take a gulp of water, sort yourself out and then let's go. I've a great surprise for you. It's no good, I can't keep it in any longer. I took the liberty of booking us a table at The Chop House for an exceptionally long, very lazy, very pleasurable lunch. We will get pissed. Then we can go and see your building".

Lunsford looked concerned, he knew The Chop House was exclusive and expensive.

"On me, of course", she said, "Get on with you, go and clean up". He turned away and walked into the bus station. He was expecting to feel shaken and weak but he felt the opposite. He was expecting to hear his voices. He heard nothing but the buses coming and going, the newspaper seller yelling a headline about Dangerous African Gangs. Two old, tartan trolley ladies were chatting about a college boy carried off by the Icene's dangerous currents and washed up, freezing but alive in Commiton by the bridge. "It always gets like that after a big snow fall. Did it in '47 and '63, and it'll do it again. People should be aware but they just forget and go and jump in to show off".

"I heard he was pissed".

"Pissed. Pushed. Jumped in. Same difference".

"Yes, same difference. Where is this bloody bus?"

"Always late, the 47, always late".

They nodded and blew warmth into their woollen mittens.

Lunsford made his way to the bus station lavatory, which was sparkling clean and looked after. He tidied himself up. He took a breath and realised he was famished.

Back at the Guildhall, Mrs Werldinham was smoking a long, slim, black cigarette. Adelaide was bored and looking for something to do.

"Lunsford! You've brushed up well. If I were a younger woman, well, I couldn't hold myself back I'm sure".

"Mrs Werldinham, you're younger than me", he laughed and looked a little more closely at her and felt unsure.

"Are you ready to eat some fabulous nosh, Lunsford? And to drink some astonishing wine?"

"I'm more of a beer drinker myself", he said.

"Jolly good, let's go, I know the chef and his wife, you'll like them very much, very down to earth".

CHAPTER 36

A SLAP-UP MEAL

1978

Before long they were standing in The Chop House restaurant where Mrs Werldinham was deep in conversation with the young woman who greeted them at the door. Lunsford only heard one side of the conversation, but it made him glad indeed that he'd come.

"Are you a pudding man, Lunsford?!" she asked over the warm hubbub. Before he could reply she grabbed his hand and pulled him forward into the heart of the small, mostly candle-lit, fantastically boothed and tabled restaurant.

"Our booth is ready, and you are in for a tremendous treat!".

When Mrs Werldinham promised Lunsford that they were going to have an extraordinarily long, boozy lunch and she wasn't joking. They sat down with the menu in The Chop House at one o'clock and didn't rise to leave until six in the evening. Lunsford had never experienced anything like it. He wished Chloé could have been there with him.

Mrs Werldinham said, "No point in ruining your own appetite with pointless wishing is there?" And there wasn't.

"Why here?" asked Lunsford looking at the menu quizzically.

"The food is wonderful. The booze is amazing. The people are fabulous. And, probably most of all, it brings new light and air into Crosschester. Innovative ideas. It's like a bridgehead from the wider, exciting world. I wanted to show you that even in this stick-in-the-mud town that thinks it's a city there are outward looking people with ambition and hope.

"In food?" Lunsford couldn't understand.

"Food is centrally important to everything, it's crucial if you think about it".

He did and was still none the wiser. Food was fuel, but he liked the feel of the place, and Chloé had recommended it to Lunsford who, he now realised, disliked new things, flavours, approaches because they were discomfiting to him and for no other reason.

A tall man came over to them, a tall, thin man with a shock of grey hair exploding from his head like a petrified ocean splash after a whale breaches and falls back to earth. He was apparently great friends with Mrs Werldinham.

"We go way back", she told Lunsford. I gave him his start out of school, when was that Marcus?"

"I cannot for the life of me remember. Try this potato with the capers, garlic, butter and black pepper. What do you think?" he shoved a small plate with a long, butter browned, potato cut in half to reveal yellow flesh.

"Bloody hell!" exclaimed Lunsford who had been expecting a

roast potato and got a lot more.

"Delicious, Marcus, absolutely first class", Mrs Werldinham enthused.

"It's Kipfler potatoes Meunière, we're trying it out to go with the skate wings poached in white wine and then roasted quickly. Good isn't it?"

"It sounds like perfection", said Mrs Werldinham, who was grinning in a most inelegant way.

"Kipfler?" said Lunsford.

"Yup, Solanum tuberosum to get Latin about it. Same family as the aubergine and tomato. Named after Austrian for croissant", said Marcus the chef.

"Bloody hell", said Lunsford who didn't understand a word that had just been said, and didn't care one bit, it was the best food he'd ever tasted – a potato.

The afternoon flowed, joyful, into the evening. Delicious dish after dish, nothing too overwrought: a slice or three of rare roast beef with fresh horseradish sauce and a dollop of mashed potato that seemed to be more butter than spud. A salad of courgette, watercress, pickled cauliflower florets, blackberries and crispy fried kale. Lunsford had never eaten kale, it was animal food, he remembered smelling it rotting in his father's unloved allotment by the cricket pitch.

The chef's business partner, Joyce walked over with two plates. On one was an egg in its shell, light brown. "Sliced with a razor blade", she explained, "and then the white is removed and mixed with chives, black pepper, clove, cinnamon, ginger before the whole thing is poached. Then you whisk up some double cream, as fresh as possible with a little cider vinegar and salt until you can see it making peaks. Add that to the eggshell and the yoke, and here you are. We hope you like it", she lowered her voice to a whisper, "We picked it up from a young chef in northern France".

On the other plate, "We have a square of beef shin that we cooked with port and butter in the pressure cooker, then you've got some cubes of beetroot, which we cooked slowly in the beef fat and some salt from Porthampton. Then there are cubes of pickled celeriac, with some walnuts for crunch and more blackberries from Hunters Wood near Shalford for zing, and a little goat's cheese from Bursley to calm everything back down".

Lunsford hadn't seen anything like either of these dishes, "You don't have any egg and chips, do you?" he asked before piling beef, beetroot, celeriac and cheese on his fork and eating it.

"Do you think we'll actually see Fawley again?" Lunsford asked in a pause between dishes.

"He said you would, I've never known him to lie before, so yes we will see him again".

"How long have you known him?"

"For as long as I can remember. Try these peas, amazing. Just cooked in butter but they flavoured the butter with acorns".

"From Hunters Wood?"

"Of course. What do you think?" He didn't like the butter, but he let that slip into the air.

On and on they went, blessed with the food and, in Lunsford's case, the Elder's IPA because try as he might, he couldn't get on with the wines that Marcus and Joyce brought over. They, he discovered, had cooked and served and eaten all over the world: Australia to France, India to Iceland and finally back to England and Crosschester.

"What brought you here?" he asked when all the other diners had left, the sun had set, and all four were sitting around the table, chairs pulled back and cigars and cigarettes belching.

Joyce spoke first, "I was brought up here, so I suppose I did. That's strange because I couldn't wait to get away from the place when I was younger. I moved to London when I was 16. Crosschester was such a small-minded place back then. Reliant on gentlemen farmers who despised change in any form in any sphere of life, who didn't appreciate what they had as anything other than a machine to process money most of them".

"Most, not all, even back then. Joyce is the categorical one of our partnership", interrupted Marcus.

"I am, and I make no bones about it. Anyway, we'd got married in Italy".

"It was a year after my wife had died", said Marcus.

"It was more like two years, love", corrected Joyce.

Despite it being late in the day, she was still clean as a whistle in her whites. There had never been a bead of sweat on her tiny frame, her hair was in a tight bun, her thin framed glasses perched on her sharp nose and she looked out to the world with her bright, ganache brown eyes. Her voice retained its county swing and was calm, measured, deep but was always assured. This contrasted with Marcus who spoke loudly, enthusiastically, at the speed of a city boy who had lived 15 of his forty years in kitchens. Where his partner dominated by authority and certainty, he did so by height and charm. Both of them, however, retained the loyalty of their staff like suns did planets.

She continued, "Anyway, the place was all lazy, chubby with its over-stated history. You couldn't get a meal that wasn't boiled, stewed or roar-roasted to char anywhere in the orbit of Crosschester City. The pubs were dark and full of old men, some of them not yet twenty years of age drinking horrible beer that hadn't changed in hundreds of years. So, I left, saw London, saw the world, learned how to work hard and make food. Then I met Marcus in Madrid and I decided that we wanted our own place".

Marcus segued in as Joyce stopped speaking, "Anyway, a very old friend got in touch. They'd started up a farming cooperative out near Shalford. Having travelled to Australia and the States they'd met a bunch of hippies who were all about natural this and natural that. They invited us over. So, we went over to the co-op for old time's sake and to see if there was anything we could learn. We were thinking of setting up a French place in an old chop house on Rose Street".

"Rose Street?" asked Lunsford.

"Near Covent Garden", Marcus paused and saw Lunsford's blank expression "In London, my town".

"Oh", said Lunsford, none the wiser.

"But as soon as we tasted the…"

"Watercress", interrupted Joyce, whose memory of the cress was a fond and foundational one.

"Yes, that. Anyway, as soon as we tasted those, we were sold".

"Anyway", he took a long drag on a cigar and swallowed a half balloon of brandy, "that acorn butter you had, subtle, a bit malty? That was an idea from the farm. And a pain in the balls to make too".

"Oh god yes. Time consuming", said Joyce.

"But worth it", said Mrs Werldinham, brandy in hand and aware of the time and of how chefs liked to talk.

Joyce nodded, "Anyway, to answer your question Mr Lunsford, this place, which had been a cafe selling terrible tea, worse coffee, unloved and unlovable sandwiches and evil, evil fry-ups became available and we thought, with the farm beginning to have an effect on a few other farms and small holdings in the county, and the county centred on Crosschester, we thought…"

"There's money to be made!" said Marcus, half-laughing, half deadly serious, "the sheer amount of cash sloshing about this place, well, it's untenable that it shouldn't be set free somehow".

"The place was far cheaper than Rose Street. There was an untapped market of people who might want to try something less stodgy, who might want to try food with actual flavour. So, here we are hoping to change Crosschester and drag it into a new world".

"And make money", said Marcus, "but yes, there's hope. At first it was the tourists, but as soon as people look through those bay windows and see the place packed with happy faces, well… in they come".

Lunsford had trouble with that given that since the restaurant opened three years previously and he must have walked past it to the bus stop at least a few hundred times, never thinking of going in. He'd been alienated by the menu at the front and the decor. He had been frightened off by the dark blue, glossily painted frontage with its dead straight typeface, by the colourfully chalked A-board on the street, but mostly by its menu, stuck inside the window. Back then "Acorn butter", "Venison carpaccio with blackberry and horseradish", "Slip sole with in oak smoked butter with Jerusalem Artichokes" and "Guinea fowl with asparagus" had less than no appeal. Although the "Rice Pudding with Vanilla Bean, Crunchy Nougatine and Nutty Burnt Butter" nearly dragged him in. Of course, Chloé had wanted to go with him, but had eventually gone with two of her friends and loved it. But not him, not Lunsford. Lunsford was old Crosschester born and white bread.

"I didn't come in", he said.

"No everyone does. That's not how it works", said Mrs Werldinham.

"No", Lunsford continued, "I mean, I thought all the food looked off-putting. Complicated. Deliberately foreign. Just strange for the sake of it. I mean, acorn butter? Butter mixed up with acorns? Crunchy Nougatine and Nutty Burnt Butter? Why burn butter? What even is falafel and a tahini cream?".

"It's delicious, if only you'd given it a chance", remarked Chloé.

"Did you like the acorn butter?" asked Joyce laughing.

"No, not really, but that's not the point".

"What about the rice pudding?", asked Marcus leaning into the table, "you seemed to like that".

"Bloody hell! Bloody hell, sir!", tipsy Lunsford stood up, "It was the best thing I've ever eaten in my life. How did you do that!? It's just rice pudding after all"

"Let's just say, Carnation Condensed Milk, eggs and a lot of sugar using Jean from Paris's recipe".

"Time is short", said Mrs Werdlinham.

"Anyway, we saw money, great local produce and just the slightest possibility that a community of people who want to look out into the world and like it, and that future could coalesce around our place", said Joyce.

"Ego, money, produce and progress. Chef's favourites", said Joyce.

"As it goes, we're leaving the place with the team here in a month and we're going to travel again", said Marcus. Lunsford looked downhearted, "Maybe I should travel more".

Marcus patted him on the back in encouragement, "There's no maybe about it. Travel broadens the tastebuds, and all other knowledge comes after that.

"The team are great, young, local, trained by us, perfect. There's always a seat for you", enthused Joyce.

"Right, the bill please, we have a place to be. Absolutely wonderful to see you again, it's been way too long between drinks, you devils", said Mrs Werldinham.

"Absolutely not! You're not paying for this. We wouldn't be here without you for god's sake", Joyce stood up and embraced Mrs Werldinham warmly.

"It's not for you, it's for the staff. Marcus, for god's sake tell her, you can't run a restaurant on bloody charity".

It was a half past seven in the evening when they finally stood in the doorway again exchanging firm handshakes and deeply felt hugs. Lunsford looked back into The Chop House and saw it as a friend sees a friend.

"I told you, didn't I, my lovely man? That rice pudding!"

"You did my love, you did. And I should have listened".

"Time for a pint I think, don't you Lunsford?"

Lunsford didn't want another pint. He wanted to stay where he was, warm, safe, around enthusiastic people. He knew he had to be at The Wulfric Hall though. There was no choice anymore.

CHAPTER 37

A FALSE DAWN

1978

Snow was falling again. Harry Mottram found himself standing in front of the Wulfric Hall dressed entirely in black from the Commando cap on his head to the steel toe-capped boots on feet. His hands were in black leather gloves, and he had a double-bladed stiletto knife in a black scabbard hanging at his back from his black leather belt. He was trying to hand out flyers to anybody who was wandering by as they headed to the Market Cross.

He had a set of flyers for the gym, a set for The Green Man's "Famous Sunday Lunch", which was only famous for managing to be both bone dry and extremely oily. There was also a set for Mrs Edith Benson's new bingo business that she was going to run out of the Wulfric Hall itself.

Harry was very cold and very pissed off. He clapped his gloved hands together and blew into them. His actual job was to point any punter who had turned up looking for the BDFP meeting to the pub. He could either tell them that the meeting was over-subscribed or that they couldn't come in looking "like that". So far, however, and with the time for the first speech only ten minutes away, only two prospective party members had shown up.

One was a lad who Harry knew from the good old days of the Natural British Front. He would have made a decent enough soldier for the cause. He was a nice enough young bloke, a regular in The Green Man, handy with a brick, always up for a scrap, never overthought things. When Harry told him that the meeting was off, the young lad simply shrugged and said, "See you up the town anyway, H'", turned on his heel and headed off towards the first boozer that would have him.

The second person to try and push past and go into the hall was a primary school teacher from Commiton. Harry recognised her from a couple of dates they'd been on and a few meetings they'd both attended.

"It's off, Charlotte. Cancelled. Events beyond our control. You know how it is". Harry gave her a peck on the cheek, she smiled.

"What's it all about H'? I read a leaflet that looked interesting, so I thought, you know, why not come and have a look? We've had some blackies come into the school last week, twins, 10 year olds. Adopted by some local do-gooders. Black as cans of boot wax. Can't stop them coming though. You'll never believe the names they have, my gosh!"

"Go on", said Harry, stamping his feet against the cold.

"Yewande and Yetunde Okonkwo", she opened her eyes wide.

"You what-ney and you dotney?", laughed Harry.

"I know! No way our white kids would have been able to cope with those names. So, the headmaster called a special assembly and explained about the two wogs being at school for the foreseeable future and that, to make everybody's lives easier, we were to call the taller one, Wendy, and the slightly less ugly one, by the name Judy. Easier to remember. Kind of him I thought".

"Fucking hell, Charlie. Whatever next!"

"Lord knows. OK then, hon', I'm off to the cinema I suppose. See what's on. Will you be around later?"

Harry thought about it for a few moments and nodded with a, "Yeah, why not?" look. Meredith had ordered him to hang around the place until nine o'clock taking names if he could. Fucking off any Reds or students who turned up looking tasty.

Harry was fucked if he was going to stay past eight, and it was nearly that now. It wasn't his problem after all. Too fucking complicated for its own good was this political life. The world just wasn't that hard to understand. Race relations were simple: you were either prepared to be flooded by immigrants from all over the fucking place or you weren't. Easy. They were either in or out of this mighty but full-up country. Harry thought of himself as thoroughly racist because he couldn't see what was wrong with that. Everybody was, blacks against yellows, yellows against browns, everybody against the whites. It was just that most people were too fucking spineless to admit it for reasons he couldn't work out.

The snowfall abated and Harry decided enough was enough. If people were stupid enough to come out on a night like tonight and listen to other people talking, well more fool them. He went into the hall and found the key holder who was sitting on one of the few chairs not stacked against the wall. They exchanged a few words, Harry didn't like him because of his nose. They parted, Harry to a drink in The Fighting Cocks, and the other man to lock up and go home on his own.

"Hello Harry, how's things?" Thomas Vyvian Sarson-Taylor, swaying from left to right, stood in front of the hall. "I hear the hall's going to be used for Morris Dancing or something or for the new Quaker meeting house, which seems fun".

"Go away cunt", Harry tried to push past the reeling drunk.

"Are you going to make me?" slurred Sarson-Taylor.

"Oh, for fuck's sake haven't you learnt your lesson you little prick?"

Vyvian dropped his balled up hands to his sides, leant against the wall and asked, "Why do you hate me so virulently, Harry? What have I ever done to you?" He looked up into the taller man's eyes for a human connection, for sympathy, even pity would do. Harry was having none of it. He looked over Sarson-Taylor's head down the street to the Market Cross. A large group of people holding flaming torches were milling about ready to march up the hill to mark the annual autumn festival, the origins of which no one could remember. The procession finished at a small patch of green land opposite The St Mary Godwin pub. Then the people would gather around a large bonfire, kids on their shoulders all cosy in their warm coats, mittens and bobble hats. Then fireworks would be let off and the people sang a song that was a mixture of Christian hymns and tunes from a forgotten time. Then the ones with children headed home while the others packed the pub. This had happened every year in late October, for as long as it was possible to remember, with no one knowing why. The words of the song were simple, and the song was short. Every singer, everybody, took the part that fell most naturally to them, and harmony was always achieved.

Oh Lord bless our beautiful county,

Your bounty of hope and of love

Oh Lord bless our beautiful city,

Held safe by the spirit above

Oh Lord bless us for what we offer

And stay with us through the cold nights

Oh, Lords bless our beautiful city,

As we worship you in our adoring praise

Everybody had to remember to sing, "Lords" not "Lord" on the penultimate line. No one knew what that might conjure up, so tradition demanded the plural and year-in and year-out that's what she got.

Harry looked on over Sarson-Taylor's head as the procession started to snake from the Market Cross up the hill, its spine alight and flickering against the snowy grey blackness of the sky. Their shadows were huge and calm against the ancient buildings that crowded the road.

Harry shivered and returned his concentration to Vyvian and his whining question.

"You're a waste of air, Vyvian. I've met Jews I'd trust more than you", this was false. As far he was aware, he'd never actually met a Jew in his life. He was quite incorrect in this assumption though, what he hadn't met were any of his imagined hooked-nosed, thick-lipped, drinkers of babies' blood.

"Vyvian, no one has the fucking time to hate you or even care for you in any way as far as I can tell. Now do yourself a favour and just fuck off. Find a new hobby, top yourself for all I care but get out of my fucking face because it's cold and I've got a shag with an actual woman lined up".

"Come for a drink, Harry. Let's patch things up. You've got me all wrong. Come on old man", Sarson-Taylor pulled Mottram's arm.

Harry punched him full in the face, and felt for his knife. Vyvian fell on his back into the slush. Grit got into his eyes and mouth and up his nose. People walked by looking down at the dishevelled drunk in the gutter, offering no help, feeling repulsed.

CHAPTER 38

THAT TERRIBLE BUILDING

1978

The freezing wind smashed into Mrs Werldinham and Lunsford with the force of ten thousand freshly sharpened knives. Armoured by hours and hours of eating delicious food and drinking wonderful booze, however, they were more than a match for it. Collars up, gloves on, hats pulled down, scarves thick and warm and wrapped around like mother-love, they headed off across the snow and up to The Wulfric Hall.

Adelaide had opted to remain with Marcus and Joyce, and their young crew. She'd been fed on scraps and was curled up by the open fire that burned for heat and occasionally a slow roast of whatever ingredient looked as if it would benefit from it.

The people of the city, including some newcomers who had heard that this was the right thing to do, were gathering by the Market Cross for the autumn Lantern Procession as the year began to die away. The lanterns were uncovered torches made from willow that was grown just for that purpose in the gardens of the College. Wax scented with sycamore, oak, ash, hazel and willow leaves. The wax was held in a willow basket at the top of a willow handle. A wick of threaded willow bark poked out and was lit for a long, multi-coloured flame.

"I used to love that walk, and the singing. It was exciting but I didn't know why. Me and Mick would go with his mother and dad. My mother refused to have anything to do with such 'pagan devilment' as she called it. Dad was too bloody lazy and the whole thing wasn't all about him. Then me and Chloé and Mick and Jeanne would go. It was good, it was simply good that was all", Lunsford whispered this.

Mrs Werldinham nodded, "I've avoided it since it became so commercialised in the 1930s. Those torches are made by the Sarson-Taylor family in cahoots with the College. They cost nothing to make, they sell them for 25 pence each. 25 new pence! When I was younger, the torches were for good purpose, and there was a meal of meat and potatoes at the end. I've no idea what this nonsense is all about. Let's go shall we, I want to get away from here for now. Can't stand that Market Cross at the best of times".

On they walked, against the flow of the torch bearers, past the snow covered awnings of the pen shop run by the Woods family since 1799 (red doors), the furniture shop run of Whittham family (green doors), the mighty Mahony's Bookshop (blue doors), and past the Bookmaker's run by Mrs Edith Benson under her husband's name (brown door).

The streetlamps were lit giving the whole scene a vaguely Victorian aspect if you overlooked the tarmac on the road, the double-yellow lines, and the Ford Cortinas, Vauxhall Vivas, Morris Marinas and Austin Allegros parked on each side all in various shades of off-yellow or green. The lights mixed with the puddles and again with petrol spilled as young boys sucked it through tubes out of tanks and into cans before rushing off to the grown men who gave them cigarettes in exchange.

Cigarette smoke competed with the fumes from the torches, and Mrs Werldinham added to that fug by lighting a cheroot. On they walked, until the crowd walking against them dissipated so the cold grew even sharper.

"Where is this building of yours?", asked Mrs Werldinham

"Not far now", Lunsford said, hoping he was correct.

"I'm afraid I need to go to the loo right now. Should have thought about it before, stupid of me I'll see you there", she ducked into the nearest pub, a narrow faced place called The Nag's Head that Lunsford had never noticed before. There were so many pubs in Crosschester that missing one or two in fifty years was to be expected.

"Nearly there, mate".

"Nearly there, Mick", said Lunsford sadly.

"It was fun wasn't it? Getting that joke of a building plan amended past Jarvis and his mob of fascists?"

"Pardon? His what?"

"Oh mate, see that's one of the reasons I loved you mate. You are so un-bloody-worldly. Some would say you have no curiosity but I know that's not strictly true. You're the only man I know who could tell me the names of every bird by its song, egg and nest; every plant, tree, flower, grass in the county, all the hills and valleys, fields and bloody copses for miles around. I never knew how you did it. But people and politics? Not the foggiest, you silly bastard.

"Yes, Don Jarvis is one of those nasty little fuckers who never actually fought anything but feels threatened by everything. Him and his bunch of mates had us design this hall and then they gave it the name they'd picked from some made-up book of British-sounding names. Their mates got the construction contracts of course. And now here it is".

And there it was: The Wulfric Hall. Squat, square, grey, with two frilly, sickly and concrete Corinthian columns dwarfing the door. Mick and Lunsford had done what they could but obviously Jarvis had got to it before the final plan was put in place. Even the beautiful, dark, rosined and polished carved oak double doors that they'd designed and had thought that their friend, the carpenter and joiner Mark Craven would make had been replaced with a sad simulacrum in what looked like treated pine. It was a miserly one-man door, the sort that wouldn't be out of place on the front of a municipal toilet. Lunsford's heart sank.

If the doors had been replaced, what chance of the misericords still being in place?

"Get your head up Lunsford, it's a lovely night!". He turned around and there was Fawley standing next to Adelaide. Lunsford could swear she was smiling with her tongue lolling out of her open mouth. He nodded at them both and then turned back to the building. His and Mick's building.

"What do you make of it, Lunsford? Is it what you were hoping for?" Fawley asked.

"No. We worked hard to turn this into something decent for

everybody in the city whether they ever went in or just walked past it.
We may have bent the brief a little, but the brief was a confused mess
to begin with. Modern but traditional, Jarvis wanted. Talks to the soul
of the People, the soil, the land, he said. I mean, that doesn't even
mean anything.

"God knows where the money went because it wasn't on these
materials. Look at it!

I quote you, I bloody quote you what Jarvis demanded,
"Gentlemen, not only must our new building speak to the spirit, soul
and intent of the People of Crosschester, but to the People of Britain, to
Britons who sacrificed and will sacrifice to our ancient freedoms!"

"I'll tell you what sort of buildings talk to the people of Britain",
Lunsford was enraged for the first time in so, so long. "A cricket
pavilion. A bowling green. A covered market selling decent stuff. A
hospital! A cafe that sells decent tea. A pub where you can sit and chat
with your mates over a quiet pint. A Bingo hall. A school with decent
playing fields for all the kids. A Lido for the summer. A bloody Public
Library. A bloody treehouse! Not this, this cheap, squat. Not this
abomination", he came to a stuttering stop.

Fawley smiled and hugged his friend who returned the hug in
equal measure before pulling away and shoving both hands deep into
his pockets.

"Fair play to you Lunsford. Let's go in though. It's cold, I've
taken a detour, and I want to see what you and Mick did, after all,
manage to make".

"Shouldn't we wait for Mrs Werldinham?"

"Push on, push on, she's a grown woman, she knows where we

are".

Lunsford nodded, stepped forward and tried to open the door. He pushed and pulled and he laughed.

"It's locked. After all these days of expectation", he said.

"You didn't say you were excited? I didn't think you even wanted to come", said Fawley.

Lunsford banged on the door in frustration. "I didn't say excitement, I said expectation. Let's go. I want a drink".

Adelaide, who had been sniffing around the side of the Wulfric Hall returned and sat down in front of Lunsford.

"Out of the way dog", he said. She wagged her tail and remained unmoved. "For god's sake!"

The door opened and behind it was a bloke about Lunsford's age who was wearing a black donkey jacket, black denim trousers, and a pair of brown boots. He had a blue and white scarf, the colours of Crosschester Rovers FC around his neck. His hair was grey like his eyes.

"What do you want?" he asked.

Lunsford recognised him from long ago by the river, with the pike, with his brother, "Terry?"

"Yes. What do you want?"

"Terry Timmons? Shalford Primary? What on earth are you doing here?"

"Caretaking. For a fucking pittance. Who wants to know?", the man seemed to be taken aback at the fact that anybody knew him. His life was a lonely one, he had very few friends and was used to being ignored and passed over. He'd spent time in prison for an assault and battery that his brother Keith had done. He'd joined the merchant navy and been raped. He'd driven lorries in Europe and been a cook in Berlin.

"I thought you and your brother had left the area, or been eaten by The Ancasta", said Lunsford.

Terry Timmons leant back and, wheezily, laughed bitterly. "The fucking Ancasta! The mad fucking fish! Fuck me. That brings back some memories. Who are you again?"

"Lunsford, Martin Lunsford. I sat in front of you at school for a while, you used to hit me on the back of the head before…" he stopped.

"Before we were moved on again, and again, yeah, I remember you. You were alright. So, you want to come in then?"

"Please, yes".

"You can't bring the dog. The dog stays outside", said Terry wanting to show some responsibility or at least authority. Adelaide bared her teeth at him and growled half-heartedly.

"Who's your friend?"

"This is Fawley, a good mate indeed. Fawley, this is Terry Timmons, an old school… a bloke I knew from school years ago".

Fawley put his right hand out, grabbed Terry's and shook it vigorously. "Good to meet you Mr Timmons. Are you staying locally? How good to meet you".

Terry shook Fawley's hand and, forgetting his usual reluctance to engage with anybody else in the world at any point, especially on personal details replied, "You too Mr Fawley. Yes, I live over the stationary shop on Jewry Passage. I've been back in Crosschester since

I left my last job in Bristol. Come back here to live out what's left of my fucking life. Anyway, enough about this old bastard, come through won't you?"

They entered the Wulfric Hall through its cheap front door in single file. Once inside they stood next to each other with Terry Timmons in the middle. Lunsford and Fawley both avoided touching the already weeping concrete walls. They pushed their hands deeper into their pockets. The hall was murkily dark, with four cheap lightbulbs masquerading as flaming torches shed grubbiness on the walls. Flickering weakly they provided just enough light so that a person wouldn't walk into the rank of yellow, plastic chairs lined up in front of the high lectern. A streetlamp's light, sick and yellow, snuck in through one of the narrow, horizontal windows. The whole place had the smell of damp and rot already.

"For goodness sake", whispered Lunsford, "Plastic chairs. No pews, no fucking pews!"

No pews meant no misericords.

"What a fucking disaster. What a fucking joke, mate", said Mick.

Fawley nodded.

"Mick, our life's work. Jesus Christ!"

"Lunsford, don't be so dramatic. It's one building out of many we designed. Remember the public swimming pool in Bursley? The council houses up in Stanley Farm estate? Loads of places better than this, we did them. Me and you, and the other blokes in the department.

"Remember, mate, we fought a war, and came back and helped to build things, actual things for actual people. This dropped bollock is Don Jarvis through and through, top to bottom. Fuck him mate". Mick was angry but correct.

"Where are these gargoyles then, Lunsford?" asked Fawley.

"Misericords! For crying out loud mate, how many times?".

Lunsford realised he'd called Fawley his mate, so quickly stepped forward, as did Adelaide who had sneaked in and was tight by his side.

"Terry, have you got a torch or something?"

Terry rummaged around in the canvas bag over his shoulder and pulled out a weighty battery powered torch that he switched it on and passed over. Lunsford walked towards the lectern searching for somewhere that the small sculptures could have been hidden. He walked up the three steps to the platform on which the lectern had been mounted and shone the torch around. He swept the light from left to right and back again. He looked up into the rafters. He could see tiny fissures in the ceiling where, had there been any starlight, it would have shone through.

The building would be condemned before it reached its fifth birthday, he knew it, his experience told him that. He scanned from left to right again, all he saw was decay and bodged work with bad materials. He felt he might cry or at least yell in outrage and frustration at the state that Jarvis and his cronies had allowed this place to become. What was the point in building something, anything so slipshod, half-arsed and ugly? No one benefited. There was no accomplishment, no reflection of the heart and bloody soul of The People. Not unless the People were misbegotten, ugly, cheap lumps of clay who were happy to be praised by valueless gangsters.

He took the three steps down to the watery floor and turned to face the lectern.

"Well fuck you all. Fuck you all", he breathed, feeling as angry as he ever had. He was angry at Fawley for leading him here. He was angry at Mick for not being here in life. He was furious with himself for being fooled into this feeble, childish moment of hope.

"That's it, let's go to the pub", he said to Fawley.

"That's your arse, mate!" yelled Fawley pointing into the rafters.

"It is! It bloody well is!" cried Mick.

Lunsford shone the torch at the ceiling and this time he saw them, carved in oak, polished, small, barely visible but visibly rude and very much there. The misericords had been repositioned. There was Mick, eyes wide, fingers pulling his mouth open, his tongue sticking out and pointing directly at whoever was speaking to the hall. His own arse, with its owner looking over his own shoulder, smiling with more teeth visible than any man had ever or would ever have was up there.

Mark Craven the carpenter had done a fantastic job. Both misericords were the size of small coconuts, both were lurking at the angles of the rafters. Both were joyous, ugly, and solidly, lovingly made.

Lunsford breathed out, unaware that he'd been holding his breath, and continued to stare up.

Terry looked bemused, Fawley and Adelaide looked at each other, then all three quietly left the Wulfric Hall leaving Lunsford to his thoughts and the broad grin that had spread over his face.

The Mick spoke for the last time, "See you, Lunsford. Not for a long time I hope. You get on with it, mate. And remember to be here when they pull his place down so they don't trash us by mistake. Rescue us won't you. Lots of love mate, lots of love".

"Bye Mick. Lots of love, mate", Lunsford was still looking up, still happy.

He looked one last time, checking to see if either the misericords were in danger of falling, then he turned and left the building.

"I tell you what", he said, turning to Terry and Fawley, "I need a pint now".

Terry Timmons shook his head, "Not for me Martin. I've got to lock this place up. I don't drink anyway, it fucks me up. But look, we could meet up later in the week before I head off again?"

"Yes, yes, that would be good. How about a walk to see The Ancasta then a cuppa at mine? Then where are you off to?"

"Well, Mr Fawley here…"

"Just Fawley, as I say, just call me Fawley", he said, kneeling to pick some grot from Adelaide's fur.

"Fawley's offered some work up in York, and I've never been up north, so, yeah, I said yes".

"How about you Fawley? A farewell pint?", he knew what the answer was going to be before he asked, but he was starting to live in hope.

"No can do, Lunsford. Me and Adelaide must get started if we're going to get to York this year. We'll be back again and when we do, we'll come to Oak Cottage and winkle you out. It's been fun after all", Fawley straightened up.

"You're taking Adelaide?" Lunsford tried not to stop his voice sounding like a small child's after being told his dog was going to live on a farm.

"Nope, she's taking me I think. To be honest, I'd not really thought about it but this way feels okay. What about you Adelaide?"

She looked up at Lunsford and barked gently and shook herself down. Then she turned and walked onto the street and began trotting up the hill towards the torchlight procession before turning back to Fawley and barking.

"Here we go, Lunsford. See you one day. Don't forget to visit Hunters Wood often. Take good care of yourself. All love to you", and he and Adelaide disappeared into the procession and the soft overlay of the light from the people's torches.

Lunsford shook Terry's hand and agreed to meet on Thursday. Terry walked off towards Jewry Passage, to a book, and bed. He was looking forward to going to Yorkshire for the first time. He'd not looked forward to much in years. Things were looking up.

Left to his own devices, Lunsford considered getting on a bus and going home for cocoa and an early night. Or maybe a visit to Dr Alice Wilson? Or a pint in The Phoenix? He settled on a pint in The Bunch O'Grapes on the Cathedral Close to warm up a little and take everything in. He started on the short walk and soon found himself under the small arch that separated the Market Cross square from the Cathedral Close.

"Hello there, Lunsford. Shall we have a small drink?", Mrs Werldinham was standing in the lamplight, smoking a cigarette. Lunsford nodded and they walked the short distance to The Bunch O'Grapes.

"After you", said Lunsford. He was content now. Not happy as much as he was more at peace with the world than he'd been since Chloé's death.

Mrs Werldinham smiled and swept through the door and straight to a small, round table close to the bar. Lunsford joined her briefly before ordering a pint of bitter for himself and a long, dark drink ("Just ask for my usual") for her. He sat back down and started talking.

"You don't have to, dear Lunsford", she whispered.

"I don't have to what?"

"Talk. It's been a long day. Lots has happened. Let's relax, watch the snow fall, listen to the hubbub. I've got a crossword. Let's just be quiet for a while".

He felt fine about this arrangement, he nodded and smiled, and gazed out of the window. The beer wasn't Elders but what was? He breathed in and out gently, the snow fell, he felt comfortable.

CHAPTER 39

VYVIAN AT THE CROSSROADS

1978

Sarson-Taylor slipped and fell away from The Wulfric Hall, stunned and humiliated by Harry Mottram's judgement and his fist. He reached for one of his flasks of whisky as he walked into the city. He took a drink and his vengefulness turned inward. He was a stupid, pointless, feckless man. He knew it. He's known it since he was told it by his mother who had spotted it early on. He took another drink and kept walking, head down, collar up, snow melting down his back.

The first pub he came to was The Bunch O'Grapes off Cathedral Close, with its public bar like the Wardroom on Nelson's Victory. He could see through the large bay window that it was full of happy tourists in couples or large groups all having a marvellous time discussing where they'd been and where they were off to next. Even the travellers who'd come on their own were mixing in and buying each other drinks and swapping stories.

Sarson-Taylor went in, bought a pint of beer and a large scotch, and slunk off to a corner seat. It was covered in purple velvet and had a fag burn slowly expanding from his centre but it offered a fine view of the rest of the bar. He was well aware that his family owned the freehold on this pub like it owned nearly every other property that could be made to turn a profit in Crosschester. Every property not already owned by the church or the College that is. If he wanted, he could have shut it down and kicked everybody else out into the snow and slush and degrading torch stems. If he wanted to. But what would be the point of that? His natural inclination was to have people like him. That was his way no matter what or how, so when a young couple in bobble hats and waterproofs came over and asked if there they might share his table he was drunkenly over eager.

"Why certainly, please join me!", he shouted too loudly.

"Oh, we don't want to be a bother, we'll just squeeze up on this end of the table," they were quite delightful.

"It's a round table, it doesn't have ends", he pointed out too loudly and too drunkenly.

They laughed, nervously, not wanting to be a fuss, picked up their drinks and went through the crowd of drinkers to the opposite corner and squeezed themselves onto a table of other similarly dressed young visitors. Minutes later laughter broke from that table as shared interests and even mutual friends came up in conversation. Vyvian was annoyed by this despite how often this sort of thing happened to him since prep school.

He tipped a measure of scotch from one of his flasks into his glass, which he then rolled around in his hand, and looked around the pub for someone to be loved by. Usual tourists, usual students, usual police informers and army men, usual peasants all. Then he saw Mrs Werldinham with that ungrateful lump Lunsford sitting too close to her at a table near the bar. She was drinking a long, dark drink, and smoking a cigarette like she was some kind of film star or one of the racier members of the Royal Family. He was sipping a pint, looking into the middle distance, not even noticing her. She was doing *The Chronicle's* crossword with a gilded silver pencil. They weren't talking. She was obviously bored by that tedious, odious, little man. He had to go over to her.

He had never seen her off her home turf, and in this new context he saw how elegant she was, how beautiful and approachable. He guessed that she was in her fifties, and she had all the poise and power that half a century could bestow on an already quite extraordinary person. He knew he was drunk, it was his natural state of being, but he also knew that he had the right to talk to her without delay and now and deeply and lovingly and finally, truthful and romantically and so he would do that. Because he had a right. Love gave him that right she would understand she would listen and learn.

She was on neutral ground, so he could get to know her, maybe she could even save him, give him something to make him useful, make him likeable, make him worthwhile. Maybe when she saw what a decent man he was, and what a staunch and noble family he came from, she would see what the others refused to see. He took another mouthful from his pint and also a nip from one of his hip flasks.

They would finally become friends. Maybe they could become more than friends. After all, she was a fine looking woman despite her age. Good legs. Great legs. Wonderful sleek body. Strong hips, fine strong hips and hair, healthy, healthy hair. She must come from excellent stock. His family would surely approve. His father would approve, or he could lump it. But he'd surely approve and give his blessing.

He took another drink, stood up and fell over.

He stood up again and made his way through the crush to where Mrs Werldinham was sitting near the bar.

"Mrs Werldinham! As I live and breathe, fancy seeing you here? What a delight, what a delight. May I freshen your drink?", he put his hands on her shoulders, she shrugged him off.

"Go away Vyvian", was all she said.

Lunsford shifted in his seat and said nothing. There was no need. Mrs Werldinham was quite capable of dealing with Vyvian Sarson-Taylor.

Sarson-Taylor knelt on one knee by the side of her chair and took a nip from one of his hip flasks. He smelled of fishing gear, whisky, delusions and grand gestures.

"Would you like a cigarette Mrs Werldinham?"

"I have cigarettes, Vyvian. Now get off your knees and go away. You are making a fool of yourself", she lit a new, long, black cigarette.

Sarson-Taylor didn't move.

"You're the only person who truly knows me, Mrs Werldinham. You've known me since I was a baby, a beautiful bouncing baby boy. You were like a mother to me until they sent me away to that school, that place", he took a long drag on a cigarette and a short nip on the diminished glass of beer.

"Eton College, Vyvian. You were sent to Eton".

"Horrid place. And when I came back you were gone. The rotten family had sent you away. Poor you! Poor me! Poor us! Poor us!"

After decades of dealing with his tantrums, grand gestures, love and hate tokens, self-pity and ego, she was finally exasperated with him. Because they weren't in The Phoenix, she didn't have to care about him. Outside The Phoenix he was his own problem.

"No, that didn't happen at all, Vyvian. You know it didn't happen", she paused, thought for a second, "and we're not going to go over your entire history. Mr Lunsford and I are having a quiet drink and I am completing my crossword".

"My history? My history! You're the only one who has ever cared about my history. Everybody else cares about the family's history, the town's history, the rugger club's history, the history of the Hunt, the history of the chapel, the history of the house, the College, the Cathedral and fucking Royal Oak! Not my history. Not mine!" His voice split the hubbub and general good humour of The Bunch O'Grapes.

"Pipe down now, Mr Sarson-Taylor if you would sir, people are trying to enjoy a drink", called the landlord from his post near the optics.

"Fuck off Donald Cousins, you fucking peasant", Sarson-Taylor thought he whispered to himself before turning back to Mrs Werldinham.

"Why do you make time for that Lunsford beggar? He's not your class, he's no class at all. And Fawley! He's a thief and a liar and a gypsy and a tinker. He's a tree-hugger and a queer, up to no good. Why him? Why not me?"

Lunsford balked a little at the slander of Fawley. He looked towards Mrs Werldinham who made the slightest of eye movements to say, "I'm fine, Mr Lunsford".

"He's the better man though, Vyvian", said Mrs Werldinham looking at 15 across in *The Chronicle*'s crossword.

"Him! Him! He's a middling sort. He's a clerk or a shopkeeper or some tired, boring sort like that. There must be a better reason! There must be!", Sarson-Taylor swayed and swigged.

"No, Vyvian, there are finally no reasons I can give you that would be useful to you in any way. Mr Lunsford is comfortable with himself today. He has been through a very great deal of unpleasantness. The kind of unpleasantness, loss in fact, that could have unhinged and then broken other people. Instead, he asked questions of himself and of his particular histories. He took help. His pride was a bolster not a brick wall. He is aware that tomorrow there may be more questions he needs to confront. That there may be no ready answers. But tonight, he is drinking a quiet pint with a good friend".

Lunsford considered what had been said about him. He certainly hadn't thought all that. He hadn't realised that anybody else had, let alone Mrs Werldinham. He looked at Sarson-Taylor, and he nodded.

She continued, "You, Vyvian, are a thoroughly unpleasant person who has had several opportunities – not even chances, no, you've had rock solid opportunities to improve yourself".

Sarson-Taylor stood up and swayed, his bright yellow corduroy trousers dusty and torn at the knee. He declaimed to the tightly packed and gently steaming pub, "I come from stock that needs no improvement. Hundreds of years of perfecting the bloodlines went into me. Careful Selection, bugger the natural variety. I am of the Unimprovable Class!".

"I rest my case, Vyvian", she said, returning to her clues and her solutions.

Sarson-Taylor let out a most theatrical howl, something between "Woe!" and "Fuck!" and jumped up. He slammed his fists into the table in front of Mrs Werldinham upsetting the ashtray before howling again and sliding down to his knees in front of her.

"Dear, dear Mrs Werldinham, I love you. I impeach you! Impeach you. I always have loved you. I love her, you see everyone, I love her!" he roared and pointed at her. She sighed.

"No, Vyvian, you don't love me. I am certain of that fact because there is no love in you. This is true of very few people but you are one of them. I have indeed known you since you were a babe in arms. If there's one skill that you above all other men need to learn is what being loved feels like. However, there's a catch…"

"There's always a bloody catch!" he moaned.

She continued, "There is no point in your constant search for someone or something to love you as deeply as you purport to love them. Love doesn't work that way. There must be no more second guessing on your part. Love isn't a gesture nor is it an obsession".

Vyvian was silent, a tear performed its ways down his cheek. The pub remained chummy, steamy and loud. No one paid much attention to him other than to be grateful that they were no closer to him.

Mrs Werldinham concluded, or tried to conclude, "In short, Vyvian, sort yourself out. You've had enough chances".

He wiped away his tears and looked up at her, "Always so judgemental aren't you? Snooty, uppity bitch", he sneered and stood up swigging from one of his hip flasks.

Lunsford made to move, to get rid of the drunken little monster. Mrs Werldinham put her hand on his arm. He sat still.

"You think you're always so bloody well right about everything don't you? You're just a glorified barmaid though, aren't you? If you think about it for one fucking moment. You're stuck down there in that shanty village, aren't you? You're no one to give advice to anyone let alone to me. You're a failure! A fucking wench with airs and graces. You're a fraud, everybody knows it. You don't even own that pub. We own your pub. We own you. Everyone knows that my father's had you. My brother Horace had you and he was queer! The whole bloody county has had you!"

She smiled and exhaled pitch black cigarette smoke into his face.

"How does it feel to be the only person in the entire county that I decided I didn't want to fuck, Vyvian?" she said.

He stood and spoke at the pub, "Look at her! Look at the old whore-fraud! Look at the hag!", everybody looked away, everybody except the landlord. He came from behind the bar and took Vyvian by his collar.

"Right then you! Out! Out of my pub! I don't care who you are anymore! This is the final fucking straw. I've just spoke to your father on the telephone and he's agreed that you're a holy bloody terror. So, now you're barred. And you're not just barred from here, you're from all the pubs in Crosschester. Just you try and find out. Just you see. We're all sick of the sight of you. Out!" The publican, a bull of a man with military experience and a usually calm demeanour picked Vyvian Sarson-Taylor up by that collar and actually threw him into the street and onto the snow covered slush. Threw him hard and far. Vyvian slid across the icy, slushy, gritty road into the iron railings that separated the pub from the cathedral grounds and its tombstones.

"You are fucking barred for life you little shit!" and the doors slammed.

CHAPTER 40

VYVIAN TAKES A LIFE

1978

Out on the street, Sarson-Taylor searched the pockets of his custom made Barbour waxed-jacket and finally found what he was looking for. A bottle of 40 year-old, single malt whisky that he had taken from his father's personal spirit store. He turned, gave two fingers and a tongue to The Bunch O'Grapes and began to walk through the cathedral grounds, past the tombstones of the great and good, soldiers, mayors, an author, and Thomas Thetcher who died of a fever brought on by drinking small beer.

As usual he toasted Thomas as he headed across the grounds towards Spitfire Bridge, which had since his childhood been a favourite place to sit and consider his place in the world. Deeply faithful making their ways home from the Taizé service at the cathedral mixed the College boys and squaddies and they all missed seeing the roly-poly figure of Vyvian Sarson-Taylor weaving from tombstone to tombstone toasting as he went across the grounds on his way. He appeared happy enough, some thought. He was obviously very drunk, said others later. He was singing, he was moaning, he was crying or sobbing, said other people. As he disappeared under the buttress arches, a few people saw him turning his head and sticking his tongue out.

"He was obviously in some kind of distress if you ask me", said one of the people who had been in The Old Vine.

"He was pissed, as usual", said another.

"Poor form. Disgusting behaviour", said his father the next day.

Vyvian reached Spitfire Bridge at the same time as he finished half of his bottle of scotch. Despite its name, the bridge was not named after the fighter plane but after the dragon that took the centre field on the Sarson-Taylor coat of arms. The bridge was three hundred years old and spanned the Icene in what had once been the centre of Crosschester. Wide enough for two horse-drawn wagons to pass each other as they went to and from the markets. It was ornamented with busts of the family, the latest being Vyvian's brother Horace Sarson-Taylor (DSO, AFC) who had died fighting bravely as a nineteen year old pilot during the Battle of Britain.

Vyvian hated the memory of him with a searing pain made deep agony by the fact that his father worshiped the dead hero son. He looked around him to see if there was anybody close and discovered he was alone as he pulled his trousers down. He climbed onto the side of the bridge and stuck his bare arse over the bust of his brother. There below him was Horace in mossy sandstone, pilot's bonnet on his head, eyes goggled, jaws like axe heads, empty eye sockets looking south east along the river. Gazing towards the open water where his plane had exploded in glorious flames, and his legend had risen in slightly less glorious saltwater steam. Vyvian strained and teetered over the water until a stream of alcoholic's thin, dark shit dribbled out and onto Horace's head.

"There, there you are, there you are you great saviour of reputations, upholder of the family name, beloved of his line, bully, queer, torturer there you are, all for you, all for you dearest brother Horror. You died for nothing, it didn't bloody matter after all, not at all, you silly, silly, silly dead prick".

He reached for his bottle and slipped. He fell forward onto the road, hard. His head bled and several of the bottles in his pockets shattered, their shards piercing him along with the fishhooks, gutting knives and the iron crucifix he carried with him and that he had forgotten about. He stood up but his bright yellow corduroy trousers, clumped around his ankles, tripped him and he crashed into the road again. Being so drunk meant that he felt nothing. He laughed loudly at his performance and pulled up his trousers. He fastened his belt and rose slowly and as carefully as any drunk can. After a few attempts he managed to hoist himself back onto the bridge side so that his legs dangled over the snow-melt, rising water and the shit covered bust of his brother. The Icene was dark and flowing quickly that night, all its creatures at rest, all its weeds still in languid action dragged by the flow to the sea as they desperately tried to remain rooted into its ancient chalk base.

Vyvian Sarson-Taylor sat drinking and thinking about how England was lost if the only people who were defending it were the kind he had recently been forced to mix with. Tedious, porcine local bourgeois, the thugs and the mean spirited shopkeepers. They had the gall to look down on him, to call him vile names and to shun his ideas. His family were leaders and were part of the warp and the weft of the country let alone the city. Over with the Conqueror, always here, always ensuring that things remained as they should.

He laughed and yelled the family name into the night and spat it down on the river and down on his brother's head. He howled it at the night air but as there was no wind that night, his battle cry just fell. He howled it and he howled it again and again and he nearly toppled over from the force of it but saved himself. Inside his jacket he was bleeding from all the cuts made by all the things he had held close.

He stopped shouting and sunk his head into his chest. He didn't care about England. He couldn't care less about what kind of people were allowed in or remained or left. People were all the same. He knew that. People were dismissive and cruel no matter where they came from. People were horrid and they victimised you, and then blamed you for being a victim. He was no victim, not Vyvian Sarson-Taylor. He was a fighter, a warrior, he knew his ground, he knew what he was due. He knew people. He knew he was a shit. A useless shit.

No one really cared about anyone other than who could do them a favour. He was sure of that. He'd practised that because that had been shown that to be the only truth about people. People at home. People at school. People in the workplaces he'd never been allowed in. According to his father, people were assets. People were assets. There were our people and there were other people, people who were not ours. Be they farmhands or gardeners or lawyers or cooks, we care for ours as if they are our children, we have a duty to them. We do not care for the people who are not ours, we have no duty to them. They can go rot. Vyvian pitied them. Then he pitied himself, his parent's actual child.

The booze was already doing a good job of lowering his body temperature close to that of a corpse when the snow started again, settling on him. As it was Sunday the shops and the cinema were closed tight. The churches and the synagogue had disgorged their choristers and cantors, and the kids who played in the trees and on the bowling green with sticks for guns and stones for hand grenades were home and in their weekly baths.

Crosschester was never silent though there was always a background throb, the frequency of a moribund pulse that moved from stone to stone and brick to brick. It was in the Norman arches and the Tudor gables, it resonated through the museums and teashops, even through The Wulfric Hall and out to Oak Cottage, and it would never stop. It was the accumulation of the pulses of everybody who had died in Crosschester and its villages from the beginning, harmonised to the point just before their death.

It was the resonance of every single thing, alive or dead that had ever been a part of the place, and it radiated from there to the next place and the next and the next, mixing and harmonising again and again until it touched every place, everywhere, for all time. It was only occasionally audible but it could always be felt. Horace Sarson-Taylor had heard it and felt it as his Spitfire hit the water. Mick Downes had felt it as Darren Craven's Ford Capri slewed into him. Darren had heard it, in hospital, and Chloé had heard it coming and going in waves as the cancer metastasised inside her, was forced back and came again. It was the sounds of all the lands of all the world and the heartbeats of all the dead reaching over to them all, easing their way, closing out the fear and their own grief at the loss of everything and everyone they knew; welcoming them, joining them, teaching them and adoring them.

Vyvian could hear and feel the pulse as he swayed on the side of Spitfire Bridge, and he cried. For the first time since he'd left his nanny's bottle and began on his father's he wasn't crying for the wrongs done by others to him, he was crying at the waste of life he had worked so hard to impose on the small world he'd inhabited for all of his thirty two years. The pulse of the city grew louder but no more urgent, it never changed its cadence because it never needed to, it was always going to reveal itself.

At first Vyvian mistook it for the sound of his own blood pounding out his heartbeat in his ears like he'd heard a hundred times before as he lay on a street as a pillow. He looked left, and then down onto the shitty head of his brother, at his own feet and into the water. He took a handkerchief from one of his many pockets and bent down to clean Horace's spattered head, and gently he tipped over the edge. He cracked his own head on that of his brother and he fell down and down into the Icene. He didn't struggle because he had no idea what was happening to him. He was dead very quickly and silently, and he began bobbing up and down gently along the only river he had ever been brave enough to swim in, floating out and away towards the sea.

Don Jarvis stood at one end of the Sarson-Taylor Road that the Spitfire Bridge carried from one side of The Icene to the other. He snorted, turned back towards town and started to walk, his hat pulled down and collars up against the snow ladened east wind.

The next afternoon two boys rushing to bunk off school along the banks of the river, with a porn magazine, a packet of Woodbine cigarettes and some cheap sweet, fizzy cider discovered Vyvian Sarson-Taylor's body. It was nestled into the carpet of detritus that clung to the central pier of The Goldberg Bridge a mile downstream outside the Crosschester Synagogue – one the oldest in the country.

The Sarson-Taylor family arranged for a quiet funeral with Vyvian interred at the back of the family plot, not in the mausoleum but in the shade of a yew tree with a view over the Water Meadows, and just slinging out distance from The Phoenix. No one made a eulogy and there was no reception with sandwiches and sherry afterwards, everybody dispersed back to their farms, their banks, their marriages and model villages. Vyvian joined the pulse of the place and nobody knew nor cared, and nor did he anymore.

CHAPTER 41

THE LETTER

1978

After Sarson-Taylor had been thrown out of The Bunch O'Grapes, Lunsford and Mrs Werldinham decided to call it a night. Mrs Werldinham dropped him off outside Oak Cottage in a taxi she seemed to have conjured up outside the Cathedral. He waved her goodbye, and she blew him a kiss. They agreed to meet again soon, but there was a sense of parting for longer which he knew was true but not forever.

He slept soundly, and before dropping off resolved to go to Pearce's Pet Shop in Crosschester the next day and find himself a dog which he would call, Lizzee and who would be just like Adelaide. He would also get a bicycle, and a fishing rod and would join the library.

When he woke, the morning was crisp and fizzing with energy. Lunsford was washing the outside windows by nine after which he had a large breakfast and considered his day. He would go and put flowers on Chloé's grave and speak to her about his future. He would buy that dog, and he would get some holiday brochures. Biting into the last piece of toast and marmalade he noticed the unopened letter. He picked up the knife he'd been using to slice into the bacon and eggs, wiped it on a dishcloth and slit the envelope open.

"My Dearest Martin,

"I hear from my colleagues at the hospital that you are home now. That your body is mended. I cannot imagine how you must have felt when you woke from your coma to discover that our beloved Mick was no longer with us and hadn't been for so many months.

"I wanted to stay and share our memories of Mick, with you, to halve our grief by celebrating the man. I am so sorry that I was unable to do this and that you suffered alone, even without Chloé. But I couldn't stay in Crosschester any longer.

"I could no longer bear the hurt that was being flung at me like dung. With Mick by my side I felt less alone and less vulnerable to them. With him gone and you and Chloé too, there was nothing to keep me in that place to be called Coon, and Wog, Nignog and Jungle Bunny and Sooty and Chalky and Black Bitch. That used to happen in whispers, Lunsford but lately I had it shouted at me on my way to work at the hospital, healing people, all the people.

"One night, when you were still in your coma, it stopped being whispered though. I was knocked off my bicycle by some lads in town just outside The Crown and Anchor. They surrounded me and they destroyed my bike. They screamed at me and threatened me with knives and they told me to go back to the jungle. To go back to where I came from.

"I am a nurse, dear Lunsford, and I am a Christian woman and I should have been there with you, healing you. I am a coward though. And this letter is an apology from my soul to your soul. From my heart to yours. Please forgive me for leaving you but my courage failed me and I returned to where I came from. I returned to Handsworth in Birmingham and my family.

"I loved your Chloé and I counted you as a true friend. My Mick loved you both, I know this to be true as a Bible story and sweet as the word of Jesus himself. I also know that you are not a religious man, but please let this old woman have her say. We laughed a lot, us four, and I would give anything to make that laughter ring again with you.

"I have written my address and my telephone number down for you. I would welcome you at any time if you can find it in your heart to forgive me.

"Your great friend, Jeanne Downes"

Lunsford read the letter twice before transcribing Jeanne's details into the address book that Chloé, of course, had assiduously kept up to date and in order. He read the letter again and this time grew so angry that he wanted to break the people who had done this to a woman he knew to be dear, powerfully good and hugely beloved. He wanted to snap them into kindling and use that to light a fire on Mizmazz Hill for everybody to see and come and be warmed by.

"She's always been a lovely woman has Jeanne. A lovely, lovely woman. A friend. And you never appreciated that, did you, Lunsford?"

"Chloé, my love, I never appreciated anybody enough. You know that. I know that now. What can I do now though? How can I make her feel better? How can I explain that none of it is her fault? Nurse or no. Christian or not. None of it is Jeanne's fault and never has been".

Nothing came. No voice. No answer. Silence. Not the barking of a dog or the words of recovery from Fawley or Mrs Werldinham. Not Mick, not his Mother. Chloé was silent, angry.

"What can I do Chloé'? What can I possibly do?" he repeated.

He looked at the letter and wondered why he wasn't crying over it. Sobs and convulsed tears and heartache, where were they? Instead, he felt angry.

The house can wait.

The dog can wait.

Chloé is patient and doesn't like flowers much anyway.

He went into the hallway and took the phone from its cradle and dialled. The phone rang and rang, and Lunsford fidgeted and stepped from foot to foot.

"Hello, Handsworth 317146, to whom am I speaking please?"

"Jeanne, it's Lunsford. I'd like to come and visit… soon if that would be ok".

"That's the way, Lunsford, my lovely man. That's the way", said Chloé's voice drifting away.

EPILOGUE

1999

On the 10th of June 1999 the local BBC news broadcast the following story at 1am to an audience of lonely, uninterested people.

"Crosschestrian businessman and long-time independence campaigner, Mr Donald Jarvis MBE, has been duly elected as Member of the European Parliament for the South West of England".

The program ran a brief piece of footage during which Don Jarvis made his acceptance speech, thanking his agent and all the many ardent, brave and hardworking members of the Britons for Independence Party for their support. Then, like the captain of a successful football team he held up a small, polished oak sculpture about the size of a large potato.

"This is Wulfric! He is our mascot! The mascot of our party! Our People! Our Dream! And soon, of our Independence! Like the brave soldiers at Agincourt, he is showing his arse to the French. Like our courageous troops in both World Wars, he is telling the Germans and Italians and Spanish what we think of them! We want out! And we will be out, or my name is not Donald Jarvis!"

Behind him stood several men, dressed in black paramilitary gear, and one tall, thin, serious woman. She smiled like a razor cut and ticked something on a clipboard.

The TV cut away to football highlights.

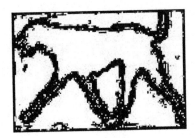